BECKY CHAN

For John Rudell

BECKY CHAN

A NOVEL

JARED MITCHELL

SIMON & PIERRE
A MEMBER OF THE DUNDURN GROUP
TORONTO · OXFORD

Editor: Barry Jowett
Copy Editor: Julian Walker
Design: Jennifer Scott
Printer: Webcom

Canadian Cataloguing in Publication Data
Mitchell, Jared, 1955–
  Becky Chan

ISBN 0-88924-300-X

I. Title.

PS8576.I8696B42 2001   C813'.54   C2001-930191-X   PR9199.3.M57B42 2001

1   2   3   4   5   05   04   03   02   01

 Canada

THE CANADA COUNCIL | LE CONSEIL DES ARTS
FOR THE ARTS | DU CANADA
SINCE 1957 | DEPUIS 1957

ONTARIO ARTS COUNCIL
CONSEIL DES ARTS DE L'ONTARIO

We acknowledge the support of the Canada Council for the Arts and the Ontario Arts Council for our publishing program. We also acknowledge the financial support of the Government of Canada through the Book Publishing Industry Development Program, The Association for the Export of Canadian Books, and the Government of Ontario through the Ontario Book Publishers Tax Credit program.

Care has been taken to trace the ownership of copyright material used in this book. The author and the publisher welcome any information enabling them to rectify any references or credit in subse-quent editions.
J. Kirk Howard, President

Printed and bound in Canada.

❁

Printed on recycled paper.

Although there are speculative references to real people and situations in this novel, this story is strict-ly a work of imagination. None of the incidents, as described, ever took place. All main and most sec-ondary characters and situations in this story are fictitious and similarities with real events and characters, living or deceased, is coincidental and unintended.

Excerpts from "Long Ago (and Far Away)" by Jerome Kern and Ira Gershwin, copyright 1944, reprint-ed with permission of Universal Music Publishing Group.

The author acknowledges the generous support of the Ontario Arts Council.

Dundurn Press	Dundurn Press	Dundurn Press
8 Market Street	73 Lime Walk	2250 Military Road
Suite 200	Headington, Oxford,	Tonawanda NY
Toronto, Ontario, Canada	England	U.S.A. 14150
M5E 1M6	OX3 7AD	

BECKY CHAN

ONE

Feng Hsiao-foon demanded to know what I'd done with his wife, Becky Chan. It was July, hot outside, and the air stank of diesel exhaust and rotting garbage. The back of my shirt was damp with sweat from a trip across the harbour to the Royal Observatory in Kowloon. I'd been reporting a story about atmospheric radioactivity. The beta activity of airborne dust samples had dropped to ninety-six pico-curies, which would come as a relief to those who worried about such things. Fallout over the China coast had been fluctuating following an atmospheric test of a hydrogen bomb in the distant region of Sinkiang. I'd glanced up at the sky over Hong Kong, and while it looked the same as it did every summer, bluish-white, hazy, stunningly bright, I almost wished for a cheery iridescence, something to physically imply the story. Becky Chan was my best friend. Feng said she was missing.

That day was July 2, 1967. I had known Feng, as well as any outsider could know him, for more than fifteen years. He was the chief of production and principal shareholder of the Great World Organisation. His greatest star, Becky Chan, was the Goddess of Mercy, and she presided over those most hallowed of Hong Kong temples, the cinemas of the Great World circuit. The 1958 super-production of *The Goddess of Mercy,* was her greatest success. It was Great World's greatest picture and she was its greatest artistic asset. She had played a dual role in that film. The first was that of

Koon Yin, the merciful deity draped with snow-white robes and lying on an emerald lotus pad that floated in a purple moonlit sea. She daubed her mystic dew from a willow branch, the dew fell through the purple sea down to our world below, and it brought relief to mankind's innumerable sufferings. She also played a poor peasant woman, whose family Koon Yin saves from catastrophe. The baroque sets, the brocade costumes, the process photography, *The Goddess of Mercy* brought great prestige to Feng's studio. The only thing it failed to do was make a profit.

The rest of Becky Chan's films, plastic comedies and overheated melodramas, all made profits, and in the jumped-up merchant mind of Feng Hsiao-foon, that made them worthier. Almost always before and after *The Goddess of Mercy,* Becky's pictures made money for Great World. Thus, you can understand why Feng Hsiao-foon was deeply concerned about his wife's disappearance.

My face must have changed when Feng said Becky was missing because Billy Fong, the *China Telegraph's* one-eyed copy boy, glanced at me twice. He stared sideways to get a focus and the gesture exaggerated his interest. It unnerved me so I looked down at my desk, fiddled with things on it, shifted a disorganized heap of papers in a wire basket. I pretended to search for something important. I glanced over at Mary Wu, the Chinese switchboard operator, visible at her station through a rectangular cut-out in the cream-coloured wall on the side of the newsroom. She was taking a message from an English-speaking caller and I could hear her bawling into her headset: "How to spell please?" Over by the entrance to the washrooms, prematurely wrinkled from worry, a young Chinese janitor poured water into a zinc bucket from a red rubber hose. A drunken correspondent from the British Press Association had once offered the janitor ten dollars to take him into the loo and beat him with that hose. The janitor had just enough idea of what sexual fetishes were to decline, though in much agony, for he urgently needed the money. Over by the window, Sonny, the Ceylonese copy editor who was apt to daydream, looked out at the weird sight of a double-decker China Motor Bus on the steep grade of Wyndham Street just outside the window, waiting for the traffic light at the bottom of the hill. The diagonal view made it look as if it had just crashed into a pit outside the newsroom and we, lords of the Oriental English-language press, sat ignoring it. Four British reporters sat on the edges of two desks, swinging their feet and talking sports.

I suddenly felt very tired. I dreaded the possibilities, that Becky might have been kidnapped, that she was lost, or dead. Many people suffer through a difficult year some time in their lives; 1967 was my difficult year. Becky's disappearance was going to exhaust my endurance. An all but overpowering urge to burst into tears crept over me. Becky was the only true friend I'd ever had. The orphan girl from the refugee shack towns that ringed Kowloon. The jade girl, the pretty teenager who had started out performing ingénue roles in Cantonese opera. The local apprentice actress who slaved for cheesy film companies that came to Hong Kong from Shanghai following their closure after 1949 by the triumphant Communists. When she joined Feng's Great World she had her best years, first in cheap but touching Cantonese stories about sacrifice and suffering, later in unlikely Mandarin comedies and dress-ups. In the early '60s she had a brief career in Hollywood in stupid, forgettable pictures with Oriental themes: *Almond Eyes, Panic on Grant Avenue, Chopsticks.* She sabotaged her own career in Los Angeles and punished herself for it by coming back to Hong Kong and marrying Feng Hsiao-foon. He put her under contract at Great World again and, because she was now his wife, he paid her no salary. Becky admired Western directness and sometimes when I put a blunt question to her she shot back with rare revelation. I asked her why she had gone back to that dreadful man's employ. "I always outlast my jailers," she said.

Becky and I got on brilliantly. She constantly came down with colds and the flu, and during those illnesses I would listen patiently to her minute analyses of each minor viral assault. She reported their progress with the intensity of a radio sports commentator. Illness and the possibility of getting sick fascinated her. She was actually disappointed when chest X-rays absolved her of tuberculosis. She told me about the hardy bacillus in an odd little lecture over tea in a hotel coffee shop. "If you have tuberculosis," she'd say to me, "and you spit on the street, the bacilli are in the spit. Even when the spit dries up it's still alive. So when the dust blows, the bacilli are carried into the air and gets into someone else's lungs. Then she's got it." She sat back and sipped her glass of Coca-Cola, looking terribly stimulated and even hopeful.

She in turn listened to my singing, something that was to have been my intended career. I taught her goofy Western novelty songs. She found their foolishness to be uncomplicated source of fun and laughed innocently and heartily. "Wally the Walleyed Mackerel," "Thanks for the Buggy Ride," "The Prune Song." I sang "The Wee Hoose 'Mang the Heather," exaggerating the Scottish burr monstrously. "Though A'm far away frae Scotland and the scenes I loov sae weel. There's a beat for the auld country that in ev'ry pulse I feel!" She couldn't have liked it more. The song was even more absurd for her than it was for me.

In our early, easy-going years we had an uncomplicated affection for one another in a city that was being strangled by the complexity of its relationships. I did not worship false goddesses. I had no other true and dependable friends. I was not married and had no possibility of becoming so. My society was Becky and I was her window on freedom.

In the 1960s, telephone lines under Victoria Harbour could be unreliable and that day the line that carried Feng's call intermittently crackled and honked as if afflicted with emphysema. Feng was angry, almost shrill, as if I were still an employee of his to be tossed about by the mighty gusts of his supreme will. He purposefully tried to confuse me so I would lose my guile and confess to crimes I had not committed. He asked me why I was harbouring Becky. I hadn't even known she was missing. I was as worried as he was. He didn't believe me.

He said she had left their home in Kowloon Tong the previous morning without saying anything. She had instructed her amah to walk down to Waterloo Road and flag a taxi. When the amah returned with the taxi, Becky came out of the house with a small suitcase. She got in, the driver turned his vehicle about, drove back to Waterloo Road and turned right. That meant she was heading into central Kowloon. The amah thought that was unusual because Becky should have been going to work at Great World's studios out in Tsuen Wan, which were in the opposite direction. Ah-niu assumed Becky was going to a location shoot and thought no more about it until the director of her current picture called the house asking where she was. The amah called Feng. That had been yesterday and Feng had yet to notify the police. "She left the baby behind," he said.

He then asked me a series of questions and provided me with alternative answers that might satisfy him, all of them pointing to my culpability in some foggy conspiracy to humiliate him or to ruin the Great World Organisation. I put my head on my hand and let myself get beaten up. The damp sweat patch on the back of my shirt was now very cold in the *China Telegraph* newsroom. Air conditioning was the worst innovation to come along in the 1960s. Workmen came in and constructed a false ceiling to hide the conduits, which made a merry old runway for the office rats. Late at night you could hear them up there, big, lusty, whiskered things, pounding the top side of the asbestos panels as they dashed above your head.

I listened to the scurrying feet of Feng's questions and gave short answers. His inquiries had a circular quality leading to an invariably terrible conclusion, like dud missiles you'd see in newsreels, the ones that rose from Florida launch pads then made pinwheel courses a hundred feet above the Earth and exploded. I told him that I didn't know where she was and I could tell by his comments he didn't believe me. He kept spinning about. Feng always assumed that something was hidden, that nothing was wholly visible and innocent. He earnestly believed that, like him, everyone had something hidden, something complicated and soundless, like that penthouse machinery that enables elevator cars to scuttle up and down dark hoist ways and disclose different places to passengers without cohesive explanation.

I could picture him at the other end of the telephone call, taking off his glasses and blinking unseeing at the air. His questions and demands suggested that he couldn't make sense of where Becky was. He had never really known her, not like I had. He did not want to see her the way I did. He saw her as something to be dug out of the ground, smelted and refined into something useful and then sold off. I really believe he thought that that. I still do.

Feng attempted an oblique threat. "It may be necessary," he said, "to call the authorities. They might come to your office and ask questions." This meant more to him than it did to me. Feng had a poor idea of what could scandalize a newspaper reporter. The police turning up at his studio office would be devastating for a senior member of the North Kowloon Rotary and one of the most socially ambitious Shanghanese businessmen in the colony. Although he was a movie showman used to generating publicity for the studio, he wouldn't do anything that undermined his sorry, sad little pursuit of personal respectability. Feng just didn't get why Chinese bankers, industrialists and colonial government officials never wanted him around.

As rich as he got, he never found the degree of respectability he thought they owed him. Highly stratified and wary of Northerners, elite Cantonese society shared their charity boards with him and invited him to their banquets – but only when they wanted him to do something for them. Or when they wanted him to write a big, fat, greasy donation to Po Leung Kuk, the society to aid women and children. But he was never a close friend to any of them. He never went to their card games or drank their tumblers of iced cognac in private rooms of fine restaurants while they opened the secrets of their social connections. No messengers hand-delivered invitations to high-caste weddings. There was no personal warmth, only utility. Such subtle exclusions only made him try harder, but in weird ways. When he failed to get an invitation to dine at Chinese New Year with the Tsengs, a banking family who lived on Shouson Hill, he issued a press release stating that thereafter, Great World's Mandarin-track motion pictures would switch from black and white to colour. He ordered a copy of the release sent to the Tsengs' offices. I suppose he thought that by adopting colour he would so magnetize himself socially that the invitations would fly to his office and stick to the outer door. He didn't know that when the Tsengs and other quality families thought of movie producers, weak smiles and charitable looks crossed their faces. For them, transistor-radio factory owners had more prestige than any crude Shanghai show-man. The Tsengs organized opera performances in their own homes, the performers they personally chose, such was their taste and knowledge of art. Movies, whether in black and white or colour, were for workmen with salty faces and factory girls with metal hair clips. Feng would always be a vulgarian.

I cared little for Feng's dainty warning about "the authorities." I was a bum with a typewriter who spoke with "the authorities" every day. I was used to sniffing around with the police, rather like an unhygienic dog. One of my best friends was in the police, Jack Rudman. Oh, that man. I tried, very hard, to be close to Jack. At the time I thought that he, unlike Feng, was a magnificent man worthy of one's complete devotion. But he wouldn't have me. Jack pushed me away, albeit with confusing irregularity. Today, I recognize Jack Rudman's behaviour to be that of a weak mind in con-flict with itself. Then, I was merely frustrated and hopeful. When he was canvassing for a police charity, Jack got me to buy a long-playing record of music performed by the Bands of the Hong Kong Police. It was courtesy and civic duty for me to buy a copy, but also, in a pathetic way, I might have been hoping to get closer to him. I even sat alone one evening and listened to the LP sever-al times, drinking too much while the police pipes and drums per-formed "The Hills of Kowloon" and "Traffic Control." I might as well have listened to a whole library of LPs. Did he sit up evenings thinking of me? Would he change his life for me? I might as well have fallen in front of that bus on Wyndham Street.

Much of what little happiness I had in those days was anchored to the hope that something might take root between Becky and me, or me and Jack Rudman. But after nineteen years in Hong Kong, I found my hope was nearly depleted. Like lone-ly people around the world who were approaching middle age without settlement, I got along with chance encounters and called it my life. Encounters with tourists, co-workers, armed-forces personnel, the oblique relations with people you brushed past in everyday life. I went to a restaurant in Stanley Street for breakfast every morning. There was a very young Chinese waiter who showed me great affection and, lonely me, I reciprocated. After a few weeks of serving me bacon and two eggs six days a week, this tender-hearted young man brought me three eggs, but only charged me for two. I must have shown encouragement through my gratitude, because the next week he brought me four. A week later there were five fried eggs and I had to tell him to stop. He seemed hurt, so now it was my turn, and I showed my escalating warmth with increasing tips until I was leaving one hundred per cent of the bill as a gratuity. One morning I came by and the restaurant had gone out of business and I never saw the young waiter again. That was all, that was it, that was one of my finer relationships.

Once, when I confessed to having a bad migraine, Becky nodded knowingly, removed a bottle of aspirin from her purse and swallowed two. She met my incredulous look with this explanation: "I think I have a headache coming on too." I could have kissed her for that. In recent years she'd become a vegetarian. She lectured me on the unhealthy nature of meat. "The human intestine," she'd say, "is like that of herbivorous monkeys: very long. Real meat eaters, such as tigers or lions, have short intestinal tracts." It could get a bit tiresome and transparent. But if I teased her about eating too many beans by making a lot of crude noises that the scatological people of Hong Kong would find hysterically funny, she would grow huffy. "I see that you're trying to upset me," she'd say with a lot of shrugs and glances out the window. "Perhaps you don't care about my health." There was an awkward moment in which I tried to ratchet down her indignation but I usually had to apologize before she would warm up again, to give some personal sacrifice of humility before she felt that I had paid enough. A few nights later we went out for dinner and she would choose a vegetarian restaurant. "I need to be with my people," she said with pretend grandiosity. "My fellow monkeys."

The way I preferred to think of Becky, the way everyone preferred to think of Becky, was as Koon Yin in *The Goddess of Mercy.* Great World shot the exteriors in Taiwan because it had unspoiled mountain vistas. The hills of Kowloon that so inspired the police pipes and drums were scabby with squatter shacks and Royal Air Force antennae that snooped the skies of southern China. The police also worshipped the Goddess of Mercy, the one they called "She Who Looks Down and Hears the Cries of the World." I attended the movie's premiere with Jack Rudman, who unconsciously leaned against my shoulder in the Ambassador Cinema, perhaps to huddle against the ferocity of the air conditioning. Or perhaps, for once, he was just being nice to me.

Koon Yin is one of the most popular celestial inhabitants among the Chinese because of her compassion. She is destined to fall short of achieving nirvana until every last mortal achieves it, so it is in her interest to end the suffering of ordinary men and women. Becky struck a memorable tableau at the denouement when a married couple, whom the story has followed, rise up and meet her in heaven. The man had been a mariner once and his ship had thrice been saved from destruction when he saw her on a rock in the middle of a stormy sea, like a supernatural lighthouse. Now, in heaven, Becky stood in her white robes surrounded by carbon dioxide clouds. In one arm she held a horsetail duster. With the fingers of her free hand, she touched the rising couple and gave them eternal happiness. In the last shot the camera dollied back irregularly, so Becky appeared to float and bob away into infinity. The picture turned up at the Edinburgh Festival, where programmers praised Becky as "a restrained performer trapped inside an over-pretty chocolate box." For a few months *The Goddess of Mercy* became the darling of European film buffs. It still didn't recoup its costs.

Feng Hsiao-foon had his secretary hold my line while he took a second call, from Great World's publicity director, whose job it was occasionally to hunt down missing performers. Becky was not the only actress to go missing. Others sometimes fled to escape their killing workloads or simply to escape Feng. They'd turn up in Singapore hotels, flat on their backs in the embrace of mundane exhaustion. Others eloped with amorous plastic-pail manufacturers who spirited them off to secluded villas in rural Hong Kong. These new husbands bought out their contracts and freed them from Feng's exhausting grind forever. Being married to Feng, though, meant that Becky would never be free until the very last movie goers had found such happiness that they no longer needed the diversion of cinema.

Today, Hong Kong movies are known in the West for their wild and violent but improbable action. They have become newly popular, even chic among irony-loving Westerners who think that Chinese movies were invented around the time of Bruce Lee's ascendancy. But there has been a movie business in Hong Kong for three quarters of a century although, like Hong Kong itself, it has re-invented itself many times. The movie business in Hong Kong in the late 1960s was a small, diverse, vigorous but not always profitable industry. It could make employees feel like family but then treat them with all the cruelty that families trade in. Dollar-a-day actresses lived in dormitories, barracked in tinsel harems, strictly regimented in their feeding, grooming, acting and public appearances.

The business churned out three hundred pictures a year. Big studios such as Great World operated twenty-four hours a day, with three shifts, sometimes renting out studio space to small independent film companies. Feng would only rent to them if they paid up before shooting began, because he knew they were constantly on the edge of insolvency.

The Kwong Yi Film Company concentrated on white-collar melodramas in which ambitious characters toiling in offices escaped their dull lives with overblown adventure and romance. Another studio devoted its output to a single starlet, Ting Ying. Nicknamed Transistor Girl, she had just one character and one costume – a radio factory employee in a grey smock. When not on the assembly line she was dating the owner's handsome and agreeably knuckle-headed son. With her irrepressible charm, Ting Ying eventually overcame the boy's family's disdain for her low origins. Other studios were openly funded by mainland China and they turned out "socially progressive" pictures about how society cruelly treats the working class. These pictures really bored audiences silly. To carry the snoozers, the socialists also mixed in gangster, nightclub or musical pictures. And there were plenty of tiny Cantonese-dialect studios that eked out pathetic livings with shabby pictures Hong Kong people called "seven-day fresh," reflecting the factory-farm pace of taking a script to finished print in just one week. One studio was so poor it had to illuminate its movie sets with discarded automobile lights wired to car batteries.

Three big studios dominated the Hong Kong industry: Cathay, Shaw Brothers and Great World. The Big Three produced the whole range of pictures: contemporary musicals, classical Chinese dramas, sword-play epics, gentle, weepy domestic tragedies and even, once, a western featuring all Oriental cowboys. The Big Three prospered. Cathay, Shaws and Great World had sound stages, distributors, theatre circuits, and they had talent. Cathay's great star was a slightly plump beauty known as Laam Toi. She made Cathay a great deal of money but she was deeply miserable and she committed suicide by overdosing on phenobarbitone in 1964. Hysterical fans at the funeral overturned the hearse. Shaws had Peter Chen Ho, Betty Loh Tih, Chen Ping and Wong Yu. But the biggest star of them all, the greatest box office draw wherever Chinese movies played, five times voted Empress of Stars at the annual All-Asia Film Week, the queen of the Hong Kong cinema: Great World's Becky Chan.

Feng almost failed to put Becky under contract when I brought her to his attention back in 1951. She was out of work and afraid of starving to death in a town packed with talented artists who had fled the Communist revolution. Feng wasn't interested in Becky: she was Cantonese and he was a Northerner. He didn't speak Cantonese yet and had little interest in making movies for that little market. He concentrated on shooting Mandarin-track films with the strange and futile hope of getting them to the huge market in Communist China. But the Communists had no interest in decadent musicals about nightclub singers and silly comedies about the idle rich. That world had vanished and in the new China, Feng Hsiao-foon was unnecessary and unwanted.

After I'd personally introduced them to one another, Becky pursued Feng relentlessly, standing outside the gate every morning with flowers or almond cookies or some other pathetic little offering. She kowtowed when his car sped in the gate of his new studios. Whether she actually lifted the hem of her skirt like other would-be actresses I don't know – and I didn't want to know. She ground him down with persistence and eventually he signed her on as an extra.

Her bit-part acting impressed him. Becky worked hard and with great loyalty. Within a year he relented to the reality that most of his Hong Kong audience understood only Cantonese so he started a local-dialect division and gave her leading roles. After she won her first award at the All-Asia Film Week in Tokyo for a Cantonese-track picture, Feng couldn't ignore her talents, and he put her into Mandarin pictures.

Becky was a big enough star to appear in every kind of picture Great World made. In 1966, I met a young man from Wyoming, a soldier on leave from Vietnam who was delighted when I told him I knew Becky. He had seen one of her comedies at the Metropole cinema in Saigon. In *The Trouble That Money Brings,* Becky and comedian Li Chi-chuen star as a newly rich couple. They take delivery of their first refrigerator, only to see it take off on the delivery men's dolly down the steep grade of Cloud View Road in North Point. They chase after it frantically. The fridge barely misses a taxi and forces a grocery-laden amah to jump out of the way. It crashes into a fruit stand and sends oranges in all directions. The affluent couple learn a lesson about the trouble that money brings. The picture was mostly tedious except for Becky and Li's abilities to chase the fridge, flailing their arms so they looked like they were running much faster than was humanly possible.

Becky had even greater success with tragedies, in which she'd played in Cantonese-track films in the early 1950s. Back then there had been hundreds of thousands of refugees in the colony. You might have thought that refugee audiences in Hong Kong, when they scraped together ten cents to go to a cinema, would have wanted happy stories: giddy comedies, costume dramas adapted from Chinese history or Eastmancolor musicals, something to take their minds off their hideous lives. Instead they favoured weepers that really punched them in the guts. Middle-class Anglo-Saxons who have never lived through a cataclysm like that of Twentieth Century China usually find the plots of Becky's melodramas mawkish. But to Hong Kong audiences in the 1950s they were the touch of an electrified wire. In the dark of her temple, where no one could see them, refugees could crouch together and watch the most excruciating sufferings and know exactly what it was like. Becky's cinema tragedies were emollients for pent-up tears.

In *A Mother's Burden* Becky played a refugee woman forced to sell her youngest daughter to prevent the rest of the family from starving. The night before the little girl is to be delivered, Becky makes her daughter some sesame cookies or something, I don't recall exactly what, only that it was the little girl's favourite treat. The sight of that innocent three year old clapping her hands in delight and the reverse angle of Becky's face in such raw, profound pain as she hands her daughter the dainty treat brought such a deep moan of agony from all sides of the Ambassador Cinema that I was chilled. The second act of *A Mother's Burden* takes place years later. Becky, still living in poverty, goes to work in a rich family's home. Naturally, the daughter she'd sold has been adopted by them. Becky realizes this but it is her sacrifice to say nothing, to admire her teenaged daughter in silence. The girl treats Becky badly, and mistakenly accuses her of stealing a necklace. Becky works hard to clear her name and the daughter flings herself into remorse and asks her forgiveness, never once realizing Becky is her natural parent.

"Have you ever been a mother?" her daughter asks. Becky is so fighting her tears that she cannot speak, only nod slightly. *"One day,"* her daughter says, holding Becky close, *"I will be as good a mother as you."* They kiss and Becky goes off into the night. She stumbles to a tram-stop and huddles against a pole, tears streaming down her cheeks.

When the film ended and the lights came up, ushers literally had to pry women from their seats. The women collapsed on the stone floor of the lobby, screaming remorse for their own hidden pasts, shouting the names of children. After some shows ambulances had to be called. Feng added a sixth daily screening, and *A Mother's Burden* played for an unprecedented three months.

Two

I asked Feng if he had contacted the police. He had done nothing, other than order his publicity man to track her down. He had made inquiries among Becky's friends and at the studio but no one knew anything. The publicity man had Telexed a lot of private detectives, overseas Chinese men who worked in Southeast Asian countries. They were watching the Manila Hotel lobby, the sitting room of the Oriental in Bangkok, and the coffee shop of the Shangri-La in Singapore.

"We have to call the police at once," I said. Feng balked. "What if she's been kidnapped by the Communists?" I said. "Or by organized gangs?"

Feng was silent for a few moments. I guess he hadn't figured that. Then he assembled an answer. "It is not suitable for Chinese people to contact the police," he said. The condescension infuriated me. I knew what Chinese people found "suitable." I'd lived in Hong Kong for almost two decades. I repeated my suggestion and again he said no. I began to have the strange and plausible idea that Feng might be of two minds about whether Becky should be found at all. She might have been his biggest star, but she was in her thirties now, a decade older than most actresses in Hong Kong movies, and she wasn't achieving the kind of box office that she used to. Her fame had been in decline since she'd returned from Hollywood in 1963.

I wanted Becky found, regardless of what Feng felt, and decided to go behind his back. She could be in danger. I told him

I would make some discreet inquiries. He considered this but became worried. "It would be very harmful to Becky," he said, "if you were to publish a story about her disappearance in your newspaper." I disagreed and said it could help find her. He became cross and lectured me about the supremacy of his decisions. He was angry because he could not control me. We left it that I would telephone friends who worked for airlines in Hong Kong to see if she'd left the colony.

I idly turned the carriage knob on my typewriter and my story on radioactive fallout slipped free. I gave it to Billy Fong to pass to the dayside editor.

"You okay?" Billy asked.

I nodded and picked up the telephone. I called some friends at the airlines: Thai Airways International, JAL and Pan Am. They checked passenger manifests for me – back then such favours were possible. They found no record of Becky on any flights. Next I tried to telephone some of Becky's colleagues at Great World, but they were all shooting on stages. There was a big musical film in production called *Life's Like That* which required lots of contract players to appear as a nightclub audience. The scale of Hong Kong movie-making meant that leading players sometimes filled in as extras on such shoots. Feng was paying them anyway, he might as well have kept them busy. I left messages for several of them.

Then I called Becky's home in Kowloon Tong and spoke with one of the servants in Cantonese. Ah-niu was the maid and had been with Becky for years. She started to cry when I spoke to her. I asked a lot of indirect questions about whether Becky and Feng had been quarrelling but she was reluctant to speak about her employers, especially over the phone. She only allowed that Becky had been especially anxious for about a month, something I had noticed too.

Finally, I called my friend in the Hong Kong Police, regardless of Feng's wishes. Jack was in the Emergency Unit, the riot police, and would not investigate personally, but he could get inquiries going much faster than I could. When I called, Jack was out patrolling in Kowloon City. I left a message.

That evening I decided to attend the premiere of Becky's newest film, *Long Ago and Far Away*. Great World employees would be at the Ambassador and I wanted to talk to them about Becky. I almost couldn't get to the theatre. The police had found a brown cardboard box left by Maoists on Nathan Road tied to the steel fence that ran down the median. Fearing a bomb, they cordoned off the street so traffic and pedestrians had to find another route through the narrow, jammed side streets of lower Kowloon. Traffic came to a complete halt and pedestrians were reduced to a maddening shuffle. It turned out that the brown box was a hoax designed to cause just such chaos. It contained an old pair of shoes and a note in Chinese that said: *"British imperialists! Use these to run away from the proletarian masses!"*

As I approached the Ambassador Cinema, a flock of startled pigeons took flight with the first frantic burst of a Maoist song issued from a trio of loudspeakers on the overhang of the Astor cinema. The Astor stood across Nathan Road from the Ambassador. It was operated by a company controlled by leftists sympathetic to China's Mao Tse-tung. The whole building was completely covered in red bunting, red lanterns with gold tassels and an enormous, brilliantly painted billboard showing Chinese industrial workers, women activists, People's Liberation Army soldiers and peasants walking arm in arm. They were smiling because above them, where the sun should have been, was a golden cameo of Chairman Mao radiating the brilliant light of his invincible thought. The picture was titled *Chairman Mao Joins a Million People to Celebrate the Great Cultural Revolution*. It came with a "supporting colour short," *The Pearl River Delta Today*, produced by the Central Newsreel & Documentary Film Studio. While such pictures were numbingly dull compared to the glamour, fun, sex and sadness of Hong Kong movies, they did find audiences with dutiful leftists who yawned through four performances a day and joined earnest discussion groups during the intervals. The propaganda music that came honking out of the loudspeakers pounded down on pedestrians packing the sidewalks, one more indignity of urban noise.

On the opposite pavement, a huge hand-painted billboard for *Long Ago and Far Away* completely masked the Ambassador's façade. A three-storey painted billboard showed Becky in a head scarf, looking sad. The disembodied heads of supporting actors, comparative Lilliputians, floated in the background at odd angles, like runaway balloons. *Long Ago and Far Away* was a tragic love story about arranged marriage. It was as free of politics as the Astor's Communist film was larded with it. The Chinese title of the picture gave a different angle on the story: *She Must Smile at a Man She Does Not Like*.

Fans were buying tickets to the premiere and I lined up to get one from the booking windows. In Hong Kong you still bought cinema tickets from a paper seating plan the cashier presented to you. You pointed to your seat, either in the front stalls or in the balcony's Dress Circle. Before the Second World War, only the British got to sit in Dress Circle, but they really had to dress – evening clothes were a requirement of admission. Now everybody sat wherever they chose, and evening clothes for Dress Circle was only a peculiar, faint memory. If it was a quality film in a classy house like those on the Great World circuit, you might get a promotional gift with admission, such as a new brand of soft drink or a tube of lipstick. Great World tried tie-in contests – to promote Becky's 1965 picture *That Day at the Airport*, which featured the repeated image of a wristwatch, Feng raffled off Tissots, the Swiss Omega company's cheaper brand.

There were a few Great World performers in the lobby, mobbed by fans. I spoke to the company's publicity chief. He was cagey and too much of a creature of his employer to reveal anything. I was getting nowhere. Then I spotted Netty Leung, a Cantonese star with Great World. Netty appeared in as many as seventy films a year. In 1964, she too had abruptly disappeared from the studio to flee her workload. She had been acting in three pictures simultaneously and her disappearance forced Feng to shut all of them down. A few days later, the general manager of Feng's Malaysian theatre circuit spotted her in a Singapore restaurant.

Netty's excuse for running away: she was just plain exhausted. Feng fined her six months' pay as a warning to other would-be bolters. For half a year she was indentured labour at Great World.

"Have you seen Becky?" I asked her. I must have appeared so upset that Netty chuckled with embarrassment and bobbed her head to encourage me to find my equilibrium. Netty said she knew nothing of Becky's disappearance. "Although," she said as she went into the auditorium, "if she walked out, good for her."

I was going to leave at that point. I didn't want to sit around in a movie while my best friend was missing. I could hear the film begin with the familiar trumpeting fanfare of the Great World Organisation. Feng, who was almost pathologically vigilant about production costs, hated colour. Back then, Feng had to double his lighting budgets for Eastmancolor. He had shot his first colour production almost in defiance of practicality, using black-and-white-film lighting levels. The performers' faces came out a bilious green, but, with typical patience, cinema-goers didn't seem to mind. At first, Feng was going to keep working that way. Part of him did want his films to look better. So up went the lighting budget. Great World didn't have a colour-processing lab for several years so Feng had to air-freight negatives to Rank Laboratories in England, raising costs and causing unacceptable delays. He ordered that all editing be done on a clipboard, with directors and film editors keeping track of film can numbers and ordering on the spot which pieces of film to use in the final product. Once the processed film was flown back from Rank, a Great World negative cutter pasted the picture together in twenty gruelling hours. Feng also committed his theatre circuit to widescreen projection using the CinemaScope process, which he renamed WorldScope. Shooting was often rushed and clumsy, so the extremities of images were blurred. Again, Chinese movie fans didn't mind – they loved the colour and WorldScope dimensions, the vast brightness a respite from their hard lives in the grey, cramped streets of Hong Kong.

I grew curious, standing in the empty lobby of the Ambassador, listening to the Great World fanfare. Feng had complained of the expense of reshooting the Great World fanfare sequence in colour: the old one had featured a revolving Plasticine globe hovering on a cloud of carbon dioxide. Technicians would have to go out to an electrical goods factory and buy a new electric motor to make the Plasticine globe spin because they had failed to keep the old one they'd used when they'd shot the black-and-white version. So he ordered that the spinning globe be ditched in favour of a beautiful young woman opening a fan in front of her face. Painted on the fan was a map of the world. She became framed by the superimposed Chinese characters *Tai Shai Kaai* and their English counterparts: "Great World."

Then Becky was on screen and I confess that I so longed to see her again that I was willing to stare at her giant projected image as a substitute. An insistent usher tugged me to my seat. *Long Ago and Far Away* was Becky's 190th film. The story was unusually sophisticated and represented a high point in the career of Becky's favourite director, Chen Lo-wen, a veteran of the pre-war Shanghai movie studios. In it, Becky plays a tragic woman riding a train through the countryside. She sits at the window with her hair fashionably swept to the side and heavily lacquered, the way smart women all over the world wore it in 1967. Like all Mandarin-track movies made in Hong Kong, this picture never exactly spelled out where the story was set – certainly not Hong Kong, a small, provincial city that Shanghanese filmmakers such as Feng and Chen disdained. It was probably supposed to take place in some fantasy of a modern, affluent China, near a middle-class Shanghai-like city that had never existed, a conceit every bit as proud and weirdly unreal as the notion of making Mandarin pictures in a Cantonese market, or a colour film with black-and-white lighting. Everything Feng did was proud and weirdly unreal.

The device on which *Long Ago* relies on is that whenever Becky's train stops in a station, she sees something on the platform that reminds her of her past. At the first stop, while a soft rain drizzles down the window, she sees a little girl in a fancy Western dress being tugged along by a happy father. That triggers a memory of the heroine's own childhood. She had grown up in a wealthy home. But from early childhood her character has been pledged by her parents to marry the ugly, cruel son of a neighbouring wealthy family. At another station, there are two happy lovers pooling their pennies to buy dried salty plums. This makes her think of how she had once met a poor but kind and handsome artist with whom she fell in love long ago and far away, putting her at odds with her family and their promise to marry her off to the cruel boy.

And so the story goes, with this train of memories pulling in and out of stations. Great World had used the British section of the Kowloon-Canton Railway and, with studio efficiency, shot the entire picture in twenty days. Becky had spent three days just riding the KCR's big olive-coloured trains back and forth while the crew filmed her. She held a hankie to her mouth every time the diesel engine roared through the mile-long Lion Rock Tunnel, spewing blue exhaust and overwhelming noise into the cars behind.

At one point, and for no intended reason, Becky sings. Even in first-class Mandarin dramas things sometimes happened for no reason – moviegoers expected a song. Feng Hsiao-foon understood this as a ritual rather than logical device and gave moviegoers what they wanted. She sings a Mandarin version of the famous song from the 1944 American movie *Cover Girl*, which justifies the film's English title. It actually carries more freight in Becky's picture than it had in the American one, serving as a soliloquy.

> *"Long ago and far away,*
> *I dreamed a dream one day;*
> *And now that dream is here beside me!"*

As Becky's character made her way down the railway line, suffering and agonizing, I glanced about the movie theatre at the patrons. This might have been the film's premiere, but it was no exclusive Hollywood-style gala. Tickets had been sold to the public at regular prices, just as with any other performance. Money had to be made at every showing. There in the audience, their faces illuminated by the screen's reflection, were Becky's fans. They were refugees: about one-third of Hong Kong's population of three million had recently fled China for the British colony. These movie-goers were middle-aged, married women with their hair pulled back into ponytails and fixed with rubber bands who came to escape the monotony of their tiny, drab homes in Kowloon housing estates – the ones where your kitchen was nothing more than a small brazier on a balcony and the lavatory was a malfunctioning communal toilet down the hall shared by twenty-four people. And there were hawker women who sold vegetables or cheap plastic goods on Hong Kong's crowded and bustling sidewalks who now sat in the Ambassador in light day-pyjamas.

There were lonely single men, mostly factory workers, who had fled China's upheavals and had become the lost souls of Hong Kong. One man used to turn up for every single premiere of a Becky Chan picture. That had been years before, in the '50s and early '60s. He always wore the tattered and faded uniform of the Kuomintang Army, which had been vanquished by the Communists on the mainland in 1949. He and other hapless Kuomintang soldiers had been forced to flee to Hong Kong when the Communists ultimately proved victorious. Had they stayed behind they might have been imprisoned in the vengeful early years after Liberation, or slaughtered. They wandered around Hong Kong like ghosts, still wearing their uniforms and trying to make a living at odd jobs.

Whenever people saw that pathetic man at Becky's premieres they spoke of "Chiang Kai-shek's lost brother." He would sit down at the front and stare up at Becky. Before *The Goddess of Mercy,* he would sit in awe and contemplation, perhaps adoration. His oily face shone in the movie reflection and you could see two bumpy cheek bones sticking out on his Cantonese face, the faded Republican Sun flashes on the shoulders of his worn-out uniform plainly and pathetically visible. He had inspired in me endless questions about where he had come from, what he had done with his life, and why he always came to worship the Goddess of Mercy. People joked at her premieres that Becky should say hello to her biggest and grubbiest fan, but so far as I know Becky never did. He wasn't around anymore; nobody had seen him in years, and I often wondered what had happened to him. Now I looked up at Becky on the WorldScope screen, so magnified, so vividly coloured. This was my friend, this was the Goddess of Mercy. She was gone. It wounded me to be left with no more than her shadow.

THREE

The following morning, I took the ferry from North Point to Kowloon City. Down on the water the salt and morning mist smelled fresh after the all-night stink of Hong Kong Island. I sat on the lower deck and stared without purpose at the airport runway, which jutted into Kowloon Bay. It was only a few hundred feet from the ferry's route and I dumbly watched a Thai Airways Caravelle thunder down the runway and climb out. A few weeks before, an inbound Caravelle had fallen short of the runway during a typhoon, resulting in many deaths. This morning, the sun was still low and a fresh South China Sea breeze was funnelling in through Lye Mun, and for the only time in twenty-four hours I felt cool and clean. The day would be scorching hot again.

At the Hongkong and Yaumati Ferry wharf in Kowloon City I walked down the stone steps to the bus bays. I was to cover an expected leftist demonstration outside a plastics factory. Feng Hsiao-foon had forbidden me to telephone Ah-niu, Becky's maid, at their home. He didn't know that I already had. Like a schoolboy, my instinct was to disregard him. In fact, I intended to visit Ah-niu in secret. At the bus plaza, three forlorn-looking palm trees invigilated over the daily ebb and flow of passengers. Young factory women, Ting Ying's Transistor Girls, stood in corrals made out of welded grey steel pipes, waiting for buses. When a Kowloon Motor Bus No. 11B swung around a curve to the bus bay, its driver trying to keep to an impossibly tight schedule, the huge double-decker leaned over precariously toward the Transistor Girls like a great red and cream-coloured slab about to entomb them. While the women pushed and shoved each other to get aboard, the driver clambered out a little door on the side of his cab with a garden watering can to top up his radiator.

I boarded my bus and rode in the upper saloon through the squalor of Kowloon City to Kowloon Tong. Crowded into the heaving bus, I read that morning's edition of the paper. On the front page was a story about a mob of Maoists paying teenagers to throw stones at passing Kowloon Motor buses. Adjacent to that story, and this was so typical of the schizophrenia of the *China Telegraph* in the summer of 1967, was an overly enthusiastic item headlined "Stars Have a Ball at New Kowloon Bowling Complex." Hong Kong didn't have a reliable supply of drinking water, people slept in the streets and Maoists were pelting buses, but we had modern bowling lanes. The story ran with a photo of young Josephine Siu Fong-fong firing a bowling ball down an alley in the new Star Bowl.

Hong Kong's Chinese movie business was regular news and avidly covered by the *China Telegraph*. The paper was losing money, and management believed we had to appeal to Chinese who read English as well as lower-class Europeans and British forces personnel who were not served by the *South China Morning Post*. The *Post* was so stodgy and tame everyone called it the "Government Gazette." The *China Telegraph* sought to reach people in the British forces in Hong Kong, low-ranked colonials and, most of all, educated and English-reading Chinese. So we followed Chinese entertainment closely.

Movie actresses, including Becky Chan, were constantly presiding over charity events, inaugural airline services and bank-branch ribbon cuttings. Siu Fong-fong was much younger than Becky and enormously popular with teenaged Hong Kong girls who identified with her high spirits, groovy Western clothes and a consuming preoccupation with romance, all of which were unobtainable for real-world Hong Kong girls. Even though Fong-fong starred in low-class Cantonese-dialect pictures and Becky performed almost exclusively in prestige Mandarin pictures, the younger actress was stealing the public's attention from her.

The bus rolled up Prince Edward Road and the neighbourhood changed as the ground got higher. The filthy tenements that hunkered around the airport under the most appalling noise of screaming passenger jets gave way to tidier flat blocks. Servants worked in the car parks, wiping down Cortinas or Impalas with long dusters made of brown rooster feathers. The bus turned onto Waterloo Road, a wide thoroughfare lined with expensive low flat blocks and numerous houses. Despite the heavy traffic feeding into the newly opened Lion Rock Tunnel at the north end of town, Waterloo Road and its side streets was the best place to live in Kowloon. Long before the British allowed Chinese to live on the upper levels of the Peak on Hong Kong Island, affluent Orientals and middle-class Europeans were living in Kowloon Tong, side by side. Feng Hsiao-foon had lived here since coming down from Shanghai in 1950. He and Becky owned a smart flat-roofed house, small by Western standards of luxury, but immensely roomy for Hong Kong.

I alighted at Suffolk Road, a quiet little side street away from the groan and rattle of green-and-red delivery vans on Waterloo Road. The Feng home had a little tiled courtyard with a ficus tree surrounded by a circular stone bench, a shady place for a poet's contemplation, but to which no poet ever came. I pressed a black intercom button. The button and the metal speaker panel were encrusted with rust from the salt air. A woman's voice squawked out of the speaker. *"Wei?"* I announced myself to Ah-niu, the amah, and she buzzed me in.

The courtyard was a bit of rockery Feng had contrived, an ersatz little echo of the great Soochow-style gardens. Grotesque twisted-looking concrete rocks surrounded a little pool filled with koi fish. The courtyard came alive for a moment. An annoying little dog ran forth from under the cool of the stone bench, making a huge, snarling, slobbering show as defender of the household. Feng had named her Chung Hsiang, after the Peking opera *Chung Hsiang Upsets the Classroom*. She barked and snarled and almost choked on her own tongue. I hated that dog so much. I wanted to take the belt out of my trousers, chase her around the courtyard and flog it, but, clever me, I knew that Ah-niu probably wouldn't let me in afterward. Anyway, exhausted and bankrupted by her brief performance, Chung Hsiang gave up the defence, retreated under the bench and collapsed in a ball of hair.

I looked at the house. Ah-niu was standing in a window on the ground floor and she had visible misgivings. It was rare that I was allowed to visit their house. Like many people in Hong Kong, Feng preferred not to entertain at home, but chose less private, less revealing banquet rooms in Chinese restaurants and private clubs. Admittance to Feng's home when he was not there was normally unthinkable so it was testimony to Ah-niu's worry about Becky. I wouldn't have put Ah-niu at risk of Feng's anger unless I felt it were important.

Ah-niu opened the big wooden front door. Above it was a stone tablet sunk into the wall. Carved and painted in gold were the characters for *"Bricks and Mortar of the Nation,"* meaning the family home. On a small sconce beside the door was a brass plaque, also tarnished by salt air, that bore the name of Master Tsang. He had been a great opera performer who had introduced that art to South China in the Eighteenth Century. Now he was a kind of deity. Cantonese opera performers and, by extension movie people, honoured him.

The amah took me to the kitchen. Feng had left for Great World hours before, where he indulged himself in the make-up department with a shave. His face lathered up, he'd watch the make-up girl slowly scrape at his chin. It made them nervous, the way he scrutinized them, and he probably enjoyed it, that complex interchange, him scowling at them, the girls holding razors to his face. He liked his female employees to be frightened of him even when they held razors to his throat. It was potent and erotic.

Ah-niu served me coffee in the kitchen on Becky's overly fancy English bone china. The nursemaid brought the baby out for me to see. I held Amanda in my arms for a few minutes, and the baby considered me with grave concentration. Amanda tended to scowl, as if she were finding her first six months on Earth unsatisfactory. She looked about the room then back at me and eased into a noisy cry, so I handed her back to the nursemaid.

Becky could have no more children. It was cruel to have lost the ability. The hysterectomy had left Becky despondent and often prompted spontaneous crying. Feng said nothing on the subject to me – I was not family and I was a foreigner. He outwardly showed only ineffable stoicism, if not sympathy, for his melancholy wife. Ah-niu told me that Feng had become angry with Becky following the operation. The best that he could muster was to sigh impatiently and, once, he told Becky in front of Ah-niu: "All this crying will prepare you for *Long Ago and Far Away.*"

Ah-niu told me that Becky had received numerous letters that bore postage stamps from the People's Republic of China. They had been clumsily stuck on – Chinese stamps had no glue on the back; correspondents had to slather paste on them from a brush bottle in post offices. Ah-niu did not know who the correspondents were, possibly activists soliciting her help or condemning her as a tool of the British. She said the letters had been addressed to "Expel Imperialism City." In the insanity of the 1960s, Red Guards flooded into the southern city of Canton, 130 kilometres northwest of Hong Kong. They were a paramilitary force of malevolent teenagers who sought to help Mao regain control of the Communist Party from his rivals. But they became large and potent and they went berserk, making mad orders – the madder the better, as far as they were concerned. They invaded the Canton post office and issued a decree that no mail bound for the British colony should be delivered if it bore the name "Hong Kong." They had unilaterally and spontaneously renamed Hong Kong "Expel Imperialism City." Any postal workers who dared question these hysterical zealots were beaten ferociously, sometimes to death. There was other madness in Canton. The Red Guards decided that since red was the colour of the Communist Party, all traffic in Canton streets should proceed on red and halt on green lights. They would stand at intersections and scream at baffled and intimidated truck drivers who had stopped on red at the city's few traffic lights: *"Go forth with the Red Sun of the Communist Party!"* the teenagers screamed. *"Go! Go! Go!"*

"Did Mrs. Feng have any doctor's prescriptions?" I asked Ah-niu in Cantonese. *"Western-doctor medicine?"*

She shook her head. *"Only painkillers after the operation,"* she said. *"But they ran out and she didn't renew them."* Becky preferred Chinese medicines over Western drugs, which she said were harsh and had no underlying unity of purpose.

The first time I met Becky was in the autumn of 1948. I was new to Hong Kong and still enthralled by the sights and smells of the colony. I'd gone over to Kowloon from my dismal flat on the island to tour the big shrine to Wong Tai Sin. It stood at the top end of the peninsula, just below the great hills that ringed the north side of Victoria Harbour. From the steps of the shrine you could see all the way down to the tip of Kowloon and in late autumn, when the air was sunny and clear, it was beautiful. The shrine was always packed because the god Wong Tai Sin had gained a fabulous reputation among refugees for coming to their assistance. His advice, conveyed through a canon known as the One Hundred Poems, led one man to start a small business sharpening knives on a sidewalk and now he owned a big shop in Laichikok. A refugee woman took Wong Tai Sin's advice on whether to marry a certain man. The poems had indicated marriage, which turned out to be successful and there were many sons.

I had grown a very red moustache in a bid to look older than twenty-two. I wore a Harris tweed jacket, which I clutched to my sides as I dodged platoons of beggars on the steps to the shrine. Mounting the curving stone staircase to the main courtyard of the temple, I saw the gate of the temple, with its slouching tiled roof and pillars. Inside hundreds of people held clumps of smouldering joss sticks in their hands as they knelt before a stone effigy of Wong Tai Sin. Some were in rags and looked truly in need of miracles. Others wore fine woollens and silks and looked as if they ate meat three times a day, and not the gristly cuts. In among them was a slender young Chinese woman in a Western-style white dress, cinched at the waist and cut low around the neck, a cheap, vulgar thing she'd probably bought in a back-street market stall, not a fine British dress shop. She was very young, very beautiful and she knelt there among the poor and destitute, the affluent and well-fed, clutching a great fistful of joss sticks. She batted the smoke away with her free hand and coughed irritably.

She saw me looking at her and winked, a shocking gesture from a respectable Chinese girl back in 1948. She examined me, my tweed sports jacket and oyster-coloured trousers and probably concluded (rightly) that I was harmless. "Hello," she said in English. She was truly a lovely young woman, even in that poor-quality dress. After she finished her supplication she asked me to help her insert the joss sticks in a huge sand-filled urn. She gave me half of them and we planted them together.

"What do you want?" she asked.

I was flustered because I thought she was accusing me of trying to pick her up.

"From him," she said, gesturing over her shoulder toward an oversize stone effigy of a bearded man painted with bright enamels. "From Wong Tai Sin?"

"I was just curious about the temple," I said.

She fired out her arm and extended her hand in a put-'er-there way she must have seen in an American movie with Eve Arden in it. "Becky Chan."

I shook her hand. "My name is Paul Hauer."

She repeated it several times to make her tongue get used to the feel of it. "You're a tourist?"

"No, I live here. I work for a newspaper."

"What do you do for it?"

"General reporter."

"A newsman," she said. "Some glamour." We finished putting the joss sticks in the sand and she clapped her hands together. "Uck, everything's so dirty here. Hey, I got a story for your newspaper." She told me that the temple was far holier than the crowds, smoke, noise, peanut vendors and playing children made it appear. "Even the Turnip Heads had to pay to harvest the bamboo stands that surrounded the temple when they were here," she said. "They were so in awe of Wong Tai Sin." She was talking about the Japanese forces during the Second World War, using the defiant slang the Cantonese used for their tormentors in the darkest years of occupation.

"Let's go ask the god for advice." She led me toward an arcade covered with corrugated tin roofs. Inside were fortune-tellers. "You want anything from the god today?" she asked. She turned and looked at me for a second then asked, "Do you see everything in blue?"

I didn't understand.

"Your eyes are blue. So is everything you see blue?"

I asked her if she saw everything in brown.

She smiled beautifully and rolled her eyes to the side. "Hey, is your hair naturally blond or did you dye it? I'd like blond hair too. It would be fun."

I couldn't resist her. She was jaunty, vivacious and a bit out of her depth with her forwardness. She must have helped my frail ego by showing interest in me then appearing vulnerable with her naïveté. I went with her to the sheds at the side of the temple. There sat sage fortune-tellers, smoking long metal pipes and examining the One Hundred Poems for answers to the questions put to them by subscribers. She sat before one man who had a couple of long wiry hairs sprouting from a mole, considered decorative, like bonsai trees, I suppose. I stood by while she fished out a couple of coins from a pasteboard purse that looked like a miniature version of a child's lunch bucket. It was pale pink and so tacky I couldn't help but smile. She was sweet, but the girl needed tutoring in Western fashions. I had enough sense not to tease her about her clothes.

Becky put her question to the fortune-teller. He gave her a tin canister, perforated at the top, which held a number of sticks. She shook the canister and a single stick rattled out through one of the perforations. The fortune-teller looked at it through his spectacles, sighed in bland recognition, then looked through a book for the corresponding poem. He read it aloud to her in Cantonese and then gave her an interpretation. All the while she listened very intently, very gravely, asked a few questions in Cantonese and then thanked the man. I stood by and watched without comprehension. When she was done the fortune-teller gave a jaunty little wave and considered me, thought I might be business and beckoned me over. I just waved politely and escorted Becky back to the main compound. "What did you inquire about?" I asked.

She gave me a cheerful smile. "French high heels," she said. "I want them so badly, so I sought advice on how to get them. They'll be lovely when they arrive." She glanced up in the air then winked at me again. "They'll be here any time soon," she said, as if they were about to plunge out of the sky and hit the ground in front of her.

Becky told me that the fortune-tellers in their decrepit sheds were the principal conduit to Wong Tai Sin's munificence. With explicit instructions from the One Hundred Poems she had, she claimed, overcome a clumsiness that had confounded her parents. They were Mother and Father Chan and they had adopted her out of the Door of Hope Orphanage and put her to work in their Cantonese opera troupe. She said that through his actions her father had taught her to come to Wong Tai Sin and ask for help.

That day in Wong Tai Sin Temple, while refugees were praying for a roof over their heads, redemption from illness or just plain money, Becky was clapping her hands in divine pursuit of French-made high heels. Or so that's what she told me. I couldn't understand Cantonese yet so I didn't know what she had spoken to the fortune-teller about. I had to laugh at her frivolity about shoes amid the squalor of Kowloon. I gave her my business card and invited her to call. "Hey," she said, slapping my arm with the back of her hand. "Is this a pick-up?" I blushed fiercely and she laughed. "Hey! Do that again. Change colour like that. Can you turn other colours? Green or blue?" We went down the steps and beheld the view of Kowloon below, a panorama today lost behind a wall of modern high-rises. She stopped before a beggar child and gave him a coin.

She looked back at me and said, "Next time I will pray to Wong Tai Sin for a telephone, so I can call you." I didn't know her yet so I couldn't tell just how thin the top layer of her frivolity was and how networked it was with fissures, like crackle-glazed porcelain. It was a such fine day in October 1948 and we were both young and more adventurous than we realized. She seemed like a fun person to me, as I said in my diary that evening, and I probably seemed exotic to her. So we began to pal around. It never occurred to me to date Becky. The fun we would have in those early years would go a long way for both of us.

I took Becky and a party of others – there was a BOAC crewman I wanted to hanging around with that year, an American reporter, and two other actresses who worked for the Southern Electric Film Company – to a gambling den. I thought it would be a fantastic adventure. The women said they didn't want to go, but the presumed authority of their Western male friends got the better of their judgement. I took them to a back street in Hung Hom, just past the old ferry dock, where there was a fetid old shophouse next to the Hong Kong United Shipyard. The shophouse sold cheap plastic housewares, but its principal activity was illicit money-lending.

I remember that one of the Southern Electric actresses started to shop for plastic tumblers until we gently tugged her to the back of the building and up a narrow set of stone stairs. You had to go through the living quarters of a small family to get to the gaming room. There was a granny lying on a cot in front of the secret door. Whether she was actually ill or just putting on a lucrative act wasn't clear. You had to wait while her teenaged grandsons lifted her up and aside. "Not again," she would mutter when she got hoisted out of the way. *"I'm so tired,"* she said, holding out a leathery palm for a coin. Upstairs we laid down one-dollar bets and thought what a smart set we were, until the police arrived with a battering ram for the steel door. I recall running down the back stone steps with Becky, while she and three other actresses shrieked, *"Fai-ti, lah! Hurry! Hurry!"* We escaped.

Becky became very quiet and didn't speak to me for a long time. I hadn't realized that my idea of boyish fun would frighten her so. It dawned on me belatedly why. She had just hustled her way into a job at Southern Electric, and if her bosses had found out about the raid they would have fired Becky. Her job was more important to her than any night of fun and I apologized for causing her such worry. I should have thought better of the risk I put Becky and the other women in. Stupid of me, but then I was a very injudicious young man.

Seated in Feng's kitchen, drinking his coffee, I asked Ah-niu if Feng had been cruel to Becky and she said no, although I suspected that she was merely being decorous. She didn't have to tell me Feng could be cold and dictatorial. When he thought that no one was listening, Feng could speak to Becky with a cutting meanness. At a banquet celebrating Great World's fifteenth anniversary I heard him mutter to her, *"You used to be so pretty. I think you're gaining weight. You know how the 'Scope lens stretches your face. You'll look even fatter up there."* Becky only looked at her coffee cup and nudged it around the table, pretending nothing had been said.

Ah-niu excused herself and hooked a rubber hose from the kitchen cold-water faucet. She ran it from the faucet to the first of four large olive-green plastic barrels in the adjacent pantry. She turned the water on and began to fill them. *"It's our day,"* she said. While the water splashed noisily into the first barrel I asked her if Feng had told her anything about Becky's melancholy and she replied, *"Mr. Feng never speaks to me about anything other than household duties."*

We said nothing for a while and I waited for her to fill the barrels. That summer, Hong Kong endured the worst drought in its history. We were subject to strict water rationing by the government: four hours of service every other day. My shower head would be gushing assuredly when I stepped beneath it, but just as I put shampoo into my hair, the water would dribble off and give a disappointed gasp. I usually forgot to fill my water barrels on the day my neighbourhood had its turn so I went without. My kitchen sink filled with dishes and glasses and I would come home on a water day to find I'd left the tap open and there was water splashing everywhere in obscene and chaotic abundance. In the slums of Hong Kong Island and Kowloon, women shoved one another in ill-policed queues next to forlorn little public stand pipes, their only source of water. They'd spend the better part of a day filling up the square metal cans and taking them back to their shacks in the hills then coming back for more. The drought had left Hong Kong reservoirs nearly empty. You could see them from the hillsides: sadly reduced ponds edged with steep chalky orange banks, wrinkled and arid in the summer sun. There had been no typhoons to replenish the reservoirs and a secondary source of water, through a pipe from China, could not be increased. No local bureaucrat in south China would dare make a decision on increasing water without worrying about whether he was going to be charged with aiding the British imperialists in Expel Imperialism City.

At most times, China seemed as far away as Europe from the cares of life in the British colony. China nevertheless could occasionally intrude on our lives with dramatic impact. My good friend, Sergeant Jack Rudman, faced down increasingly militant labour agitators who had been emboldened by bullying Marxists in the nearby Portuguese colony of Macau. Eager to gain favour with Maoists on the Mainland, Hong Kong leftists launched the biggest period of unrest Hong Kong has ever known in peacetime and Jack was getting it in the face. While I covered stories about demonstrations, riots and bombings for the *China Telegraph*, I would see Jack and his men in the Emergency Unit, firing tear gas into crowds of young people waving Mao's *Quotations*. In turn the leftists would hurl back anything they could lay their hands on: flower pots, sharpened bamboo spears, metal bars, rattan chairs and all sizes of stones. In one riot an enormous sledge hammer came whirling through the air at Jack. It missed him, but struck a Chinese colleague, breaking his shoulder.

I would call Jack every evening to see if he was all right. Sometimes he was too tired or weary of stimulation even to take my calls. He showed all the tedium that came from too much excitement. "The only thing I want to do at the end of the day," he said, "is go back to quarters and wash the tear gas out of my hair. It's a simple thing, and I wish more people realized that. Please don't call again until the weekend." I felt like a nuisance and I was a bit ashamed of my preoccupation, as though I were a fretful old woman.

And so I devoted myself to my news stories. The agitators' disruptions to daily life were often ingenious: teenaged boys boarded buses and released bags of snakes, creating a blind panic that almost resulted in a crash. Little schoolgirls, hounded and intimidated by leftists, were instructed to position themselves between the demonstrators and the police. They would stand there with their arms linked, caught between two determined forces. You could see them crying in terror and wanting to bolt. The Communist press was standing by to witness a brutal police attack on little girls so it could publish stories and photographs of the cruelty. I heard one leftist hectoring a little girl who was about to break ranks and flee, using a threat understood only by the two of them: *"Li-li! Remember what I warned you! I* will *tell your father what happened!"*

Ah-niu finished filling the water barrels in the pantry and placed lids on them. She put the hose away and looked out the tiny window over the sink. There was nothing to see but the wall of the house next door. All at once she burst into tears and turned her head away from me. *"Gangsters have kidnapped her,"* she said.

She wiped a handkerchief over her face and tried to busy herself in an already tidy kitchen. She plugged the electric kettle back in to make more coffee.

"How do you know that?" I asked her.

"I don't. It just makes sense," Ah-niu said. *"She wouldn't just run away. She has to work hard. She has a new baby. She has many responsibilities."*

"She wasn't happy. She hasn't been happy for years," I said,

Ah-niu thought the remark irrelevant and it showed how far apart our worlds were. *"What is happiness? Happiness is for the idle. She has a family to feed and care for. She has a hard job."*

"Do you think that Mr. Feng has hurt her?" I asked. *"Do you think he arranged for her to go away?"*

Ah-niu pulled the plug of the kettle out of the wall. *"Perhaps,"* she said. *"Mr. Feng has been very cold."*

She brought me a fresh pot of coffee. I drank a cup in silence. When she thought I wasn't looking, Ah-niu sneaked her hand into the sugar bowl and took out a single cube. She put it into her mouth, closed her eyes and concentrated on the sweetness. Becky did the same thing all the time. The gesture made me think of her.

Ah-niu let me look around some more but she was growing nervous with the length of my stay. I was snooping about the Feng household shamelessly. Ah-niu walked behind me to scrutinize my every move, polishing a sofa table after I'd touched it, as if Feng would lift fingerprints when he got home. She was keenly aware that my presence could get her fired. I went into the main bathroom and opened the medicine cabinet. Inside were little pots of make-up creams, lipsticks and eye shadow. There were also capsules of Peking Royal Jelly, a box of purgative tea, aspirin, mouthwash and deer horn extract. Under the sink, in the cupboard, there were a few boxes of Hazeline Snow face powder and five aerosol cans of hair lacquer.

I quoted an old saying which Ah-niu took to and she repeated to herself: *"Beautiful women are ill-fated."* It was what women in movie audiences explain to themselves on why the blessedly glamorous really are damned, and how they, the ordinary women of the world, have the real advantages.

Feng was an inveterate showman who loved to trot out his pretty wife at lavish parties, like a prize chicken. In Cantonese slang, associating women with chicken is an obscene comment, but in my poisoned opinion not at all inappropriate for Feng. Like Cecil B. de Mille, whose movies condemned extreme depravity but showed it in loving detail, Feng Hsiao-foon knew how to indulge the public's sex fantasies while vigorously decrying them. Many of his "decadent" Mandarin-track pictures were about nightclubs, rich people's idle cares, airline stewardesses, singers and the police. In films such as *Pink and Deadly* or *Don't Bargain with Fate*, Becky plays nightclub singers who turn their back on normal domestic lives with husbands, children and in-laws so they could perform on stage. It is pre-ordained that the adventuring woman head ends in ruin, reassuring the audience about their mundane domestic arrangements, but the public got a good gawk at the fun she had before the end. Yes, beautiful women really were ill-fated.

Ah-niu's anxiety peaked when I went into the Feng's bedroom. It was wildly over-decorated in a Louis XIV style, with blue satin cushions and oppressively over-carved furniture that Feng and Becky had shipped in from the United States. I sat on the edge of the bed and looked at the items on Becky's night table. There was a script for an upcoming picture. Recorded at the bottom of the title page, in Becky's hand, was idle gossip of no great importance. So-and-so spent $4,000 on legal fees to petition for divorce. So-and-so's wife is pregnant. It told me nothing about Becky. There was a Royal Doulton figurine of a woman holding the edge of her billowing yellow dress. Her right hand was missing, chipped off probably when it had got knocked to the floor. There was a big book of Chinese medicine, detailing cures for various ailments. Chinese cinnamon to treat yang-deficiency in kidneys. Clove tree to counteract vomiting. Powdered oyster shells for heart palpitations. Wild turmeric for chest pains and semi-conscious states. There was no bookmark, no annotation, nothing to indicate just what Becky had been looking through these medical journals for. It told me nothing more than she had a general interest in disease, illness and its treatment. It was the first time I'd ever set foot in her bedroom and I noticed something missing that caused me a moment of sorrow and emptiness. Despite our two decades of close friendship, there was nothing in this room, or anywhere in Becky's home, that showed any physical evidence that I had a place in her life. No little photo of me in a collection of similar pictures on a side table, none of the trinket gifts I'd given her over the years. I sighed and put the books back on the night table. Ah-niu had become so anxious about my sitting on the bed that when I stood up she frantically swept the creases out of the bedspread.

I thanked Ah-niu for her cooperation and left. I stepped outside. The day was growing very hot. I glanced up at the words over the front door, *"Bricks and Mortar of the Nation."* Chung Hsiang came to life again, for just a moment, when I came out the front door. She barked and slobbered furiously, trailing me to the metal gate and, once satisfied that I had closed it behind me, turned and went back to the shade in triumph.

FOUR

How different Becky's movie roles were from the beautiful but gawky and naïve young woman I first met back in 1948. Both Becky and Hong Kong offered a new start for me, after a bad life in Canada. Like the refugees from China, I found a safe haven in Hong Kong, far from personal turmoil. I had once dreamed of a career as a singer in Canada (I referred to myself as a "song stylist") but I never got further than paying for two years of university at United College in Winnipeg by performing part-time. I appeared during intermissions at the Uptown Theatre, a cinema on Academy Road. Between the shorts, co-feature and the main film I would rise grandly out of the basement on an elevator platform, surrounded by an eight-man orchestra. I sang dance numbers, my specialty being animal songs. I performed "Arfie the Doggie in the Window," "Mr. Bluebird," and "Wolf Call," which I spiced up with realistic howls. While I performed, little gold lights in the blue ceiling of the Uptown would twinkle like stars.

My father disowned me, quite violently. A letter from the United College dean's office arrived at my home, addressed to my father. It stated that the college had expelled me. My father disbelieved it at first and made an increasingly humiliating telephone call to the dean's office, hotly denying the charge of "personal indecency." After my father raved on the telephone to the dean about how preposterous the sexual allegation was, I quietly took the phone from his hand and hung it up. "It's true," I said very quietly. Then the police arrived, I was taken in and formally charged. My father grew furious, first with them, then with me. His doubts began to spread around the edges of his confidence in me like slime on a favourite swimming hole. In silence he drove me home from the police station on James Avenue. I wanted to bolt from the car when we crossed the Redwood Bridge and dive into the brown waters of the river, so frightened and ashamed I was. The idea actually fascinated me for a few minutes. When we were home again, I had one of those scenes everyone dreads: the increasingly hostile examination by the father, the palliative cups of tea from mum, her feckless attempts to calm the father, the steadily rising timbre of his questioning. It ended with him giving me four or five good hard smacks on my face with his fist. I fell clear over the back of the chesterfield. Mum got a raw steak from the fridge, then started to cry quietly as she pressed it to my cheek. It's been half a century since then, and I still don't like to talk about it.

I had been caught in bed with my history professor and a mechanic who worked for Grey Goose Bus Lines. We had been introduced to one another through a very private and secretive circuit of men in Winnipeg into which I had only just insinuated myself. The Winnipeg police (who in contrast to their counterparts in Hong Kong had very little with which to preoccupy themselves) had been keeping an eye on the professor for some time. They burst to his house, I yanked the sheets over myself, the professor sputtered about search warrants and the bus mechanic fell off the far side of the bed. The professor went to jail briefly. As for myself and the mechanic – I remember he had bus grease under his fingernails and it made him terribly exciting – we were given suspended sentences. The whole city learned of it somehow. Winnipeg was a hostile place. No man even used an umbrella back then, since such devices were considered effeminate. And if a simple black umbrella were a lacy parasol in the minds of right-thinking Winnipeggers, sex with another man was beyond abomination. People whispered when I walked down Portage Avenue and some morally outraged young man in front of the Lyceum Theatre threw a Coke bottle at my head.

My father informed me that I was not his son and that I was to get out of his house by the week's end. I went to my room, examined the relics and mementos of my recently concluded childhood and had a quiet cry. When I finished, my mother knocked on the bedroom door and pushed our ancient black Labrador, Duke, into the room. "He wants to see you for a while," she said and closed the door again with barely a sound. I was so grateful for Duke's cataractic gaze, his white muzzle on my lap.

As I told myself with brave nonchalance the next day, my fortunes lay elsewhere. My mum put me on a Canadian Pacific train to Montreal; my father refused to take time away from work to see me off. While we waited in the depot she kept scratching Duke's neck and talking only to him. "Poor old Duke," she said. "You're so very sad that our Paul is going away, aren't you? You don't know what you're going to do, do you?" She didn't always talk exclusively to the dog; only during times of personal crisis. Everything of significance went through the dog. She walked Duke up to the train platform to see me off. The train pulled out of the CPR station in the middle of a blasting rain storm, and I felt about as wretched, ashamed and condemned as any twenty-one-year-old boy could.

It was the era, of course, but every time I saw a soldier, sailor or airman on the train I felt even more intensely wicked. A whole pack of them boarded at Fort William, looking so brave and heroic, even when they told each other obscene jokes or picked their noses. These were men who served their countries and honoured their families. All I had done was disgrace mine through sexual perversion. My carapace of guilt only began to break in Montreal, where I looked for work as a nightclub singer. Some of the irrepressibility of youth returned when I saw the *boîtes* of St. Catherine Street. It proved more difficult to break into nightclubs in Montreal than I'd expected. Managers didn't think that intermission singing in Winnipeg cinemas was sufficient, and more than one actually walked out during my audition song, a childish anthem called "Let the People Sing" that was utterly inappropriate for Montreal's champagne-and-gun fire nightclubs.

I did not stay long in Montreal. I managed to get myself run out of town there too. I was caught in bed with a nightclub dancer. He was thrilling, he was muscled, he was from Martinique and he called himself "Othello." He let me wear the shark's-teeth necklace he used in the Folies Nègres routine at the Club La Framboise and he showed me how to do the splits. Even more thrilling than Othello was getting caught in bed with him by the police. Othello knew his way around Montreal and had the sense to lick off five ten dollar bills from a small roll in his pocket for the good constables. I didn't, so I was arraigned on gross indecency yet again. While I was awaiting trial I went to the Canadian Pacific office and bought a ticket on the next boat for England. A few months later, from Hong Kong, I wrote to my United College history professor, who was now lecturing the cons in Stony Mountain on Benjamin Disraeli's career and dodging them in the showers, and told him that I had decided to go east. I just hadn't realized just how far east I would go.

I arrived in the colony feeling renewed, blue-eyed and hearty. With the last of a lot of money my mother had given me secretly, I bought a ticket on BOAC to the Far East. My idea had been to become a foreign correspondent in Japan. When the BOAC flying boat splashed down in Kowloon Bay, the British authorities put me off because I had no accreditation to continue on to U.S.-occupied Japan. In Hong Kong I found a job with the weakling rival to the *South China Morning Post*. The *China Telegraph* was a small broadsheet that the managing editor called "a working man's newspaper." The managing editor was a man named Trebilcoe, a veteran of second-rate newspapers in Britain and India, and, like his colleagues around the world, he was going to pieces on alcohol. He had a pink face and his grey-blond hair was malodorous. You could smell gin on his breath at ten in the morning, thanks to a twenty-sixer in his desk's lower drawer. "May your career at the *China Telegraph* be a long and restful one," he said on my first day. This wreckage was no place to make friends for an eager young man who had just rescued himself out of Canada.

Mr. Trebilcoe must have invested in me the last of his tattered hopes because he made sure that I was always busy, covering every sort of story there was, as if I were a surrogate fresh start for him. Mr. Trebilcoe was one of a breed of itinerants who spent a few years in any city in Asia that had an English-language newspaper: the *Bangkok World,* the *North China Herald,* the *Straits Times,* the *New Straits Times* and one paper I thought had a most charming name, the *Borneo Bulletin.* After editors like Mr. Trebilcoe grew tired of the town and the inner trembling about their lives became external, they would move on. Such a life and the deprivations and internment of war had left these men preternaturally aged, tired and bibulous. At the time my perception of Mr. Trebilcoe varied between being picturesque and a pathetic nuisance. I was more than once dispatched at five in the afternoon to scour the bars for him. I found him in the back of the Seventh Heaven Restaurant on Wyndham Street, leaning over a triple and close to tears. "I didn't work today," he said, visibly shaking and hunched forward, "but I'm sure I would have if I had." I guided him down the Wyndham Street sidewalk, a treachery of intermittently placed sloping steps, back to the *China Telegraph,* where he functioned for the remainder of the evening.

Hong Kong was sports-mad back then, and every day the *China Telegraph* featured two whole pages of local amateur sports round-ups: cricket, rugby, soccer, softball and field hockey. I was responsible for contributing hearty coverage of local matches.

The China Telegraph
Sport and Sportsmen

The stands at the Police Sports Ground in Boundary Street were overflowing yesterday when South China B played Kowloon Motor Bus. KMB attacked from the start, and their finishing touches in front of goal were spectacular. Just before half-time, Lee Chun-fat of KMB held the shot but the ball rebounded into play. After the interval, South China B began attacking and in the eleventh minute Colin McLinn opened the scoring....

Beyond the sunshine world of Westerners in the colony there were darker things in 1948, stories I covered usually with a Cantonese-speaking interpreter and, as I learned more of the dialect myself, on my own. Far from British arrogance bred of easy accomplishment, and even further from the Chinese merchants and professionals who were, even then, quickly growing rich, were the refugees who huddled into Hong Kong from the endless turmoil in China. I could never have imagined, when I first arrived in the colony, the squalid depths to which people could sink on those hills covered with packing-board shacks. It is hard for young people in Hong Kong today to realize that their parents and grandparents came close to extinction in those harsh years after the war. Husbands pimped their wives and daughters to make enough money to fend off starvation. A paternal nation, Father China, had collapsed and its spiritual casualties were those heads of households strewn over those hills, selling their wives, stealing food, killing one another and finally giving up and fleeing their families. It was at this time that the intolerable pressures of life drove many despairing men to one of the most hideous of fates, heroin. You would see them gathered up in police raids, starving stick men, unable to close their mouths, their eyes rolled up so only the whites showed.

I covered stories at the Criminal Sessions, including an all-too-frequent crime of "acid throwing." Mrs. Cheung Mei was accused of tossing hydrochloric acid at another housewife in Kowloon City in a case of convoluted neighbourhood tensions gone out of control. It was hard to disentangle who had done what to whom. Then there was a high-class prostitute from Shanghai known obscurely to her clientele as "Coca-Cola," who was found poisoned by an angry customer in her Happy Valley house. Mr. Trebilcoe instructed me to identify her discreetly as a "cabaret artiste."

For the first few months I stayed at the Tsimshatsui YMCA, then known as the "European" Y. All winter I rode the Star Ferry every morning, travelling second class to save money, and freezing on the open decks. In my leather briefcase was a flattened roll of toilet paper for use in the ill-equipped *China Telegraph* washrooms. The newsroom usually smelled of rotting paper, even in chilly winters, when you had to wear fingerless gloves to type. The inmates of the European Y were much poorer and often far stranger than the Oriental idea of what a European was. Some were older men excessively preoccupied with Edwardian poets such as Siegfried Sassoon. And there were Anglophillic Chinese bachelors who had lived abroad and were capable of breaching the racial barrier by "taking rooms" at the European Y. They reincarnated themselves as cut-rate English gentlemen with authentic eccentricities. One man was fanatical about railways. His eyes actually blazed and he addressed me in an over-rich Anglo-Cantonese accent about the nature of mixed trains. "That is to say, trains that mix passenger carriages with goods vans. One never attaches livestock vans to mixed trains. It's just not done because of the odour that would attend passengers. Yet in the evolution of mixed trains not all the world's railways came to this realization quickly. Our own Burma Railways, for instance ..."

The British residents of the Y were no less inimitable, and at best distant, decrepit relations to more refined commercially important persons from Britain. These fatigued lower-downs in print dresses and serge pants gathered in the YMCA canteen and waited for their meals with a freckled poise, looking pretty shabby. Between them and the doddering, comedic Chinese waiters they called "boys," it was difficult to assess who was more likely to drool over the plates of food. "Oh, Jess!" two women crowed in unison on the first morning of my residence. They were greeting a third who made her way into the canteen with the benefit of a cane. "How'dja sleep, luv? Poor Jess, you look all in already." Jess, whose badly mottled skin reminded me of marbled cheese, came and sat down and began to enumerate all the miseries of trying to sleep in a tropical climate. What she and the other women were doing in Hong Kong I never found out. Probably visiting their sons in the British Forces garrison or, like my Mr. Trebilcoe, possibly castaways who had roamed from colony to colony until they were out of money and hope. Either way, here they lived and every morning discussed their miseries with the intensity of young sports reporters at KMB games.

Initially I was very lonely and still really very sad over my father's dam-burst of hatred for me. He never, in the rest of his life, wrote me with any indication of reconciliation, and I guess I never made much of an attempt to seek forgiveness. It was over between us, and it was over completely. Even in 1967, almost two decades after, it still ate at me with regret and, increasingly, unfocused anger.

The first flat I rented was in Causeway Bay, then a sleepy neighbourhood on the edge of an extremely unsanitary typhoon shelter, a little basin of breakwaters stocked with decrepit fishing boats and excrement. My apartment toilet was criminally mischievous: it flushed efficiently enough but then several minutes later would suddenly regurgitate its contents up through the drain of the bathtub (this sometimes happened while I was entertaining guests). The apartment's builder had prized privacy above views. He had fitted the windows with frosted glass, and I was left scratching my head as to what was going on around me. Wavy wrought-iron typhoon bars on the inside made it impossible to stick my head out the casements and see what was out there. At night I could hear mah-jong games clattering in the next flats and the voices of the players, but I never saw who the players were. The streets were often just as unyielding. I passed a pawn shop on Fleming Road in Wanchai which had saloon-style louvred doors just high enough so that I couldn't see inside. I was too shy to go inside to look but I could hear clients haggling with the pawn-broker, their voices rocking off the green stone walls of the shop. When a deal was consummated, the pawnbroker brought his chop down on the sales agreement with a clap. Someone with a small treasure wrapped in an old smock once bustled in through the spring-loaded doors, affording me a momentary view of the brokers in their cages. But the doors swung back and hit me in the nose, bloodying it.

My loneliness amid the fusty wrecks who worked for the *China Telegraph* propelled me into making friends with a new generation of Hong Kong people. In need of company my own age, I went to a few bars in Wanchai where the matelots hung out, but the fighting and the bar girls made me uncomfortable.

Through the press club I met young Europeans and Chinese who mixed freely at inter-racial parties. This was considered brazen and unwise by our European and Oriental elders so we felt stimulated even more to flout their expectations. Being young.

I started one evening with some work-mates from the *China Telegraph* and the *South China Morning Post*. We had drinks at the Press Club in Central, watching the tinhorn society come and go. An American who did a music program on radio station ZBW came in wearing a navy blazer on his shoulders, affecting a European look that took some imagination to appreciate. He came with a young woman named Arden Davis who worked in the public relations firm of Feltus and Robertson and she was an exception to the cheap pretenders in the room. She was a smart creature in a beret and white angora sweater that should have been impossible to keep clean in the Orient, where dirt clung to everything. I asked Arden how she did it. "It's because," she said, signaling the waiter for a Manhattan, "Americans are among the great dry-cleaning peoples of the world." I adored her immediately. She had the best teeth I had ever seen. Arden, who became a life-long friend, contrasted sharply with the dishevelled-looking woman who edited the women's page of the *China Telegraph*. Mildred always looked like the heat had wilted her, even in winter; her hair was plastered flat on her head. After a little coaxing she suffered her male companion to order her a martini. He had on a bow tie and a coarse tweed jacket and corduroy trousers that he wore even on the hottest days of summer.

That evening, I ran into Becky Chan for the second time, at a party in Kowloon Tong. Arden, a few *Post* reporters and I stopped by the Hongkong Hotel for another aperitif and then popped into Mac's Grill for steaks and whisky. We were a little tight and not at all comfortable on the ferry ride across the choppy harbour to Kowloon. We walked into the party with shouts to the hosts and bottles of Scotch under our arms. There were men and women, Chinese and Western, in every room of the house. It was only a few weeks after I'd met Becky at the shrine to Wong Tai Sin. She wore a cheap and ineptly made teal-coloured dress.

The décolletage came down in a V-shape, culminating in an unnaturally large artificial blue rose in the centre of her bosom. She was seated by herself and had just poured a bottle of Coca-Cola into a tumbler. She uncovered the sugar bowl on the tea set next to it, spooned sugar into the Coca-Cola and then tried to dissolve it with a vigorous stir.

"You're making quite a sweet drink there," I said.

"I like it this way. It brings out all the flavour," Becky said from the sofa. "You're the guy from Wong Tai Sin, aren't you?"

I was glad that she remembered me. "Did you get your French heels?" I asked. She held her feet up and showed them off with such a gleeful look. She hunched her shoulders and giggled. Becky was bursting with energy and fun. Through the back window came the sound of a late-night train clattering up the Kowloon-Canton Railway toward China. I couldn't bear watching her dump even more sugar into her soft drink.

Becky had just finished a picture at the Southern Electric Film Company, a tin-bucket little Cantonese studio. They had exactly three sets, which they painted and repainted. A skyline backdrop, frequently viewed through a fanciful window featured just a single building painted on canvas (Becky said they couldn't afford more than one building). It was no joke about getting the job, though. She had pursued Southern Electric's managing director relentlessly, shoving her face in his car window when he arrived each morning at the front gate, almost yelling at him about what a good actress she was. She was a glamour girl standing in a gown in the dust beside a collection of shacks that made the studio. Coolies with shoulder poles and baskets full of night soil stared at her and muttered sexual speculations to one another. It wasn't pretty or dainty, and Mildred would have found her grotesquely unladylike, but Becky aimed to survive.

Eventually, to get her out of his face, the Southern Electric man hired her at one dollar a day. She got a place to live in the studio dormitory with twenty-five other girls, sleeping on bunk beds. In the narrow spaces between the beds she'd perform a ribbon dance for the girls of the sort one saw in Chinese cultural movies put out by the Communist studios on the Mainland. Instead of orbiting long strands of colourful ribbons in great circles, Becky made do with two rolls of toilet paper that she slowly unrolled on her fingers. It was actually kind of artful until the spools of toilet paper slipped off the inner cardboard tubes and flew in opposite directions across the room, leaving her with nothing but the tubes on her fingers, which she stared at in mock confusion. The other girls loved it – they clapped their hands, screamed with laughter and called her *"toilet theatre goddess."* It was all so innocent and earnest.

"Come and meet some people," I said and made her leave her Coca-Cola. I introduced her to some European men and she charmed them just as she had charmed me, with big handshakes and American slang culled from the cinema. But when I guided her toward some Western women, she pulled back on my arm. "I left my drink in the other room," she said, her voice getting smaller. I said to never mind that and brought her over to meet Arden and Mildred. Arden had good manners and returned Becky's howdy handshake in similar spirit. But Mildred assumed a dryness and spoke in a tiresome *morgue*. "How do you do, Miss Chan?" she said. "Tell us about your family." Mildred pronounced it "fem-lee" and closed her eyes, feigning a London suburbanite's idea of how aristocracy behave. Being in charge of the *China Telegraph* society pages meant Mildred had to set some sort of standard of behaviour. She continued in on Becky. "Are you a Hong Kong Island Chan or a Kowloon Chan?" And here Mildred gave off a great horsey noise.

"Mildred, what a weird joke," Arden said, and Mildred's face grew a little taut. Becky didn't have a clue what Mildred was talking about.

She wasn't finished, she still saw some sport in Becky. "What a lovely creation you're wearing," she said. Becky knew enough to be wary because she had closely scrutinized Arden's up-to-the-minute bouclé sweater and silk skirt. Becky was learning that she was cheaply dressed. "It's a bit loud, isn't it, Miss Chan? And that big blue rose right here —"

"Let's go get your Coke," I said to Becky and guided her by the arm back to the other room. I glanced over my shoulder at Mildred but she had closed her eyes and stretched her mouth wide as if victory was hers. But as we left the room I could hear Arden revving up, something very direct, something like "you scrawny pompous cow ..."

Becky said nothing about it for that evening. But when I took her to dinner one evening she asked where she could read about Parisian fashions. We went to the City Hall library on a Saturday afternoon and went through current issues of *Vogue*. She snapped the pages of the magazines as she turned them and they gave off little firecracker noises. She stopped on a photo feature and pointed at a gown.

"How do you say that?" she asked.

"Givenchy."

She repeated it with a Cantonese spin, "Ji-bon-ch'i," she said. "Where do I get a Ji-bon-ch'i in Hong Kong?"

"They cost a fortune."

"I'll make one just like it."

And she did. Using fabric she bought in the Gilman Street cloth market she refitted her wardrobe with homemade approximations of Givenchy and Chanel. She stayed up late in a corner of her dormitory at Southern Electric, sewing by hand with a peculiar technique of keeping her thumb pressed up against her palm. You couldn't even see her thumb when she sewed. She also cadged time on the costume department's sewing machine. In just over one month she reinvented herself as a chic young woman. If you felt the cloth with your fingers you realized it was second rate, but it was good enough to present to the tin horns.

The night I brought her in on my arm to the lounge at the Press Club the European women turned around and gaped at us. Arden rushed over and shook her hand. "Atta girl," she said. "Knock these sad hens dead." The European men jumped to their feet as we approached, their mouths forming little rictuses. They politely wished her good evening and made room for us to sit down. It was too wonderful. And Becky adopted a newfound hauteur, her make-up toned down, her hair grown longer and given a soft permanent wave. She even stopped yelling at waiters to come to her table, the way she had done when I first met her. Now she began her requests to them with a whispered *"Mm-koi?"*

This anecdote, the sort that Sunday supplement writers thank God for when it falls out of the sky at their feet, ended in a way that confused me at the time. Becky grew oddly unhappy with her new wardrobe. She said she didn't deserve it. I had no idea what she meant. "Of course you do," I said, "you made it." But she didn't wear the dresses for a while, choosing instead extremely plain Chinese dresses, like you'd see sales girls behind the counters in Lane Crawford wearing. Then one day, the mistress from the Southern Electric costume department (it was more of a back storage room than a department) asked to borrow the dresses for use in movies. Instead, Becky demanded rental fees. They dickered, agreed on a price and suddenly she felt much happier about her clothes. She started wearing them again.

Becky never lost her dry-eyed approach to making a living. I recall an incident at Great World, during the making of *The Goddess of Mercy*. A payroll clerk came on set and gave her the weekly pay-cheque. Resting against a diagonal board to protect her costume and head-dress, she snapped open the pay envelope and scrutinized the deductions hawkishly. There was just one penny too great a deduction. At once, the Goddess of Mercy stood up from the slant board and marched off to find Feng Hsiao-foon. She argued over the penny until he was fed up with her and ordered a corrected cheque cut. It was no wonder that the women refugees of Hong Kong had such a bond with her.

We found a camaraderie in physical complaint, Becky and I. It was in Hong Kong, during those early years that I first fell victim to crashing headaches that began with jagged violet lines pulsating before my eyes, followed by crippling pain and finishing up with some good hard retching. I sought out an American physician, who had a practice in Alexandra House. He diagnosed migraines and prescribed cold compresses. But the headaches were still agony. Becky found out about them over coffee one afternoon.

"What's wrong?" she asked.

"Nothing."

"What's wrong?"

"A bad headache."

"I knew it. I knew you were the sickly sort. I will make you better." She insisted that I be treated by a Chinese herbalist at once. We couldn't wait until I felt better: we had to take care of it right then and there. In my agony I boarded a bus with her and we trekked out to a Chinese medicine shop on To Kwa Wan Road in Kowloon City. Becky insisted we go there with the fervour of the mixed-train enthusiast at the European Y. No other shop would do. The place was nothing to look at: very dark and open to the street on one side. It had a lot of drawers, painted black and standing in rows right up to the ceiling, each one labelled in gold paint with a single Chinese character. The drawers contained dried roots, leaves, bugs and animal parts. The smell would have been pleasant if I hadn't been suffering from a migraine, which magnified potent odours. The medicine man declared that my gall bladder was out of whack and prescribed *prunella vulgaris* to cool my internal fires and restore the flow of vital energy up to my head. I took it for years but with only variable efficacy.

The actual truth was that this young actress was not interested in cures, at least for herself. She was trying to make herself very sick, which sometimes worked and she would succumb to raging headaches and stomach pains. She confessed to such self-loathing, but only rarely. She would become lugubrious at lunar new year or during the Moon Festival. "Don't forget," she would explain, "I'm an orphan." She would let the comment out as if it were a lone soldier banished from a heavily fortified citadel. She would let no more information forth. At first I pressed her but then I learned she was an intensely private young woman who rationed information about her real self. For most of our long friendship she told me little of substance, and never as a response to a direct question.

Becky loved movie-studio costumes and sometimes made little contra deals with the Southern Electric costumer, her faux Givenchy, for whatever they had in stock that month that looked like fun. When she was more confident about her appearance she arrived at a mixed-race evening in dark red lipstick and wearing a monocle and floral hat covered in a coarse veil – Chinese and Europeans alike recognized a spoof of Mildred, and we laughed knowingly. She especially favoured big ball gowns with enormous, fluffy skirts. She turned up in a taxi outside at a party in Kowloon Tong with a skirt so big it poured out the windows of the tiny cab like an enormous pile of rising bread dough. Inside the hostess's flat, she used the dress to antic effect when the hostess, a tea service on a tray in her hands, looked about bewildered for the coffee table. "You've got it under there, haven't you?" she said. "You've got the whole table under your dress." And Becky would be standing there in that fluffy skirt, her hands behind her back, looking up at the ceiling, trying desperately not to laugh.

FIVE

Even as a child in Canada I invited peril as a kind of thrill, a plea, a punishment, a dare. I had great fun walking across the black steel railway bridges in Winnipeg, hoping a freight or passenger train would catch me at mid-crossing. Once, a livestock train did. I was right over the middle of the Red River when it came and I stood on the tracks and waited until the last possible moment, before skipping to the edge of the bridge, clutching one of the thick diagonal trusses. I must have been eleven years old and after the train had passed I cried violently, and that made it even better. What if my leg had slipped between the creosote-stained timbers of the open bridge deck and become wedged there? I *couldn't* have got out of the way. Too horrible. Too wonderful. I possessed a foolishness that I've never completely shaken. When I was a teenager I saw Niagara Falls with my family. As I stood at the edge of the water, a few yards above the precipice, that hypnotic current racing past beckoned me, as if to say, jump in, ride down the cataract with me, tumble about at the bottom and swirl among the boulders there. My dad stood there with me, oblivious to my urges, and asked, "What do you think of it?" I replied: "Lead us not into temptation." He only looked blank and then back at the water. I often wonder if my dad lived out the rest of his life thinking his son was psychotic.

The China Telegraph

Rioting spreads to Central

By Paul Hauer
China Telegraph

Mobs of leftists laid siege to Central District for seven hours yesterday, stoning Hongkong residents, tourists and journalists, and causing extensive property damage.

In the morning, left-wing union representatives took to Garden Road with the intention of laying siege to Government House, but found their path blocked by police just outside the Lower Peak Tram station.

Using loudhailers, police ordered the group to disperse. They refused and resorted to demonstrating outside the Hongkong Hilton. By early afternoon police took up positions at road junctions around the hotel and forced crowds to retreat to the waterfront.

A group of 40 stick-wielding rioters knocked an American journalist to the ground, punched and kicked him and smashed his camera. Members of the Emergency Unit made baton charges and fired four tear-gas cartridges before the crowd dispersed.

At the Fire Station in Harcourt Road someone tore down the Union Jack and burned it in front of a cheering, slogan-chanting crowd.

Mr. Anthony Benbow of MacDonnell Road was seriously injured by rioters outside Central Market. He was taken to Queen Mary Hospital and is said to be in satisfactory condition.

By 7.20 p.m. the mobs had dispersed and the situation was calm. Police arrested 44 people during the disturbances.

I can still recall quite plainly the sound of the policemen's paint scrapers shrieking over the surface of the windows on the building that housed the Hongkong and Kowloon Rubber and Plastics Union in July 1967. It was a few days after the riot in Central. I had gone out with a police patrol for a story. They were removing what were called "big-character posters," inflammatory polemics glued to windows. By early July 1967 the colony had entered a new and hysterical phase of Maoist agitation. One of the posters read as follows: *"Plunge yourselves into a struggle against factory management's devices to step up exploitation! Smash the British imperialists and the Hong Kong capitalist running dogs!"* While two policemen, both Chinese, scraped the posters off, a British officer photographed the remaining ones. This was going smoothly enough when suddenly a melee burst upon us. It was very wild and very dangerous. I, of course, was fascinated by the fighting and, just as I had been tempted by the current at Niagara, I instinctively walked toward it.

Rubber and plastics workers rushed out the entrance of the union building and came right for us. All the built-up anger, frustration and want in every Hong Kong man's heart, the poison of bitterly hard lives, came to the surface, abetted by the rhetoric of the Communist bosses who'd taken over the union. I confess that I stood there foolishly with my pen and notebook, like a maitre d' steeling himself for an onslaught of unhappy diners. I relished the riot coverage and would later write without irony of a fierce attack by "rubber men." They came at us with bars and knives. One crazed young man swung about wildly with a fluorescent light tube, deeply wedded to the idea of smashing it in someone's face. The street filled with noise. It was very sunny and hot. The two Chinese policemen dropped their paint scrapers and drew their pistols. The British policemen pointed at the unionists and told them in Cantonese to withdraw. He could hardly be heard above the awkward chants about *"Invincible Chairman Mao Thought"* and *"We will deal harshly with British imperialists!"* They were just as filled with hate for the Chinese policemen working for the Hong Kong Police as they were for the British ones, and they chased the three of them back down Canton Road.

I remained standing amid the leftists, getting jostled and shoved as they passed. I hardly moved. It was later said by another reporter present that I appeared to have achieved some kind of professional rapture. Then, in an instant, something made me snap to. A macabre group of young women came toward me bearing brilliant green plastic toy water pistols. I knew this trick because they'd used it before on others: they'd filled the pistols with highly corrosive industrial acid. They ran toward me squirting the toys madly and I bolted up Canton Road.

I was met by a squad from the Emergency Unit marching south. These were the riot police and they wore coal-black helmets with gas masks on their faces, giving them an impersonal, almost robotic appearance. They carried black hardwood batons, lightweight and flexible circular wicker shields, pistols and Greener guns. To be caught between factory workers with acid-filled squirt guns and charging riot police is a clarifying thing. I finally retreated at a right angle to the confrontation and fetched up beneath a shophouse arcade. Two policemen hoisted a black cloth banner on bamboo poles that warned in English and Chinese: "TEAR SMOKE."

By now the rubber men had been joined by a larger crowd. Apart from the Communists, much of the rioting in the summer of 1967 was run by what the Chinese called "Ah-feis," what the British police called "corner boys" and North Americans called hoodlums. They conducted much of the havoc to mask petty crimes such as burglary, extortion or racketeering. Sometimes just for badness. Nevertheless, the Communists lionized them and frequently characterized in the left-wing press some nasty little Ah-fei the police had collared as a "proletarian fighter."

Some rioters engaged the police with a variety of savage weapons culled from the storehouses of an industrial city. They swung sharpened bicycle chains or lashed out with gloves impregnated with nails or stabbed wildly with copper water pipes filed into sharp spears. Once, when a riot platoon raided a trade union office, they found that the concrete stairs leading to a second-floor arsenal had been washed down with cooking oil then sprayed with water, making them virtually impassable.

I followed the Emergency Unit back down Canton Road. The young man with the fluorescent tube had made contact with another young man, perhaps an enemy of Chairman Mao or perhaps just another aimlessly angry young man. The victim lay on the ground, clutching his bleeding face and screaming about his eyes. He was surrounded by little bits of glass and there was a fine powder all over him.

The EU fired tear-gas canisters, which left a white trail in the air as they arced upward and came back down amid the rioters. Several riot policemen had affixed wooden tubes to their guns and fired them into the crowd. The projectiles were very painful but usually did no serious injury. The crowd began to break apart and run down side streets. It looked like it was almost all over until someone on the roof of the Rubber and Plastic union lobbed a small refrigerator off the roof. Through some ingenuity they managed to set the refrigerator alight. The EU backed away as it slammed to the pavement and popped open as it bounced. Inside, a huge carboy of gasoline smashed and gushed forth fire with a terrific concussion. It blew the fridge door down the street. Despite such fine showmanship, the Maoists lost the day because the fire forced their own ranks to scatter. The riot evaporated.

While plain-clothed investigators sealed off the union building with wooden hobby horses and went inside to make arrests, the EU boys began to relax. The tear gas had blown south, away from us, so the police removed their masks. I found my friend, Sergeant Jack Rudman, among them. There was a large sweat stain on the back of his tunic and sweat poured off his face. Rudman's dark eyebrows sank in a fierce V toward a beak-like nose, parallel with a widow's peak, which made him look stern and all-seeing. Few people could see so much of others as Jack could, and yet he saw so little of himself. He was still breathing hard and scanning the windows of buildings above us for trouble.

"I'm glad you're all right," I said.

He gave me an examining look but did not respond. He flicked his head to get the sweat off his brow. Drops fell on my hand. "Yeah, I'm fine," he said then looked about at the civilians at the side of Canton Road. "But what about you, mate? You almost got a sting there, pursued by those dollies and their toy guns. Why the hell did you stand there …" He paused to think of a literate-sounding metaphor, then said: "… like a garden gnome." He looked back to me for a moment and added, "Trust you."

I tried to make a joke, knowing that I'd been foolish.

Inwardly, I was very unhappy that Jack couldn't have been a little more sympathetic. He could have murmured a kind word or something, at least expressed the most oblique thanksgiving that I hadn't been injured. Otherwise, what was the point of standing in harm's way? He looked about to satisfy himself that none of his fellow coppers had been injured in the fight. They got his tender concern. I envied them for having his loyalty.

Fire engines came down Canton Road to put out the gasoline fire, bumping over rioters' stones and EU projectiles, so we went and stood over by the harbour side of the street.

"Got your message about your girlfriend," Rudman said. "Been too busy."

I told him I understood.

"I feel like a steak," Rudman said.

"I'll buy," I said too quickly. "Tonight."

Rudman surveyed the wrecked street again then glanced back at me. This time he had a look of warmth. He touched his sweaty hand to my jacket. "Yeah, all right." He even smiled.

When I returned to the newsroom in Central shortly before noon there was a message from Chen Lo-wen at Great World. Chen was Becky's favourite director and the creator of *Long Ago and Far Away*. He had come down with Feng from Shanghai after the Communists took power and had laboured for Great World for little money ever since. The studio directors were grotesquely underpaid relative to their commercial value. Actors frequently planted rumours in the mosquito press about imminent retirement from films; actresses hinted they were getting married to rich businessmen and were leaving the screen. It was the only way to guarantee a meeting with Feng Hsiao-foon to discuss their lousy pay. He kept everyone waiting in strict silence out in Miss Chin's anteroom, where she gave them hard, disciplinary looks until they were cowed into thinking they were badly spoiled children exploiting the studio's father. Confucian deference to Feng, as well as highly restrictive contracts, meant that performers rarely had the sort of tantrums and upsets that Hollywood performers indulged in. They almost never complained on the set, issued few protests, and if they did, Feng would punish them with fines and a lecture. A couple of months before Becky vanished, Tina Ti from Cathay Studios disappeared for a few days without explanation. She washed up safe and sound at the studio a couple of days later, citing a curfew surrounding the Maoist riots in Kowloon. She may have just wanted a few days off from her hectic shooting schedule. Most top actresses had a reputation with audiences for inaccessible glamour, but the reputation they had with impecunious and dominating studio lords like Feng Hsiao-foon was something else: they were dispensable goddesses with short shelf lives who wouldn't have known how to put on lipstick if it hadn't been for his instruction. Becky hadn't, before she went into the movies. Many performers had miserable lives – some were actually refused permission to marry. Others were never allowed to travel abroad for fear they wouldn't come home. They all fought bitterly with Feng and sometimes walked out, paying contract penalties or launching lawsuits to free themselves.

Feng didn't mind the atmosphere of anxiety at all. He made sure that no one ever really knew what he was thinking – he would only sit behind his desk and nod his head while employees vented their spleens, wept furiously or shouted feeble threats. Then he would simply say: *"Go back to work now and stop making a fool of yourself."* Humiliated and no wiser or richer, they just went back to work. The only time I had ever seen him unnerved was when a young actress hung herself in her dormitory room at the Great World studio. They brought Feng to see her body, gently swaying and swollen. He had the room exorcised.

As a director, Chen Lo-wen had even less latitude than the performers. He was so beholden to Feng, who had kept him all these years, that his complaints were few and he worked very hard, often at great personal sacrifice. Chen gave himself a serious groin pull loading one of Great World's heavy old Mitchell cameras into a truck for a location shoot on *The Herdsman and the Weaver.* Feng told him to keep working or lose pay for every day he was off. Chen was in such pain that he miscalculated in lining up a close-up shot of Becky's climactic scene because the Mitchell used a range-finder rather than the through-the-lens reflex system. When the film came back from Rank, her face was away off to one side of the frame, one eye obscured. I thought the shot had an appealing quality because it made it look as if the weaver were trying to hide her sorrow over her husband's long absences. But Feng was furious. He ordered the whole scene reshot and expenses charged against Chen's pay. Why Chen stayed with Feng was a testimony to not only his loyalty to the studio father but also to the desperate oversupply of Shanghai movie directors.

I called Chen back. You could hear the upset in his voice and I assumed it was because of Becky's disappearance. "Have you learned anything?" I asked him in English.

He made a lengthy and suspicious protest: "I do not want any harm to come to Miss Chan. No one has told me anything about her going away. I had nothing to do with it. I know nothing. No one has informed me of anything."

His answer was peculiar so I poked about with a few questions. When had he last seen her? How did she seem at the time? I had no strategy in my questions to cause any direction to emerge so I gave up. I just put my head in my hand and rubbed my eyes. "I don't want her hurt," I said.

"Neither do I!" Chen said. "You must run a story in the *China Telegraph* saying that I do not know anything about her disappearance! Please telephone Mr. Feng at once and tell him the same. I have told this very same thing to *Cloudburst!* You must not tell Feng that I spoke to *Cloudburst.* They get everything wrong in that paper and I want to make sure they understand that I had nothing to do with her disappearance. I am no one. I am just a quiet man who does his job."

It was pathetic to hear a senior Great World director whinge like that. And to admit that he had gone to *Cloudburst* with a story was especially undignified. Among all the mosquito press in Hong Kong, *Cloudburst* was the most notorious for its scandal reports, celebrity gossip, corruption reports and bilious crime reporting. The paper's name was Cantonese slang for female orgasm. It got away with such crudeness because the British barely knew it existed and polite Chinese society pretended it didn't. But *Cloudburst* and its vile sisters were much relished by taxi drivers, day labourers, amahs and fruit market women. In recent weeks they had run stories speculating on Becky's marriage to Feng, suggesting that she was deeply unhappy about his lovemaking and that she had a secret European lover. That would be me: they had so characterized my friendship with her before. I actually wrote them a letter once correcting them on the point and they built a story around it: *"The tall blond Canadian forced Great World's patriarch to wear the green hat! Now he hotly denies his sweaty passion for Feng's wife!"* Wearing a green hat was an allusion to being cuckolded. I gave up and ignored the occasional subsequent reference. If Feng knew about these stories he steadfastly ignored them.

Becky had been the centre of mosquito press swarms for years. I was furious when I read all sorts of explicit but fictitious slop about Becky's sexual activities. I asked her if it bothered her. She was distant but you could tell that it really didn't. "What they say," she said, "isn't true. I probably deserve their scorn." Then she looked at me in the eye, just a flick of a glance, no more, and she looked away again. "None of it matters. I still have to work." And she did. It mattered more to her that she still had a job, food to eat, and dry shelter than all the stories in the mosquito press.

I questioned Chen Lo-wen some more about what was happening at the studio and whether the publicity chief had any results from his investigators in Southeast Asia. "He is too busy with the new campaign," Chen said. Feng had ordered that *Long Ago and Far Away* be retitled in English and Chinese to *Where is She?* Even as we spoke, display artists had taken down the six plywood panels of the billboard on the Ambassador Cinema and were painting over the floating faces of the supporting players and replacing them with question marks inside yellow bubbles. And this bastard, this filthy bugger, insisted he didn't want a scandal. It was no surprise that quality Chinese society avoided Feng Hsiao-foon.

Did Feng love Becky? I had never seen open affection, but that was not unusual in the private world of Hong Kong family life. He had certainly pursued her for many years and divorced a dowdy woman during the 1950s to focus his attention on wooing Becky. It was said that Miss Chin, Feng's secretary took great pleasure in her boss's divorce of the first wife. Someone at Great World had claimed that she used to refer to this woman as "No. 1 Wife, a term used by concubines." It could have been waspish gossip or it could have been a real angle on Miss Chin's view of herself.

Whenever I telephoned Feng I would hear a soft click on the telephone line. It was probably Miss Chin. She had picked up the telephone at her austere grey steel desk just outside Feng's office at Great World. I could picture her sitting there, in one of the glum-looking olive brocaded dresses she favoured. She wore them because she saw older actresses in Feng's movies wearing them. In real life, fashionable Chinese women laughed at her clothes; they were a cliché of what matrons wore. She had funny kinds of nylon stockings that only went up to her mid-calves; you could always see the tops of them. Her hair was dyed an improbable black and she pulled it into a tight bun that looked almost painful. Becky had once told me Miss Chin had learned that from the Great World make-up department: pulling her hair back tightened the wrinkles on her face. Miss Chin wore gold spectacles with lenses so thick you couldn't quite see her eyes. She always eavesdropped on Feng's more important conversations, slipping phone extensions off their cradles and cupping them in her hands, like precious little children with vital secrets to impart. She would daintily slip a hand onto the mouth piece and her black eyes would dart back and forth at objects on her desk while she listened. She did not eavesdrop for crude fun. She had an urgent need to know. She wanted to know everything so she could better protect Feng. He could not help but know she listened, but he never objected. He might even have encouraged it.

Becky tried to be oblivious to all this nonsense. She attained the height of her popularity during the late '50s, playing women who endured their trials or, even better, were mowed down by them. As she played them, these women had little self-awareness. The characters scarcely knew why they were the way they were. But that was melodrama as practised all over the world, an unawareness of the causes of life torments. That didn't mean she couldn't deliver a wallop. In *Mother's Love Endures All*, Becky played a woman forced to sell her body to pay for her good-for-nothing son's school fees. Becky starts the film as a beautiful mother who wears virtuous high collars and spends the day scrubbing her home and doting on her medical-student son. Her husband kills himself, unable to endure the humiliation of a fall from respectability to poverty. The only way she can raise the tuition for her son is by removing her high collar, painting her face and leaving the home in the care of her dutiful daughter, who is a younger duplicate of Becky's virtues. Becky dons brocades, paints her face and becomes a prostitute. Despite her humiliation she manages to play the seductress expertly. But her first client proves to be the first man she ever loved – and still secretly loves. He recognizes her and is so disgusted that she has succumbed to whoring that he throws a handful of money in her face. The look on Becky's face as she gathered the money up had the Ambassador Cinema's female inmates honking into their kerchiefs. These women never worked as whores but they knew all about humiliation, sacrifice and the depths to which a mother was willing sink to help her children. In the end, the wastrel son conveniently dies, but not before declaring his remorse at having pushed his mother to such sacrifice. The first lover returns, having learned of Becky's selflessness and throws himself before her, asking her to marry him. Becky and her daughter gather round the man and a new family harmony is forged. It played for 43 days at the Ambassador. Every afternoon and evening, female audiences went home reassured that sacrifice and forbearance really do foster happiness.

I kept my promise of a steak dinner for Jack. I took a bus out to the Unmarried Policemen's Quarters near the airport. The police informally called it the "peach garden," a reference to the "peach-garden brotherhood" that the Chinese god Kwan Ti entered when he agreed with two other heroes of the Three Kingdoms era to raise an army to fight crime and disorder. Kwan Ti was the god of righteousness and loyalty, and all Hong Kong policemen, British and Chinese, worshipped him. Jack liked that story.

He preferred that I wait down at the guardhouse of the residence rather than come up to his room. He came down and checked out with the guard. "Just out for a bit to eat. This man is paying," he said to the guard. They talked about whether an off-duty policeman should be walking the streets of Kowloon but our instincts about the peaceful nature of Hong Kong overrode that and we set out. As we walked I unconsciously crowded him on the sidewalk. I was completely unaware that I was doing it until he put out his palm and gently shoved me over. I could smell Jack's blokeyness from twenty feet away, the sweat, the excessive barber's cologne, the hair oil, even the mushy smell of the starch in his shirts failing in the night heat.

Conder's Restaurant was at the corner of Argyle and Luen Wan streets on the edge of Mongkok. It was an unusual location for a European restaurant, far away from the tourist districts and big Western businesses of Central. It served the British Forces stationed at Osborn Barracks and the big police dormitories. Conder's was a congenial place with a Continental menu. The owner, Jack Conder, who billed himself as "the most popular host in the Far East," had caught that year's craze for bowling and opened a few lanes. Rudman and I had a few beers in the bar then went to the dining room.

We'd met via a self-important little jerk by the name of Tony Pinch who always had chalk dust all over the lower pockets of his suit jacket at the end of the day and he never thought to clap it off. He managed to infiltrate the press club a couple of times, through some arcane and mutually beneficial conspiracy with Mildred. I was introduced to him there. When he learned that I used to sing in Canada he gave me a hard sell on his amateur theatre group, the King's Park Players. "I'm not at all familiar with what amateur theatre is like in Canada," he said, "but the British carry their love for performing everywhere they go." My mind flickered on the Press Association correspondent who'd tried to bribe the *Telegraph* janitor into beating him with a rubber hose. I don't know why I thought of that.

He was directing a production of *Pirates of Penzance* and needed more singers. "British operetta is one of the highest expressions of theatrical entertainment," he went on. Blah blah blah. Gilbert and Sullivan. Blah blah blah. But I went along to audition because I wanted to make some new friends.

Like Mildred, Pinch made a socially ambitious suburban Londoner's maximum attempt at gentility. He had me out to a King's Park meeting and I met the other members. His digs fell short of his gracious ideal, smelling of Woodbines cigarettes, musty books spoiled by the semi-tropical humidity and more than a trace odour of cat sick.

One of the other auditioners present was a young British policeman, Jack Rudman, who also sang. Afterward, Pinch volunteered an assessment of who in the group "showed promise" as performers and who was to be avoided socially. He warned me off forming any sort of society with Rudman, saying that he was just a "policeman type." I asked what that meant and Pinch told me the sort of person Rudman was. "Quite apart from the fact that he's, you know, a copper, he says things that give him away."

"As what?"

"He says 'serviette,' instead of 'napkin.' I expect he would say 'horseback riding,' instead of just 'riding.' You know, not the sort of language we want to have round us."

I must have given him an uncomprehending look, because he grew fatigued, almost faint. "You're from Canada and may think that these matters are not important, but they are if we're to set any sort of example for the Chinese. They're up and coming, you know, and they'll want to know how it's done."

I got a part in *Pirates* and performed shoulder to shoulder with Rudman, whose limited yet earnest, creative nature had been drawn to the comic characters of the Penzance constabulary. He too was looking for friends, in his case people outside the peach-garden brotherhood. I wasn't sure at the time, but I suspected that he had inclinations toward perversion, just like me. Eventually he stopped coming to the amateur theatre group and retreated back to be among the police, as if he had confirmed his own differentness. The only person from the group he continued to see was me.

To my mind Jack Rudman was a marvellous man, hearty and robust, virile and sincere. And, yes, being from Canada, I couldn't care whether he said "serviette" or "napkin." He loved trout fishing and Wendy Hiller. He tried to coincide his home leave to Britain with Miss Hiller's stage appearances. He smoked a vile and obscure brand of pipe tobacco that he liked to discuss as a connoisseur. He had a record collection of the compositions of Arthur Bliss, not because he thought the *Colour Symphony* and *Things to Come* were great compositions but because he believed it was a cultivated thing to have, so he listened to them very carefully, and without much discernment. Every time he met someone who was a writer, even reporters like me, he would speculate at length on some piece of information he'd picked up somewhere. Was it not true, he asked, that there are only thirty-nine different plots in all of literature, that all books are just variations on those thirty-nine plots? As no one ever gave him a categorical reply, he kept asking, a determined flatfoot seeking admissible evidence of his literary notion.

Rudman used to boast, rightly, that no group of men in Hong Kong lived in greater racial harmony than the police. British, Australian, New Zealand and even Canadian and American men worked side by side with the Chinese constables. All the Western men spoke Cantonese – it was essential for their work on the streets – and they came to love their Chinese brothers, members of what they called the "great little army." When one man, Chinese or Western, got promoted they cheered him heartily; and when one died he was mourned fiercely. If he were killed in the line of duty, which before 1967 was rare, all were thrown into deep trauma. The Chinese policemen were greatly fond of their Western mates. While the work was sometimes dirty and usually met with indifference by a thankless public, the policemen took great comfort in their peach-garden brotherhood.

Although people in Hong Kong were suspicious of the police and corruption was a problem, there could be real warmth for them. Jack pulled people from burning buildings, broke up fights, and nabbed petty criminals. Little children in back-street markets were attracted to his pale green summer uniform. They ran to him whenever he patrolled and went through his pockets for the sweets he always carried for them. I had a photograph in my newsroom desk of him standing in uniform on the stage of a Cantonese opera charity performance, towering behind a fund-raising group of Chinese doctors and lawyers.

Rudman would talk about how he and the mates had done a "sort out" of the various corner boys, yobbos and thugs hanging around San Po Kong Sub-District. Young criminals he referred to as "characters." They infested Tsat Po and Luk Hop streets and got either arrested and charged or exported to another police sub-district. Occasionally Rudman would meet me for a drink and direct me to write something for the Sunday social notes section of the *China Telegraph,* something, say, on the recent marriage of a young constable in the San Po Kong Emergency Unit. He once even handed me the preferred wording, which ended with: "... all of us at S.P.K. wish the new Mr. and Mrs. a world of happiness." When I said I would pass it on to Mildred, he looked at me as if I were shirking.

"At San Po Kong our motto is," he said during a toast he gave at a policemen's association dinner in the Hotel Miramar, "if it moves, salute it. If it doesn't, paint it!" This would get a roar of knowing and affectionate laughter from other policemen, a kind of understanding attained only by other coppers. Like Maoist sloganeering, it sounded plodding and dumb to my ear. And yet it was moving to see just how close Rudman and the other policemen were to one another, as evidenced by that jolly, bland joking. And it reminded me of just how inevitably distant civilians like me were from them, their work, their lives, their hearts. "And in closing," he said in his toast, "I'd like to remind you that if you drive, don't drink. And if you don't drink, don't bother to come out to San Po Kong."

At Conder's that night we dined on bacon-wrapped filets and heavy red wine. Jack wanted to talk about cricket and the things "the men" were turning up in raids on Communist hideouts around the colony. He was fascinated by a specially rigged gun that fired seventeen shots instead of six and speculated at length on just how that was mechanically possible. I listened dutifully for a while then talked about Becky. I explained what Feng had told me about her disappearance. Jack seemed indifferent at first. He didn't know Becky personally and thought film people inconsequential. It really annoyed me, his thinking of her that way.

"Of course," said Jack Rudman over the filet, "there could be an explanation for your girlfriend's disappearance."

"She's not my girlfriend."

He looked about the dining room – he was always scanning rooms, back and forth, and sometimes it was annoying because I'd think that he'd seen something important and would turn around to look too. This time all I saw was an obese European man in the corner, dining by himself, bent over a magazine. He reached around and scratched his back with his dinner fork. I looked back. Jack had been scanning the room, nothing more. He did little things like that and it angered me so.

"Could have been kidnapped," he said.

"Her amah said she left with a suitcase."

"Anyone to corroborate? Maybe the amah is in on it."

"She suggested that Becky might have been kidnapped too."

"Yeah, there you go. She'd be a cunning little confederate, covering her tracks like that." He poked at his salad, rejected it and went back to his meat. "I'll say this here and now," he said, "because I've seen these things. I seen a lot of things in my time. To some characters, a woman in trouble is a beautiful thing. If she's in some sort of trouble she might as well undo the front of her frock and say come and have a go at me. I've seen it in my time, you know. And in this case I see two possible groups: leftists looking to create yet another disturbance or co-opt her to the cause, or just plain criminals. Gangs would have a field day with Feng over his lovely lolly of a wife. And she's his biggest asset too, isn't she? I'm surprised Mr. Feng let her run around town without a bodyguard all these years."

We waited until the waitress, a pleasant young woman from Newcastle, cleared away the plates.

"Feng would never spring for a bodyguard," I said. "Too cheap."

Jack shrugged. "Penny-wise," he said.

"Can you make inquiries?"

"No. I'm in the Emergency Unit, matey. What do you think the Criminal Investigation Department is for?"

"They're not taking a lot of calls from the public right now, with the disturbances. I'd be obliged if you could kick-start them."

"Why?"

I didn't have a good answer and hemmed a bit and just said: "For me?"

Jack looked annoyed. "Besides," he said. "Feng hasn't reported her missing to the police. But if you want I'll see if I can call around."

"Would you mind?"

Rudman squinted across the room, as if he saw something. I turned and looked over my shoulder, then realized he was only searching for a reply.

"I'm sorry, you've got a lot on your mind," I said. "But this is so very important to me. Please, I'm very worried about her."

He shrugged and agreed to look into Becky's case. We finished our wine and talked about soccer. Conder had trifle on the menu for dessert, so we ordered that. "Have no fear," Jack said. "We'll get your girlie back." After the trifle arrived he looked at me for the shortest of moments. "I'm glad she's important to you, Paul. I really am."

SIX

She who looks down and hears the cries of the world. Thus the ten-cent program Great World sold in its theatres reminded movie goers who saw *Goddess of Mercy* in 1958. What I recall most vivid-ly of the picture was the one day I was on the set. Becky had com-pleted one half of a difficult process shot: she was to look down from heaven while, in a double exposure, a poor farmer whose roof had just blown off the family home in a typhoon looked up. Becky waved her hand to make the rains stop and magically produced a neat pile of timber and fresh clay tiles for constructing a new roof. The farmer says, *"She does hear our cries! She does!"*

So far as classical myth tells us no one ever looked up and heard the cries of the Goddess of Mercy. Her grief went unheard and unremedied. She silenced whatever troubled her and worked at her job year after year, without complaint.

That is why I did not believe that Becky had left her home voluntarily. If she got into a cab with a suitcase someone had to be blackmailing her. But for what? She was the Goddess of Mercy in her greatest picture and countless other fantastic women, vamps in comedies, nightclub singers in dramas, ingénues, a Buddhist nun contemplating love in *Longing for Worldly Pleasure*. Feng had asked her to shave her head to play the part because Buddhist nuns shaved their heads. She almost did it until the director Chen Lo Wen reminded Feng that Becky would be need-ed on *White Snake,* her next picture, within a week of completing

Longing for Worldly Pleasure. She would need a head of hair. So they put a latex skull cap on her instead. She kept on acting in one picture after another, always haunted by the need for steady work. It was not that Becky earned a lot of money, the pay was microscopic compared to Hollywood. It was also such a regulated, dawn-to-dusk existence that it was impossible to find the time to get into trouble. I couldn't imagine what anybody could use to blackmail Becky.

Her output and her talent had been so great that she won the title Empress of Stars five times in her career. All-Asia Film Week was a festival put on by movie companies in all the free nations of East Asia. In 1967 Becky again won the Empress of Stars award there. It came into her hands as a free-form gold sculpture that reminded me of a small table lamp without a shade and bulb. The Tokyo studios hosted the festival that year, and in the way of fair-minded parents, the organizers discreetly ensured that every country's participants received some award. Over the festival's life, just about every major production house had won loads of table lamps. No one lost face. The greatest awards, equivalent to best actor and best actress, were "Emperor" and "Empress of Stars." That year, Becky won for a weepy drama called *Love Calms the Goddess.* In that picture, the goddess was not mythic but rather a beautiful mortal who rebuffs many suitors until she falls for a tender, sensitive type.

The award ceremony was held at an awkward banquet where, with so many languages being spoken, few people completely understood what was going on. It was an amalgam of glamour, small-town warmth and awkward conversation. There were plenty of empty smiles and bewildered looks. All the actresses of the region's cinema wore fabulous French gowns – not home-made ones – paid for by their production companies. Even Bo Bo Fung, a child actress from Hong Kong, came in a miniature Chanel. Japan, Hong Kong and the Philippines had the most people at the festival, thanks to their huge output of films.

Becky had asked Feng not to make her go. She was eight months pregnant with Amanda. He virtually ordered her to, no doubt because he had been told ahead of time that she was going to win again. Once Japanese reporters had interviewed her after the ceremony I sat down with her for a short interview. She looked profoundly weary; she had drawn herself in, huddled against the pressure. Her bare elbows almost touched one another over her swollen stomach as she cringed in a banquet chair in a corner of an assembly hall of the Imperial Hotel. There could be no thrill to becoming Empress of Stars anymore. The first time Becky had won was in 1952 for *The Tram Conductor*, a surprise, because the picture had been in Cantonese and carried no prestige or even much semblance of production value. It had been filmed aboard a double-decker tram on Hong Kong Island. There was no money for post-syncing the sound so there was a lot of background noise in the picture: honking horns, the tram's moaning, pedestrians yelling and trucks gearing down, and it occasionally drowned out actors' lines. But it was a great hit and the award boosted Great World into the world of prestige picture makers. Feng snapped up an offer from Toei in Japan to buy the rights to remake the scenario. Toei had wanted to hire Becky then dub over her voice with that of a Japanese-speaking actress but Feng sensed rightly that Becky was becoming a valuable performer so he kept her at home, graduating her to Mandarin-track production.

By the time Becky signed with the Great World Organisation in 1950, she had already made twenty films for small, rickety outfits like Southern Electric, which were in and out of business all the time. Long before she became a movie player, long before I met her, Becky had worked for a ramshackle little Cantonese opera troupe named "Tales of the Little Phoenix," owned and managed by her adoptive parents, the Chans. At first her duties with the troupe were little different than they had been at the "Door of Hope Orphanage for Little Children." She swept a little apartment that twenty people lived in, including five children, and she aired out mounds of bed linen. Cantonese opera, unlike the more famous Peking opera, was far more experimental and only began to flourish in the Twentieth Century. When Becky began to perform little incidental roles on stage, first playing maidens then graduating to ingénue parts, Cantonese opera had come out of a brilliant period of growth. Its performers, clustered in Canton and Hong Kong, tried and developed lyrical singing, big orchestras, even performing entirely with Western musical instruments such as violins, drums and horn sections. Instead of the rigid minimalism of northern opera, the innovative Cantonese troupes used richly painted backdrops that sometimes adopted perspective illusions. Or they used tables, chairs and other props, which were never used by Peking troupes. The busy Taiping Theatre showed a new opera almost every week. There were two gruelling shows a day of four- to eight-act plays, from noon until five and then from seven to midnight. Sometimes there was a third performance on Saturdays, all-night performances to mark special occasions.

Tales of the Little Phoenix was, to Cantonese opera sophisticates, a lousy troupe. Devotees dismissed them as derivative and undisciplined, lacking in finesse and charisma, and knavishly imitative. Father Chan had a gentle demeanour but he nevertheless made Becky uneasy. *"We need girls for our opera troupe,"* he said. *"We need healthy girls."*

In a private room at the orphanage, out of the sight of the nuns, Mr. and Mrs. Chan walked slowly all the way around Becky, examining her. Mrs. Chan stood behind her, took the clip out of Becky's ponytail and felt her straight hair. It was coarse and dry from much scrubbing with cheap soap they made right in the orphanage. She flicked at it contemptuously. *"I don't know why I bother,"* she said, as if Becky were an inferior purchase in the market and she wanted to talk down the price.

Father Chan put his face up to her neck and rubbed it against her skin. Then he took her arm, raised it straight up and began sniffing loudly into her arm pit. *"Nice,"* he said. *"You have a vital odour that is compatible, highly compatible. Now, be a good girl and show Mrs. Chan your teeth."* Becky bared them and Mrs. Chan asked her to breathe into her face. Mrs. Chan inhaled loudly and was pleased. *"She's healthy,"* she said. The Chans adopted her and took her away from all that she had known for ten years in the Door of Hope Orphanage. The nuns wished her well, gave her a few presents and instructed her to be a good girl, loyal and servile to her new parents. *"Without your new parents, child, you would become a barren spirit and be returned to us."*

The Chans operated out of Kowloon, in an old house where Austin Street veered off from Austin Road. They lived on the third floor and Becky spent the first afternoon looking out in ambivalent fascination at her new neighbourhood. The Kowloon Cricket Club was across the street and she could see European men in white shirts and trousers playing cricket. There were other children in the crowded flat, all her own age, and for a while it was fun, but fun was not the point. Fun was for the idle, for the audiences. The point was to train the children in performing arts, but the training the Chans gave them was erratic, sometimes contradictory and showed the obsessions of each parent. Mother Chan kept teaching the girls how to pantomime sewing on stage. *"A lady,"* she lectured, *"never shows her thumb when she sews. It must be tucked in. You must look dainty, refined and restrained."* Father Chan taught the boys tumbling. While the girls pantomimed sewing around the perimeter of the main room of the flat, the boys went rolling up and down the floor. They could barely get one somersault in before they bumped up against the far wall. Sword-play using long sticks was even more problematic. The boys would whirl the sticks in circles the way Father Chan taught them, inadvertently hitting Becky and the other girls.

Father Chan liked to boast of his great taste in building opera troupes and in finding "golden boys" and "jade girls," young people to train in the art of opera. He shunned the brokers of children, men and women who brought the offspring of poor farmers in southern China to Canton and Hong Kong to learn opera. The farmers surrendered their children for a fee and these boys and girls trained at singing and tumbling for several years with troupes. *"Those brokers,"* Father Chan said to Becky, *"they often dress the girls up in long sams and powder their faces to hide their peasant complexions. I'm smarter. I wet a handkerchief and rub their faces to get the*

rice powder off and see if they're brown and spotty. I lift the skirt of the
sam and examine their legs to see if they're shapely or if they're big,
bowed and muscled. After you, from now on I'm going straight to the
orphanages to find good girls who aren't painted up at all. And best of
all, you don't cost anything!"

The Chans were fooling themselves when they complained
that the opera profession was colluding against them, that the
whole business was rife with cronyism. They played at the fabulous Taiping Theatre only once and it was a morning performance
for children. Impresarios waved them away as unfit for adults.
Father Chan had to hustle up work at rural festivals, from newly
wealthy businessmen with uncultivated taste, and from charitable
temples. Much of their work was done at the low-quality amusement parks in Laichikok Road and out by Kai Tak Airport. There,
the Little Phoenix had to fight for the public's attention with old
movies, Peking and Swatow opera troupes, nightclubs, striptease
shows, a grimy and inhumane zoo, a roller-skating rink, a "floating ballroom" patrolled by undernourished dance-hall hostesses,
an ice rink, pinball machines, rides, game stalls and outdoor
restaurants. This was not a place that nice middle-class Chinese
came to. It was loud, vulgar entertainment that a coolie could
afford and only a coolie would appreciate. There was a snake swal-
lower at Laichikok that you had to pay to get in to see. I made the
mistake of seeing him after eating a meal. He would show his
audience a small writhing serpent in the palm of his hand. Then
he pushed it into his mouth and concentrated very hard. After a
few moments, in a horrific display that was sure to traumatize the
kiddies, the snake would slither out one of his nostrils. Even more
sinister and elusive were the illness brokers who hung around
there. If you had a sickness, you got referred to them and they
arranged to make you well, either with questionable herbs or with
bizarre superstitions. Some men with syphilis believed that having
sex with a child could migrate the syphilis from them into the girl.

Into these raunchy and unwholesome places came teenaged
Becky. She made most of her early public performances at Kai Tak,
including an all-night show during the festival of Tin Hau. You

paid fifty cents and you could spend the whole night lounging about listening to *Giving the Pearl on Rainbow Bridge,* visiting with friends and taking refreshments. It was an astonishingly atmospheric place, even if the performances were third-rate. Through heavy clouds of smoke from Chinese pipes and American cigarettes you could see older men sitting on benches at brown wooden tables that rocked perilously when you put your elbows on them. They nodded their heads in recognition of melodies that brought back such memories of youth in an idealized Canton from before the war, a time when they had been young, vigorous, forceful and in control of everything, a time before China had been humiliated and wrecked by Japan, before it had collapsed beneath civil war and social disorder. These faded men now sat in the tents at Kai Tak Amusement Park and ogled the ingénues, no doubt wishing they could share rich men's ability to host opera troupes in their home for prestigious private performances. The shows were intermittently drowned out by Royal Air Force Dakotas, which roared overhead on finals into the nearby airfield. Patrons came in and out of the tent several times during a performance, going for drinks or to see other attractions and then coming back to chat noisily with friends. Few people sat through the entire performance. The smell of the palm-leaf mats that sheathed the tent's roof, the rolling melody of the butterfly zither played with little bamboo hammers, the dried nuts to munch on and the eerie singing about events and intrigue among the immortals of heaven. The shows began with an overture played by sixteen musicians. The overture didn't necessarily highlight melodies from that opera; they could be any popular tunes the orchestra's leader fancied, and occasionally you heard an excerpted bit of Cole Porter's "I Get a Kick Out of You" creep out of the three-stringed banjo. Sometimes they performed with Western trumpets; nothing was out of the question in the highly creative milieu of Cantonese opera. When the curtain went up and performers playing extras entered to crashing percussive patterns knocked out with the quickening of taps on wooden blocks and bracketed with cymbals, you could see the smiles creep on the faces of men in the audience.

Through Father Chan's persistence, Tales of the Little Phoenix made one film in the late '40s, now lost to archivists. It gave Becky a start in films. It was merely a photographed version of a Cantonese opera, and the Tales of the Little Phoenix had to bring their own costumes and sets. These filmed operas were popular with moviegoers and cost nothing to produce. The camera was fixed in one spot and the actors merely moved about on a single stage. Not even a close up here or there. It has been alleged, not implausibly, that the film directors assigned to oversee Cantonese opera pictures merely set up the lighting and the cameras, yelled *"Action!"* then went out grocery shopping while the troupe took care of its own performance. The camera operators changed their own film magazines and kept shooting until the performance ended several hours later. By then the director had returned with his purchases just in time to yell *"Cut!"*

After that film, the Tales of the Little Phoenix finally ran out of gas. Pursued by creditors, denied bookings, nudged out of even the Laichikok and Kai Tak amusement parks by more competent and more desperate opera troupes that had sailed down the Pearl River from China in leaky boats, the Little Phoenix went boots up. Mother and Father Chan told Becky and the other kids in the troupe their services were no longer wanted. Never mind that they were legal guardians to their exploited jade girls and golden boys. The Chans just disappeared into the back streets of Kowloon and the kids were on their own.

Becky went to the studio that shot the opera film but they had no work. They did tell her about a big film being produced by a reputable outfit newly arrived from Shanghai. The picture was *Sorrows of the Forbidden City,* made by the grandly named Yung Hwa Motion Picture Industries. *Sorrows* was what they called a "super-production." Budgeted at one million Hong Kong dollars, it was the story of Emperor Kwang Hsu and his Pearl Concubine, and featured plenty of performers, big, beautifully rendered sets and gorgeous costumes. By Hong Kong standards it was a first-class picture. *Sorrows of the Forbidden City* gave the Hong Kong film business a big, hot, post-war start, and it got

Becky before the cameras. Her first performances after serving as an extra in *Sorrows* were non-speaking roles in another Yung Hwa super-production, *Tales of the Manchu Court,* and then a Peking opera picture.

Becky made several small appearances in subsequent Yung Hwa films before working as a supporting player at United Southern Film Corporation. United Southern put her in speaking roles in *The Terrible News* and *The Cockatoo.* Both pictures were in Mandarin and at the time Becky didn't speak a word of it. She learned her parts by rote, repeating each difficult word over and over, the "sh" sounds so common in Mandarin and non-existent in Cantonese caused her the most grief. Her final role for United Southern was as a bit player in a super-production, *The Queen of Heaven.* That picture was a colossal bust for United Southern and they went out of business.

Becky was out of work and hungry and she literally threw herself at the managing director of Southern Electric, the Cantonese studio where she worked when I first met her in 1948. Southern Electric films were unbelievably crappy. The studio's sole producer had just seen David Lean's *Brief Encounter* and he wanted to use fancy music too. He featured a Rachmaninoff piano concerto for the title music of one film, but played a phonograph recording of it at a sluggish seventy-two RPM instead of seventy-eight in an uneducated attempt to avoid paying a royalty on the recording.

These pictures were cheap and crude. One Southern Electric screen-writer, whenever he couldn't think of a joke for a comedy, would simply insert the sound of a toilet flushing in the background. The characters would pause in their jokes or those rhyming sing-songs that punctuated Cantonese comedy, and they would listen to the toilet. Usually it got a laugh from the audience. The sound was uneven, and frequently you heard technicians on the soundtrack. They'd drop equipment with a clang or mutter to one another to go get something. In one picture in which the lead actress was pouring her heart into a crying scene, you can faintly hear a man say, *"Don't go to that noodle shop on Shun Chi Street. Everything tastes like pig shit."* There was no money to rerecord the sound so they threw it in and audiences laughed heartily during the poor actress's big scene.

Becky appeared in a series of tear-jerkers for Southern Electric that were, by the standards of the studio, very profitable. It was the Pei-ling series that began with *A Smart Girl*. A young woman remains faithful to her mother even though she has been accused of murdering her cruel husband. Then Becky made *A Smart Girl Falls in Love* as a sequel, followed by *A Smart Girl Returns* and so forth. For a while, she worked hard and ate regularly. Then Southern Electric abruptly decided to get out of filmmaking. They sold rights to the *Smart Girl* series to newly constituted Great World and used the proceeds to invest in automatic knitting mills. Its all-purpose industrial name carried over to the new enterprise, Southern Electric did very well forever after, happy to be out of motion pictures. Becky was on the street again and hungry. It was a terrible time, and I felt extremely badly for her.

She lost her confidence and trailed after the Southern Electric people to the site of their new factory in Tsuen Wan, pleading with them for work in the knitting mill. They told her to come back in six months when the factory was built. Becky would have starved by then. So she went next door to another factory already up and running, the Jade Bracelet Wig Co. To her surprise, the owner was only too eager to hire her, or anybody for that matter, since most women in Hong Kong at the time thought the human hair used to make the wigs came from dead people. *"Women sell me hair,"* he explained. *"I've got brokers in the East Indies and Europe buying it from smart girls who know how to make some extra cash."* He put Becky to work in the bleaching department, stirring skeins of human hair in acrid chemical baths. No longer in need of the smart permanent wave she'd given her hair to impress the people in my press club, she cut it very close and sold it to the factory. The owner, a man name Kwong, paid her the lowest rate, forty Hong Kong dollars, because her hair was Chinese. *"I really need Italian hair,"* he told her. *"Their hair is the best in the world."*

When I found out from one of the former Southern Electric actresses that Becky was working in a factory I went there and waited at the gate at quitting time. When she saw me she marched right past, and walked down to the bus stop at Castle Peak Road with other factory girls. I followed her. Before I could say hello, she said without even looking at me: "He's paying me good money."

"That's good," I said. "You have to eat."

She stopped and turned and finally looked at me, almost angry. "Yes," she said. "I have to eat." I examined her grey smock and head scarf and asked her what she was doing in the factory. She said she was dyeing hair. Then she took off the head scarf and displayed her short hair, cut as short as a boy's. "And," she said, "I'm selling my body."

"So long as that's all you're selling," I said.

"I have to eat!" she shouted and resumed her course.

"Wouldn't you rather act in movies?"

"Movies are for idle people."

"They have you dyeing in that factory? Becky you can speak English. Not just any girl can do that. You should be working in the managing director's office. You could model wigs for them or something."

That never occurred to her, it never occurred to her that she could take the advantages she had to improve herself. She more expected to bob along and endure whatever setbacks happened. All she said was, "That's no certain thing."

"Did you tell him you could speak English?"

"I've got a job, I don't want to lose it," she said.

She always had that quality of physical desperation. "I have nothing," she would sometimes moan. Even when Becky became affluent, even when she no longer needed to pray to Wong Tai Sin for high heels, she was desperate. The shoes came in boxes from smart European shops in Central. She even owned a few wigs, which sat on faceless styrene-foam heads on the top shelf of her closet. She carried an air of destitution that you could see in the way she handled food. If Ah-niu finished a jar of store-bought Hoi Sin sauce Becky would pull it out of the trash and inspect it to make sure that every last drop had been scraped out. She seemed to value a flexible rubber spatula for digging out food remains from jars more than her acting coach at Great World.

I'm sure that Becky would have kept working in that wig factory for the rest of her life if she hadn't got laid off. After the Communists swept through Canton in late 1949, the first of the great waves of refugees from the Mainland poured into Hong Kong. Suddenly, there were thousands of women desperate for work. They were not as fussy about handling human hair. The price of labour in the Jade Bracelet Wig Co. plunged, and Becky was let go in favour of a cheaper woman from the countryside. Becky pleaded with Mr. Kwong and said she would take less money. *"I can speak English,"* she said. He told her he didn't need anyone who spoke English.

With the refugees taking factory work, Becky was destitute. She was about to lose her bed in a small Kowloon dormitory and go out on the street. I gave her 100 Hong Kong dollars. She wouldn't take it. "It's a loan," I said. "From a friend."

She was sobbing when I offered it. "What is the interest rate?" she said.

"Becky, you can't be serious. I'm your friend. I don't want interest, I want you to get back on your feet. Pay me when you can."

The man guilty of introducing Becky to Feng Hsiao-foon of Great World Studios was me. I was determined to get her some work and he was setting up his Hong Kong film operations. He and his family had only just arrived from Shanghai following the Communist revolution. They were a higher order of refugees, people whose idea of sacrifice was having to leave four of the ten servants behind.

I had called one day at their chaotic house in Kowloon Tong. My editor had assigned me a feature story on the so-called refugee movie producers who were pouring into Hong Kong from China in the aftermath of the Communist revolution. Feng Hsiao-foon was only too pleased to meet with me since I represented a minor entrée to English-speaking Hong Kong society. British Hong Kong could be useful to an ambitious man.

When I got to their house, a big, new, boxy, white thing behind a wall on Essex Crescent, the place seemed to have more files, boxes of photographs and film cans than furniture. Feng showed me about the packing crate maze with airy confidence. He and his two brothers (who for years had followed the instructions of their dictatorial youngest brother, Hsiao-foon) were trying to bring organization to the chaos. I was not allowed to look very closely at any of the boxes, lest I see some secret of the family business. Instead, an overworked domestic servant was ordered to clear a place on the balcony where we could sit and have tea. Actually, it was a measure of just how much Feng wanted to cultivate an English-speaking reporter that he saw me at all. The Fengs have always been extremely secretive, always listening attentively to what you said and commenting little. I was still new to the newspaper trade in 1950, but I was experienced enough to know that Feng was prepared to tell me no more than what he wanted me to hear.

He told me of his bitter feelings toward the Communists, who had taken over his family movie business, Golden Heaven Film Co., and made the Fengs employees. This was intolerable, he said, because the Fengs loved freedom, free enterprise, free expression, blah, blah, blah. Although he was a cunning speaker, Feng slowly betrayed that he loathed the Communists, not because they denied him artistic freedom, but because they denied him the autonomy to make as much dough as he could.

"It was all we could do to flee with the clothes on our backs," Feng said, with manufactured sadness. He spoke in Shanghanese, which was translated by an office assistant. In a few years he would master enough Cantonese and English to function, a not inconsiderable feat for such a busy man. *"We had to leave our equipment behind, and the actors and scenarists, the cameramen, the lights, the costumes, the sets. We are ruined now. We have to start all over with nothing. It will be a courageous struggle ..."*

Denied access to the immense mainland movie audience of 450 million people that would have made his operations more profitable, Feng had to focus on an overseas Chinese market of fewer than twenty million. He complained that fewer than half could understand Mandarin. Worse: he had to pick over the scraps of refugee filmmakers who had come south to Hong Kong to find useable talent. His one great resource was staff director Chen Lo-wen.

There wasn't much in the rhetoric Feng issued that I could use for a story. But he did tell me a little of how one could finance a Chinese motion picture on virtually nothing. First you had to have a script, and stories were hard to come by. One movie company offered a script-writing contest for the general public, that's how desperate they were. Then you needed a handful of airplane tickets and a lot of bluff. You flew to Southeast Asian cities to meet owners of cinemas catering to overseas Chinese. Singapore, Kuala Lumpur, Bangkok, Rangoon, Saigon, Manila and, most of all, Taipei. You met with the cinema owners and told them that you had some of the biggest stars in Hong Kong movies lined up to do a whopping good story. Gee whiz, it was going to be a great picture! You showed them the script and fed them lavish meals. When the owners were very drunk, you got them to pay out advances, preferably in U.S. dollars. With their money you flew back to Hong Kong to make the picture and hoped that the final product would be good enough to earn back the advances. If it was, you made a slender profit, enough to repeat the process all over again.

The trouble was that Hong Kong was full of movie producers in 1950, also refugees from Shanghai. A-class studios, which were well-equipped and financed, could make super-productions, but most producers ground out small, trashy, cheap product that failed to find a market. And, as I've already said, many refugee producers from China preferred to make pictures in Mandarin rather than Cantonese, even though the vast majority of moviegoers in Hong Kong understood Cantonese exclusively. Otherwise-astute businessmen were so sentimentally attached to old Shanghai and the Mandarin dialect that they clung to a virtually foreign language. They associated Cantonese with Cantonese movies – cheap, quick little pictures that appealed to the folksy instincts of vulgar, illiterate and unsophisticated Southerners. Feng and his brothers clearly wanted to be a big studio, but it was going to take money, and at the time Feng claimed that he had none.

Feng sent out beautifully printed press releases, the quality of which outstripped the importance of their content. They triumphantly outlined the Great World Organisation's plans for a major movie studio. There were also releases on his gifts to Hong Kong charities. He joined the board of the Tung Wah Group of Hospitals and volunteered to raise funds for Po Leung Kuk. He turned up at meetings of the Chinese Chamber of Commerce and the Chinese Temples Committee. All organizations of the highest quality and influence. He dropped by Government House to leave his business card, knowing that Governor Grantham was in the habit of automatically inviting every person who left a calling card to the annual garden party for the King's birthday. Hundreds of ambitious people did it.

Feng did not always run a high-class operation. He also found cunning ways of cutting corners that were either brilliant or dastardly, depending on whether you were taken in by them. He bought the services of well-known performers similar to the stature of Ng Chor-fan, the great legend of Cantonese cinema. But he paid them by the hour, gave them cameo roles they could perform in the morning and then be home by lunch. In turn, he advertised the picture as featuring these big stars as if they were in leading roles. And he was always curious about what independent producers were working on when he sublet Great World stages for overnight productions. These were the impoverished refugee companies who could only afford stage time after midnight. Feng would ask them about their scenarios: if they had a really hot idea he would rush a picture into production and slam it onto the circuit before the poor bleary-eyed fools of the night got theirs in the can. Feng was also not above using old, tired stories with a new title. Becky made one picture many times over. She starred in *Rich But Hungry* in 1957, remade it as *Girls Demand Excitement* in 1958, and then again as *The Millionairess* in 1964. Sometimes Feng didn't even bother to remake the picture; he just reissued it a year or so later with a new title and different advertising, a cheap trick that audiences really resented.

In their Shanghai days and before the advent of sound recording, the Feng family had produced a full slate of pictures: quality dramas for the sophisticated Chinese of the port cities and cheap, quick productions for rural illiterates much less demanding in their tastes except that they required a bare minimum of titles. What the Fengs wanted to be in Hong Kong was another Yung Hwa Motion Picture Industries Ltd. At first they piggy-backed distribution through China United in Hong Kong and on the Majestic circuit in Malaya and Singapore. But because there was no money to be made in merely producing films, they took on their own domestic and overseas distribution. Great World Pictures marketed the studio's output throughout Southeast Asia and in the Chinatowns of North and South America. By the early 1960s, the height of Great World's success, Feng had 110 theatres in Singapore and Malaysia alone, held by his subsidiary Great World S.E.A. Pty., and as a Chinese cinema proprietor he was second only to Shaw Brothers. He had twice as many theatres as Cathay.

Right from the beginning, the Great World Organisation, through its operating unit Great World Studios, produced shiny Mandarin-track romances, comedies and classical dramas. There was no need to build up capital; the Feng family mysteriously seemed to have plenty, despite Feng's protests of ruin at the hands of the Reds. Although he spent money on his Mandarin-track pictures, he was punishingly cheap with the Cantonese unit. His directors wanted crane shots but Feng would not release the studio's only camera crane from the Mandarin unit, so the Cantonese crew made a huge teeter-totter. The camera operator sat on one side of the teeter-totter with a big heavy Mitchell camera while five scrawny technicians pulled down the other end, trying not to grunt. Once, they lost their grip and the operator and camera came crashing down. They ran the footage shot by the falling camera in the final picture because there was no money for retakes. It made for a very amusing piece of film, especially the expressions on the faces of the startled actors. Feng fined the technicians for risking damage to the Mitchell and pocketed the money.

When I introduced Becky to Feng Hsiao-foon, he looked incredulously at her short hair and said to me through the English interpreter, *"This is an actress? She looks like a prison-camp inmate."* I don't think he disliked her short hair so much as he wanted to talk down her hiring price, akin to Mrs. Chan at the Door of Hope. Feng didn't know Becky understood English (or maybe he did). I told him that she had starred in the *Smart Girl* movie series, the rights to which he'd just picked up. *"It's just Cantonese crap,"* he said. Still, he took her on and had a scriptwriter dream up an excuse for her short hair. *"She fell into a tub of glue,"* he suggested, *"and she had to cut all her hair off!"* Feng didn't care how stupid it sounded, and he was actually going to go with that as a story line. They didn't in the end, but I don't recall what the excuse was. They revived the series and kept playing out variations on *Smart Girl* until the public was weary of them. The *Smart Girl* films made money right up until the end, all twelve of them.

The first week she was at Great World, Becky began paying me instalments of two dollars a week on my loan. She would give me the coins tightly closed in her fist, so no one saw what she was giving me. "You really are my friend," she said.

She never forgot I helped her out and, given that I introduced her to Feng, I never forgave myself for having helped her. He put her in ingénue roles in his Cantonese unit and she did well with *Those Kids,* and then came her first Empress of Stars award for *The Tram Conductor.* She appeared in her first Mandarin-track feature with *Two Beauties* in 1953.

Nineteen years after she entered motion pictures, Becky looked tired when she accepted her trophy for *Love Conquers the Goddess* at the 1967 All-Asia Film Week. She wanted to fly home immediately and have her baby in quiet and peace. But here she was in Tokyo, sitting on an uncomfortable banquet chair in a clamorous room at the Imperial Hotel. Becky was showing signs of crumbling in ways I would never have expected. Perhaps her youth had shielded her in the past. Young people often have a resiliency that wears away as they age and what was once merely something to tough out later becomes insurmountable. It wasn't love conquering her, it was fatigue.

I asked her how it felt to win Empress of Stars. She didn't even stop to think. She just rattled it out: "Being Empress of Stars is a heavy load to carry when you're eight months pregnant, weary, aching and exhausted." I was surprised. I failed to write it down. I just looked at her. It made me wonder if she had said this because she was speaking to a Westerner and could be more direct. Perhaps it was a revelation of just how unhappy she had been for many years. Then she asked: "Is this for the paper?"

I said: "Give me one."

"I am very honoured and touched to have been so named by Asia's greatest movie makers. The Far Eastern cinema is marching ahead, keeping abreast of progress and artistic refinement." She spoke almost like an automatic device. Becky knew what was required of her.

SEVEN

Nathan Road, the main artery in lower Kowloon, was shut down again by police after they found mysterious packages on the pavement. Someone reported they had seen an old car driving up and down Nathan Road with a hole in its floor. And through that hole, a passenger had been dropping small boxes and rag bundles onto the pavement. Traffic came to a halt and the authorities began the long and awkward task of clearing the sidewalks of the nightly crowds. I was standing at the corner of bustling Jordan and Nathan roads, with huge flat blocks on all four corners, while the police were pushing back pedestrians for their own safety. Jammed together, hot in the summer night, frightened about bombs and indignant about the police shoving them, the crowd grew restive. Near the corner stood the Ambassador Cinema with its three-storey billboard of Becky's tearful face looking down on the disorder below. I saw that the alterations to the billboard had been completed so the name of *Long Ago and Far Away* was now *Where Is She?*

I telephoned the *China Telegraph* offices on Hong Kong Island and said it was impossible to get back that evening. The ferry boats had stopped and Government Information Services had just announced that the governor had imposed a curfew to clear the streets. So I was stuck in Kowloon and didn't have enough money even for a Chinese hotel. I dictated my story over the phone to an editor then took one of the last buses north to Lok Fu in the foothills of northern Kowloon.

Lok Fu was a public housing estate, built of concrete by the government of Hong Kong in the late 1950s as a solution to the frequent, ghastly conflagrations that destroyed refugees' hillside shanty towns with terrible regularity. Housing estates like Lok Fu sprang up on the hilly suburban fringes of Kowloon, providing solid, sturdy and fireproof concrete flat blocks that were a world away from the chaos, dirt and hazards of the packing-board shanty towns. They were still grim places though. Lok Fu was barely half a mile straight east of Suffolk Road, the smart street where Becky and Feng Hsiao-foon lived. But it was a world away in terms of conditions. There was one toilet for every twenty-four people and all cooking had to be done on small charcoal braziers set out on the external corridors. Every passing resident and visitor could look upon the women of the buildings preparing their suppers, meals that got sprinkled with dust and grit thrown up from nearby construction sites where more such dormitory buildings were rising to house still more refugees. The neighbourhood was notorious for robberies and peepers. As I walked through the sterile courtyard between buildings distinguished only by giant coloured numbers on the ends of each block, I came upon a Maoist poster showing a dog with a man's face wearing a policeman's hat. The dog was getting a hard knock on the nose by a disembodied flying fist, presumably fired off the arm of a Communist trade unionist.

It was in Building No. 5 where a Chinese friend lived with his parents and siblings. When I knocked upon the flat door I saw a glimmer of green through the peephole and I knew at once that Benoit Ng was home. The green belonged to his favourite kimono.

Benoit opened the door. He was a man past thirty and, like me, a man more or less cursed by marriagelessness. He was stocky, given to pudginess and was dark-skinned for a Cantonese. His hair was receding. Benoit stood there with the steel door of his family's flat ajar, peering through the steel accordion grate, and he gave me a look of cultivated weariness. He wore the long emerald-green silk dressing gown – French-made, not Chinese. He pulled the accordion grate back and it gave off a nasty, dry screech. Benoit said the same thing he always said when we met: *"Dites-moi de l'amour."*

"I'm sorry to call so late but I'm stuck."

"The riots," he said and looked up and down the outdoor walkway. "I'll fix a mat for the floor."

Benoit's Chinese name was Siu-hung, but he had abandoned it for many years in favour of the French one. We sat in his family's living room, which was illuminated by a garish overhead fluorescent tube. It hummed annoyingly. An electric fan cooled the room. We had cigarettes, first my American ones, then Benoit's French ones. Benoit said that he heard there had been more trouble that evening. He drew the green silk kimono closer to himself and muttered about the stupidity of the Maoists.

Benoit Ng didn't work in the plastic-flower factory with the rest of his family. Assembling plastic flowers was a simple task that any unskilled worker could do. Benoit wasn't unskilled: he had been the chosen son in his family, the one on whom they had spent all their savings, educating him so that he could find a better job. It was not possible to educate all the children, so they'd concentrated their meagre resources on their eldest. They'd hoped that by doing so, Benoit would get a good job and lift the entire family with his eventual earnings. But the scheme put a terrible strain on the schoolboy, adding to emotional pressures that were impossible for his parents to see, much less appreciate.

Benoit graduated with a business diploma and became an office clerk for Rediffusion, the British broadcasting-equipment maker. Rediffusion sent Benoit to a Waterloo Road subsidiary, Reditune. I met Benoit in a basement bar in Central called the Dateline. We went out to dinner and he gave me a long and enthusiastic explanation of the scientifically proven benefits of Reditune. He recited what his employers had told him about how Reditune boosted staff morale and put customers in a placid buying mood through the clever, subliminal use of background music piped through loudspeakers embedded in the ceilings. Rediffusion had convinced Hong Kong banks, hotels and large Chinese restaurants to install the Reditune system so customers could hum along with soft American-produced music. This what came of Benoit's family's scrimping and sacrifice: so that their son might raise the family fortunes on a wave of elevator music. It would strike middle-class Westerners as undignified, but nobody in the Ng family cared whether the product was tawdry or ironic, only that it helped pay for food and kept the family together.

It was Benoit's job to install and maintain the music systems. I once chanced on him atop a step-ladder just outside a carved-ivory store in the shopping arcade of the Hongkong Hilton. He was screwing a white circular loudspeaker into the ceiling while a whistled version of "Poor People of Paris" flowed out of it. He hummed along with the music, looked down at me and said, "The poor people of Paris must be wonderful."

For Chinese people in the 1960s it was the pinnacle of Hong Kong chic to hear "Go Slow" and "Ebb Tide" playing when they sat down to dinner at, say, the Kum Wah Chinese restaurant. Reditune never played Chinese melodies – only American-produced music. The closest it came to Oriental music was a string-heavy version of "Sukiyaki." You could see nascent, naïve, glimmers of sophistication when customers dryly complained to the Kum Wah waiters about the inferior quality of the music Benoit's machine had delivered and then made specific song requests from the invisible machine. *"Play 'I've Grown Accustomed to Her Face,'"* they'd order maitre d's.

Benoit was not like the other young Chinese men you'd see in the Kum Wah Restaurant, the ones who sat in their white shirt-sleeves over lunch, their elbows on the table and their hands hold-ing cigarettes to their mouths while they stared off into the middle distance and intermittently discussed their business and amorous ambitions. Benoit was different. His business-school classes had convened in Tsimshatsui, the Kowloon tourist belt. He was coming home from class one night when he had a remarkable encounter that changed him forever. He was walking along Granville Road, heading for the bus on Nathan Road, when his eyes locked on to a tall, dark-haired Western man. The Western man asked in English for directions and then said the code words that such men used to say back then: "I think you're my kind of fellow." Siu-hung's English wasn't good then and he couldn't dis-cern that the man had a different accent. But he instinctively understood the lingering glances that ordinary men would never give one another (unless they were about to knock each other's brains out). The Westerner took him to a cheap Chinese hotel where they had sex. His name was Chouinard. He was French-Canadian and he unwittingly transformed Siu-hung.

Chouinard was a steward for Canadian Pacific Airlines. He flew weekly between Hong Kong and Tokyo and courted his young Chinese friend during his layovers. Chouinard brought Benoit gifts from Japan, trifles with which a Westerner would be amused – paper fans, wood-block prints, even a *yukata* dressing gown. But Benoit was much more interested in the Black Cat cigarettes Chouinard smoked and the smartly cut three-button suits he wore. Benoit wanted a slim-looking charcoal-grey business suit and narrow black tie like Chouinard's. They went to dinner at the Café Parisien in Central. Chouinard asked all sorts of questions about Chinese customs and said he wanted to visit Benoit's house. Benoit said he would arrange it but put it off, so ashamed was he of his family's two-room flat in the Lok Fu housing estate. Benoit was more interested in hanging around Tsimshatsui and Central with Chouinard, and got him to take him to the Cock and Pullet Restaurant in Duddell Street. Chouinard thought the restaurant's name extremely funny, but Benoit didn't understand. He was more interested in dining on what he believed was French food: beef Stroganoff and steak and kidney pie. Benoit knew nothing of the French, much less French-Canadians, but he saw they represented style, quality and, most of all, escape from Hong Kong's dreary poverty and mediocrity. Benoit and Chouinard had a lovely romance every Thursday, when the steward flew in from Tokyo on a DC-6, and it lasted until Saturdays when he flew back. Each man had a beautiful time, even if neither understood in the least what the other sought.

Eventually, Canadian Pacific reassigned Chouinard to its European routes, and the break up was palpably tragic, quite embarrassing really. Chouinard had become so enamoured with Benoit that he pleaded with him to emigrate to Canada. The last time they saw one another was at Kai Tak Airport, where the

French-Canadian wept copiously and unashamedly in front of his fellow crew members. He pleaded for Benoit to apply to emigrate as soon as possible. In a moment that carries such resonance for twenty-two-year-old lovers, Benoit gave a solemn pledge that he would follow Chouinard to Canada. The Chinese boy received letters from him every month, telling him he was planning a home for them near Dorval airport in Montreal. He sent Benoit packets of Canadian government information on immigration.

Benoit never went. His parents had asked him about his "European" friend, but Benoit was too ashamed of what he was to tell them the truth. He had only once brought Chouinard around to Lok Fu to see the family and only because Chouinard insisted on seeing what a Kowloon home was like. Chouinard was horrified, Benoit was ashamed and that made him angry. His family was only baffled as to why a Western man would want to come to Lok Fu. Even as they sat down to tea, Benoit began to rise up in an unexpected self-propelled indignation that surprised even himself. He asked Chouinard how often he saw his parents and the French Canadian said only once or twice a year. "A good son," Benoit said, "sees his parents every day." And he repeated the remark in Cantonese so his parents would appreciate his loyalty before an outsider. "Family," Benoit said, "is the most important thing anyone can have. You Westerners with your airplane travel and smart clothing don't have strong families." Chouinard started to object but stopped, allowing Benoit his defensiveness. "We work hard in Hong Kong," he went on, "for every cent we slave and it all goes to the family's general welfare."

So when Chouinard began writing to Benoit and pleading for him to immigrate to Canada, Benoit failed to reply. After many pleas for an answer, Chouinard gave up and stopped writing. Benoit told me that he wanted Chouinard to come back to Hong Kong, to take him to Canada personally. "I said prayers," Benoit said. "I lit candles." But I knew that it wasn't Chouinard's fault. Benoit would never leave his family, he would never make room in his life for Chouinard.

That did not stop Benoit from re-inventing himself as a kind of Oriental Frenchman. He saw the Hollywood movie *An American in Paris* six times, then went to a street market in Mongkok where he searched and searched through cheap clothing stalls until he found a wine-coloured beret. He depleted his pocket money in a Mody Road tobacconist for Gauloise cigarettes (he felt Chouinard had misled him when I told him that Black Cats were Canadian). He learned to sing "La Petite Tonkinoise" phonetically and even performed it – just once – at an amateur-talent night in a North Point nightclub.

That had been ten years before the summer of 1967. Now, with me sitting beneath the humming, aggressive fluorescent light of his family's sitting room, Benoit lit up a Gauloise and surveyed the sitting room, his own little concrete cubicle of sophistication in the middle of Kowloon.

"You know what they're doing up on the roof of our building?" he said. "They're making firecracker bombs. We find the red paper fluttering down everywhere. Terrorists are unwrapping firecrackers and sifting the powder into big glass jugs with fuses in them. Those people are disgraceful."

At that moment, Benoit's mother called from the bedroom. *"Siu-hung? Is that you?"*

"Yes, Ma. I have a friend, the foreign gentleman from the British newspaper. He can't get back into the city."

"Don't leave the light on too long," she called. *"The electricity."*

"I won't, dear. Go to sleep now."

Benoit looked at me, a little sorrowful and a little defiant, as if he had to explain his affection for his parents. Then he said: "You won't tell anyone that I said they're making firecracker bombs on the roof? We would get into trouble."

I assured him I wouldn't.

"We're quiet, hard-working people."

I told him that I would mention to my policeman friend that I had received an anonymous tip. Benoit felt uneasy about it because he disliked Jack Rudman intensely. I had introduced them in the basement bar of the President Hotel. Rudman, after watching Benoit's French affectations, thoughtlessly dismissed him as a "whoopsie," a word Benoit had no difficulty deciphering. Thereafter Benoit referred to Rudman as "Her."

"She smells," Benoit said.

I agreed that sometimes when he was off duty Rudman was intemperate with his use of cologne.

"No!" Benoit said sharply. "*Kwailo* smell."

I said that Jack had inquired into Becky Chan's disappearance. Benoit was interested in the news that Becky had vanished. He had just taken his parents to see *Long Ago and Far Away* and hadn't understood the newly painted question marks on the billboard of the Ambassador Cinema. He softly sang a verse from the title song in a lovely warbling baritone:

> *"Chills run up and down my spine,*
> *Aladdin's lamp is mine;*
> *The dream I dreamed was not denied me.*
> *Just one look and then I knew*
> *That all I longed for*
> *Long ago was you."*

First he sang in English, then Cantonese and indicated where the differences were. "For one thing," he said, speaking softly to not disturb his sleeping family. "Chinese people might not know who Aladdin is. And we wouldn't say that dreams are denied you. We are not entitled to have dreams in the first place. We only work hard and thus sacrifice dreams." He lit another cigarette and looked a little sombre. "Well," he said, "you get the idea."

His parents had nagged him for years to get married. When Benoit showed no interest, his mother colluded with Lok Fu women to bring their daughters around for his consideration. They had told him he needed to start a family, but now they were growing weary of nagging and were reconciling themselves to Benoit's eccentric bachelorhood. It was getting very bad for poor old Benoit. He was too old to be attractive to European men and too encumbered by his circumstances to meet a Chinese man. Just as he said, he never dreamed of leaving his family after they'd sacrificed so much for his education.

"Are you still mooning over her?" Benoit asked.

"I don't 'moon,'" I said.

Benoit shrugged. "Ignore her." He said that I could have picked a less impossible figure to fall in love with. "You think that she's ever going to fall in love with you?"

"I'm not asking for that," I said, although that was precisely what I wanted to happen.

Who was Benoit to lecture me about impossible love? Here he was trapped in a cell-like tenement in Lok Fu, denying he had dreams of love even when every moment of his imagination lay elsewhere. It was far from Hong Kong, ironically, a place that warmed the imaginations of tourists on Canadian Pacific Airlines. But for Benoit, the far-off world was a place that created his expensive cigarettes, his French dressing robe, his smattering of French words. These were appalling self-indulgences in a place where hard sacrifice was expected and given.

The fact that Benoit went to bars such as the Dateline, with their high-priced drinks, was a shocking waste. I had met him there, listening to Herb Alpert songs on the juke-box or to live Filipino singers who enthusiastically imitated Mexican pop. Benoit preferred to come to places like the Dateline since most of the patrons were Western men, mostly itinerants: tourists and military men. This way he couldn't be found out by Chinese society; this way he could keep his unentitled dream hidden.

"Are you all right?" Benoit asked.

I put my hand to my right eye and said that I was.

"Then why are you crying?"

I really didn't feel at all upset. Quite calm really. It was more like I'd sprung a benign leak from a malfunctioning duct. "It's all the dust in the air out here," I said. "From the construction."

"You're not thinking about that policeman are you?" Benoit said.

I told him I wasn't the least bit interested in Jack and, if anything, I was worried about Becky.

"She's not worthy of your attentions. She's a trifle from far away." Benoit lit another cigarette. "She would only be too happy to see you in a jail cell after she had raided one of the bars you were in."

I gave him a fierce, confused look and he backed off.

"Western romance is inferior to Chinese romance," he said. "I know both." We considered the room, the hum of the overhead fluorescent tube, the dust in the air, a dainty carved camphor box on the sideboard, and we listened absently to the electric fan oscillating back and forth, something in its mechanism giving off a click now and then. "Everything Chinese is better," he said.

"It's not a romance," I said.

Benoit got up and put a reed mat on the floor for me to sleep on. Before he went to bed he made sure all the butts of his Gauloises were out. He snapped off the ceiling light and looked through the stripes of the burglar bars on a small front window. There was a dim light bulb in the walkway outside, which threw the shadow of the stripes on his face. He said softly: "She hasn't written me in years."

I spent a miserable night on the floor of the Ng family's flat, turning in the humid heat. My face felt filthy when I woke and my shirt was dirty. I thanked Benoit and his parents then stopped off at the Lok Fu District police station. I spoke to the duty officer about what I'd heard about the bomb factory on the roof of Benoit's building. They agreed to let me go along with their investigation. They found shreds of discarded firecracker papers on the roof. I got a story out of it, but they found no one to arrest.

EIGHT

There were three phone messages waiting for me at the *China Telegraph* newsroom. Two were callbacks on stories I was working on for the Sunday edition. The third was from Jack Rudman. It said he had located Becky Chan. I immediately called his number at the San Po Kong sub-district station. A Chinese officer said that Rudman had been mustered for expected disturbances from the Kowloon Motor Bus transport workers. I also telephoned Great World Studios to tell Feng Hsiao-foon that Becky had been found, but his secretary, Miss Chin, told me that Feng had gone to a Rotary Club luncheon. Great World had put out a press release announcing that Feng was to give a speech in praise of the Tung Wah Hospitals Foundation. Miss Chin told me that it would be impossible to disturb Feng on this important occasion. He wasn't about to cancel Rotary just because his wife was missing. I decided against leaving a message about Becky, just to be a bastard. Miss Chin nosed about, asking me why I was calling, but I dodged her and hung up.

I put off a scheduled interview with another Royal Observatory meteorologist on latest fallout figures from China. Then I quickly engineered a new assignment. I told my editor that I'd received a tip there was going to be trouble with bus union militants in San Po Kong. My editors let me go, and I ran from the *China Telegraph* offices on Wyndham Street all the way to the Star Ferry's Hung Hom boats.

When I found Jack, he was on the street outside the San Po Kong sub-district station with his men. "There you are," he said. He pulled his gas mask slightly to the side so he could speak to me. He held a lightweight woven rattan shield, carried a long black truncheon in a belt loop and had a Colt .38 in a side holster. "I found out where your little Chinese actress got to."

I opened my notebook and started to write what he told me. His news was brief and undetailed. "She's in China," he said. "She's gone over to Mr. Mao's side. You can expect that she'll have some explaining to do to that hubby of hers if she ever comes home. Which I doubt."

I asked Rudman how he knew this. He said he had confirmed it with British customs officials who had processed Becky's documents at the Lo Wu train station on the day she'd disappeared. I couldn't get anything more out of him. All he said was – and this was through his gas mask so I couldn't be sure I heard right – "She'll never come back to Hong Kong!" He gave me a hard look, as if he were about to do battle with Becky herself. "She's finished."

What he'd said didn't make much sense. Becky had no interest in politics. She had never expressed any views about the Mainland, especially given her husband's public anti-Communist stance. It didn't figure.

After he'd spoken I looked at him through the Plexiglas panes of his gas mask waiting for more, some small information that would help me understand. But he only scowled back at me, as if *I* had something to account for, as if *I* had done something wrong. He went to join the other members of the Emergency Unit.

The trade unionists were demonstrating over arrests of their comrades who were, at the moment, inside San Po Kong police station. The EU was to prevent them from getting inside. Jack looked over his shoulder and his eyes had changed. He had almost a warm look as he went shoulder to shoulder with his mates. He pulled aside the mask again, pointed at me with a free hand and said: "This place may be one of the hotter corners of hell, but you know it not!" He must have been quoting some obscure hack poet he thought sounded classy. If it was cheap, it was still a kick in the head when he said that. At that moment I couldn't have cared if the Maoists broke his head in. Jack blended into the common ranks of men in black helmets.

They formed a line across the street against the advancing demonstrators. The leftists were singing raggedly.

"The East is Red! The sun has risen!
China has brought forth a Mao Tse-tung!
He works for people's happiness!
He is the people's great saviour!
Chairman Mao loves the people!
He is our guide!"

With a group of other reporters, Chinese, Japanese and Westerners, I followed at a distance. The police planned to concentrate their will on a group of rioters many times their number. These showdowns were often truly frightening to watch, which is perhaps one reason I hung about them. Jack never felt the morbid excitement I did. He averred that he got very frightened, but only after a riot, after he had done his job. "Someday," he'd told me, "I may wake up one morning and say, 'My God, I can't do that again.'" But he kept doing it.

I had to sieve everything Jack said for the motive. Was he saying something to make me feel badly? Was he lording inside information over a reporter? I could be sure of one thing: Jack was not lying, speculating or manipulating me; he was meticulous about hard realities. Maybe he had been telling me that I was all wrong about Becky, that I was a poor judge of character. Maybe he was telling me that I really wasn't worthy of his friendship. To the casual observer, our friendship had the markings of ordinary male companionship. The shared evenings of drinking, exuberant exchanges of useless facts about mechanical things and history, impractical reminiscences, all that makes merry the hours shared by men. We had a long and thoroughly enjoyable discussion comparing and contrasting the Vitaphone and Phonofilm sound-recording processes. We went together to the City Hall library to find documented proof of the existence of the DC-5 airplane after an American serviceman we met in a bar insisted that Douglas had never produced one. We couldn't find any documentation, but we both swore that we'd once read something somewhere that Douglas had produced a handful. I felt very good that evening with Jack.

It was, perhaps, the sort of night that gave me even greater pleasure than the physical kind. Back when I first met him, back when we were performing Gilbert and Sullivan for the King's Park Players, we went drinking after rehearsals, in the British-style pubs of Tsimshatsui. We would burst into a chorus from *Pirates of Penzance* every once in a while, entertaining the American tourists and, not surprisingly, entertaining the music-loving Chinese even more.

> *"Take one consideration with another –*
> *A policeman's lot is not an 'appy one!"*

One evening, after a few drinks at the Gaslight Lounge, I invited Rudman home for a nightcap. He downed the last of his whisky and said, "Let's go."

We rode the ferry over to Wanchai singing. At the time I didn't twig on just what a sorry, risible comment on circumstances the song had.

> *"Our feelings we with difficulty smother*
> *When constabulary duty's to be done!"*

We took a taxi out to my flat in Paterson Street humming this song and glancing at one another, naughty smirks crossing our faces. Like anyone who has ever tacitly agreed to go home together, we felt the intrigue was behind and now we could say and feel whatever pleasures we wanted, unencumbered by device. Sometimes we laughed for no apparent reason. He smacked me on the knee and we sang another chorus. The Chinese cab driver loved the song and grinned at our high spirits. We went up the tiny elevator in my block, the kind with a swinging door you had to pull open with your hand. We paused to talk, in a blokey way, about the clever electric lock that prevents people from opening the elevator door when the car is away from that floor. Mechanical talk had been part of our mutual seduction. We would have discussed automobiles if either of us had one. I opened up my flat, made us another round of drinks and Rudman stood at the window, jingling coins and keys in his trouser pockets and humming the song. He stood at the window and examined the domestic activity through the windows of other flats. "You know what?" he said. A large brown beetle, probably a cockroach, came droning in on awkward, waxy wings and both of us looked at it with dismay. I banged it hard with the Island phone book and killed it.

"What?"

"I think I've got you figured, mate."

I brought over the drinks and asked him what he meant.

"I think that you're my kind of bloke."

"What kind is that?"

Rudman gave me that searching look that all policemen give suspicious characters: the eyes darting back and forth, that examination for hidden evidence, the felonious little plan. It was Rudman's equivalent of Feng's circumlocution. But his look had more to it, a certain familiar and unsettlingly prolonged glance. From outside, we heard a group of mah-jong players in another flat mixing up the tiles, preparing for a new round, and his eyes darted in the direction of the sound. "Let's move away from the window," he said.

Afterward we lay side by side, slick with sweat. It was the first time I had it on with him and it was to be the last. The whole thing spanned no more than fifteen minutes and it was easily the best quarter hour of my life. The only time I had ever felt more alive was standing in front of that train in Winnipeg or planning a caper over the edge of Niagara Falls. I ran the back of my hand over his chest hair, my only unfulfilled wish being that I had bought an extra pack of smokes before taking him home. The only way it could have been even better an experience was if it had never happened at all, if I had gone through life only fantasizing and longing. Now he was here at last, the dream I dreamed was not denied me.

This is what he said, this was Jack Rudman's tender pillow talk, this is what one guy said to another at such an important moment, this was my man talking to me: "We could get six months to a year for this."

I looked at him. I didn't say "you son of a bitch," though in retrospect I really should have. The bedroom window was open and the sounds of mah-jong games, radios broadcasting Cantonese opera and China Motor buses gearing down to the terminus on Paterson Street came in. "But then I'd have to arrest myself," he said, "and bear testimony against same said individual. So I guess it's not on."

Our affair did not remain one for long. It wore off, and Rudman became interested in some transient American tourist. It was safer to have sex with Western tourists, who were in town one day and then on an plane for Bangkok the next, than to have it with a local, someone with traceable habits. Tourists wouldn't hang around, become nuisances and try to blackmail you. "I have to be careful," he told me. "Very careful, mate. A lot of men are counting on me."

I wanted to smirk at that, confect a double entendre, mock him for his self-importance and apparent disinterest in my feelings. But I didn't, because I badly hoped that he would change his mind.

Benoit Ng had no patience with my anger and my heavy drinking after Rudman pushed me away. He sat, twirling his wine-coloured beret in pouting circles at the end of his index finger and watched me in the Cellar Bar at the Ambassador Hotel while I clenched my fist around my glass of rye. Thelma Quasado was singing that night. The management had told Benoit to take off his beret or leave, so Benoit was cross too.

"*Ai-ya*, you live in Hong Kong," he said. "You should eat rice. Not potatoes."

"It's not like that," I said. I could have crushed the glass I was holding with my hand. "Don't make it crude."

After my love thing with Rudman I tried the best I could to be his pal, his only functioning friend outside the police force. For Rudman, my one saving grace was that I was a newspaperman, and that meant, in some overly logical way, acceptability for Jack.

Newspapermen wrote about crime and disorder, they hung around police stations seeing the coppers doing their duty for the people of Hong Kong. We had a place in their firmament, but it was a far-flung orbit and they could ignore us most of the time. I'm sure that in Jack's mind I would never be more than a distant friend, a person from a foreign country. Once in a while he would lecture me about all the things he saw, things to which ordinary residents of Hong Kong were oblivious, like foot patrolmen having to pick up the bodies of refugees who had died and been left in the gutter. Back when he had still been an ordinary constable, he had come across a dead coolie on Temple Street. He bashfully told me that rather than face disposal of the body at the public mortuary and the ensuing lengthy paperwork, he'd picked up the corpse and dragged it across the street to the opposite gutter, which was the territory of another patrolman. On another occasion he let me in on a few more little secrets. "There's a little buggery game going on at the back porch of St. John's Cathedral. As soon as the beadle complains we'll have to do a sort-out, so don't get caught there, because I won't be able to get you out of it. I won't even know you if I have to take you in."

Jack used to work in the Criminal Investigation Division, but something had happened to him there that he wouldn't discuss. He personally requested a transfer into the Emergency Unit, and it was granted. Rudman never told me what had happened but you could guess at it from the contours of his promotions through the police. He had gone from a prestigious position as an investigator to working in the roughest job in the force. It was classic male psychology, but I stayed away from that guff. It does no one good to pick apart a man's motivation. I wouldn't like that done to me and I wouldn't do it to Jack.

The leftists were about to challenge Rudman and the Emergency Unit. They were, for a mob, very disciplined. They mimicked one another's hand gestures, flicking their copies of Mao's *Quotations* back and forth over their heads and repeating the same slogans in unison. When they moved, they moved together. If the front ranks stopped, everyone behind them stopped. They could change directions like a massing flock of swallows. They believed, and so they could. And yet all this fervour, the bombs, the terror, all of it was a mild distillation of what was happening just across the border in China. In recent days I had been assigned the regular duty of riding the trains of the British section of the Kowloon Canton Railway to interview Chinese Hong Kong residents returning from China. Since foreign reporters were not allowed into nearby Canton, we were obliged to probe returning Chinese who had been visiting relatives on the Mainland. Most travellers refused to talk to me but a few would tell vivid stories of what they had seen, always on the condition of anonymity. The only verification of their comments I could make was matching spotty reports by the Kyodo News Agency out of Peking.

The China Telegraph

Half million to rally for Mao in Canton

By Paul Hauer
China Telegraph

Chiang Ch'ing, wife of Chairman Mao Tse-tung, has arrived secretly by air in Canton to take charge of a massive rally for "class struggle," said travellers returning from China yesterday. A 60-year-old businessman from Hong Kong told the *China Telegraph* that Madame Mao had arrived to "light the fires and fan the winds of cultural revolution throughout Kwangtung Province."

Canton workers were said to be building arches and decorations to welcome Madame Mao.

Kyodo reported that Canton was gripped by fear and apprehension over a call by pro-Mao forces for a demonstration by 500,000 people next Friday. Tension was reported to be high, and some travellers predicted new street battles between pro-Mao and anti-Mao forces over the weekend.

The clash between Hong Kong's leftists and the Emergency Unit that day in San Po Kong was difficult to follow and it came on so fast that I wasn't quite sure how it happened. Much of what I am about to tell I did not know until weeks afterward, when the sequence was reconstructed in criminal court. We reporters stood to the side of the police and watched them force the crowds back along King Fook Street, away from the Magistracy building where they were to protest the arrests and detentions of other leftists.

It began when a bottle came hurtling through the air toward the police. No one will ever know just who threw it for no one was charged and proved guilty. The bottle was full of gasoline and had a burning rag attached to it. When it crashed to the pavement at the feet of Police Constable Chan Chi-kin, it burst into a fiery pool that engulfed his legs and ran up his rattan shield. The crowd drew back to avoid the flames, and Chan Chi-kin staggered backward and rolled to the ground. But the gasoline clung to him and it seemed like ages before another policeman came forward with a fire extinguisher and enveloped him in white fog.

At this point the "TEAR SMOKE" banner went up and off went the guns, volleying tear-gas canisters streaming across the lines. One group of police fired wooden batons at the mob. You could hear a popping sound as the guns went off, different from the crack of a pistol. The crowd broke apart. The police were grabbing some of the ones in front and dragging them back to police vans. People were screaming and coughing and a group of police had surrounded Constable Chan to keep the crowd from further attacking him. I saw one officer fire a wooden projectile at the stomach of a man in a white shirt who had a nest of stones tucked into the crook of his arm. The man with the stones fell backwards with a cry. His stones flew into the air and rattled down the pavement. I saw blood on his stomach. Other policemen were besieged by a chanting trio who were swinging bicycle chains at them. They retaliated with some hard coshes to their heads with wooden truncheons, and I could hear the sticks hitting rioters on their heads, amazed at how the same stick could make a different sound on each skull. The Chinese policeman with the fire extinguisher was screaming obscenities in Cantonese at the crowd and discharging the extinguisher into their faces. The rioters in the front put their hands to their faces and tried to draw a breath of oxygen but they were suffocating. They had to fall back. The police grabbed some more rioters and hauled them away.

The crowd broke into disarray and everyone began running back down Hong Keung Street. But just when it seemed that the riot had been broken, the protesters began firing bottles back at the police. I retreated up Foo Yuen Street to avoid the tear gas which was drifting backwards. The bottles contained acid or gasoline and they started smashing all around us. The crowd came back, throwing more bottles and the narrow street lit up with pools of orange flames and columns of black smoke. The soles of my shoes felt spongy from walking through corrosive acid. I dreaded slipping and falling on my hands in the acid. One of the policemen turned to me and screamed to get the hell back. It might have been Jack for all I know. Not that he would have cared whether I lived or died. With the tear gas drifting backwards and in their favour, the crowd advanced again and threw more acid. The police were retreating now.

You've never really been a reporter until you've had to run to save your skin. I saw two correspondents, one from Agence France Press, the other from a right-wing newspaper, *Kung Sheung Daily News,* get caught by the mob and beaten. I clutched at the sleeve of the guy from *Kung Sheung Daily News* to pull him free but the whole arm of his sports jacket came off in my hand. Somebody punched me in the ribs and then the side of my head. I bolted for the San Po Kong Police Station and ran in the front door, pursued by two screaming men with sticks.

Inside, the Report Room was chaos. There were detained rioters held up against the wall of the staircase leading up to the entry. The police had drawn pistols and were holding them to the faces of the rioters while they screamed at them not to move. They had lost all discipline and control. Someone began pushing me from behind. I turned and saw the boys of the Emergency Unit, who'd retreated from the street altogether. I couldn't quite see the entrance because of all the men in black helmets. The police station itself was now under siege and they drew shut the two great steel doors at the entry. We could hear stones and bottles breaking against the doors and screams from the crowd. One of the detainees in the stairway took up a chant of *"Resist! Resist! Resist!"* Other demonstrators took it up too. A policeman pushed at me and shouted to go downstairs for my own safety.

I went down the steps. It was the lockup. I didn't actually walk down the stairs, I fell feet over shoulders, clutching my notebook. When I stood up, rubbing my neck, I saw that there were about ten demonstrators in a cell and about an equal number of men from the EU. I saw Jack Rudman there in a rear cell. He had just flung off his gas mask and helmet. The helmet was still rocking uneasily on the floor, where it had landed on its back like a doomed black turtle. There were huge sweat stains on Jack's shirt and his hair was streaming. He held a long black shiny truncheon in one hand and a demonstrator, seated in a chair, in the other.

"Did you throw that gasoline?" he screamed in Cantonese at the demonstrator.

The demonstrator said nothing.

"Answer!" Jack screamed.

And at once he began slamming the truncheon down on the demonstrator's head over and over and over. Oh Christ, it was awful. I could hear the thuds from across the room growing softer and more liquid each time. *"Answer!"* he screamed with each and every blow. Two Chinese constables were holding the demonstrator by the arms, stretching him wide before Jack. They were yelling too and one kicked at the demonstrator's feet. Then Jack put both hands on the black truncheon and raised it over his head. I recall this only too clearly because it was one of those moments that seemed to move so slowly. He held it over his head for a second then brought it down. Amid the yelling and the clamouring I distinctly heard the popping sound the stick made when Jack hit the protestor on the top of his head. The prisoner's legs shot out straight and he went entirely limp.

Rudman stepped back, faced the other demonstrators and shouted, *"Which of you bastards wants it next? I'll kill you one at a time if you don't say who threw the gas!"* He made for another and raised his truncheon and held it aloft. The leftist ducked down, put his hands before his face and wept loudly. The body of the demonstrator Jack had beaten slumped over and fell heavily to the floor.

Jack looked at the body and put his hand on the green-painted bricks. He seemed about to weep too. The two Chinese constables picked up the rioter and eased him back into the chair. They glanced at one another. One said, *"Wai! Take a pulse."* The second put two fingers against the rioters neck then shook his head. Both of them stepped back from the body, newly aloof and contemptuous of the corpse. One of them seized the truncheon Jack was still holding with one hand and took it away. He left the lockup with it. No one ever saw the truncheon again.

Jack began to recover himself. He stood up straight and full, reappraised his surroundings and turned about. He looked at his men, then the prisoners and finally he saw me there for the first time. He stared at me, really stared. He was so frightened. No one else spoke. Jack looked at me. I looked at Jack. I was seeing him and he didn't like it. We just stood there, facing one another. I loved him at that moment. I'm sure he could have returned it. But no. No.

Jack pointed a finger at me and shouted in a furious great roar that transformed him beyond anything I had ever seen in him before. "Get that man out of here!" he shouted. Everyone turned to look at me.

"I said get him out! Get him out!"

The other cops started pushing me backwards with batons. Not hard and bruising, just enough to get me moving. I staggered backward, still looking at Rudman who was returning my look with great fury. The guards closed the inner steel door of the lockup so I could no longer see into the cells. They kept pushing me along, up the stairs to the report room. At the top of the stairs they shut the lockup door. They kept bunting at me and yelling to get out so I staggered out of the report room and they closed a third door. Finally they pushed me into the street, where I could smell burning rubber and the lingering threads of tear gas in the air. The rioters had dispersed and the street was empty. The police forced shut the two big green steel doors, and I was left on the outside. I stared stupidly up at the police station, as if some answer or explanation was going to be found on its outside walls. A small slit in one of the big doors flicked open. The eyes of a Chinese policeman looked out at me for a few seconds. Then the slit snapped shut and I was alone on the street.

On my way back to the *China Telegraph,* I recalled what Rudman had said about wanting to wash the tear gas out of his hair. I had a lingering sweetish smell about me that became nauseating. There was a bump rising on the side of my head and my suit was dirty. On the HKY ferry to Central, I stood at the stern and looked at Kowloon receding behind me. I couldn't take much more of this, I thought, and actually started to choke on tears. I put my elbows on the railing. Its varnish was sun-cracked and flaking off. The crust clung to the sleeves of my jacket. I'm glad I stood at the stern, facing away from the other passengers so I could contort and twist my stupid face in an all-out bid to get myself under control. In the air, a Pan Am 707 banked on finals into Kai Tak. In the harbour, a fishing junk cut across the ferry boat's wake, its high stern bobbing up and down. On the ferry two women gossiped noisily. I pounded my fist on the cracked varnish and sobbed abruptly, then stopped, just as abruptly. I opened my notebook to catch up on my reporting. I gave off a few sighs, slapped my eyes with the back of my hands and wrote down my account of the riot.

I arrived back at the newsroom in Central composed and ready to write my account of the confusion, pulling in official comment supplied by telephone from Government Information Services. When I got the GIS man on the phone I asked him about the death of a rioter in the San Po Kong Sub-District lockup. He said he knew nothing about it and that it was probably just a rumour.

I hesitated. I asked a few other questions concerning the number of arrested, injuries and cost of damage to private property. Then I mustered my nerve and said. "Actually, I was in the lockup when it happened." The GIS man was silent for a few moments then said he'd call back. When he did, all he said was, "The government has no comment at this time concerning allegations of a demonstrator's death in any police station. Any further announcement, if there is to be one, will have to come from the Crown prosecutor's office." I asked if any police officers had been charged with offences. He repeated his first sentence then hung up.

I mentioned the incident to Bill Dunn, the duty editor.

"You saw it?" Bill said. "Who did it?"

Suddenly I felt very unwell and wanted to go home. I couldn't. I sat there.

"Well?" Bill said. "Who did it?"

"I didn't quite see their faces," I said.

"But it was the police?"

"I think so."

He said that if the government refused to comment on it then there was no story to be done. I know that sounds strange. You must remember that this was Hong Kong in the 1960s, and gutless English-language newspapers were slavish about repeating the government's line. So I didn't do a story on it.

I telephoned Feng Hsiao-foon's office and asked Miss Chin for an appointment with Feng that evening. This news would hurt him and I was looking forward to it.

NINE

Feng Hsiao-foon probably hadn't seen the *Ta Kung Pao* news report yet. He wouldn't touch a Communist newspaper and no one in the studio would dare tell him about the story, so afraid were they of him. *Ta Kung Pao* had learned from a source inside China that Becky had arrived in Canton and was now working for the Southern Film Corporation in aid of Chairman's Great Proletarian Cultural Revolution. I would be the one who would tell Feng this. Oh, the pleasure of something to look forward to, especially after the horror of the San Po Kong police station and the news about Becky. I took a taxi out to Tsuen Wan, northwest of Kowloon, to the big Great World Studios complex on Castle Peak Road. The area was building up, with ten-storey industrial buildings that housed transistor-radio factories, artificial flower works, and makers of vacuum-flasks, wind-up toys, wigs, knitwear, plastic utensils and small electricals – everything, that made up the Hong Kong economic miracle, including motion pictures.

Great World's studios looked little different from the big concrete buildings dotting Tsuen Wan except that they were low and spread out over several blocks. Despite the glamour and excitement created inside the studio complex, the five low buildings had dreary concrete exteriors and were all painted a uniform sandy yellow. In the humid semi-tropical summers, black mildew spread up from the base of the buildings, giving them a grubby look. The front office was near the entrance to the cramped four-acre lot. On the roof was a simple sign painted with red Chinese characters on white background and the English equivalent: "The Great World Organisation" and illuminated at night with incandescent lights fixed to arms that stuck out in front. Inside, there was a reception desk nestled under a curving staircase. All the windows were glass brick, which admitted light but distorted views of the outside. The old Chinese porter at the desk recognized me. This was Uncle Lo, who had been with Great World since the Feng family came to Hong Kong from Shanghai in 1950. He wore day-pyjamas and a very bad toupee, cast off from the costume department. It accentuated his big ears. He remembered me from the late 1950s when I had worked briefly for Great World as an English-language publicist, greeted me with a bow, then announced me with a deaf man's shout over a heavy old telephone to Miss Chin.

Miss Chin came down the winding staircase and shook my hand. She gave me a severe look and said that Feng was having his dinner. I told her that I would wait, but she ushered me up. We passed through her small fore-office. There was her grey steel desk, which stood forlornly in the middle of a virtual concrete shell. The walls had been lightly stuccoed and painted over in a dated cream shade. The floor was red stone tiles rimmed with gaping black rubber moulding instead of proper baseboards. There wasn't a single picture on the walls, not even a Great World movie poster. It was as if she wanted to keep herself in prison-like austerity.

Feng's office was a riotous contrast. The walnut-panelled walls were completely obscured by a neat grid of photographs depicting Great World stars, Chinese and Western businessmen shaking Feng's hand and a few foreign celebrities who had worked on pictures in Hong Kong. William Holden, Ray Stark, Curt Jurgens, Robert Wise. There were lobby cards of his greater pictures. There was also a large photo of him standing on the top of the first-floor overhang of the Ambassador Cinema with his arms outstretched, the unabashed showman. Behind him in the photo was an enormous hand-painted billboard of Becky Chan costumed for *The Goddess of Mercy.* But the real pride of place was a plaque that had a clear space around it, directing the eye to its surface. It was his perfect-attendance plaque, awarded by the North Kowloon Rotary Club.

Feng was seated in shirtsleeves behind his desk and had a cloth napkin fixed to a button on his chest. He abruptly stood up and ordered Miss Chin to get me a meal too. I declined. Miss Chin stared at me through her thick little eyeglasses, as if I had committed some rudeness. I glanced at her but you could never quite make out her eyes through those glasses. She only left when I yielded to accepting a cup of tea.

When I'd come in, Feng had been speaking on the phone in Cantonese. He went back to his call. He always assumed, as did many people in Hong Kong, that foreigners couldn't wrap their heads around the dialect. (Many northern Chinese like Feng had difficulty mastering it too, with its sharp sounds and extra tones not used in Mandarin or Shanghanese.) He cupped his hand over the phone and said, "I'm speaking to His Excellency, the Governor." I nodded and waited, pretending not to listen. He wasn't speaking to Governor Trench. He was speaking to a junior aide and the junior aide was giving him the brush-off. Feng, undeterred, kept slugging along, telling him how important it was for the Governor to attend an upcoming Great World movie pre-miere. He suggested that it would be good for public confidence to see the Governor attending a movie, a sign of stability. Finally, he said that Trench had attended Shaw Brothers and Cathay pre-mieres but had never come to one of Great World's. *"This is unfair,"* he said. The call ended inconclusively. When he hung up, Feng looked at me through his spectacles and said in English, "Governor Trench will be making time in his busy schedule to attend one of my premieres very soon. He is very excited about Great World's success."

I congratulated him. We made small talk about Feng's health, my coverage of the disturbances and the pictures Great World was making at that moment. Feng took momentary delight in telling me that one of Hong Kong's left-wing studios – Phoenix – was on the verge of suspending production. "They're paralysed with fear," he said almost gleefully. "They don't know what their big bosses in

Peking want them to make." Feng was very pleased with this. He added that "the Governor" had informed him that he was going to ban the American film *The Sand Pebbles,* which had been shot in Hong Kong the year before, because it might further inflame the leftists. He seemed to relish the thought that a big American company's product could get banned in his own territory, as if that somehow cut Twentieth Century-Fox down to his size. He chatted on about American and European movie trends, so I let him circle about for a while. *The Letter,* which was to have been shot in Hong Kong, had relocated to Madrid. He said several foreign projects were coming to town. Some of the projects were American, but many were German, French or Italian. The Europeans rented Great World equipment for such shoots. The American companies brought their own. They said Feng's cameras and sound-recording equipment were out of date. He took offence at their bluntness.

Then Feng was quiet for a moment, frowned, pushed his dinner tray back and said, "What have you learned?"

"I spoke with a friend in the police force. He consulted with customs and the Immigration Department and they said that Becky has left the colony."

We spiralled down to the news. Feng wanted to know if she had been seen at the airport. I said no. He asked if she had been seen at the Macau ferry docks and I again said no. I didn't have to tell him where she had been seen since there was only one other way out of Hong Kong: through Lo Wu, on the Chinese border.

He was too guarded and private a man to provide me with a reaction. He merely stared into space for a few moments and then removed his glasses to rub them clean with his napkin. He picked up his telephone, punched a line and said to Miss Chin, *"Take this food away."*

I waited while Miss Chin came in with my tea. Then she examined Feng's food tray and muttered something to him in Shanghanese, which I do not understand, though I believe she was concerned that he hadn't eaten enough. He spoke sharply with her and she smiled in embarrassment and took the tray away. She came back in with a sweater and carefully draped it over his shoulders. He seemed to come back to attention and said to me, "Is the air conditioning too cold for you?"

"No, it's fine. Don't worry."

"I can get her to change the setting."

"No, please."

"I will get Miss Chin to order out some food for you."

"Thank you, but I'm fine."

He insisted. I presumed that he wanted to be in control, and his anxiety so locked up our discourse that I relented and let him order me a paper box of noodles from a nearby shop on Castle Peak Road. Miss Chin went away again but not before giving me another severe look, as if she wanted to punish me for having upset her employer.

Miss Chin was never far from Feng's side. She cut his food for him when he ate European meals because he felt awkward holding a knife. She sometimes held his hand when he walked, not romantically but more the way a nurse does with an elderly charge, as if he were prone to stumbling. She had nothing in her life but her career and she gave of herself to Feng completely. She knew him, understood him and protected him fiercely. I had once offered to buy Feng a present for his birthday, a silver cigarette case, and I conferred with Miss Chin. She shut down the idea, absolutely refusing to agree with my suggestion. I asked her what I should get him and she said, "Nothing." She didn't want others crowding her ministrations. Surrounded by glamour, she was relentlessly dour, as if putting up a stoic defence in the face of mighty onslaught. Tittle-tattle at Great World insisted that she was in love with Feng; I'm certain she never had an affair with him. When I worked for Great World in 1958, I learned that she actually arranged women for him, mainly movie starlets with short careers. She lived conveniently near the studio and sometimes gave him the keys to her apartment so he could take women back there. Miss Chin lived with her elderly mother, who had come down from Shanghai with her when she followed the Feng caravan to Hong Kong. The mother spoke only Shanghanese and rarely left their flat, except when Miss Chin evicted her so Feng could have sex there. Mother

Chin was obliged to sit in tea shops all afternoon or on a stool in her daughter's office, miserable and silent.

Now Feng waited until Miss Chin left his office, then asked, "Who have you told about this?"

"No one, until now."

"Will you write a newspaper story?"

"It's in today's *Ta Kung Pao.*"

Feng made a note on a scratch pad, probably a reminder to call the *Ta Kung Pao* editor and threaten to pull Great World cinema ads. His concern about publicity was wholly inconsistent, given that he had altered the *Long Ago and Far Away* billboard at the Ambassador Cinema with question marks to exploit Becky's disappearance. But he was never consistent. He put his pen down and said, "You are trying to destroy me."

I told him I didn't see it that way, that everything was beyond our control at the moment and people would be sympathetic to him for having lost his wife. Or they would have been sympathetic if he hadn't changed that billboard. But then I realized I was sounding more like Feng's old publicist and not Becky's friend. I stopped and we were both quiet for a while.

Destroying a man like Feng Hsiao-foon would be difficult. President and chief shareholder of the Great World Organisation, officer of the Rotary Club of North Kowloon, past president of the Tsuen Wan General Chamber of Commerce, a one-time adviser to former Governor Grantham on matters pertaining to entertainment-industry licensing (there was a picture on his office wall of Feng shaking Grantham's hand), a raiser of funds publicly cited by the Tung Wah Hospital Group for meritorious service and, with the Shaw brothers and Cathay's late Loke Wan Tho, one of the most powerful men in Chinese motion pictures. Not an easy man to destroy, nor an easy one to understand.

How Feng's family got involved in motion pictures quickly became a myth that Feng Hsiao-foon was only too happy to cultivate. The story went that back in the 1920s, Feng's father, a

Shanghai textile broker, had been playing cards with a real estate owner who ran out of money during an all-night game. To pay off his debts, the man gave Feng's father a decrepit cinema in Chapei district, Shanghai. The truth, as Becky once told me, was far blander. The family had simply bought an entire block of Chapei property as part of a move to diversify out of textile brokering and into booming real estate. A cinema, the Golden Heaven, happened to be on that block.

The Feng clan had been in a fallen state when they'd arrived in Shanghai at the end of the Nineteenth Century. They'd come from Hupei province, where for generations they'd been scholars. Warlords and social disorder put an end to the great imperial network of schools that employed people like the Fengs. They went to Shanghai to find work and Feng's grandfather discovered that he had an acumen for business. But being a textile broker was a second-rate, vulgar pursuit compared to the purity and social respect of being a scholar. Although the family grew rich and invested their money in Shanghai's hot real estate, they were acutely aware of their newly acquired crassness. Feng Hsiao-foon hated his father's obsessive accumulation of wealth and strict pressure on his sons to succeed. He ordered the eldest of Feng's brothers to study classical Chinese literature in a funded attempt to recreate the family's former respectability. The eldest boy, at least, would amount to something. Young Feng Hsiao-foon received no such opportunity at redemption and was doomed for business.

One drunken night in the bar of the Metropole Hotel, his eldest brother cried for twenty minutes uninterrupted. He didn't want to be a scholar, he said, he wanted to be an actor or a musician. The older brother claimed that he was intellectually incapable, just a performing monkey in a white collar and cuffs. He started making monkey sounds and slapping his own face in a seizure of shame. Hsiao-foon had to hold his hands down until the urge passed. Feng resented his brother's weakness. His brother had been given so much, such an opportunity to be a quality person, and here he was sobbing in a hotel bar. He hated him more a few weeks later after the older brother stood on the railing on the roof of the Cathay Hotel for a full hour, trying to muster the courage to commit suicide. He couldn't and took the elevator down to the lobby and went home.

Feng's father took the family out to Chapei to see the Golden Heaven cinema he'd purchased. He was the sort of man who seldom wasted time by idling away afternoons in cinemas so he had a difficult time seeing any worth in it. What they found confirmed his suspicions about the sort of fools and deadbeats associated with such places.

The Chinese government had arbitrarily decreed that all soldiers could get into cinemas free, and they took up the expensive seats. Before the film began, attendants in grey shirts and loose gowns handed out wet towels so customers could refresh themselves. Many of the patrons refused to return the towels but kept them for household linens. Then the picture ran. Afterward, the attendants went around with tattered straw baskets to collect money for the showing. Many people wouldn't pay, complaining that they hadn't liked the film. The attendants argued and bullied but got money from only about half the audience. Feng's father asked the cinema manager why he didn't collect money from customers before they even went into the auditorium, the way the big European-owned cinemas over on Nanking Road did. The manager said that he had tried that but Chapei residents were notoriously impecunious and refused to pay for something they hadn't inspected first.

This is where the Feng family's prowess for showmanship first indicated itself. Feng's father told the manager to begin the next performance but to stop the projector after a few hundred feet of film had run. The manager did, and a story of illicit love in old China flickered to a halt. The engrossed audience began clamouring and stamping for the rest of the picture. They eagerly paid to see the rest, and even the soldiers had to dig down. Feng senior told them the government allowed soldiers into the theatre free, but they had to pay to actually see the movie. Golden Heaven was suddenly making money.

The films it showed were terrible. This was back in the days of silent pictures, and the Chinese films produced in Shanghai were a poor distant cousin to American films. Their only advantage was their low production costs. Most of the pictures retold stories from classical Chinese literature: *The Monkey King Creates Havoc in Heaven, Wang Hsi-feng Disrupts Ning Kuo Prefecture, Lady White Snake.* But the filmmakers had no money for costumes, so the actors performed in simple cotton smocks. And the actors merely walked back and forth in front of a stationary camera, gesturing in crude pantomime. It was grossly inferior entertainment compared to live Peking opera, with its colour, its music, its effects, the brilliant costumes, the acrobats, makeup and renowned stars. Even rickshaw coolies could afford cheap seats at the opera. Movies were such poor competitors that it was rare for them to fill a theatre for the entire week of their run.

Feng senior needed better product so he called on his younger son, Hsiao-foon, to investigate local movie studios. Hsiao-foon consulted a Shanghai business directory and found one at random. He took a rickshaw out to the Yellow Sea Studios in Chapei and found a large, dirty, sagging villa. The company was in a brick-lined courtyard, idling the day away with badminton. The producer had gone off gambling two days before to raise enough money to pay their wages and continue work on a picture. He hadn't returned. While they talked to Hsiao-foon, a few clay tiles slid off the sloping villa roof and crashed to the floor of the courtyard, prompting everyone to laugh about the crumbling state of affairs at Yellow Sea. Sensing a benefactor, the employees showed Feng around the editing room, where a technician spliced film together, the dressing rooms made out of big wooden packing crates and a flimsy canvas-backed set on which had been painted an approximation of imperial court. Everything was shot under sunlight to avoid paying for electric lights, and sometimes a breeze made tablecloths and costumes move even though the scenes were supposedly indoors. The actors put on a little bit of opera for Feng's entertainment and he was hooked. When the producer finally returned, Feng asked him how much he wanted to sell the operation for and by the end of the afternoon he came away with a complete movie studio for 200 Yuan.

Feng's father was furious with him for having bought the first movie studio he'd seen without examining other ones. He accused him of wasting family money. Even his eldest brother, the scholar, laughed at Hsiao-foon's first business decision. To save face, Hsiao-foon became determined to make the old place work. He changed its name to Golden Heaven Studios, after the Chapei cinema, and spent every waking hour there, watching the cameraman shoot pictures, the director instruct actors and the editors cut the film. But he also imposed a financial discipline on the operation – forcing everyone to keep to a rigid production schedule, hurrying them up, so that every week a two-reel motion picture went to the lab. At first, the pictures failed to attract audiences and Golden Heaven's output went largely unseen. But Feng pleaded with his father to give him larger budgets so that he could rent costumes from Peking opera troupes. When he spent the comparatively huge sum of 4,000 Yuan on an adaptation of *The Butterfly Lovers,* his father was enraged and humiliated him in front of the whole family. He said no one would ever pay to see a black-and-white silent-movie pantomime of a Peking opera when they could go to live theatres and see – and hear – the real thing.

But when his father saw Feng Hsiao-foon's production of *The Butterfly Lovers,* he knew immediately that it was going to succeed. Unlike other Shanghai movies, which were static and stagy, Feng's camera moved about on a little wagon with omnidirectional casters which he had personally built. The camera lovingly examined details of the actors' make-up and costumes in extreme close-ups that couldn't be experienced in live theatre. And Feng had condensed the tragic but lengthy story of student lovers denied one another into a fast-moving narrative that ended lyrically with the dead boy and girl lap-dissolving into butterflies playing over a field of wild flowers. *Butterfly Lovers* played for an entire month at the Golden Heaven and eventually transferred to second- and third-run houses in Chapei where it played for weeks more. Made for 4,000 Yuan, it returned 10,000 Yuan.

His father instructed Hsiao-foon to grow the business, with constant vigilance about costs. He stretched his resources both as an exhibitor and producer. He sold tea and salty dried plums in the auditorium during reel changes. He reused studio sets, repainting them slightly. By the end of the industry's silent era, Feng Hsiao-foon had five cinemas in Shanghai and was producing seventy-five two- and three-reel films a year and making tens of thousands of Yuan in profit.

He would travel about Shanghai in rickshaws wearing a hybrid of the long traditional Chinese man's robe with high mandarin collar, but tailored out of fine English pin-stripe wool. On his head he wore a Homburg made of German felt. Lots of young Chinese businessmen dressed like this, one foot in the Oriental past and the other in the Occidental modernity onto which Shanghai opened. When young Feng deigned to notice beggars running alongside the rickshaws with their palms outstretched, instead of giving them coins, he would give them cinema tickets.

When sound pictures began, Feng had his first huge successes. Suddenly, the American films that dominated Shanghai cinemas no longer made sense to the Chinese and local audiences began to flock to the first Mandarin-language pictures. More serious artists in other media derided Shanghai films as "ice cream for the eyes." Feng's defiant response was to sell ice cream out of portable freezer chests in his theatre lobbies.

But what Feng needed more than anything else was movie stars. The Chinese were as mad for stars as anyone and Feng needed somebody to compete with other studios' great performers, Wu Hu-tieh, Wang Ren-mei and Ruan Ling-yu. He lost his first discovery, Li Loh Tieh, after only her third film. He had cast her in a sword-play epic, a genre much beloved by coolies who filled the ten-cent seats of Feng's cinemas and gaped at the swirling action. Sometimes Feng gave Chapei-area coolies parts as extras and, untrained, they frantically swung their wooden swords at each other in fight scenes, almost always injuring one another. In her picture, Li Loh Tieh was required to fly, so the crew tied a cargo rope around her flowing white robes and hoisted her into the air.

The rope was run around an open rafter. After the scene began, the rafter creaked ominously and suddenly broke, sending Li twelve feet to the floor, then to hospital, where she issued her resignation.

When Japan invaded China and absorbed Manchuria, Shanghai movie producers woke up to their motherland's peril. They produced patriotic pictures, which did well at the box office. Feng imitated them. But no amount of rousing the nation's spirit could turn back Japanese militarism. After the Second World War Feng and Golden Heaven tried to rebuild, but the old days were over. The struggle between Nationalists and Communists raged on until the Communist victory in 1949. The following spring, the Communists entered Golden Heaven Studios and took ownership of everything, offering Feng a job as an employee. Feng and his family fled to Hong Kong with only a few household possessions.

When I met him for the first time, I couldn't figure out how the Fengs blew into Hong Kong in 1950 with only furniture and clothes and could be producing pictures again within a couple of weeks. A mysterious supply of money got poured into the construction and equipping of Feng's new studio in Tsuen Wan. He named the new operation Great World, appropriating the name of the famous amusement complex in Shanghai, evoking that city's reputation for big fun and quality entertainment – something Hong Kong had never possessed. In Hong Kong, it was less urgent that you had a compelling photo play full of twists and turns, or fine performances, attractive sets and beautiful original music. It was enough for the working poor of the audiences, those wretches who toiled in cramped factories and lived twelve to a flat, to see glamorous and beautiful young men and women in fine Western clothes driving sporty automobiles along winding mountain roads or simply lounging in the incomparable luxury of a large room with fewer than five people in it.

Feng survived a near-strike by employees sympathetic to the Communist government on the Mainland who argued that all Great World pictures should be socially progressive. Feng had quietly made friends with the British authorities in Hong Kong and got many of his more troublesome workers legally banished to

China. He then went on with the business of making profitable pictures that audiences wanted to see.

Those first successful years in Hong Kong quickly turned down, and it looked like Feng either was going to shut Great World or cut back drastically. Yung Hwa, the studio that gave Becky her start, had gone out of production. By the mid-1950s there was no chance of getting commercial Hong Kong movies shown inside China, and the Nationalist government on the island of Taiwan, the other big overseas market for Mandarin pictures, was increasingly protecting its own shattered film industry from external competition. Too many Hong Kong speculators were getting into the picture business, drastically driving up the number of films available to exhibitors and driving down the quality. Everybody in the Hong Kong movie business was on the verge of bankruptcy and so was Great World. Then a brilliant idea fell at Feng's feet while he was attending the weekly luncheon of the Rotary Club of North Kowloon. The guest speaker was from the United States Information Service and his topic was defending democracy through modern communications.

Feng made an appointment to see the man, whose name, fortuitously, was Banks. In exchange for financial support, Feng offered to make Mandarin-dialect movies with anti-Communist themes. At first, he pulled a blank. The American was new to Hong Kong and had no idea that movies were even made in the colony. But after he checked with his superiors, everybody got fired up about the proposal. They exchanged cables with Washington and Feng took the U.S. consulate staff out to a lavish Chinese banquet and energetically pledged himself to fight Communism through the magic of movies. The Americans were very pleased. They spoke importantly about the success of their agenda, and pledged $300,000 U.S. over three years, subject to regular inspection of Feng's books by their own auditors. Feng fought over that point but eventually conceded. After twelve months, Mr. Banks was reassigned to the USIS office in Saigon. Everyone at the U.S. consulate forgot about Feng. They also forgot to turn off the supply of money, which ran and ran. He never made anti-Communist movies. He made musical comedies. He ploughed some of the dough into building up his cinema circuits, Great World (S.E.A.) Pty. in Southeast Asia and a Western Hemisphere distributor, Great World Pictures Ltd., which served Chinatowns in Canada, the United States and Peru. As far as I knew, Feng was still receiving cheques from the USIS in 1967, giving him good reason to hate the Communists on the Mainland.

"I am going to Taiwan tomorrow," Feng said. I picked over the box of noodles Uncle Lo had brought in. Feng said, "I have to look for Becky there."

It was as if he hadn't even heard what I had told him. Just one of his weird responses, I thought. He added: "If you run stories about my wife in your newspaper, you will be plunging a dagger into my chest."

"I'm sorry, I've got my job to do," I said.

Feng became angry in a stagy sort of way so I decided to leave. I wished him a good trip to Taiwan and left. As I was going he picked up the telephone and asked Miss Chin to come in. We passed one another. I closed the door to Feng's office just as she said to Feng: *"The tickets are here."*

I glanced down at Miss Chin's desk at two air ticket folders bearing the symbol of China Air Transport, an operation owned by the U.S. Central Intelligence Agency but actually run as a real airline, quite a good one too. I was curious why there were two tickets so I opened the folders. One had Feng's name and the other bore that of Hannah Szeto, a new young actress recently put under contract with Great World.

TEN

Suddenly, her face was everywhere. Women news agents, squatting on plastic stools on the sidewalks with their newspapers and magazines surrounding them, offered Becky Chan in more than a dozen publications. The Chinese newspapers went berserk. Most of the stories in the apolitical mainstream Chinese press merely reported her arrival in China, nothing more than what *Ta Kung Pao* had revealed. But one of Hong Kong's Communist papers, *The New Evening Post*, reported that Becky Chan was in China to rehearse a new motion picture called *Triumph at Li Hsian*. It was to be about a woman revolutionary who organizes peasants around Mao Tse-tung thought. The project was to be the first of a new order of pictures being produced under the personal supervision of Mao's wife, Chiang Ch'ing. All filming had stopped during the Cultural Revolution because China's studios were confused about what was required of them. Hysterical teenaged gangs of Red Guards banished artists to the countryside. *The New Evening Post* hailed Becky as a revolutionary hero who had smashed the chains of her Chinese and British slave-masters. The *Tin Fung Daily* had found an old publicity still of Becky looking stern and pointing a finger accusingly at somebody not in the photo. The still was from *Mangoes and Coconuts* ("beach hotel owners cope with madcap guests," the advertisement said). They captioned it with a purported description of her firm criticism of British imperialists and their Hong Kong Chinese lackeys. The mosquito press favoured a different approach. *Cloudburst* hinted that Feng had been unfaithful to Becky and that drove Becky out of Hong Kong to the one place where she could return a blow to his anti-Communist reputation. *"She can match him insult for insult!"* exulted *Cloudburst*. The English papers, mine included, stuck to bland facts and noted that a handful of other actors had gone to the mainland to help the Cultural Revolution. Kit Masters on Radio Hongkong's English service spent fifteen minutes discussing Becky's defection on "Topics" one night. The movie commentators on Cantonese Commercial Radio couldn't stop talking about her.

It was not the sort of publicity any movie company would have wanted. I knew too well what sort publicity Feng wanted – harmless pap, venal slop that worked hard for a living. When I accepted a lucrative offer to work for Feng Hsiao-foon at the Great World Organisation in 1958, I was tired of the newspaper business after ten years of general reporting and I fooled myself into believing that it would be fun to work in a movie studio. My job was to get publicity for Great World films in Hong Kong's English publications. Back then, papers devoted almost no coverage to Chinese entertainments. Although the European relationship with the Chinese had changed markedly after the war – Europeans no longer pretended to be supermen – there remained a broad ignorance about exactly what the Chinese were all about. Rather than pay attention to the latest Chinese movies, the China Telegraph devoted its meagre entertainment coverage to flat-footed American films on local circuits such as *Barricade* ("It's Kill or Be Killed 100 Miles from Nowhere – And a Woman Is the Treasure to Fight For!"). There were a few European-attended private film societies in Hong Kong, but they contented themselves with whatever Western documentaries they could borrow from libraries: English industrial developments in *This is Britain* or brisk travelogues produced by the New York Central Railroad.

Becky had just appeared in *Get Out of My Way*, a Cantonese film, which was rare for her since she usually stayed in prestige Mandarin-dialect films. *Get Out of My Way* followed on the heels of a much fluffier Mandarin picture, *Girls Demand Excitement,* and Becky insisted on doing the new picture in Cantonese. She played a successful businesswoman who turns her back on her family, newly arrived in China, because their shabbiness and unsophisticated speech are an embarrassment to her and compromise her social ambitions. She neglects them even when her niece's youngest daughter is gravely ill and needs an operation. Her sister, who frantically works at two jobs, runs across the street to avoid being late for one of the jobs and gets run over by a delivery van. In her grief and remorse, Becky cries her way to the family's hillside shack and takes them home, renouncing her social ambitions. The little niece gets her operation and the audience explodes in tears, thoroughly and completely entertained.

To boost coverage I had to get thinking. One of my first bright ideas was to plant a feature on one of Becky's most peculiar film fans. He was that Nationalist army veteran I've mentioned, the one who turned up at all of Becky's premieres, who sometimes appeared in the background at her public appearances. He was there when she helped open a new clinic run by the Tung Wah Hospital Group, when she appeared for a photo stunt at the Air France check-in counter at the airport, and when she presented a cheque to the Door of Hope, the orphanage that raised her. He had never spoken to Becky, or even come near her at the public appearances. He was just there, quietly admiring her from afar. He was the sort of poor man who would have been repudiated by Becky's character in *Get Out of My Way.* I told Feng about my idea for the story but he rejected it at once.

He said that Becky's fans no longer wanted to be reminded of poverty. And this man was poor: he still wore the Nationalist army uniform even though the civil war ended with the Communist victory in 1949. He probably lived at Rennie's Mill, a squalid enclave of displaced and destitute Nationalists and their families. Rennie's Mill had once been a pristine place, named for a Canadian businessman who opened a flour mill there, but now was a hopeless, crowded slum of shacks, crawling with Nationalist veterans cast off by Ch'iang Kai-shek when he fled to Taiwan in

1949. What I didn't know at the time, and nobody else did either, was that the dirty, hungry-looking veteran who followed Becky's career from a distance was her natural father.

It was only many years later that Becky told me she had known her father. This is the story she told me of her parents.

Her oldest memory was that of picking rice kernels out of the heaps of hulls. It was near a tiny rice paddy her family rented in a small village south of Canton, in China. She recalled seeing her mother rhythmically pounding a wooden hulling mallet with her foot. The device had a pedal connected to a big club that smashed down into a small pit in the ground, about one foot across. In the pit was the family's newly harvested rice. The mallet would bash the rice until the hulls fell off. Becky sorted through the rice hulls and picked out kernels that missed the pounding. Every grain was important to poor peasants. It seemed to her she'd been picking out the leftover kernels since the beginning of time. She sorted pebbles from the kernels, listened to her father scythe the rice straw for later sale in a nearby village. It was a pleasant brushing sound. Sometimes Becky's father called out a song, to which a farmer in a distant field replied with the second verse. Her father and that man shared a water buffalo that, when not toiling in the fields, lay on its knees in a barn: huge, placid and inscrutable. One day the water buffalo was gone. Becky didn't know what happened to it.

She said that she distinctly remembered looking up from where she was squatting on the ground near the hulling pit and seeing her mother. She was telling her some big news.

"We're leaving the farm," she said. *"We have to look for a new place to live."*

Becky must have asked why, because her mother said something about not making enough money to pay the rent on the land.

"Where will we go?" she asked.

"To the city to find work."

That meant nothing to a small child. She had no idea what a city was. She might as well have said to the temple or to the shops.

It was just another word, until she said that Becky's family were leaving everything behind.

"What about the babies?" she asked, squinting up at her mother.

"Oh jeh-jeh, don't be a burden to me with your questions," she said. Becky's parents nicknamed her *"jeh-jeh,"* which meant sister, even though at the time Becky had no siblings. She had been a sister once. The "babies" were the buried remains of three other children who hadn't lived more than a few months. They rested in a hillside cemetery on the outskirts of their village, all buried together in the same plot, because there was no money to bury them separately.

"Why do we have to go to the city, mameeyah?" little Becky asked.

"I don't know, that's what people do," her mother said.

"Can't we stay here?"

"We can't afford the rent anymore. It's gone up."

"Why has it gone up?"

"I don't know why! It just goes up." Becky's mother knelt down and spoke more gently to her. *"Do you want to be a good girl, jeh-jeh? Do you want to make me happy? Then don't trouble me with questions that have no answers. I have enough on my mind. We'll leave you behind if you don't behave."*

She started to cry but her mother walked away and got on with her work.

Becky didn't remember much about moving to Hong Kong. She could recall her parents going to the village cemetery to fetch the "babies." In order to pay for their trip to the city her father agreed to vacate the cemetery plot, which he in turn sold to a wealthy family. Her parents went to the cemetery with little wooden boxes and dug up the graves. Becky said she always remembered the sight of her father half-submerged in a pit, pulling up three rotting cloth bags and laying them out on the mound of fresh earth. Her mother opened each bag and looked inside. Becky started yowling that she wanted a look but her father cuffed her with a dirty hand and told her to be quiet. Her mother sifted the contents of each bag into a small wooden box. Becky could see the tiny tibias and femurs turned brown, also a miniature jawless skull. The bones slid out and into the box, all done very neatly and very solemnly. The graves empty now, Becky's father went to the wealthy family for payment and thus they had enough money to move to Hong Kong.

The other thing she remembered was standing at the very top of the Tai Po Road, looking down at the entrance to Kowloon. It was their first glimpse of Hong Kong, the first glimpse of a city, and it both amazed and mystified her parents. The motor cars and trucks that laboured up the Tai Po Road might have been metallic spirits, incomprehensible in their complexity and foreignness. There was a troupe of grey monkeys that lived at the top of the Tai Po Road and they watched Becky and her family standing at the crest. Becky's father told her that the monkeys were definitely spirits and they had to be supplicated. He gave a third of the meagre supply of fruit they carried to the monkeys, who clustered round the little stockpile, pushing and biting one another to get at it.

Becky and her parents lived on the pavement at first. She would awake to the sound of trucks passing the spot where they camped for many months. She looked up from her mat on the ground and saw the cloud of dust thrown up by the truck. The street was cold and wretched when it rained for there was no place to take shelter. She and her parents had to endure the rain and then wait until the sun came out to dry them off again. Their only possessions were a few bed rolls and a rice pot. They lugged their household goods with them everywhere, fearing that if they left them beside the road, they would all be stolen.

Her mother found work with the police, cleaning out the barracks at Kowloon City. She took Becky along to do the same work, even though Becky was probably less than seven years old. She was fascinated by the policemen's uniforms, every one of them dressed in exactly the same colour, and to Becky this was highly peculiar. Why would anybody who could obviously afford good-quality cloth want to make their suits all the same?

At the time, Becky wasn't clear on just what her father did for work. He didn't clean out barracks. He was supposed to work at unloading the big Pearl River cargo boats down at Holt's Wharf, receiving a handful of uncooked rice at the end of the day as payment, which he was to put in his pocket and bring home for supper. Other times he collected scrap wood to sell to charcoal merchants, but this was so competitive in Kowloon that he soon gave it up. He tried the filthy task of working on a coaling barge in the harbour. He would come home completely black except for spaces around his eyes and nostrils. Becky was terrified the first time she saw him like that but he made a joke of it and got her laughing. Still, he was so tired and miserable at the end of the day, with no more than two coins in his pocket.

For a while he worked digging out the outdoor toilets behind houses. The stink was awful when he came back to the roadside camp every night, for there was nowhere for him to wash. At one place, he noticed men going in and out of a white stone house. All day they came and went. Some came out laughing with joy, others appeared with their hands on their skinny backsides surveying the sunlight and sighing, *"Ai-ya"* in a slow, sad and defeated way. They shuffled off and more men came, crowding in the front door. Becky's father could hear shouting and calls of encouragement. Finally he went to investigate, but at the back door a big man leaning on the handle of a banana machete refused to let him come in. *"Come back when you've had a bath. You stink of shit!"* the guard said.

So her father stayed outside all day, working on those outdoor toilets, gazing about at the neighbourhood with affected aloofness, although his thoughts always circled round to the same subject – what was going on inside that house? The men came and went, some went away slapping their friends on the back, others grumbling beneath their voices. He could stand it no more so he tried to breach the back door again. The same big man with the machete blocked his entrance. Her father craned to look in at what was going on. *"Go wash off!"* the big man said.

"What do men do here?" her father asked.

"Become happy."

"I want to be happy!"

"Then go wash off." The man called to a twelve-year-old boy. He gave the boy a few pennies and told him to take her father to a public bathhouse. *"With my compliments,"* the big man said.

Becky's father thought this thug a wonderful man to give him the money and he gratefully followed the boy to the bathhouse. The boy paid the admission. Inside, men in thin towels were sluicing pails of water on their heads that they drew from a concrete cistern. He bathed in this way, then walked back to the house. *"Come in, you're welcome now,"* the guard said, and he gave Becky's father a few ten-cent coins, what the guard called "seed rice."

The place was dark, virtually unfurnished and smelled of cheap pipe tobacco. In the centre of the room there was a circle of men all squatting on their haunches. One of them was picking up Western-style playing cards from a frayed deck, lifting each card over his head and tossing it down, face up, with a grand flourish of his hand. When it was a good card the other men would groan with delight, when it was a bad card they said nothing. So Becky's father watched this for a while then went to the next room where men were play-ing fan tan. He watched intently as a game master counted off dirty little porcelain buttons drawn from a bin. The game master waved to him to join them. He stayed all day. He had come in with little more than twenty-five cents in his pocket and left with five dollars. He went back to the roadside camp and gave half the money to Becky's mother. She was so happy she danced in a little circle; her father clapped his hands in rhythm and hummed one of the tunes he used to sing in the fields back home in a whining, nasal voice.

The next day, the family rented a cubicle subdivided from a flat on a side street in Hanoi Road. There were big banyan trees growing on the pavement. Invigorated, Becky's father forgot about digging toilets and went back to the gaming house every day. Most of the time he came back sullen and nervous, his head jangling from the excitement of the games. *"Give me all your money!"* he snapped at his wife.

"No, it's for food and the rent!" she said. He slapped her face and took the money anyway. He seemed to shut out any concern for his

wife and family, like he had closed a door to an unneeded back room. It was a rotten time to become addicted to gambling because Becky's mother was pregnant with what later turned out to be twins.

Edgy after a day of playing cards, Becky's father knew he had to find food for his family. With all his money gone from gaming, he hung around the back doors of restaurants, pleading and begging for scraps of twice-cooked vegetables and greasy rice. Usually the cooks turned him away, waving a chopper in his face. Sometimes they relented and gave him something out of the square steel garbage bins by the back door. He endured the heavy scorn that balanced the charity of cooks who ladled the food, uneaten stuff that had been scraped from customers' platters, into his hands. He had to put the scraps into his pocket to carry home. *"Wai!"* the cooks shouted, *"Don't come again! We're not in business to feed trash like you!"*

"I don't know what's inside your father's head," Becky's mother told her one day. They were scrubbing walls in the police station and her back was aching both from the exertion and from carrying twins. *"It's like it's full of insects. He can't keep his attention on anything. He wasn't always like this. Back in the village he'd stay out too long at the wine shop getting a snoot full. But that was only once in a while, and his cousins always shamed him into coming home. His cousins were good people. I miss his family. I miss the village. I miss them all."*

After the twins were born, things got better. The twins were girls, Man-ling and Cheung-mei, and her father happily said that he was now a king with three princesses. *"He doesn't have to nurse the princesses,"* Becky's mother griped to another woman in the flat who helped deliver the babies.

Just before Becky's shirt fell apart in tatters, her mother nicked some money from a small cache of gambling proceeds her father had stuffed in his one other pair of shorts. She bought Becky a new one, plus a new pair of trousers and a little black pin to hold her hair out of her ears when she worked in the police station. Becky was overjoyed with these gifts. *"It's because you're such a good girl and work so hard,"* her mother said.

Soon a boy was born, whom they simply named Yee. Becky's father lost more and more money gambling. He rarely worked. They couldn't make the rent on their cubicle and so the family they'd sublet the space from threw them out. They went back to the roadside but found no space large enough to camp on. People like them had arrived from China and taken all the space. So they went into the hills overlooking Kowloon, where a petty entrepreneur had built a jumble of shacks out of packing-crate wood. He sold one to Becky's father, making a modest profit, and the family had a roof over their heads. It was just a big rickety box with a door and a window but it was better than sleeping in the street.

After they moved up into the hills, Becky stopped cleaning the police station. It was her job to take care of the three small children. She was all of eight years old and she became a familiar sight among the other migrants living in the hills walking back from a public water standpipe with baby Yee tied to her back in a cloth carrier. Becky would stop and consider the view of Kowloon below, with Wong Tai Sin Temple in the foreground. It was being built up back then into the splendid complex it is today. Her father went there often to seek the god Wong Tai Sin's advice on gambling and making money. He paid fortune-tellers to discuss the significance of certain numbers relative to the days of the month and then recommend combinations. He would come home from the great temple, rubbing his hands and fidgeting. *"Eight!"* he said over and over. *"Eight is the key, you know. It has always stood for prosperity. In combination with the number six, such as in the sixth day of the week or the sixth month of the year, preferably both, it could lead to a very great fortune. Now if we can hold out until the first Saturday of June, everything will change!"* From her vantage point over Wong Tai Sin Temple, Becky thought that there had to be something in the fortune-tellers' words, because her father abided by it all so closely. She would admire the orange and green tiled roof then plod on, up to the little shack where she could hear the twins crying for something to eat. All the while, her mother scrubbed the police station and her father slapped playing cards on the stone floor of a gaming house.

Then he learned about money lenders and how they were there to help him attain prosperity. He began running up debts so that he could gamble more. Even though she was barely eight years old, Becky knew that this was bad, for a few times he would come back to their campsite with his face red, blue and black and one eye swelled up so big it wouldn't open. Frustrated and insulted, he would in turn beat Becky's mother, blaming her for pushing him all the time.

One day he didn't come home. Becky's mother stayed up all night waiting for him. The next day she didn't go to the police station but searched the streets. She even went to the gaming house and asked for him. They wouldn't let a woman inside and refused to discuss him. She pleaded with them, giving long descriptions of his looks but they feigned no knowledge of him. *"Just another coolie,"* the man with the banana machete said and gave her a shove. She searched all day for Becky's father, starting at the tin shed of the fortune-tellers at Wong Tai Sin Temple then walking up and down the streets of Kowloon, ending up at the Star Ferry wharf, looking across the harbour at the great mountains and British commercial houses of Central. She couldn't afford the ferry ride to search there so she walked all the way back through Kowloon to her shack in the hills. She sent Becky to Wong Tai Sin Temple to watch for him for several days. He never appeared. Becky clapped her hands and prayed to Wong Tai Sin to bring her father back. She thought if she concentrated her will on praying that he would reappear. But he never came back.

I asked Becky what happened after that. Her answers were fragmented, portions rationed to me over many occasions. But the emerging answer was that her mother disappeared one day as well and Becky was left alone. She never told me why her mother vanished and why she took Becky's brother and sisters with her but not Becky. It was all horribly sad and private and I knew not to inquire any further. Until I worked on publicity for Great World I knew none of this; I had no idea that the little, greasy-faced man in the Nationalist army uniform was her father.

The Chinese newspapers' frenzy over Becky's departure for China
began to die after a few days. I didn't have a story to do, but I called
the Government Information Services out of curiosity. Were
Becky's political activities in China such that she would be barred
from ever returning to Hong Kong? The spokesman said that
Becky had left the colony of her own will. And if she were to return
there probably would be no problem, so long as she did not advo-
cate or assist in the creation of violence or disorder. But there was
nothing to suggest that Becky would ever return. She was free of
Feng and all the unhappiness that Hong Kong represented in her
life. But I was left with a question. Becky hadn't been a mother for
long but she had been a good one for Amanda. Why would she
abandon the baby to the wintry possession of Feng Hsiao-foon?

The GIS man gave me another bit of information. He read
off a release that was about to circulate: three police officers from
San Po Kong Sub-District had been detained and charged with
manslaughter in the death of a Communist demonstrator in the
Sub-District's lockup. They were Police Constable Li Kwai, PC
Wong Kai-yu and Sergeant Jack Rudman. "Just thought you
should know," the GIS man said.

ELEVEN

With the coming of jet airplanes, Hong Kong emerged as a stopping place for celebrities – the hugely famous, the moderately so, and the obscure but interesting. Back then, Hong Kong still was a truly exotic place for Westerners. These global travellers were fascinated with the colony, and we in turn were fascinated with them. It was often my daily assignment to greet people coming off flights and ask them what they would be doing in Hong Kong. We knew who was coming because the airlines freely gave out passenger lists in exchange for being mentioned in stories. "The British entertainer Huch arrived from San Francisco by BOAC yesterday ..." I'd write. "Bob Markworth, self-styled 'King of the Bow and Arrow,' arrived by Air France from Saigon Tuesday, after a week of performances in South Vietnam with his charming wife and principal target, Mrs. Nancy Markworth ..." One afternoon I patrolled the customs area to buttonhole John Steinbeck, who stepped off a Garuda flight. He was visiting a son who'd flown in from Saigon, where he was serving in the U.S. forces. Steinbeck clearly wished that I would go away. Another time I met Aldo Rocca, an artist who had grown rich painting doe-eyed, tragic clowns. He was in town for a showing at the Chatham Galleries and comfortably dismissed his many critics as "undiscerning."

When the American actor William Holden came to Hong Kong in the 1950s, he really heated up the neighbourhood. He made *Love is a Many-Splendored Thing* here, and returned for a holiday after shooting *Bridge on the River Kwai* in Ceylon. He was back again in 1959 for an independently produced picture called *Almond Eyes*. It was a significant film in Becky Chan's career and it would make good money. *Almond Eyes* was her first American film and it was the beginning of her short and highly unsuccessful career in Hollywood.

The Americans did a lot of auditioning of local performers for the lead before they heard about Becky. At first, she didn't want to make the picture and Feng Hsiao-foon wouldn't release her. But the Americans offered him a big, fat loan-out fee and he was only too happy to take it. Becky was intimidated by the foreigners, with their big budget and brisk methods. But once she started work on the picture she enjoyed it in a way that she never had at Great World. The pace was leisurely, compared to hectic Hong Kong-studio shoots. Both the director and the American star were helpful, generous and disarmingly uncomplicated. "They're just like you," she told me when shooting began. "So simple, up here." She pointed to her head and laughed. "They're foreigners." Becky began to have fun.

Almond Eyes was about an American private investigator who comes to Hong Kong to investigate the disappearance of an heiress. He gets unwanted help from a Chinese nightclub singer, played by Becky. She's fallen in with the fast company of the heiress and knows too much about the American woman's wastrel habits. Now, mystery men are hunting the nightclub girl because she knows some secret. At first, Becky's singer and Holden's investigator dislike each other intensely. She thinks he's laughing at her vulgarity and he can't abide her peppery behaviour. But they take a liking to one another and fall in love. In the end, the heiress goes to a richly deserved death, Holden dispatches the thugs, blah blah blah. The script called for Becky's nightclub singer to be both sexy and "China-doll dainty," as the producer put it. Becky's galvanic performance in the singing scenes impressed the Americans greatly. She turned a silly cha-cha, "Gesundheit," into something erotic and funny at the same time. She started each stanza with big breathy prefaces to sneezes that sounded suspiciously like the sounds of incipient orgasm. Everyone in the company thought she was the sexiest thing alive. But all the real activity in the picture was Holden's, and Becky's character was merely a trophy. The climax of the picture saw her tied to one of the big cables on the Peak Tram, screaming. Holden was battling the villain on the roof of a tram car that rose above the panorama of Hong Kong harbour 1,100 feet below. The higher the car rose, the closer Becky came to being crushed by the giant fly wheels of the tram's wheel house. This was all highly problematic filmmaking, since the polished roof of the tram car was too slippery to stand on. They had to shoot it at Wader Motion Picture & Development Company's studios in Tsuen Wan with a backscreen projection of the scenery. And if Becky were really tied to the cable of the Peak Tram, she'd be forced to ride over the top of big round pulleys spaced every fifty feet, which guided the cable. It wouldn't have been thrilling; it would have been funny, seeing her bump over those things. They had to shoot it so there were no pulleys in sight. As for saving Becky, Holden had to somehow get off the tram car roof in time to stop the whole thing. I forget now how they got out of it but it was something unspectacular, like Holden climbing inside the moving tram car and sitting on the big hand brake. After the tearful salvation, Becky and Holden are united, he with his fiery Chinese doll, and she with her Pinkerton in a sports jacket.

It sounds foolish today; it sounded foolish then, and it was consistent with the sort of pictures American and European filmmakers made about the Orient back then. Apart from the tourist colour of old ladies punting sampans and the shots of Tiger Balm Gardens, there was a new preoccupation movie-makers had with the Orient: sex. Han Su-yin's novels of interracial love and Richard Mason's famous book about Hong Kong prostitutes, *The World of Suzie Wong*, fascinated Western men, as if Hong Kong women were simmering volcanoes of easy passion. The reality is that Hong Kong is about the least sexual place in the world. If it had any sexual quality, it was that of fathers selling their ten-year-old daughters into prostitution to pay for food for the rest of the family. No Western sex fantasist wanted to deal with that.

Filmmakers from Europe were the most intent to portray their sexual preference. They flew out to Asia: small, reliable commercial film companies or wealthy men who had purchased an Arriflex camera with which to record privately their fantasies. This second group blew in from Munich or Rome and made pictures that no one ever saw, with titles like *Ting Tang, Whip Goddess of the China Sea*. They had to hire prostitutes, since real Chinese actresses at the time wouldn't disrobe.

I didn't actually meet William Holden until well into filming, when the production company set up a photo shoot for local press. It was Becky's twenty-eighth birthday and the Americans had commissioned a beautiful cake. It was built like a Chinese merchant's house, with a tile roof of white icing sloping upward in the corners. It came on a golden crate adorned with the "double-happiness" icon. When Becky blew out the single candle on the roof of the cake, a little door opened and out flew two white pigeons. I still have a terrific photograph of it. Becky is laughing and clapping her hands as the pigeons take flight. Around her are members of the company, including Holden in a white open-necked shirt and grey sports jacket, his hands in his pockets. Unfortunately, the *China Telegraph* photographer snapped it just when Holden was blinking and he has a sleepy look on his face.

One person who wasn't pleased with the photograph, or the whole *Almond Eyes* shoot, was Becky's first husband. Before she married Great World's Feng Hsiao-foon in 1964, she had already tried married life with a young movie actor, Leung Kai-yu. He was a pretty but scrawny young actor with exotic dietary habits, endowed for no particular reason with the English given name of Chickee. His habit was to eat only a Chinese soup-spoonful of any one course at meals. If there were a plate of noodles, he'd have one spoonful, if there was a pork dish, just another spoonful. He said he did not want to make a pig of himself just because he was a rich film star. Chickee had come from a poor family. Other Hong Kong people who'd risen from the ranks of refugees to the enclaves of the rich ate everything in sight, and often became obese. Chickee behaved the opposite. He mentally spiked and

stabbed at his own guts with the remembered sufferings of destitute refugees and never with the slightest hint of dignity.

Chickee was jealous of the whole *Almond Eyes* shoot. He was
jealous of William Holden, he was jealous of the foreign film company producing it, he was jealous of Becky's appearance and he was
really sore that he flunked an audition for a small role in *Almond
Eyes*. Apparently, there were good reasons for that. The producer
on *Almond Eyes* said Chickee was a "crummy" actor, with few talents beyond looking pretty, he spoke "lousy" English and "he's got
a weird name." The American frankness got back to Chickee and
he was even more unhappy. He threatened to have members of the
film company beaten up by Chinese thugs. Nobody took that seriously. It was like listening to a Paris fashion model threaten to
shoot up a runway show. The day he lost the *Almond Eyes* audition
Chickee spent an entire morning in the men's room at the
Gloucester Hotel, throwing up.

He really got mad over a publicity event involving the U.S.
Navy. My friend Arden Davis over at Feltus and Robertson worked
very hard with the U.S. consulate to arrange a visit for the leading
players in *Almond Eyes* to an American warship in Victoria
Harbour. She set it up for *Life* magazine, which came to town to
do a feature on Hong Kong movies. The captain and crew of the
U.S.S. Midway received Becky and Holden one afternoon. The
senior officers came down to the flight deck to shake Holden's
hand. The ordinary seamen had different interests. They obviously liked Becky, and she played up to their whistles and shouts by
waving to them and alternatingly hunching each shoulder forward
in a spoofy imitation of seductiveness. One young man with an
important-looking piece of equipment, which turned out to be
nothing more than a flight-deck washer, shouted several times to
Becky that she was "a beautiful chick." He was a hairy little bugger with two-toned glasses and a nascent pot belly.

The magazine took photos of Becky doing some sort of
Hoochi-Koochi dance she dreamt up on the spot for a small group
of crewmen and which *Life* declared was a traditional Chinese art
form. Holden was seen standing to the side and grinning at Becky.

The film party returned to Queen's Pier on a U.S. Navy tender and the trip gave the reporter from *Life,* a man named Albert Zieman, a chance to talk to Becky. "What do your parents think about you having an acting career?" Zieman asked. "It's not a traditional thing for nice Chinese girls to do."

"They do not mind at all. They're proud of me," she said.

"Does your mother like your films?"

"She would prefer that I not make so many pictures about nightclub singers. She thinks that 'nightclub performer' is a euphemism for another thing." Becky stumbled over the word "euphemism" and had to repeat it four times before she got it right. Zieman was charmed. *Life* went ahead and printed it.

This mother talk was a surprise to me. I heard about Becky's remark from Arden who sat in on the interview in the Navy tender. I asked her about it when the first air-mail copies of the magazine arrived from New York. Becky became flustered and upset. She started to laugh over and over, masking her acute embarrassment. "The reporter made an error," she said. Arden told me later that no, Becky had explicitly mentioned having a mother to Zieman. She had even described her "mother" for Zieman: short, hair pulled into a bun, wearing dated Chinese brocade dresses with knee-high nylon stockings. She was describing Miss Chin, Feng Hsiao-foon's dreadful secretary. Miss Chin was definitely not Becky's mother. It was a complete fantasy but if that's what Becky wanted to tell Americans, that was her business.

During filming of one scene on a double-decker tram on King's Road in North Point, the hairy young sailor from the Midway turned up, running along the pavement beside the car, shouting for Becky. "I love you!" he kept saying. "Marry me!"

"Sorry!" Becky called from the upper deck, clearly amused. "Already married!"

"But I love you!" he said. He hung around all the in-town location shoots and the producer eventually had to hire an off-duty policeman to keep him away. It turned out that he had gone AWOL and was facing charges. Becky wasn't frightened by him; she admired him for such an unabashed display. She put a finger to her lips in an almost sexual way when she looked at him. He was, she said, so foreign, so unencumbered, so free and unfettered. It was like looking into a world where nothing mattered, where life could be a lark, like chasing a pretty girl riding a tram.

It was precisely this that made her husband Chickee so sore. Becky had married Chickee without consulting anyone, as if it were a lark too. But the whole courtship seemed so dreary to the rest of us that it seemed more like a grim duty than a romance. Becky's fans loved it: the Great World movie queen and the handsome young actor. They didn't know that Chickee was prone to fretting and incontinence, or that Becky was stricken by headaches, illnesses and charcoal melancholy. Suddenly one day, there was an invitation in my mailbox to attend the reception at an expensive Mongkok restaurant. After the wedding Chickee briefly attained some of Becky's stardom, and their marriage accorded a special newsreel item in Great World cinemas. They were now a glamorous couple.

Chickee was subject to peevishness if he thought people weren't taking him seriously. His nagging bowel problem became public and, among the scatological Cantonese, it became the fulcrum of much hilarity and ribbing in the mosquito press. *Cloudburst* was especially mean-spirited and revelled in calling Chickee *"Great World's hot-to-trot young actor."*

He was from a tailor's family and he understood clothes, as he told people. He constantly studied his own films and thought about the way he appeared. Instead of greeting people with "Hello," he would say, "How do I look?" He had the prissiness of a woman and every morning argued with the make-up artists at Great World. But this pretty clothes-horse also harboured a social conscience, which none of us could take seriously either. One grew used to seeing beggars on Hong Kong streets but they always upset Chickee. If they got too close he would scowl and wave them away. A trio of them once besieged him during a location shoot on Nathan Road and Chickee lost all control. At first, he gave one three dollars, far too much. So the others pounced on him, pleading for the same. They shoved grim-faced children at him, who lifted up their little hands pathetically and whimpered. He screamed at them to go away, to get jobs and become useful. And yet he was constantly labouring at charity appearances for the poor, and even wrote papers, manifestos and essays on sanitary housing proposals for refugees, which Chinese-language newspapers kept rejecting because they were incoherent. *"Stick to wheelbarrow movies,"* an editor at the *Economic News* told him, a reference to a famous love scene in *Girls Demand Excitement* in which he sang to Becky while they lay together in a giant wheelbarrow.

After the beggar assault he retreated to a nearby hotel to sit on the toilet for several hours. Chickee claimed he had an intractable parasite, but one of the costumers up at Great World told Becky that Chickee kept a secret stash of laxatives in paper rolls inside a pair of shoes in his dressing-room closet. He could offer endless analysis of each bowel movement and what it told him about his health and mental state. "It was very plump today," he'd tell her. "And tender. You could have parted one with a pair of chopsticks."

Why Becky married him, I don't know. Perhaps because he was handsome and popular with the public, at least for a while. Or maybe it was indeed a lark. Perhaps she was punishing herself. I can guess why Chickee did it. Her popularity outpaced his and his career got a boost by marrying her. But for Becky to blunder into marriage spontaneously was so unlike her – and yet so like her. I thought the whole thing was disgraceful. She could have done better.

I asked her why she did it.

"Don't you think I deserved it?" she said.

It was a pathetic remark, an abdication of her responsibility to herself. Becky was an influential woman. As the biggest star at Great World she was a woman with some power. I disliked her for her response.

"I'd take better care of you than he will," I said.

"You're not my husband."

"I could be. I'd do that for you."

"You?" she said. "A man like you?" It was the only time she ever mentioned, however obliquely, what I was. What I am. I was very sad with this, her own reaction and for a while I stepped back from our friendship and let her get into all the trouble she wanted.

Chickee wrote a letter to the producer of *Almond Eyes* and hinted that he had "muscular friends" should anyone try to compromise his wife. The producer referred the letter to the police and things just got worse for Chickee. The police came around and interviewed him, warning him that intimidation was a crime. He immediately ran for the men's room. I know that Becky had a big fight with him about it. *"Keep your stupid, pathetic friends away from the foreigners!"* she told him. Years later, I learned that Chickee's sole "muscular friend" was a martial-arts student who doubled as a gigolo, servicing foreign women who came to town on tours. He worked through hotel bell captains, offering a discreet service for the adventurous. He had damaged himself permanently when he tried to improve his stamina with harsh chemicals. Becky laughed so hard about it and said that *"he had burned his own chopstick."*

Chickee was just as defensive about the Americans' frank dismissal of the Hong Kong movie industry. He told an American technician that his Hong Kong counterparts worked "ten times as hard."

"Pictures are still boring, though," the American replied.

They were both right, I suppose. Certainly Becky worked her heart out in those years. Between 1950 and 1959 she had graduated at Great World from such Cantonese-track pictures as *Those Kids* (young people foil crooks) to her first Mandarin picture, *Two Beauties*. It was a knock-off of Shanghai-style films from the 1930s and followed the lives of two young singers, one who studies at a fine music academy, the other who works in nightclubs. She went on to *Pink and Deadly*, playing a Shanghai-style "bad girl" who tries to steal another woman's fiancé. She stopped working full time in Cantonese-track pictures in 1954, after *Love Gets in the Way* (their lives in Hong Kong ruined by a misunderstanding, a sailor and a shop girl plot a getaway by sea). The film co-starred Chickee, although I recall that he looked less like a sailor and more like a sunburned shop clerk in a bad mood. It really was a boring picture. In *Four Shrieks of a Monkey*, a quartet of stories by the dramatist Hsu Wei, Becky played a monk re-incarnated as a prostitute. In 1956 Becky starred in a string of bad but successful Mandarin pictures, each one more plastic than before: *Candy Pink, Boastful Women, Demon Woman* and *Temptress*.

The next year she starred in *Meteorite of Love*. She played a vamp, what the Chinese called a "flaming creature," a woman who shows herself off so she can devour other women's husbands. In one scene, the comic actor Li Chi-chuen, with whom she appeared in many comedies over the years, arrives at Becky's plush apartment wearing the coveralls of a newly hired tradesman. Carrying a box full of tools, he struts in self-importantly. He's heard that the pretty girl in Apartment Two always needs repairmen so he lets himself in and calls: *"Hullo, Miss! I'm here about your leak!"*

Becky appears from the bedroom wearing a floor-length satin gown. Her hair falls over one eye. She slowly walks over to Lee, who grows so sexually alarmed at the sight of this goddess that the tools in his box vibrate noisily.

"I'm from the plant department!" he stutters.

"I just adore roses," Becky says in a deep voice, drawing closer.

"N-n-not that kind of plant!" Lee says.

"Oh," she says, touching a finger to one of his coverall straps. *"You mean ... physical plant."* The bottom of Lee's tool box opens and everything crashes to the floor.

Becky thought the role unbelievably stupid and one to which she wasn't suited. (Besides, all the best laughs went to Lee Chi-chuen and the other performers.) Anyway, it didn't matter, since the picture was completed in only fourteen days and she immediately had to make another, a domestic tragedy, the sort of picture she preferred, and *Meteorite of Love* was gone.

When it opened on Easter weekend, 1960 in the United States, Canada and Britain, *Almond Eyes* did very well. It cashed in on the Hong Kong colour but also Holden's popularity and Becky's performance. By the time the picture entered release, Holden was already back in Hong Kong to make *The World of Suzie Wong*, this time with another luminous Asian actress, Nancy Kwan. *Suzie Wong* would make Kwan an even bigger star in the West than Becky. Still, Becky was immensely liked in Hollywood for her impertinent performance and ability to hold her own next to an established star. The result was a visit by a representative of The Canning Wallace Agency. He offered to represent her for work in the United States. The talent agent told her that she could have a much bigger career in Los Angeles than she ever could in Hong Kong. Becky took the offer very seriously. But she still worked for Feng Hsiao-foon and Great World and he was not going to release her from a three-year contract. Perhaps for the first time in her life Becky saw opportunity. She saw a possibility to do more, to achieve more and be happy, to escape the hardship that clung to her, and the failures, such as her marriage to Chickee, whom she considered to be a nuisance and a mistake. She began to talk to me about getting a divorce. "It would be so wonderful to work in the United States," she said. "The Americans are so nice, like you, Paul."

And then I understood why she kept our friendship alive. I was an outsider, I was free of much of that which trammelled Becky. It would be another year before Becky thought of a way of dumping Chickee Leung and her career at Great World. What Becky did was buy herself out of her contract with Feng. It took all her precious savings and parting with that bit of financial security caused her amazing anguish. But for once in all the time I knew Becky, she wanted to pursue something that would make her happy, so I encouraged her to go. Getting rid of Chickee was another problem.

TWELVE

My assignment for the *China Telegraph* was to wait at the airport
for a Cathay Pacific flight from Singapore carrying a pack of 27
young singers. We had been alerted by the American consulate
that the group was a photo possibility. The youngsters would
launch a short concert in the arrivals hall, which we were told
would be spontaneous and unprompted. The young singers,
equipped with guitars, called themselves "Let's Go '67" and had
some obvious but unacknowledged backing from the U.S. government and American churches. They were part of what was
known as the "Moral Re-armament Movement," an antidote to
growing anti-Vietnam War protests in the United States. These
were an Asian copy of American spiritual singing groups such as
"Up with People," not unlike hastily counterfeited wristwatches
sold in Kowloon tourist markets. They were a good approximation but something seemed indefinably wrong about them, and
without regular maintenance they were prone to malfunction.
Their American creators believed that by dressing Asians up as
Americans and having them perform like Americans, everything
would be dandy. Whether these young people were there for the
money the American government gave them, the opportunity to
perform, or because of genuine conviction I couldn't say. When
they came through customs, a group of Filipino boys in neatly
pressed suits pulled guitars out of black carrying cases and sang
about human unity, equality and peace. The girls, many of whom

were from the Philippines but also Japan, Hong Kong and Vietnam, were freshly scrubbed and briskly exercised, with tidy but not dowdy dresses and white gloves. They looked like they'd been lovingly wardrobed by a church matron from Minnesota. The girls more or less automatically arranged themselves in a line behind the boys, who crouched with their guitars. They swayed and clapped their hands joyously. I interviewed a Hong Kong boy who was a member of the group and he gave a doughty, vague statement about the need to love one's homeland, one's family and one's parents. An America wire-service guy waspishly noted it was the first time he'd ever had air sickness on the ground.

The China Telegraph

Peking issues Hongkong threat

China today openly called on Hongkong Chinese to prepare for a possible call from Peking to overthrow British rule here.

In an unusually tough commentary on the Colony, China's communist leaders ordered Hongkong Chinese to mobilise themselves to "launch a vigorous struggle against the wicked British imperialists."

An editorial in the Communist Party newspaper, the People's Daily, said the Hongkong Chinese should "be ready at all times to smash reactionary rule." The article, the toughest statement about the Colony since the Communists came to power 17 years ago, came three weeks after Peking called on Britain to meet the demands of Chinese workers in Hongkong who triggered the current riots.

It erased any doubt that Peking was growing disinterested in the current situation in Hongkong.

– PAUL HAUER

The evening after I wrote the above story I got home to Causeway Bay and saw three European men waiting in the elevator lobby of the ground floor of my flat block. That in itself was unusual, because I was the only foreigner living in my building. One man touched my arm almost imperceptibly. "My name's

Soutar," he said. "I work with Sergeant Rudman." He was about forty-five, balding, wore a suit made at the coppers' favourite tailors and smelled strongly of pipe tobacco. "Might we have a talk?"

I asked him if he were there on official business and he hedged. I took him and the two other policemen to my apartment. Soutar said he understood the Crown was going to call me as a witness on "certain allegations of irregular police procedure" that took place at the San Po Kong Sub-District station on the afternoon of Thursday, July 20. I told him that I had already given two statements to the police, one at San Po Kong and another at Kowloon East District headquarters.

"Yes, we have your statements in hand," Soutar said. "But I wonder if you might want to reconsider how well your memory served you on that afternoon. There was a lot of upset and you might have been mistaken."

Did I react with indignation? I did not. I simply listened to what he had to say and then, with palpable uncertainty, said: "I can only tell the court what I saw."

Soutar put it to me that my initial police statements were wrong. "Now then, what do you intend to tell the court?"

"I can only tell them what I saw."

"Mr. Hauer, Hong Kong is currently torn by ongoing political disturbances of a very serious nature. Most of the community has rallied behind the police and for that we are grateful. It would be your civic duty to stand by the police in this most troubling case. Sergeant Rudman could be jailed for many years based on your testimony."

I just stared at him stupidly, completely lost in my own home.

"I implore you, sir," Soutar continued. "As a good citizen."

"Get out," I said.

"He's also your friend," Soutar said. He'd begun stuffing a pipe he'd taken out of an oilskin. "Or so I understand," he added, glancing up at me like a church minister with a Bible lesson. His implication was that one stands by one's mates, no matter what happens to them. When I showed no outward appreciation of this he lit his pipe and sat back. There were swirls of blue smoke, a well-conceived piece of stage work meant to elongate my discomfort. He flicked his match into my ashtray, where it landed with a faint tink.

At last he spoke, though not to me. He glanced up at one of his colleagues, who'd remained standing behind me throughout the interview. He said to the man, "Bring him in."

I stood up.

The other cop went out. Soutar and I waited in silence. He kept his eye on me.

I could hear the elevator door in the corridor whisk open and bang shut. The other policeman returned, escorting Benoit Ng.

Benoit was dressed in work clothes, white shirt, black necktie and a cheap grey sports jacket. He didn't look at me when he came in.

"Benoit Ng?" Soutar said. He pronounced Benoit's first name "Ben-oyt," extending the second syllable into a harsh twang.

"Yes," Benoit said quietly.

"Would you care to tell this gentleman what you told us?"

Benoit mumbled something no one could make out.

"I beg your pardon, Mr. Ng," Soutar said. "Didn't quite hear that."

"He buggered me."

"Who did?"

"This man."

Soutar asked if he knew my name.

"Paul Hauer."

"And would you be prepared to testify in a court of law to have been subjected to an uninvited indecent act committed by Mr. Hauer?"

"I would."

"Thank you, Mr. Ng, we've no further need of you tonight. We'll stay in touch."

Benoit left, almost casually, looking untroubled, almost as if he'd been providing tourists with directions on how to get to the Hilton.

Soutar reminded me of how many years I could spend in prison for buggery in Hong Kong and how I'd be banished from the colony afterward. Then he gave me his business card and told me to get in touch with him when I wished to discuss my testimony about Rudman. He said good night and left me alone. His pipe smoke hung in the air.

The sound of the elevator car faded away and I was left in my unkempt apartment in Causeway Bay with the lingering smell of pipe smoke, the sound of a mah-jong game starting and the buses gearing down to the terminus on Paterson Street. I sat in a chair by the window for a long time, feeling paralyzed, cheap and ashamed. In that, Soutar had done his work well. I merely allowed what had just taken place to wash over me: Soutar's request, Benoit's performance, which lingered in my mouth like a dry piece of old cake, and the final threat. It was the way Becky Chan responded to such moments, to bob along with them. The difference was that Becky found the means of staying afloat. I felt in danger of being swamped.

Finally, I stood by the window and looked out at the other flats in the buildings facing mine. This was not the Hong Kong of today, with its chubby men boasting on cellular phones in the backs of Mercedes sedans. It was a different place thirty years ago. It was a city where young men and women had lean faces, bony cheeks and hungry looks, where desperation was never far below the surface. Real desperation, not some affected anxiety of the well-fed and estranged to be turned on when the conversation was conducive, but doubts about whether the family would get enough to eat that week, and the realization that if they didn't eat no one would come to their aid. I stood at the window of the sitting room and looked through the typhoon bars at the flats on the opposite side of the light well from me. People in one flat were assembling brightly coloured plastic components into toys: piecework done at home. The finished items were little men in boats who, when wound up and put in a tub of water, could row about frantically. In another flat, five people were resting on cots, fanning themselves with ten-cent magazines. In a third, a woman was cutting out fabric pinned to an onion-paper pattern. She went about her evenings quietly, peaceably, industriously. And yet, you couldn't help speculate some nights on what secrets all these people must be harbouring – what lay beneath Hong Kong's orderly and energetic exteriors. The guilty little secrets so insignificant they mattered only to the holders who guarded them fanatically or the ones so horrific they transformed people forever. In how many other places in Hong Kong that night were people witnesses to events of the gravity I had just been subjected to? What were they plotting to escape these dramas?

I recalled a time when I had been walking with Rudman on a patrol and he had found a lost child. The little girl was very grave and refused to speak, even to tell us where she lived. So we had taken her back to Rudman's station and waited for someone to claim her. Her parents finally came. The adults and the child considered one another in silence and then left together without explanation. Their family secrets remained intact.

As I stood at the window looking at the other flats, the water in my kitchen faucets came back on after several days of inactivity. It was the beginning of my neighbourhood's four-hour rationing period. I had again forgotten to turn the faucet off when it had last expired. The water gushed out of the faucets and splashed noisily over a pile of three-day old dirty dishes in the sink.

THIRTEEN

Gerold Blofeld, the most incompetent businessman ever to set foot in Hong Kong, was dead. Someone at the Button Club in the Mandarin Hotel told me about it over pre-show drinks. I went to phone it in to the *Telegraph*. Blofeld was a sincere but not very talented businessman from West Germany who had followed his passion for petite Asian women to the Far East. Here he set up several increasingly disastrous businesses. The final bankruptcy was a huge wig factory in Kwun Tong. It was never as successful as the Chinese-owned wig companies, never made the kind of money made by the Jade Bracelet Wig Co., for which Becky had worked. Blofeld called his outfit Zsa Zsa Fashion Wigs (S.E.A.) Ltd., until he got a letter from a lawyer in California. He changed his signs and packaging to So So Fashion Wigs, and everyone said that it was unfortunate Blofeld didn't have a better understanding of English. It had been essential to maintain two production lines, one using expensive Indonesian women's hair for the U.S. market, the other cheap hair brought in from mainland China. U.S. government rules forbade truck in Communist goods, even Hong Kong-made wigs if they were from Communist hair. But the warehousemen didn't understand such strange American sensibilities about hair, and they got the Communist hair baled in with the capitalist hair. When Blofeld couldn't prove categorically that his wigs didn't come from commie hanks, U.S. Customs embargoed all his shipments and he was ruined. He resolved to drown himself by jumping off the kaido ferry to Sok Kwu Wan. But shortly after he hit the water, he was run down by the Jumbo Floating Restaurant, which was under tow. It was hard for people not to laugh even at his death. Blofeld's life stank of failure, and that was taboo in the colony.

Failure in Hong Kong wasn't a mere setback as, say, Americans would have it; failure was a catastrophe that everyone in Hong Kong faced every day. Failure was death, from starvation and exposure to the elements. Hong Kong people refused to fail, they couldn't, or all would be lost. Without a flicker of sentimentality for the past, its people reinvented the colony whenever their survival came into doubt. When I arrived in town in the '40s, Hong Kong was still an entrepôt port, trans-shipping goods made in China to overseas markets. After the Americans embargoed Chinese exports during the Korean war, Hong Kong people started manufacturing original materials. The colony pulled itself up. You couldn't stop Hong Kong with a hydrogen bomb. It was startling how nimble the people of the colony were, especially compared to the mire of self-destruction that was China. I was the only person who did not insist on laughing off Gerold Blofeld's death.

The same week Blofeld died, Jack Rudman went before a hearing in the Kowloon magistracy at which he and two police constables were committed to trial. I stayed clear of the hearing and read about it in my own paper. The Crown had instructed me not to contact Jack or other members of the police. I did not tell them of the visit from Soutar. The morning after Jack's committal hearing, I received a summons to appear as a witness.

Becky's marriage in 1958 to Chickee Leung Kai-yu had come as an astounding and hurtful surprise. Although I knew she was seeing him, she never told me they were that serious. I was sore that Becky never warned me.

The wedding reception took place in a Mongkok banquet room. Becky kept to the traditional habit of sitting in a separate room away from the groom and the main herd of guests. She sat there receiving small groups of people, a few at a time. I joined

her and a bunch of mutual Western friends for a spell. We had
drinks, toasted her and wished her happiness.

"Here's luck," she said, hoisting an extra-sweetened Coca-
Cola. She sat in a satin and silk evening dress, an Italian design. I
don't remember who made it; she hadn't.

She asked me if I was mad at her. I only said that she might
have told me about her engagement in advance.

"Why?" she asked.

"Just so I'd know."

"So you could write about it in the paper."

"No, that's not it at all." I didn't want to bicker on her wedding day, so I changed the subject and asked her where she was
going for her honeymoon.

"Scotland," she said. Feng was sending her to the Edinburgh
Festival with a copy of *The Goddess of Mercy*, which was going to
screen there. I asked what airline they were going on and she said
BOAC and I said have a good time.

Some Chinese friends came in and Becky reached out to the
women and grabbed their hands as they came in. The women
held her hands and chatted happily with her. She said in English,
almost inaudibly, "I wish my mother were here today."

I gave her a questioning look, enough to bid her to continue.

"That's all," she said. "I just wish she could have come."

I nodded and said it was a pity she couldn't.

"Not all mothers are bad, you know," she said.

"I didn't say they were," I said. "Why couldn't she make it?"

She immediately changed the subject and became cross if I
circled back to it. I grew exasperated and went to talk to her
new husband.

A week later, I arrived at the air terminal at eight on a sunny
August morning. I carried one suitcase and a portable typewriter in
a steel case. It was hot and humid so I slung my seersucker jacket
over one arm and cocked a trilby back on my head, glad to be getting out of town. There was a row of flags flying, the colours of various airlines serving the colony: Air India, BOAC, Macau Air
Transport, Pan American and PAL. It was very still; they were bare-

ly moving that morning. There was a huge construction project on the site: engineers were finishing a long new runway that would jut out into Kowloon Bay when completed. Most of the airport was built on such infilling and there were two existing intersecting runways which were hemmed in by the grey-green craggy mountains that hemmed Kowloon. I stepped out of the sun and into the terminal shed, put my bag on the weigh scale at the BOAC counter and fanned my head with my hat. The journey hadn't started, but already I felt so full of fun for the occasion that I dropped by the bar to celebrate with an early-morning drink. Then I felt that old-fashioned Canadian guilt about drinking before noon so I returned to the main waiting room. I had to feel guilty about something.

"Ah-Paul!" a woman's voice cried from the opposite side of the terminal. "Ah-Paul!"

It was Becky, dragging that new little husband of hers behind.

She wore a flat disc-like hat out of white velvet and it had a coarse little white veil that dangled down like a half curtain in front of her eyes. She wore white gloves and looked so endearing that I wanted to hug her. She came to me and squeezed my hand. Chickee was soldiering along with three small train cases. Becky called back to him over her shoulder. *"Wai! Did you check in the rest of the stuff?"* she asked him in Cantonese.

"Hai-ya," he said, grumbling in Cantonese. "Hello, Mr. Paul," he said, switching to English. "Come to see us off?"

"Good morning! How are the handsome honeymooners?"

"Our honeymoon! Isn't it fantastic?" Becky said.

Becky noticed I was carrying the typewriter.

"Actually," I said. "I'm going to Edinburgh too. The paper is letting me cover the festival, especially since there's a Hong Kong film on show.

Becky was delighted, Chickee less so. "Oh, that will be fun," he said, his voice trailing away as he made the realization. "All of us together on the honeymoon."

"Now, I'm not going to tag along with you," I said, trying to be as casual as I stared into her face. "Let's get that clear from the outset." Becky said nothing, only looked out the windows of the terminal at a taxiing airplane. The sun was getting hotter. Someone switched on the ceiling fans and they began a low and lazy whirl. "Can't we just have a little fun together?" I said. "It'll be so dull otherwise."

Chickee went over to the BOAC counter.

"You like Chickee, don't you?" she asked.

"Yes, of course," I said. Now, however, I felt badly, for risking spoiling her honeymoon. Which is funny, because that's what I had intended to do.

I hadn't gone psychotic. It wasn't as if I started collecting twigs and bird droppings and carrying them in my briefcase. I wasn't going to her premieres in a shabby army uniform and never approaching her. I just had this foggy yearning, the sort of yearning the Goddess of Mercy had as she stood on a rock surrounded by carbon dioxide clouds, trying to make everyone happy so she would find some peace. That's it, I just wanted her to be happy, so I would have some peace. I had looked up and heard the cries of the Goddess of Mercy, cries she didn't know she was making. She'd never be happy with Chickee. I'm not the only one who said that. The actress Grace Lo said the same thing. Even Feng Hsiao-foon, although he had encouraged the marriage as a boost for business, knew they weren't a good match.

Our airplane taxied the runway extension that crossed Prince Edward Road. There were traffic signals clanging like a railway crossing. Two barriers dropped into place. A row of delivery vans and buses waited while our plane crossed the road, turned about on the button of the runway, then accelerated. Once we were airborne, the plane swept to the right to avoid Kowloon Peak and headed out over the sea. No sooner had we levelled off when a Chinese BOAC hostess came to the back of the cabin and chattered to Becky. She called her "Pei-ling" after her series of *Smart Girl* movies. *"I cried all the way through The Blue Lake,"* the hostess gushed. *"I so wanted to be an actress like you."*

"You're very kind," Becky said.

"Wai! What about me?" Chickee said. *"Doesn't anybody recognize me?"* The hostess smiled and nodded at him but she

was more interested in Becky. Chickee sulked and looked out the window.

The plane stopped in Bangkok. Becky went to the ladies' room to change her stockings. I sat at a tiny bar table opposite Chickee, who was gazing out at the blistering Don Muang tarmac. There were U.S. and Thai military aircraft on the opposite side of the field, big grey machines, and I tried to identify them. C-46s and C-97s. Chickee wore a plain white shirt with black trousers, not looking any different from any other young Chinese man of the time, except for an amber and brown tie he wore in deference to the formality of plane travel. His eyes flitted back and forth between civilian aircraft and the military base off in the distance. Then he spoke. "I wanted to go to Hawaii. We could have afforded to fly to Hawaii. It's not like we're poor, you know. We're movie stars!"

"You should have. I think Hawaii is a romantic choice."

"I suppose you would have come along there too."

"Is that what you think?" I said, trying to look hurt and surprised.

"You know, I'm not a fool."

"Chickee ..."

"I'll thank you to call me Mr. Leung from here on out. I'll call you Mr. Paul."

"Mr. Hauer would be the equivalent."

"Okay, Mr. Haw, I want you to know something. I want you to know that I'm not so foolish as to miss you cook this up because you want Becky for you. I know your reputation with lots women. That right, Mr. Haw?"

Chickee was such a little fool.

"I'm going to Edinburgh to cover the festival."

"Be true with me," Chickee said, his English decaying with his rising temper. "Is she your lover?"

"Most emphatically, no. Mr. Leung, I can tell you with a completely assured conscience that she is not my lover. Nor has she ever been my lover. Nor will she ever be my lover." Nor would anyone. Ever. Ever. Ever.

"Then why do you want my honeymoon?" Chickee said, his anger growing. "You think me fool?"

"I don't. It's a coincidence we're even on the same flight. Look, where are you staying? During the festival, I mean."

Chickee took out his travel documents and read them. I knew their hotel was the Caledonian, I'd got the itinerary from Great World. I waited as he sounded out the word Caledonian slowly, stumbling and restarting several times. I made no effort to help him pronounce it.

"Oh. I'm staying there too," I said. "Well, I go to the festival tomorrow morning and I'll have my nose in interviews the whole time. It just won't be possible for me to see you, or her, after this flight. The only thing is, I may need to get a quote from Becky after the *Goddess* screening."

Becky returned from the ladies' room and sat down with a bright look for both of us, encouraging us to get along. Chickee went off to the men's room. Probably to puke or something. I hoped he would miss the flight.

We were met at Heathrow by a reporter and a photographer from a Chinese newspaper published in Britain. They asked for a photo of Becky and Chickee on the stairs of the Britannia. So the crew asked them to wait while the rest of us deplaned. I was the last off and Becky asked if I wanted to be in the picture. "No," I said, but she insisted and even Chickee, to be nice, insisted. So there was a picture of me standing behind Becky and Chickee next to a BOAC hostess at the top of the stairs. Becky and Chickee had movie-star smiles. The hostess had a BOAC smile. I merely looked uncomfortable. Now I was feeling foolish. I'd paid for the trip out of my own savings and I was ruining my friend's one bit of happiness. When we came down the stairs, Chickee asked the reporter not to mention that Becky's Canadian friend had come along for the honeymoon. *"He's not supposed to be here,"* Chickee said. I could have smacked him on the head for that.

We shared a cab from Heathrow to Euston. I sat on a flip-down seat facing the newlyweds, my hands on my knees. Chickee was doing some kind of annoying googling of Becky the whole way into town, clutching her hand and nuzzling her neck. She fended him off so she could look at famous sights. I wanted to yank him off her, like an aggressive chaperone or a mental-hospital orderly. I just sat there.

The festival received *Goddess of Mercy* politely. Some members of the audience yawned loudly, others laughed at awkward English subtitles such as "The typhoon on my roof aggravates me." However, the cinephiles, as they called themselves, boasted that with Hong Kong they'd found an important new film culture. (They hadn't seen Becky in *Candy Pink* or *The Smile of One Hundred Fascinations*, which were altogether less noble productions.)

I left the festival early to travel to London. It was in Trafalgar Square that I again ran into Becky and Chickee. Footsore and hungry, they were looking for a place to sit down. It was cold that day, even though it was August. I'd eaten a half a sandwich and was tearing off bits of bread to feed the pigeons. Becky found me with pigeons attending me eagerly. They stood on my shoulders and all around my feet. The sight of my shoulders occupied by those foolish birds made her laugh and I instantly felt better.

"Hey! Where'd you come from?" she said. "Oh boy, let's have some fun now."

I was too contented and charmed by seeing her to say hello and then leave them alone. Chickee poked a cigarette into my mouth then lit it. "Hello, Mr. Paul," he said, cheerful again, no doubt pleased that I hadn't followed them all over Scotland. "Are these birds good for eating?"

"How were the Highlands?" I asked them. "Did you have a good time?"

"It was cold," Chickee said.

"Chickee had the trots, so he was in a poor mood," Becky said. "That's the expression, isn't it? Trots? You taught me that."

I said to her: "You know, you needn't tell me everything."

"And he thinks my breasts are too big for a Chinese woman."

Chickee laughed to cover his embarrassment.

For a while, with pigeons on my shoulders, I pointed out landmarks of the square, ending with Canada House directly opposite us. Becky even took my arm as I turned and pointed, and considered what we thought was a persistent bird on my shoulder but it turned out that it had hooked a talon on my jacket and couldn't free itself. I nudged it and it got free and flew a few feet away.

Chickee suddenly professed to be feeling unwell. His trots were back, and he headed back across the square in hurry, leaving me to see Becky back to their hotel.

When he was gone, I asked her if we could sit and talk. She was disingenuous, shrugged her shoulders and said, "Sure!" in a chirpy little voice, full of fun and ease.

"Becky, I want to ask you about Chickee. Why does your husband have to have such a stupid English name? I always feel like an idiot talking about him."

"I like it. 'Chickee baby.'"

Like a little bird. "I want to ask you about Mr. Leung."

"Yes."

"Why did you marry him?"

"Ai, kwailos, so direct."

"Yes, I'm being a brutishly blunt kwailo but that's what I am. Are you in love with Mr. Leung?"

"It is essential for harmony to feel love for one's spouse."

"Do you love him?"

"No. Yes. Sure. Maybe-ish."

"Why did you marry him, Becky?"

"It was a studio marriage. You never hear of studio marriages?"

It wasn't a studio marriage. They rarely ever happened in Hong Kong. It wasn't Hollywood.

"Ah-Paul, too many questions. Can't we just have a nice time today?"

"Why?"

"I want to have children."

"That's news."

"Who are you?" Becky demanded, raising her voice now. A couple of British teenagers, a boy and a girl, looked up from a bench.

"Go back to your pigeons," she said, too harshly. "I want to go back
to the hotel. What makes you think I don't want to have children? I
do so! Go away now. I am sorry I ever came to this filthy country.
Chickee is right, we should have gone to Hawaii. There, we would
have had some privacy that newlyweds need. I could hate you for
your mean-spirited probing. Go away and leave me alone. I do so
want children, more than anything else, more than my career."

"I'm sorry." I told her that I wasn't trying to be mean, that I
was her friend and that she always baffled me with why she did
the things she did. Let's say she wanted to have children. I asked
her if she shouldn't have waited until she found a man she could
be in love with.

"I love Chickee."

"No you don't. I can tell you don't. You'd rather spend this
honeymoon with me than your own husband."

"You have no right to say these things."

"No, I don't. You're right. Let's drop it."

She went back to her hotel by herself and I walked around the
square for a while longer, stupidly still clutching the bit of sandwich I hadn't eaten. I broke off more bits and tossed them at the
pigeons. They came over and others, seeing that I had a supply of
food fluttered in. I longed for Becky, not in the way that other
men did, but just as a companion, someone to knock around
with. Now she had her sweet little hubby, and there would be no
room for me. I was done. I tossed the last of the bread and
clapped my hands clean. The pigeons bobbed and flicked at the
bread until it was gone then flew away. An old geezer in a dirty
trench coat and a paper bag full of dried bread crumbs had arrived
on the scene and the pigeons chased over to him.

They were married for just three years. They lived in a good house
in Kowloon Tong, but they lived in disarray. Becky's high heels
were strewn about her bedroom like ill-fated box cars in a train
wreck. With her career soaring, she no longer had to pray to the
refugee god Wong Tai Sin to send her shoes. They came in great

armies, an infantry dispatched from European stores in Central
for her private consideration. She was preoccupied with con-
sumption then, eating up more purchases all the time. Chickee
was equally preoccupied with clothing, and if they didn't have servants to pick up after them they would have buried themselves in
his suits, ties and her jackets and ensembles. I thought that the
Leungs would be bankrupt before their marriage failed. That, I
now realize, was Becky's greatest terror. I started to call it a
"pigeon marriage," which in Cantonese was euphonious.

Throughout this time, Becky showed wavering control. On
the screen, Becky had a way of putting her fingertips over her
mouth tentatively, as if she were unsure whether emotions might
come bursting forth. When she was upset in her movie roles, it
looked as if it was all she could do to contain herself. It was a quality that Judy Garland had, an early warning of an earthquake. She
was almost always controlled. Only once, in the weeks leading up
to her divorce from Chickee in 1960, did she lose control. She
was having a European-style party in her home and I was helping
her make hors d'oeuvres. Suddenly, she burst into a wailing sob:
"God strike me!" It came out of nowhere and went right back
again. She completely throttled whatever had brought it on and
never explained the episode.

Divorce in 1960 in Hong Kong was an extreme scandal. Becky
had to get out of her marriage. After she made *Almond Eyes* with
William Holden, she had a new opportunity to go work in
Hollywood. There was no place in her future there as Mrs. Chickee
Leung. It became necessary for her to find a device to break the marriage. We talked it over. I don't know why I did it, but I agreed to
serve as co-respondent. Officially, and nothing more, Becky and I
had committed adultery. Chickee saved face, Becky got her divorce,
and I got nothing. Maybe it was a fantasy for me, like I suddenly
belonged to someone by pretending to be Becky's lover. The court
bought it, the mosquito press loved it, the divorce went through.

Everything changed on a Saturday while I was out of town,
spending the weekend in Macau, gambling and picking up money
boys on the steps of the ruined cathedral. When I came back to

work on Monday there was a press release on my desk from the Great World Organisation announcing that Miss Becky Chan had reached an amicable settlement with the corporation. She would thereafter be pursuing a motion-picture career in Hollywood.

FOURTEEN

Becky Chan's professional records are in my possession. They
vary in number depending on the period of her career. For a
variety of technical and legal reasons that are of no interest now,
there a great many accumulated from the early 1960s. There are
no records from after 1967. I have thought of donating the
material to the archives of the new Hong Kong Motion Film
Archive and recently went through them to see what was his-
torically valuable and what was still in good condition. They
should be in the care of professional archivists: unless properly
cared for, the documents break down in the semi-tropical
humidity of Hong Kong, wilting with mildew. The damp is
everywhere: old envelopes with letters inside reseal themselves,
re-enclosing the past, and there is mould that undermines the
integrity of the corrugated cardboard box that holds these
records. There's something of an unintended joke printed on
the side of the cardboard box by its originators, a noodle company, which labelled the carton "Chewy Men." Inside this box
are scrap books of publicity photos, English- and Chinese-language newspaper clippings about her career and public life.
There are numerous old issues of an in-house magazine that
Great World Studios gave away in its cinemas. They had lots of
photos of stars and articles that told the stories of then-current
films. I have merged all this material with my own personal files
and they give something of the flavour of what went on then.

Together they trace the failed trajectory of Becky's American film career.

Here is a letter, handwritten:

> *Dear Paul:*
>
> *I have arrived.*
> *You made a great sacrifice to your reputation. I'm very grateful. Come visit me here.*
> *Becky*

The postmark on the envelope reads "Los Angeles, Calif., Oct. 4, 1960." Beneath it I have placed several letters of correspondence between Becky, Great World's solicitors, an American film production company and a talent-management company in California, The Canning Wallace Agency. The agency co-ordinated Becky's move from Hong Kong to Hollywood. Becky hated Hollywood from the moment she arrived. It was not because they were mean, exploitative or blatantly racist with her, or because it was a foreign country and far from everything she knew. The United States, she found, was actually quite a wonderful place, and there were many times when she marvelled at the uncomplicated, unencumbered beauty she found there. Americans proved inordinately friendly, kind and astonishingly generous. No, it was precisely these things that caused her to hate California. She could be happy there.

In the cardboard box there is a Cable and Wireless telegram from the Wallace agency that confirmed a memorandum of agreement on representation. The ink has slowly bled out from the letters on the paper so it looks blurry, like a gradually altering memory that becomes imprecise. Beneath the telegram in a well-ordered progression comes a Japan Air Lines ticket receipt. The cover shows a winged crane cradling the airline's initials. Below that is a souvenir certificate of passage JAL gave out to every passenger who crossed the Pacific Ocean for the first time.

Proclamation of the Seven Deities of Good Fortune

Know Ye By These Presents

that, having entered the ethereal realm of the Sun, the Sky and Moon, while spanning the Pacific on the Wings of the New Japan,

MISS B. CHAN

has crossed the International Date Line, and thus has jumbled Yesterday, Today and Tomorrow from their mundane, time-worn order.

Now, therefore, know ye, that the Seven Benign Deities of Good Fortune, Happiness and Longevity do hereby extend their eternal blessing to this esteemed individual.

The professionals that she handed herself over to at The Canning Wallace Agency were cheerful, self-absorbed young men who talked incessantly about matters so arcane, so peculiar to their profession as to be incomprehensible to her. They told Becky that the American film business was in big trouble because of television, that it was in something of hard times. But by the vastness and opulence of the studios and sets she'd seen, it was no crisis that a Hong Kong film performer could understand.

Her agents had brilliantly sunlit offices with wall-to-wall windows that would have looked out onto the Los Angeles hills if they weren't sheathed in gauzy curtains. Her assigned agent was a young blond man named Morris Feinstein, who sat at an oval teak desk. There was very little furniture in the office, and the wallpaper, white with little specks of gold, was broken by huge abstract paintings, which Feinstein pointed out when he escorted her into the office. "That's a Mark Rothko," he said.

Becky considered the painting. "Very nice," she said. There was another man waiting for them. He was only slightly older than Feinstein, and sat in a chrome and black-leather chair. Feinstein introduced him as a co-agent.

"This is Miss Becky Chan," Morris Feinstein said to the man, who was named Meikle. They all sat down. "Becky is a very big star in Hong Kong and we intend to make her an even bigger one here in America," Feinstein said.

Becky was flattered but growing uncomfortable.

"Hong Kong," Meikle said in a hoo-whee way.

"Tell Mr. Meikle how many pictures you've appeared in," Feinstein said.

"One hundred and seventy," Becky said. "Including the small parts."

Feinstein told him that Becky was only twenty-nine years old and Meikle whistled.

She assured them that none of her films were any good compared to U.S. productions. Meikle replied that plenty of American films "aren't so hot" either, but she insisted on her unacceptability. She talked about her lack of polish, proper training and depth compared to American actresses. Meikle said that she should think like a winner or she was bound to get overlooked. "You'll do fine if you give it your best."

"You'll probably do a lot better since you're free of that guy you were working for in Hong Kong," Feinstein said. "That one who put up all the flack over your contract? Please excuse my language, but that Mr. Feng is a venal bastard."

They discussed what sort of work they saw her doing and at once it became both exhilarating and disappointing. There was a big call just then for Asian actresses. But Feinstein told her to forget about ever playing roles that white women played. "It's not going to happen," he said. "However, your timing is perfect for Oriental work. We're going to sell Universal on you for either the lead or a supporting role in *Flower Drum Song*. They're in casting and they're desperate to lay their hands on every Chinese performer they can get. Can you sing 'I Enjoy Being a Girl?'"

Becky had never heard of it.

"You know," and here Feinstein sang a bit from the song in a soft, thin voice: "I talk on the telephone for hours, with a pound and a half of cream upon my face ..." He laughed at the extreme absurdity of a man singing a woman's song. "I like that song. It's a good song. Why can't there be more songs like that?"

"You're thinking that she could have played the Nancy Kwan role," Meikle, said. "Nancy sings that song. She's already signed to play the nightclub chick."

"You know Nancy?" Feinstein asked Becky. "Nancy Kwan?"

"No," Becky said. Feinstein seemed surprised she didn't, as if Oriental performers around the world all knew one another.

"I see Becky in the seamstress role," Meikle said. "Sort of tragic, gorgeous and nicely constructed."

"Speaking of nice construction," Feinstein said to Meikle. "You going to the party Andy DeColla's throwing tonight?"

"Yeah."

"You taking that girl with the nice construction? What's her name? Nancy? Nancy something or other."

"Nancy Kwan?"

"No no, not Nancy Kwan. Red-head. You know the one I'm talking about." Feinstein snapped his fingers trying to recall the last name. He was a surprisingly young man to be a senior talent agent. He took out a cigarette, lighted in and left it in his mouth. He put his hands behind his head, leaned back in his swivel chair and looked at Becky. "Sorry about the crude language," he said, not looking away. "It's the way we talk." The cigarette bobbed up and down while he spoke.

"What other Orientals could Universal use?" Meikle asked.

"James Shigeta. Jack Soo. They're committed to *Flower Drum Song*," Feinstein said. "Jack Soo's a funny guy. You met him?" Feinstein continued to address Meikle exclusively. "Funny, funny guy." Feinstein looked pleased, cosmopolitan in his acquaintance with an Asian-American actor.

"Who else is there?"

"Miyoshi Umeki."

"Oh God, that little pixie thing? Too sweet." Meikle imitated Umeki's faltering, tiny voice: "Yeste'day, I woo ha been berry happy to had you lub me — She'll probably get the lead, you know. She's not even Chinese. They cast a Japanese as Chinese. Can you believe it?" Meikle turned to Becky and said without expecting an answer: "Does that offend you? Casting a Jap as a Chinese?"

"Anna May Wong" Feinstein said.

"Is she a lesbian?"

"She's really old. I think she died recently."

Meikle held his arms wide apart. "Can't play the picture then! Reiko Sato? Juanita Hall?"

"Yeah, Juanita Hall always passes for Oriental."

"Little bit of wax for the eyelids and a black wig and anybody's an Oriental. They could make me into an Oriental." Feinstein and Meikle looked cautiously at Becky for her approval since they realized that they may have gone too far. Becky gave them a game, bewildered smile and they relaxed again.

"Tell you what," Feinstein said, leaning forward and putting his hands on his knees, "we'll arrange an audition for *Flower Drum Song.* They're screaming for every Oriental they can get their hands on."

"Maybe," Becky said at last. "With a little wax and a black wig you could come along too."

Feinstein and Meikle laughed heartily. "You're okay, Becky."

Becky didn't care for the idea of having to audition at Universal International. Back in Hong Kong they had been perfunctory affairs. Film producers in the early 1950s were more concerned that you could stand upright and remember lines and look presentable in costumes more than any acting suitability. The Canning Wallace Agency sent her to a music coach who worked with her on a song from the show. They stood in a carpeted room surrounded by acoustic tiles with little holes in them. The coach made her sing over and over. He thought it would be amusing if she knocked her head from side to side while she sang, sort of imitating an inverted bell clapper. She had to keep smiling the whole time her head wobbled to and fro. At Universal's Revue studio, she auditioned with a charming American, James Shigeta, who was not only extremely handsome but a superb singer. Well, I thought he was extremely handsome. I don't know if she did.

"'How do I look?'" he said, reading lines from a script.

"'If you had a pigeon on your head, you'd look like a statue,'" Becky read. She worked at altering her British-English accent to more of a North American one. She told me afterward she thought of the way I talked while she rehearsed.

Based on her looks, singing and dancing, Ross Hunter, the producer, awarded her the role of Helen Chao, the wallflower seamstress. The big challenge was to be a long fantasy dance scene after the seamstress finds her love for Shigeta's character is not returned. Becky was dreading it. She hated her own dancing. She thought her hips looked too large on the screen. Even before shooting began she started getting sick and was missing rehearsals. It got to be a problem immediately.

The cast got to see the elaborate street set Universal was building for the film. It had four corners, there were building fronts on each side and it was large enough for a steady stream of automobiles to pass back and forth. There was a ramp receding into the distance and when cars came down it they made a low rumble. Becky found the script peculiar and she had to have it explained to her why the characters spoke to each other in stilted salutations such as "my father" and "my brother's wife," rather than the simple "Ma" and "Auntie" that real Chinese used. The reason came back that it sounded more "Chinese" to Americans. Becky was supposed to rehearse the ensemble portions of the "Chop Suey" song but she called in sick or arrived late every day. A dance-in replaced her whenever she was away but she fell behind. Her dance director yelled at her for not knowing her work, she walked off the set in tears then stayed home for three days in a row. The other actors knew of her vast experience in Hong Kong movies and they complained that it hadn't taken her long to become a Hollywood prima donna.

Universal sent over a Chinese-American actress named Barbara Lane, who was in the *Flower Drum Song* cast, to convince her to go back to work. They figured that she would have more rapport with Becky than a white person would. They figured wrong. Barbara arrived in black deck pants, a man's pink shirt untucked at the waist and turned up at the collar. She stood in the middle of the living room in a bungalow Becky had leased in Rancho Park and scowled at her in contempt. "You might have been a big deal in Hong Kong but you're nobody here," she said. "And because you're an Oriental you'll always be a nobody here. Get it? Got it? We want to work for a living and this is a rare big opportunity, so stop holding things up for the rest of us."

Becky cried at hearing this and expressed great remorse at having jeopardized the jobs of others. "I don't deserve to be here," she told Barbara, and Barbara softened. They had a long talk during which Barbara told Becky she should be much happier working in the States than Hong Kong. "I've been to Hong Kong," she said, "to see my relatives. It's great to be over here, away from all that shit. That shitty family and that shitty society. My relatives suffocated me. You'll be much happier here and not around all those shitty, smothering people."

Barbara got Becky to go back to rehearsals. Then Becky missed two more days after that and the producers could hold work up no longer, certainly not for a secondary performer who was no one at the box office. They fired her and replaced her with Reiko Sato.

After the failure at *Flower Drum Song* the agency got her work in two cheap pictures being produced by an independent company for Twentieth Century-Fox. Each called for beautiful Oriental women and each picture was forgotten soon after release. The first was a lame, prurient comedy called *Chopsticks* about two amorous Pan American Airways pilots who juggled stewardess-girlfriends in a Hong Kong apartment. Pan Am objected to the characterization of its pilots and at the last minute the airline's name was changed to a fictional one, forcing reshoots. You can still see minor references to Pan Am such as timetables on the fictitious airline's counters and on a hangar in the background of one shot. There was plenty of exterior location work done in Hong Kong and a bad pastiche of Chinese music that depended greatly on the skills of the xylophonist. Otherwise it had little to distinguish it as a story about Hong Kong. Everything to do with Becky was shot in Los Angeles – she never came to Hong Kong for any filming. She played an overheated Filipina stewardess who spent most of her screen time either kissing the male leads or yelling at them in staccato rapid fire. When it was released in Hong Kong, *Chopsticks* opened at the Hoover Cinema in Causeway Bay. I recall the audience was more preoccupied with pointing out photographed local landmarks to one another than in Becky or the story. I admit that I was diverted by a live cat that the Hoover's management had assigned to the ornate, crumbling auditorium to cut down on rats. While Becky delivered her lines this mangy marmalade tabby patrolled the stage in front of her.

The following year, she made her second Fox film. It was about an organized Oriental crime syndicate in San Francisco called *Panic on Grant Avenue*. Jeffrey Hunter filled the male lead, which had been turned down by Rod Taylor. He rescued the beautiful and passive Chinese-American daughter of an antiques dealer from a Chinese gangster. Hunter made a number of pictures in the '60s related to the Far East, supplanting the position William Holden had occupied in the decade before. *Panic on Grant Avenue* was the sort of picture that rightly outraged Chinese-Americans in later decades for the colonial overtones of a white American guy rescuing the helpless Chinese babe. It was also a lame, dull, studio-bound movie that disappeared after two weeks in the United States. It was booked for the Queen's Theatre in Hong Kong but never even opened.

Becky had caused problems on the shoot. This surprised me when I learned about it in her personal records. She had never been a temperamental performer in Hong Kong. Unlike Hollywood performers with their tantrums, peccadilloes and demands, the Hong Kong actress obligingly did what she was told, uncomplainingly, punctually and at a bargain price. And yet when Becky arrived in California she was so uncomfortable with her new career that she began to book off sick for trivial illnesses and discomforts she would have worked right through in the Orient. It got to be so disruptive that her own agent sent her a letter.

THE CANNING WALLACE AGENCY

ARTISTS REPRESENTATIVES   HOLLYWOOD, CALIFORNIA

FROM MORRIS H. FEINSTEIN
SENIOR ASSOCIATE, THE WALLACE AGENCY

Miss Becky Chan
310 Lorenzo Drive
Los Angeles, Calif.

June 2, 1963

Dear Becky:

It has come to the agency's attention that you have been repeatedly late or absent for shooting on Panic on Grant Avenue. Mr. Furness, the executive producer, lectured me at length on certain facts about motion-picture companies, namely that they are guardians of two precious commodities: time and money. He telephoned me twice today regarding your conduct. Although, for the record, we disagree with his portrayal of your behavior as frivolous and disruptive, I must remind you of your contractual agreements with his company. Any alleged lack of professionalism would reflect adversely on this agency and we could be associated with such conduct.

Irregular appearances are wasting the Panic unit's time and money and that must not continue if you are to avoid a bad reputation and build a successful career. If you have difficulty coping with the shooting schedule I will contact the unit management personally to discuss a possible compromise.

Sincerely,
M.H.F.

What Becky found in Los Angeles was that the illusion of movies was all that much more of an accomplishment, given the city's vast mundaneness. Instead of glamour everywhere there were six-lane streets, the centre of each white concrete lane streaked with dots of black motor oil. There were car washes and auto-parts dealers ringing Paramount Pictures, motels with enormous, ugly signs on high pillars outside Twentieth Century-Fox and an endless roar of traffic along Santa Monica Boulevard which so terrified Becky she never learned to drive. A po-faced Mexican chauffeur took her everywhere. People in Los Angeles worked in stores, factories, distribution depots, snack bars, plain and simple places of commerce. Rather than a fairyland of wealth and beauty, Los Angeles was full of toiling ordinary people, wealthier than those in Hong Kong, but no more exotic or effete than the weary masses of Kowloon going about their eternal grinds, only looking up from their burdens once they'd settled into a fifty-cent seat at the Ambassador Cinema to watch her on the screen. That Hollywood could make beautiful entertainments amid the banality of everyday life was all the more remarkable.

She began to get sick very often, frequently missing shooting on her two sorry little movies because of illnesses. She'd stay at home in the modest bungalow in Rancho Park. It was through Barbara Lane that Becky learned about vegetarianism. Barbara warmed to Becky after she had been fired from *Flower Drum Song*. That failure seemed to erase the hauteur that Barbara had imagined Becky carried and made her more like Hollywood's Chinese-American marginals. Barbara took Becky to see specialists in West Hollywood clinics, where they explained the complexities and rigid rules of pursuing better health through vegetarian diets and supplements. She eliminated pork from her diet and felt one hundred times better. Then she cut out beef and improved even more. With this newfound vitality she stayed in evenings, telling American friends and her agent that she was too weary to go to those chat-up parties that might be useful to the advancement of her career.

Here is another letter that lies beneath the others in the cardboard records box. It was to have been a good supporting role in a very big, prestigious picture being released through MGM:

FROM THE DESK OF BERNARD SMITH

Dear Becky:

I'm delighted to inform you that we have decided to cast you as Ofelia, the Arapaho Indian girl in "How the West Was Won." We look forward to working with you on this exciting epic. Scheduling material will follow shortly concerning rehearsals, costume and prosthetic fittings. If you have any questions please contact my office.

Sincerely,
BERNARD SMITH

BS:kk

In *How the West Was Won* Becky played a young Indian woman who teaches George Peppard's character, Zeb, to understand the dignity of the Arapaho tribe, motivating him to take a stand against an insensitive railway engineer. Because the bad-guy engineer sneers at the Indians as savages and ignores their complaints about the railway pushing through sacred grounds, the Arapahos cause a herd of bison to stampede and destroy one of his new railway towns. Becky liked working with George Peppard and the sequence's director, George Marshall. And she liked the trip to Custer State Park in South Dakota, where parts of the Indian sequence were filmed. The location shoot seemed such a lavish affair compared to what she had done in the Far East. Here, there were caterers working out of house trailers and several floors of a hotel in Rapid City reserved for the company. In Hong Kong, Great World budgets were so slender that she had once been obliged to take a public bus to a location shoot. She loved the costume that designer Walter Plunkett created for her and thought the idea of a Chinese woman playing an American

Indian was a hoot. She marvelled at the choreography of wranglers who managed to goad a big herd of buffalo kept in a paddock at the state park to stampede carefully and repeatedly before the big Cinerama cameras. Things were looking up.

The reason why Becky does not appear anywhere in *How the West Was Won* has nothing to do with bad behaviour. It was just one of those things that happened in movie-making. Attached with a paper clip that had grown rusty in the Hong Kong humidity, and transferred an orange shadow of itself onto the paper, was another letter from the producer from the same year.

FROM THE DESK OF BERNARD SMITH

Dear Becky:

Sometimes, in the course of producing a large and lengthy project like "West" certain difficult decisions have to be made. This is one of them.

We have decided to reduce the overall length of the picture from 210 minutes to 155 minutes. To achieve part of that cut we are dropping two subplots, including one that features your character. Becky, let me assure you that this decision in no way reflects our estimation of your abilities as an actress. Your performance was very fine and moving but we decided that it was not absolutely central to the story "West" is telling.

I understand that you will be disappointed by this news. I look forward to working with you again in the near future.

BERNARD SMITH

Becky had never been cut from a picture before – no Hong Kong film company, even Great World, could afford to waste money removing major portions of a completed film. The cut only further damaged her morale. Barbara Lane referred her to psychiatrists and therapeutic dieticians. She further instructed Becky to rake her agent for what had happened, but Becky was too depressed at being cut from the film even to mention its title. She blamed herself, saying that her performance had not been up to standard.

In the cardboard box, there are a whole stack of memos between production companies, Becky's agency and others, including one from a completion-guarantee company complaining about Becky's spotty attendance. She received scripts for or worked on numerous pictures: *Operation Jade, China White, The Corrupt Ones* and *A Lotus for Miss Quon*. She either turned them down for no good reason or became so difficult that she got fired, sometimes even before shooting began.

One morning, when Becky was home with sinusitis, a courier dropped off the following letter:

THE CANNING WALLACE AGENCY
ARTISTS REPRESENTATIVES · HOLLYWOOD, CALIFORNIA

FROM MORRIS H. FEINSTEIN,

Miss Becky Chan
310 Lorenzo Drive
Los Angeles, Calif.

October 22, 1963

Dear Becky:
    We have received your letter dated the twenty-first of October and after much consideration concur with you that owing to your race, it would be difficult to predict much work for you in the coming years.
    However, we do not agree that this agency has treated you "contemptuously" and "without due consideration" for the future of your career.

We have repeatedly expressed our concerns about your keen reluctance to cooperate with production companies. Naturally, we try to accommodate all of our agency's clients in their needs and wishes. However, there comes a point where non-cooperation becomes an unacceptable impediment.

Your refusal to cooperate, coupled with the limited opportunities open to you brings us to an unavoidable conclusion. We believe that it is to our mutual benefit that we terminate our memorandum of agreement with you. If you will have your attorney contact our Legal Department the technicalities of termination will be effected. Any permanent clarification of your status with the U.S. immigration authorities will be your sole responsibility.

Good luck in your future endeavors.

M.H. Feinstein

MHF:ig

It didn't take Becky more than one month to have her belongings packed by a shipping company and forwarded to Hong Kong. She surrendered the lease on her Rancho Park bungalow and bought a ticket. She called a few American friends to say good-bye then quietly left the United States for good.

She didn't call me after she got back to Hong Kong. Everybody knew she was back in town because the Chinese-language press had reported that she was again under contract to Feng Hsiao-foon at Great World. She hammered out Mandarin-dialect pictures again, the first being a stupid piece called *The Big Doll* about a department store mannequin that comes to life and creates havoc for a window dresser. I recall that a feature writer for the *South China Morning Post* laboured hard over a metaphor on what the plot said about Becky's recent American misadventure. He had even more tedious fun with the plot line for her next slated picture. It was about a young secretary who apparently murders her employer. Feng threatened to sue, the *Post* ran an apology and the feature writer got fired.

I eventually reconciled myself to never seeing her again. Then I received an engraved invitation in the mail to attend the wedding of Miss Becky Chan and the president of the Great World Organisation, Feng Hsiao-foon.

FIFTEEN

Chen Lo-wen, Feng's favourite director at Great World Studios, phoned me at the *China Telegraph* in confidence. He said he wanted to pass on a tip, which made me suspicious. Nobody at Great World passed on tips. They were too afraid of Feng Hsiao-foon. Chen was even more distressed than on the day I had spoken to him about Becky's disappearance. He told me that Great World Studios was closed.

The whole place was in an uproar. Feng had ordered the gates locked then instructed his personnel department to begin firing every single employee. He shut everything down after a loud but otherwise orderly demonstration by left-wing activists outside the property gates. Inside, anonymous employees had pasted inflammatory posters on building walls. They'd depicted Feng as a rat dining on the bodies of fellow Chinese while under the protection of giant British colonial bosses. The posters had condemned him as an exploiting capitalist boss who'd found common cause with British imperialists. Feng had gone berserk when he saw the posters and ordered the whole company, from his managers down to Uncle Lo, the gatekeeper, dismissed until someone came forward to identify who had been agitating workers inside the studio. So far, only two semi-skilled carpenters had come forward to admit Communist sympathies. Once they came before Feng in his office, they changed from otherwise passive and quiet workers into firebrands. With nothing left to lose, they began mechanically chanting Maoist slogans condemning Feng and other "feudalist bosses" and celebrating the "powerful fist of the working classes." He ordered them off the lot and had the police charge them with vandalism. Feng believed that there were others at work in his company because the leaflets had been drafted by the *Great World Studios Committee for Anti-British Persecution Struggle.* In his indignation he saw a big plot and he was going to root it out.

This had Chen Lo-wen very frightened. He had worked for Feng since before they fled Shanghai in 1950 for Hong Kong. He had suffered all the indignities Feng cast upon him and kept working. He did some of the best work of any Shanghai director in Hong Kong. But he had never made much money and he needed to work. Chen was ageing and was afraid of destitution in his old age. He had a large family of children to finish putting through school. But what Feng didn't yet know about the venerable movie director, nor did any of us, was that Chen had been leading a secret intellectual life. Under a pseudonym he had been writing a column on Marxist thought for the Communist newspaper *Wen Wei Pao,* and he had attended Communist lectures at Pui Kiu Middle School. He had been seated at a rally in the Silver Theatre in Kwun Tong when the police raided it and closed it just a few weeks before. Now Chen was terrified that Feng was going to find out about his attendance and cast him out of the fold.

Feng had personally interviewed everyone in the film lab and was beginning to interview everyone in the art and scenery department, then he was going to work his way down through the front office. He started to sort out the actors, picking through them like an enraged grocer searching for a rotten smell in the vegetable baskets. *"Did she have anything to do with this sabotage?"* he asked them. The "she" was understood by everyone. Becky, defector to China, humiliater of husbands, it was her. She was pulling unseen strings and lashing out at Feng. The performers expressed their frantic loyalty to Feng, although some of the bolder older actresses who were too eager to retire from the burdens of sixteen-hour days at the studio offered him criticisms, as if they were tempting him to tear up their contracts. They said that he was being paranoid and that any trouble at the studio was just spill-over from the streets outside, more like a political fashion than the epidemic of evil he was looking for. One of them told him to go take an aspirin. Another, even more desirous of leaving his employ, told him to go take a shit.

He would not hear their contempt. And if you remember that Feng's Golden Heaven studio in Shanghai had been confiscated by the Communists after they came to power, one could appreciate that he had practical reasons to be concerned. Yet his sense of betrayal, that his own employees would draw pictures of him as a rat and then post them inside *his* studio, had blinded him to reason.

One of the contract actors, whom Chen had stopped using in his pictures because he considered him to be supremely untalented, settled a score. He told Feng that Chen was a Communist and that he wrote for *Wen Wei Pao*. *"Go ask the paper, check him out,"* he said. I learned afterward that Feng called Chen into his office and interrogated him for an hour. Miss Chin was in on it. She sat in a chair by the window, took notes or glowered at Chen. By Chen's own account Feng did everything but make him kneel and confess to crimes. He accused Chen of having slandered him, of having deluded and brainwashed his wife into leaving him and, worst of all, he accused him of betrayal. Chen said almost nothing in his defence, so guilty was he made to feel. At the end of the hour, Feng demanded that Chen make a choice.

"Whom do you support?" he asked Chen in Shanghanese. *"Whom do you support? The Communists or me? Tell me now and I will save you,"* Feng said.

Chen took a long time to answer. *"I support you. I have worked hard for you all these years because I support you."*

"Then you renounce Communism, and you admit that you brainwashed my wife into defecting to the Mainland."

It was a compound accusation and Chen immediately denied the latter half. *"No! Never!"* he shouted.

Feng took that to be a refusal to renounce the former half of the accusation and thus he had found the enemy. Feng told

Chen that he was personally responsible for having disrupted Great World production for a day. He said that Chen was personally responsible for Becky's defection to the Mainland. He said that Chen was a dangerous traitor and could not be tolerated. He fired him on the spot. A thirty-year partnership was over instantly.

This was not a moment of passion Feng later regretted. The following week he would bar Chen for life from the studio property and would never speak to him again. He even forbade small film companies that rented Great World studios overnight to use Chen as a director. He completely turned his back on his longest-serving employee.

I admit that, as wretched as the end of Chen Lo-wen's career at Great World was, it did not preoccupy me for more than a few minutes when I heard of it. During this time, my mind was so disorganized that I felt I was wading through a dark, steadily deepening pond. I did my job automatically, filing newspaper stories, serious and ridiculous. I went out every evening to nightclubs or parties. I had received a summons to give testimony at the trial of Jack Rudman and two other policemen for manslaughter. It would be my duty to tell the court what I saw Jack Rudman do on the morning of the riot in San Po Kong. The Crown would expect me to sit in the witness box and look at Jack in the prisoner's box and recount how he bludgeoned some hapless slob to death because he was struck with fury and grief that another policeman had been downed by a gasoline bomb. I had to face the man I was so very much in love with and condemn him. And so I spent nights, without the warmth and reliability of my old pal and confidante, Becky Chan, with no one to talk to except strangers and friends I did not care for. I had nothing familiar to cling to except empty mechanical acts.

The China Telegraph
Reds punish would-be escapees

Communist troops in San On District have been arresting people trying to sneak into Hongkong.

According to arrivals from Canton, the border guards on the Chinese side have intercepted escapees and turned them over to Red Guards in Canton. There, the Red Guards parade them through the streets carrying placards with the words: "I am a rebel against cultural revolution."

The Red Guards force them to wear tall paper hats and carry brass gongs which they must strike to draw attention to their public humiliation.

– PAUL HAUER

My American friend, Arden, took me out to a do her public relations firm had set up. It was a "chuck-wagon night" for Trans-World Airlines. She asked me along because she knew I needed cheering up. Arden knew that Becky had gone to China and she assumed that I was pining for her. She did not know that I would have to give key testimony in a manslaughter trial a few days later. Arden had been interested in me first but when I showed no more interest than pally friendship, she seemed to come to an understanding and accepted her role generously and with all the easy-going mirth that Becky used to have.

Arden's firm, Feltus and Robinson, had organized the chuck-wagon night to introduce TWA's new Asia passenger-sales manager to Hong Kong travel agents. Arden's people had transformed a banquet room at the Hilton with bales of real hay flown to the colony from the United States in the belly of a TWA 707. Barn board covered part of the Hilton's flocked wallpaper, and there were spurs and lassos hung from nails. A TWA man greeted each guest with a complementary straw cowboy hat. Most of the women in high-crown hairdos declined to wear them. Arden took me aside to survey the crowd and pointed out people she thought would make a good social note for the *China Telegraph.*

"Look at that woman's dress," Arden said. "Look closely at the pattern." It was a white dress with little red figures on it. And if you looked closely you realized that the red bits were crabs. "That woman's dress is covered in crabs," Arden said. We had a laugh over that, and I felt relief for a second. The woman in crabs listened with almost religious devotion to the passenger-sales agent's speech. When he was done, his TWA staff gave authentic cowboy whoops and crab woman applauded through her white gloves. Arden introduced me to her. She was the wife of another TWA executive who had just relocated to Hong Kong from the States and she had a clench-jawed, strangled way of speaking, as if her throat were besieged by a deadly allergic reaction. I asked her for a quote and she rambled about how the chuck-wagon night made her feel just like she was back home in the USA. A kind of clammy pride overcame her, as if the chuck-wagon party really meant something to her. She assured me that she was very happy to be in Hong Kong. "I've seen the bathrooms here," she said through her teeth, "and they're just fine." It was the only quote I could get and I would have loved to have used it.

Benson Fung, the editorial cartoonist for the *China Telegraph,* took us out for supper on one of the dinner boats that cruised around the Causeway Bay typhoon shelter. The dinner boats were nothing more than sampans with tables in the middle and plastic chopsticks with bowls. You ordered food from cooks who floated around the shelters in other sampans. They fried up food on gas-rings while you waited. There was even a beer boat that sold big quart bottles of San Miguel. We were heavily into them all evening and I recall that because there was no washroom on a sampan, we simply relieved ourselves off the side. I remember Benson, very drunk, wobbling ominously on the edge of the dinner boat, urinating while singing heartily a dirty Cantonese version of "Three Coins in the Fountain."

*"Three queers in the men's room,
Each one seeking happiness!"*

I was so sick of Hong Kong at that moment. Every encounter, whether I was working on stories for the paper or I was out on the town, only seemed more unreal and appalling than the last. The British woman, a wife-of, listened to me at a party with her chin placed on her knuckles, looking very intent. You could never be quite sure whether she was listening to you or BBC short-wave coming in on her earrings. I met naive British and French academics on their way into China to celebrate the Cultural Revolution. Even when the Communists threw them out for being totally useless, these silly men and women came back from China with Mao caps and jackets (purchased at big mark-ups) with praise for everything they'd seen. They cheerfully explained away atrocities as either justified or extravagant lies. There were other nightmarish people too. I almost stepped on a double-walleyed beggar on Nathan Road who stared upward with unseeing white eyes, his tale of tragic abandonment written in chalk on the sidewalk in front of him by a confederate. A British sailor on shore leave turned up in front of me in Tsimshatsui at three in the morning, completely naked, very drunk and weirdly out of control. I had to do a report on a sea-borne invasion of tailor-shop touts who shimmied up the ropes of the cruise ship President Wilson when it docked at the Ocean Terminal in Kowloon. The touts flooded over the decks haranguing frightened tourists with aggressive demands to visit their tailor shops. I saw an electrified expression on a woman shopping in Jardine's Bazaar when a six-pound rat, panicked by the crowds around it, ran right up her skirt during a dash for cover.

I went to the Cellar Bar at the Ambassador Hotel and ran into two Chinese friends, both of them travel agents and both of them uncomfortably fey. One had given himself the English name Dandy and the other made a trivial patriotic point of sticking to his Chinese given name, Yiu-ming. They had just watched a drinking contest sponsored by Sapporo Breweries and were giddy from rooting for all the big Caucasian contestants making pigs of themselves with beer. (The winner scarfed down five bottles in fifty-nine seconds and was now being very ill in the washroom.) A high-spirited Filipina singer named Dimple Ding Ding joined the combo in the corner of the lounge and sang "An Occasional Man."

"CPA!" Dandy shouted at me when I went over to him and Yiu-ming. "CPA! Do you know what it stands for?"

"Canadian Pacific Airlines," I said.

"No! Can't Promise Anything!"

They'd coined new and unflattering meanings for airline abbreviations on the ferry ride over from their agency in Alexandra House. Yiu-ming had one. "CAAC: Cancel At All Costs!"

"Do you know what Lufthansa stands for?" Dandy said. "Let Us Fuck The Hostess And the New Steward's Ass!"

Benoit Ng came in the Cellar Bar. He was wearing his wine-coloured beret, a white shirt and dark trousers. He looked about to see if any friends were there. He saw me and rushed back out.

I was sickened a few days later to see news photos come in from the previous night. They were so shocking we couldn't use them in the paper. One showed a Scottish policeman who had pulled at a suspicious airline bag left in Yee On Street in Causeway Bay and tried to get it off the tram tracks. He was trying to put a string on it and drag it off the rails. A bomb exploded and tore both his legs right off. There was a photo of him there with dark splinters for legs. He died later. The other was of a man holding his three-year-old daughter. She had found a Communist bomb and unwittingly played with it. You could only just make out that what the man was holding was human. The killing of the little girl was the beginning of the end for the public's forbearance of the Communists in Hong Kong. Even the Communists now realized they had gone too far.

Somebody at the Foreign Correspondents' Club started a rumour about young Chinese boys' "cherries" being auctioned to rich Europeans, among others, at secret parties. Instead of leggy Chinese women in cheong sams, the hostesses in this story were perfumed naked boys. Some of the "buyers" were so well-known that they wore silk masks across their mouths and dark glasses to conceal their identity. In this rumour, the boys came from poor refugee families who received a premium for young males over what they could get if they sold off a sister. The whole story was baloney, but oh did it make those round blue eyes go wide. European residents of Hong Kong, long inured to the exotic colour of the Far East that so attracted tourists, were totally vulnerable to imagined sexual hi-jinks. The reality was a world in which there were few private places for men to go to, resulting in, at best, furtive glances and quick pawings in semi-public places.

One such place was Yuk Tak Chee, to which I resorted frequently in the days after Becky disappeared. Yuk Tak Chee was just another shophouse in Mongkok, but it had an enormous, lovely green and red neon sign out front, by far the property's biggest asset. The place was usually the exclusive preserve of Chinese men. Some were straight men who went for the steam, others were looking for sex. They had entered into unhappy, joyless marriages out of duty, the kind of nuptials that Benoit had been expected to embrace. They passed through their lives quietly, their only moments of reality spent in Yuk Tak Chee. Inside the bathhouse, the twenty-foot-wide building housed a basement swimming pool, which was really more of an ambitious bathtub. The lockers were clustered around a wooden desk presided over by an old man in a white tunic and black skull cap with the specialized aesthetic of a big mole on one cheek with four long wiry hairs hanging down about eight inches. Yuk Tak Chee was full of drowsy men in towels. Those who paid for a massage retreated to glassed-in rooms and lay on green leatherette tables that had holes in one end where you sank your face when you were on your stomach. Some reclined in orange leatherette easy chairs affecting the air of potentates and submitted to pedicures. Others reached out and touched one another in dark alcoves to get the fire out of their systems and go home to their cramped flats full of children, brothers, sisters, grannies and granddads.

The Vietnam war brought two kinds of Americans to Hong Kong: officials to preach the government position and soldiers on leave.

Feng and the Rotary club and the Lions clubs and the U.S. consulate were always having Washington shills to lunch. They hosted film nights in the U.S. Information Service auditorium in Duddell Street, where you could sit through thrillers such as *Minnesota – Star of the North* presented in English or *Basic Principles of Power Reactors* in Cantonese. Or something tiresome and pious about the Vietnam war itself, something with a lot of colour photography of whooping helicopters that offered the viewer nothing unless he were an eleven-year-old boy. American Rotarians came to lecture their Oriental counterparts about democracy; their wives came with them to shop. Becky had been obliged to dine with several of these women. "Are Chinese children fussy eaters?" asked one crushingly sincere young wife in a pale lime dress. "Well of course, they wouldn't be," she said, answering her own question. "They have so little to eat they'd grateful for what they could get." She was surprised that Feng's wife was a Chinese movie star. "My, you certainly must have an interesting life over here."

As for the ordinary Americans, the sailors, the soldiers, the airmen, it fell to the girls in overpriced sex bars of Tsimshatsui and men on the pavement like me to keep them entertained. Every night you would see the American sailors in the streets of Tsimshatsui, hungry game fish rendered goofy and injudicious by warm waters, looking for sex with young Chinese men. The lonely boys from big cities and small towns, the gangs of antic inebriates, the over-masculine non-commissioned officers who were looking for other over-masculine men, the fatherly figures who came looking for young Mister Butterflies.

In the panic days before Rudman's trial, I played a very dangerous game. I brought home a big heterosexual brute on the promise that I could line him up with two yummy Chinese "hostesses" for five U.S. dollars. The American was drunk and he took the bait. When we reached my flat in Paterson Street, I picked up the phone and dialled my own number then held the phone to his ear. "It's busy," I said. "We'll have to wait." I poured him a big Scotch and gave him a couple of pornographic magazines that featured nude Chinese women. He got drunker and hornier and I kept phoning my own telephone number. Finally, he was so far gone he let me have my way with him. Well, if Feng Hsiao-foon used to get cinema owners to back his early movies by getting them drunk and flogging a flimsy script, why shouldn't I use the same technique? We got what we wanted.

Booze was beginning to be a problem with me. It had killed my first managing editor at the *China Telegraph*, Mr. Trebilcoe. He had been a warning about the state of being without wife, home and family. Now I feared becoming like him, a lost soul drifting downward. Mr. Trebilcoe would open a new gin bottle in the newsroom first thing in the morning, breathe deeply of its vapours and affect a joke about bibulous Irishmen by adopting an accent. "Takes me back to my childhood," he'd lilt. No joke could distance him from the reality that he was a drunk. Mr. Trebilcoe used to reflect on his own youth, back when he still had hope he could turn things around, back when he still cared enough to wipe his armpits before going out to lunch with important people. I felt much more empathy for poor old Mr. Trebilcoe. It was frightening.

I called Feng Hsiao-foon's office to hear if he had learned anything about his wayward wife. I couldn't get past Miss Chin who demanded more information from me than she was willing to give about Feng. I hung up on her in a pique. The whole lot of them had me fed up, Feng, his secretary and Becky. At that moment I began to think how much better life would be without her around, without her ambient melancholy, her hobby of rehabilitation from imagined chronic diseases, the encumbrances of her marriage to Feng. I didn't care if she married Chou En-lai. "It's not as if I had anything at stake," I muttered to my shaving mirror. "I never wanted to marry her." I knew everything changed when she had the baby. It was the beginning of the end of our friendship when she got pregnant. I was going to be replaced. Well, that was fine by me.

It was probably good for her too. It would put another person directly between her and Feng, and not an outsider like me.

Feng never got over his suspicion that I had made him a cuckold. Becky would be able to devote her familial affections to the infant and not waste them on a husband who had demanded that she marry him as a condition for returning to Great World Studios when her Hollywood career flamed out. She got her job back and he got a beautiful wife, a prestige performer and an employee who worked for free. He also expected her to provide him with a male heir. Feng could have learned a lesson about the hazards of male heirs from me. What a bust I turned out to be as a male heir. My father wouldn't even say good-bye to me at the railway station when I left Winnipeg forever. The dog, old Duke, subbed for him. I never went back to Canada, not even for my parents' funerals. True to the sexual invert's contrarian form, I had fled in terror from Canada, a country to which thousands of terrified foreigners fled.

In the days before Jack Rudman's trial I couldn't bear to go home at night. I spent far too much money in hotel lounges and nightclubs. I saw the Archdale Sisters twice in the Eagle's Nest in the Hilton. I used the excuse of the unveiling of a solid copper dance floor at the Miramar Hotel to spend the entire evening there getting hammered on free drinks on condition that I did a story in the *Telegraph*. I wrote a glowing report. There was a sense of global unreality in Hong Kong's clubs and rooms. El Trio Los Chambelanes appeared in the Dragon Boat Bar at the Hilton with a happily hollered greeting: "*Buenos aires, amigos!* We sing for you!" I wrote a gusher about the big-name acts who had appeared recently at the Button Club atop the Mandarin Hotel in return for unlimited Johnnie Walker.

I went to The Scene, the new discotheque in the basement of the Peninsula Hotel, but it was too noisy for me. Three Western teenaged girls, who styled themselves the Telstar Dancers, were performing their whining theme song. There were affluent young Western tourists on the dance floor and in the banquettes around the edges, next to the fake Chinese junk the Pen had installed as part of a nautical decor, was an almost invisible stag line of Chinese men. The Chinese guys had blown several weeks' savings on admission and a glass of Coke for the chance to look around for dates, and they weren't looking for women.

The China Telegraph

Troubadours off to the South Pole

German folk singers Ernst Luehr and Manfred Mueller end their Hongkong engagement this week before heading to Saigon to entertain Australian troops. Next month they will appear in Australia and then continue to New Zealand and Antarctica to entertain scientific missions there. They hope to appear at the South Pole – the first entertainers ever to make the trip to the bottom of the world.

–PAUL HAUER

I picked up a story from the police over the phone about a middle-aged Japanese tourist who suddenly snapped in the lobby of the Hongkong Hilton. He accused his tour guide of stealing his jewelry and started hitting everyone around him. It took fifteen minutes to subdue him. He was brought down like a bonkers animal: three Sikh security guards sitting on him while the hotel doctor pumped tranquilizers into his arm with a syringe. They packed him off to Queen Mary Hospital for observation. And he wasn't the only one to go barking mad. A British couple attacked a policeman in the Star Ferry concourse. The missus threw her shoe and the mister tried to beat him up. At the Waterfront Police Station she started slugging more coppers and, to inflame things further, she removed her skirt and was about to drop her knickers before she was restrained. In the past, I would have viewed these people as odd and entertaining fodder. Now I had a new empathy for them.

Eventually, I had to go home at the end of evenings, much as I dreaded it. I would be there alone with my thoughts. When I got off the elevator on my floor, the neighbours, women in grey and brown day-pyjamas, were conversing in Cantonese in the uncarpeted hall. Their raucous complaints about some trivial daily event echoed back and forth on the tiled walls. I went into my flat and switched on the air conditioner, which I'd inherited from a previous tenant. It was elderly and clicked grudgingly several times before obliging. My little sitting room had a kind of sectional made out of three curving pieces, all of them upholstered in red leatherette with buttons on the seat backs that were beginning to pop out spontaneously. I'd be lying in bed at night and I'd hear a little popping sound as the sectional released another button and the next morning find the seat more dishevelled than before. I used to have an olive green rug to go with it but it rotted in summer humidity so I replaced it with a reed mat I bought at the China Goods Emporium, a Communist-owned department store in North Point. The mat did its best to trap great mounds of dust and grit blown in the window. At the end of each summer I used a trowel to scoop it all up. The bathroom was tiled in hospital green. The matching green toilet had long ago ceased to function correctly, so I ran a rubber hose from the basin faucet to the toilet tank for refilling. For days without running water, I kept a huge olive-green plastic water barrel next to the toilet in which I floated an old pot for refilling the tank. On the wall was a water heater with gas jets that sprang to life whenever I took a shower. Beside the heater was a paper sticker from the Town Gas company depicting a cartoon lady in a dressing robe who reminded me in Chinese and English never to forget the "open-window rule." (In Hong Kong you had to bathe with the bathroom window open, even during frigid winters, lest carbon monoxide from the gas heater build up and leave you a well-scrubbed corpse.) I pulled back a heavy cotton curtain that limited the air-conditioned air to the living and bed room and went out to the kitchen. It stank. The garbage pail, lined with newspapers, was heaping. The porcelain sink was full of dirty dishes and coffee mugs, just as I had left them for the past several days while the water supply was cut off. I turned on the tap, but the faucet allowed only an urgent gasp and a single drop of water. It was not my neighbourhood's day for water and I had, as usual, forgotten to fill another plastic barrel in the kitchen that I'd bought to store water for the off days. Over by the window, an enormous cockroach was airborne and looking for a place to light. I yanked the casement window shut to prevent it getting in. There was one bottle of Carlsberg left in the refrigerator, nothing else, so I took it out to the front room and sat down on the leatherette sectional. I found an errant red button next to me, considered it and put it on a small glass-covered end table, next to three others.

Alone, I had to think about what I was going to do. I just didn't know. My old pal Becky couldn't advise me. I would never see her again. Obviously I couldn't speak to Jack. I hadn't communicated with him since the day of the incident. I admit that I had picked up the telephone several times and put my finger in the hole for the number three, the first digit of his number, then hung up. Jack and the other two policemen were out on their own recognizance and the Crown prosecutor had instructed me not to talk with him or the police lawyers. The closest I got, and I admit that it was a pathetic thing to do, was to trail Jack and the co-accused constables to a shrine for Kwan Ti, the Chinese god of righteousness and loyalty. I just wanted to watch him bow before the statue of Kwan Ti, with its long black cement beard and red enamel lips. Jack lit some joss sticks and clapped his hands three times. Here was the devoted man, the man I loved. Now I was to condemn him with testimony that would send him to prison and out of the Hong Kong Police forever. He would hate me (why shouldn't he?) and I would never see him again.

When Jack and the other cops left, I so hoped that Jack would turn his head just a little and notice me out of the corner of his eye. He never did, or at least not in a way that I could see. But police were good with indirection, as Jack frequently told me, and he probably caught sight of me through the cunning exploitation of a wall-mounted mirror or even a polished red pillar.

I had run out of strength. Suddenly I burst into loud, convulsing tears at the window of my apartment, unconcerned if the neighbours outside could see me through the window. I hunched against the wall, my clenched fists up against my face like a bewildered boxer. I'd had a realization: for the first time in my life I saw just how close to oblivion I was. It was a very sudden understanding, it came to me belatedly: that by standing in front of freight trains on bridges, contemplating jumping into Niagara Falls and pursuing the love of a policeman, I was a dreadful, deranged man. I was like someone who's been walking along the edge of a cliff on a moonless night and had suddenly realized the peril he's been in all along. The difference with me was that I knew that I could not flee the danger of going over.

SIXTEEN

Jack Rudman's trial was held at the North Kowloon Magistracy. There had been a big demonstration there a few days before. Leftists had attempted to storm the building to release colleagues being detained on public mischief charges. They plastered the building with big-character posters calling for the lynching of Governor Trench and death to all Chinese "dogs" who ran with the imperialists. After the police dispersed the demonstration with tear gas, there was a lot of debris left over: cloth banners, leaflets, arm bands, women's shoes, a pair of trousers, one handbag and a glass eyeball.

But on the day that Jack's trial began, it was peaceful, the demonstrators had moved on to other government buildings. The trial date was only a few weeks after the alleged crime. Back then, court calendars were uncrowded and justice was efficient and uncomplicated. At the magistracy, cops stood on the front steps, waiting to go in. I arrived with several reporters who were covering the trial. My editors had obviously excused me from this one. Among the coppers was the Deputy Commissioner of Police of the Administration Wing who'd come as an observer. He was from Hong Kong Police headquarters in Arsenal Street, an address that always brought a smirk to the faces of the ordinary cops in the Uniformed Branch. I also glimpsed Soutar, the cop who had come to my flat in Causeway Bay to pressure me. He was smoking his pipe and looking at me intently, making sure that I saw him, and more importantly who he had with him – Benoit Ng.

Benoit stood there in a sports jacket and stingray sunglasses, looking at his shoes, no doubt wishing he was elsewhere, up a stepladder in an outlying branch of the Chartered Bank wiring up Reditune speakers, scarfing pastries in the Place Véndome in Paris, trolling the furniture department in Eaton's in Montreal, anywhere but on the steps of the magistracy, being a Chinese dog running at the heels of the British police. I hadn't talked to Benoit since the night he spoke against me to Soutar. Indeed, we would never speak to one another again, too angry, ashamed and frightened as both of us were.

My editors told me to take a week's leave of absence during the trial. I had filed my last story the day before the trial.

The China Telegraph
Sex-change starlets among dead in BOAC horror

Five cabaret artistes who had been slated to perform their "Bonsoir Carrousel de Paris" show at Hongkong's Mocambo nightclub died in Saturday's BOAC jet disaster at Bangkok. The quintet were all former men who had changed their sex and gone into show business.

The ill-fated entertainers were, with their stage names in parentheses: Conilade Vincent (Kismie) 23, French; Loie Morvan (Lady Cobra) 26, French; Christian Roman (Christine) 33, French; P. Schmiell (Coco) 26, German; and C. Spencer (Sonne Teal) 37, American.

It was hard not to think of Jack. He once bought me a long-playing record that I had been searching for, a collection of songs by the great French singer Fréhel. When her lover, Maurice Chevalier, dumped her for the charismatic *chanteuse* Mistinguett, Fréhel attempted suicide then left for Eastern Europe. The booze and Eastern food got to her and she returned to Paris thirteen years later much the worse for wear. She also brought back an annoying

new style of singing that nobody went for. Fréhel died in a Pigalle
boarding house, alone and forgotten. Jack didn't get my inherent
interest in her but he made a thing of presenting it to me one hot
summer night in an open-air restaurant in Yaumatei. It was at a
time when I'd thought he'd completely lost interest in me. I asked
him to sign the back of the liner but he declined, ostensibly because
it would reduce the resale value of the record, but I couldn't help
wonder if he was avoiding a trail of evidence.

He only came alive on the beat. I saw him show rare rapport
with those tiny lost Chinese children, speaking to them in a light
voice, in sing-songy Cantonese that won their trust. I saw him
work telephones, pace the San Po Kong neighbourhood asking
the locals if they knew anyone missing a child and finally track-
ing down the parents, who were both slaving in knitwear factories and had no idea their little one had gone astray. He'd give the
child a small toy from a collection the station had in a drawer in
a metal filing cabinet. It made the sort of story that reporters like
me loved to put out in the Sunday edition and middle-class sen-
timentalists like me ate up with their breakfast. And I saw him
club to death a demonstrator who was directly responsible for
nothing more than throwing a few stones. A policeman's lot is
not an 'appy one.

Sometimes I got so fed up with Rudman's stories of his constabulary duties – always talking wearily about how he and the
men had to scrape up the dirty stuff from the streets: the petty
criminals, the domestic murderers, the bodies crushed by runaway trucks that came slamming down that steep grade at the end
of the Chai Wan Road in Shaukeiwan. It was the wearying
reportage of a mother starving for love but pushing it away with
floods of complaints about how much she suffers for her family.
He just did it to sound important and substantial and I got so
bloody sick of it, and him.

Jack stood in the prisoners' dock with Constables Li Kwai and
Wong Kai-yu to hear the charges. Jack wore a grey wool suit

which had been made at the Ambassador Tailors, a shop that took its name from the Great World cinema in whose arcade it was situated. That was the shop all the coppers went to. They always asked for the same suit, so Sammy Lo, the chief tailor, kept a supply of half-made, smaller sizes to fit Chinese constables and bigger ones for the European men. Li and Wong had similar suits. Jack looked completely sensible and stolid in his Ambassador suit and he stood there with his hawkish look, his wavy hair neatly combed and oiled.

The judge sat beneath the coat of arms of the British Crown Colony of Hong Kong, a lion and a dragon rampant. The judge, the defence lawyers and the Crown prosecutors wore powder wigs and black robes. At the front of the public gallery there were reporters from *Sing Tao, Tin Tin Yat Po, The Commercial News, South China Morning Post* and the *China Telegraph*. I sat midway back.

The court heard that the victim, Kwok Chan, had worked in an illegal lard-boiling factory at 220 Tung Choi Street in Mongkok, a vile place that gave off smoke and stinks day and night and gave local residents endless offence. Lawyers for the defendants tried to transfer the transgressions of the lard-boiling factory onto the victim, as if it was a proving ground for menacing criminals. Kwok had a brief career as an Ah-fei; he had previously been charged with vandalism after he had thrown a pole soaked in kerosene under a Kowloon Motor Bus to earn five dollars from an agitator. The bus drove off and left the pole behind. No harm done.

A forensic pathologist who had examined Kwok's body said that he had suffered a fractured skull and internal hemorrhaging as a result of many blows to the head, as well as bruising on the face and legs. Then an ambulance attendant testified that when he arrived at San Po Kong police station he found Kwok face down at the bottom of the stairs leading to the lockup, his head turned awkwardly to one side. He testified that the police recorded that Kwok had run down the steps during the melee in the report room, tripped and fell to the bottom on his head.

The Crown prosecutor, a man called Culley, had extremely poor eyesight. A tall man with dark hair, he needed thick glasses to see distances and a second pair of thick glasses to read with. So when he read his notes he wore one pair and when he looked up at the witnesses or the magistrate, he took that pair off and put the other ones on. It became quite tedious watching him switch spectacles constantly and it made me anxious. It was probably supposed to make me anxious.

Culley spent a great deal of time asking a police official about the course of Jack's career. Jack had begun, like every policeman, as a patrol constable in the Uniformed Branch. It was entered into the record that Rudman had, in 1962, placed first in a class of twenty-six police officers from a dozen Commonwealth countries in a police work course at the Metropolitan Police Training School at Hendon in Britain. The Inspector General of the Colonial Police awarded Rudman the Baton of Honour for his keen performance in studying criminal detection and criminal law. Jack had returned to Hong Kong and, following service in the Criminal Investigation Division in Kowloon East subdivision, applied to serve in the Emergency Unit, even though CID records showed him to be a promising criminal investigator. Culley wanted to know why Jack asked to transfer to the Emergency Unit, which was one of the roughest jobs a policeman could do? The answer came simply: "personal differences with CID staff." Culley read a police memo reprimanding Jack for some disagreeable conduct in a meeting which would have meant nothing until it was introduced in a trial. Then Culley took his reading glasses off and put on his distance glasses and repeated questions to the police official about Jack's reliability. He was searching for something to prove that Jack was disorderly, possibly violent. He was so far off the beam it should have been amusing. The official held his ground. Whatever Jack was in his private life, whatever outrage that represented to the CID, he was still enough of a policeman for his mates to rally round him at his trial. They weren't going to let the Crown cloud Rudman's reputation by suggesting that he was a bad copper.

Three days later I was called to testify before the court. There is, sometimes, one moment in your life that suddenly makes you. This was to be my moment. I was surprised at how quickly it was over.

The court heard about my career as a newspaper reporter in Hong Kong, undistinguished but steady. They heard of the single year I had spent working for Feng Hsiao-foon at Great World. The Crown made a point with my curriculum vitae of showing that I was likely to tell things accurately. Culley asked me to recount the circumstances of the morning of Friday, July 28, 1967, right from the time I got up in the morning. He asked why I had gone to Kowloon from my newsroom in Central. I said I'd been given a story to do on a possible disturbance at San Po Kong. I did not mention that I wanted to talk to Jack about what he'd learned about what had happened to Becky Chan.

"Would you tell the court what you saw in the lockup on July 28?"

I gave enough of a pause to be credible. I stared at an Exit sign over the door at the rear of the courtroom and just let my mind drift along, as if I were bobbing on an inflatable mattress in a swimming pool. "I don't recall," I said.

The Crown prosecutor looked up and switched glasses again. His blurry eyes locked on to me in genuine surprise.

"What don't you recall?"

"Anything," I said. I spoke very slowly, for I did not wish to slip.

Culley gaped at me, his eyes enlarged through the lenses of his glasses. He stared for so long that the judge ordered him to continue. He looked back down at his notes.

"And yet you told the authorities," Culley paused to switch to his reading glasses, "that you saw Sergeant Rudman repeatedly beating a prisoner with a truncheon while PC Li and PC Wong held the prisoner in a chair. Did you not say that?"

"I do not recall."

There was a bit of conferencing that I failed to follow, such was my concentration. Culley then returned to the pursuit.

"Mr. Hauer, I submit to you that you have been intimidated by the police. I ask you, sir, has someone demanded that you change your testimony?"

Whether I glanced at Soutar I don't recall. I'm sure that I didn't, as I was merely bobbing about.

"No, sir. No one has approached me."

"Then how do account for these earlier statements you gave the police?"

"There had been a riot outside. I saw a police constable get torched by a gasoline bomb. There was a terrible crush inside the San Po Kong police station. I suppose I was upset, frightened and confused."

Culley switched eyeglasses and read lengthy portions of my statements to the police after the arrest of Rudman and his mates. It went on for about a minute then Culley switched eyeglasses and peered at me. "You, sir, are a newspaper reporter of nineteen years experience —"

"Eighteen years. I worked for one year as a publicist —"

"Eighteen years. You gave extensive detail in your comments to investigators. And you now say you were merely mistaken because of fright and confusion?"

"I didn't write a newspaper story, did I?" I said. "Nothing appeared in print even though I was in the station. Because I couldn't be sure of what took place."

"Then how do you explain the death of the victim?" Culley said, growing angry.

The policemen's lawyer interjected that his learned colleague was asking me to speculate. The two sides sparred, the judge relieved me of the request to speculate, but told me to consider very carefully my testimony, reminded me of the penalty for perjury. I showed great piety, but stuck to my lie. Culley got no further.

And so the trial ground to a halt. Beyond the coroner's report and a bit of forensic evidence that showed only how Kwok died, there was no one to testify what they had seen. The other police who had been present wouldn't. No prisoners who were in the lockup could be found to testify. They had vanished or had been warned to vanish. And so the judge directed the jury to return a verdict of not guilty, which they did, and it was over.

After the judge discharged Jack, I asked some of his copper pals if I could speak to him. They went off to ask permission from the court's barracks corporal. He came back and said, "They've gone." I asked them where I could find him and he said he didn't know.

So I called the San Po Kong Sub-District day after day until he finally agreed to take my call. We would meet at Conder's Restaurant for, as Rudman put it, "one last drink."

We never made it to Conder's. I went to the Unmarried Police Quarters ahead of time and met him in his flat. I wanted to be alone with him. He was clearly nervous about the idea. Jack always kept the venetian blinds in his sitting room open, even at night. He liked to watch the courtyards downstairs, the men coming and going, or impromptu volleyball games. Shirts vs. skins. But when I arrived that evening the blinds were completely shut.

Jack's single little room was very masculine, very tidy. He had hung reproduction paintings of trout and salmon, like pages out of one of Audubon's studies and there was a carefully arranged shelf of books, many by Daphne du Maurier. There was a bed against one wall with an olive-green spread over it, tucked very straight along the pillow line. It was in this room that I undertook what I now describe as "the lunge." I reached out and pulled Jack toward me, by the shoulders. He let me do it and, after hesitation to show me that he was thinking the better of it, returned the embrace. I could feel by the way his shoulders relaxed that it gave him the same relief it gave me. In fact, he put his palms on my face and kissed me, very sweetly and very long. There was a sigh, either of relief, surrender or weariness. Probably all. Then he tightened up and moved away. We sat down opposite one another, him on the edge of his bed and me in an easy chair, our hands on our knees, considering the carefully vacuumed rug.

We had smokes and a tot of brandy and talked rubbish for a long while. I talked about what I thought Governor Trench should be doing about the emergency. Jack talked about a fishing trip he was planning for Scotland when he went home on leave after the Communist disturbances subsided. We talked about the Star bowling lanes and about cricket test matches

"You see that picture of Catherina Ko in your paper?" he asked, referring to a Cantonese movie starlet who worked at Cathay. "It ran the other day. Somewhere inside. She went round to the Eastern station to visit the men on a morale booster." It was starting: calling fellow coppers "the men," the circumlocution about women. There is nothing more bankrupting than listening to one of us try to be one of them. "She wore a bikini and stood there for a photograph with a riot shield in front of her, and the riot shield covered the bikini so it looked like she was nude."

I held out my glass for more brandy. "Some fun," I said.

Rudman sighed again, ready to quarrel, but then he changed course, as if he wanted to be good to me for having saved him from twelve years inside Stanley Prison.

I tried to be nice too. "She did eighteen movies in six months," I said. "She'll be on crying jags and hoofing it out of town before long."

"Yeah," he said.

Then I worked up the nerve to ask the question indirectly. "Is there any room for me, Jack?"

Rudman started peering at something over my shoulder, as he so often did. It compelled me to turn around and look at his Baton of Honour from the Hendon police school, up on a shelf. I wanted to wince at this cheap effect, this little bit of melodrama.

"You lied to the court, mate," he said. "That's something you should never have done, even if you wanted to save me." I should have known better than to feel like a weakling male, a father who stands at the side of the wharf and watches another, braver man jump in and rescue his child from drowning. I should have known better but I didn't care; I fell right into the pit he dug. "A gentleman would have told the truth no matter what," he said. "I can't be associated with that kind of conduct." He looked at his baton again and I wanted to pick it up and hurl it out the window, watch it go whirling down into the ball court below, and hear it clatter on the pavement.

"I want to be a better policeman," he said. "I want to stay tight with my mates. And I want my pension, my retirement in Scotland and time to write my memoirs. And that means steering clear of blokes like you." He poked his finger in the air, as a substitute for my sternum. He was quite categorical and gave me the look of a controlled bearer of bad news, waiting for me to break down and sob like a woman so he could soldier along, bravely in control of matters. I regret to inform you, madam, that your husband has been killed in a traffic accident. I regret to inform you, sir, that I cannot have a homosexual love affair with you.

My brandy glass coddled in my hand, I sat very still for a while, saying nothing. Jack had the courtesy to let me have a bit of time. After that, we stood, shook hands all gentlemanly and polite, and it was over. The only time I ever saw Jack again was when he was in the streets in uniform or in bars down in Tsimshatsui. We acknowledged one another with a nod or a sunny, fake "hullo there," but neither of us wanted to say much. That was that.

SEVENTEEN

I started to drink more during the days that followed Rudman's trial. I did it to pass the time. At home at night, I stared out the window at the people in the other flats. The echoing sounds of Cantonese opera being broadcast over radio seemed to come from everywhere. Or I would go to the Mocambo nightclub in North Point. After the regular acts were done, after the regular patrons had all gone home – the tourists and the respectable Chinese and Western residents of Hong Kong – the entertainers, movie people, high-caste prostitutes, gigolos, reporters and other deviants came in.

I sat at the bar and watched for a while, waving to people I knew. Somebody sat down next to me and we started to chat. It got quite hilarious. The drunker I got, the faster I blabbed, like an auctioneer, going on about everything. I had a lot of incisive off-the-cuff suggestions for the colonial government on how to handle the left-wing disturbances. Shaw Brothers, Cathay and Great World could have learned a lot from my perspectives on marketing cheap entertainment to Third World audiences. And the United States had no idea what it was doing in Vietnam.

Then I got all personal and maudlin. I polled interchangeable drinking partners whether I should have stayed back in Canada and got a good job in the post-war boom there? Public relations in an aluminum corporation? Mining was huge back home, so was petroleum. People had a good life in Canada, incredibly good. Or, like so many other Western hacks in the Far East, I should have moved on to another city as soon as I got stale in Honkers. Guys in Hong Kong who turned mouldy shifted to Thailand to work on the *Bangkok Post* or the *World*. They shunted along the informal Asian circuit between Tokyo and India and down to New Guinea and Australia. Now I had a hankering to work for the *Borneo Bulletin*. It was analogous to the low orbit used by entertainers in the Far East. The brightest spot, Saigon, was the big-money place. Entertainers made a lot of money getting booked into Saigon in the 1960s, four times what they could in Hong Kong. So could newsmen. There was so much money in Saigon and there was real action to satisfy a newspaperman. A real newspaperman. Not a slob like me. I wasn't a decent man; I was an unsavoury loser and a Criminal Sessions liar. Drag artiste Princess Tam-Tam was on stage at the Mocambo when I started to cry for the third time. "Remember everyone, practice makes perverts!" and she launched into a double-time version of "Sing You Sinners."

It was an okay thing to do, to sit in mental disarray at the bar and babble to strangers, since the Mocambo was often filled with other late-nighters grappling with unregulated neuroses. This, at least, was a kind of peach-garden brotherhood for me. Jack Rudman could stay with his effing coppers. Benoit Ng had once told me that I needed to get married and have children. Then, he'd said, I would have a family of my own, and everything would be all right. At this point in my life I had to agree. Something had to happen.

I rolled home, one night with an American service man, the next with a British tourist. The American proved too rough when he drank. He kept banging on doors of the other flats in my building, broke a brandy glass in my kitchen, his playful punches were a bit too hard. In the bathroom, he could not urinate unless he ran the water in the sink, and since water was being rationed he was in agony. I had to walk him back to the liberty ferry because he said he couldn't remember the way and he was getting belligerent. The lapping of the water against Fenwick Pier stimulated him and he finally relieved himself with an immense sigh onto a moored sampan. He carried a Bombay taxi horn, which he'd bought at Cost Plus, and he honked its rubber bulb at weary Chinese labourers coming home from work. For his part, the British tourist had prodigious flatulence and vomited in the elevator of my building after he got really plastered.

Other nights I would just go home alone, drink a bit more, then fall asleep. I got along.

In the fall of 1966, Feng Hsiao-foon had invited me and a few other friends, Westerners and Chinese comfortable with Westerners, to a dinner at the Eagle's Nest in the Hilton. He had been hosting a series of these evenings. We were the last and least illustrious group to whom he wanted to show off his Paul Harris Fellowship, which the North Kowloon Rotary Club had given him. I scrounged up Arden Davis to serve as my female date as there was to be dancing afterward. We were introduced to two Australian television performers who'd been booked into the Eagle's Nest, Dawn Dixon and Terry Holden. They were gratifyingly informal, over the top with their jokes and blissfully incognizant of the tensions that informed Feng Hsiao-foon's evenings out. They could not see the glances, the carefully chosen words, the gestures Feng made to test responses, all the while giving away none of his own feelings. The Australians blew it by not knowing or even pretending to care what a Paul Harris Fellowship was.

When the De-La-Rue Folies came on, Becky took me into the bar for a talk. She ordered Coca-Cola and asked for sugar cubes. "I want you to congratulate me," she said. She dropped the sugar cubes into the Coke and jabbed at them with a spoon to break them up. The bartender watched, fascinated. Becky said: "I'm going to have a baby."

I had to put down my drink and look out the window. From the Eagle's Nest on the top floor of the Hilton, you could look down on the mainland Bank of China across Queen's Road Central, festooned with huge portraits of Mao Tse-tung on three sides. A slogan along the roof declared in Chinese: *"Mao Tse-tung's Thought Opens the Gate to the Engine of Life!"*

Becky glanced at me, curious about why I withheld a response. Her news, had it come from anyone else, would have been a joyful announcement, lots of hugs for Westernized Chinese women and handshakes for the proud daddy. But I didn't see the happiness. I just saw a jumble of motives. "Why are you having a kid?" I asked.

"Because I want one," she said, too hard and pressed flat even to pretend at maternal joy. She stared at her Coke as she twirled the spoon in it.

"Are you going to give it up?"

She didn't answer for a long time. She chit-chatted with the bartender who asked why she put sugar in her Coke. Finally she replied, "I see that you're trying to ruin this evening for me."

I was so exasperated with her. We had been through with idiotic marriages, her illnesses, her ruined career in the United States, her use of me. Now a baby was going to be one more set piece.

"Is the baby going to —" I stopped, for I was about to ask her if she expected the baby would cure her of all her troubles. She reminded me of Jack Rudman's story about a superstitious woman in Wanchai who was found in bed with a couple of hired children strapped to her body because she believed she could transfer leprosy out of her body into theirs.

Becky suggested that I didn't like children and I awkwardly denied it, the way single men do. We spent more time at the bar in silence than talking. Finally I said, "I hope that the baby doesn't replace me as your friend."

"Oh no," she said.

"I've made such an investment —" Again I caught myself from suggesting outright that I had listened to her neuroses for so many years and now she was putting me aside for a new little friend, maybe a miniature duplicate of herself, upon whom she could transfer all her cares and terrors.

Dickie Forsythe, a television comic who was in Hong Kong as part of British Week, was on the stage when we returned from the bar: "Our mother superior gathers the young nuns about her and announces ever so gravely, 'Sisters, a case of syphilis has been found in the convent.'"

We sat down, each of us stone-faced, and the others at our table had the sense not to pry.

"From the back of the group one not-so-swift novice pipes up: 'It'll make a nice change from Beaujolais!'"

When Amanda was born in early 1967, Becky surprised me with her abilities as a mother. By this, I don't mean that she stood in a sunlit window with lacy blankets holding the baby then tossed her over to Ah-niu for changing. In fact, she quickly learned to read Amanda as if the baby could already talk. Becky learned which was a cry of boredom, which was a cry of discomfort and which was the sort of cry that sends mothers up the stairs two at a time. She showed maternal erudition in analyzing the contents of Amanda's diapers, vigilant against illness or disorder. I regretted that I did not acknowledge this to Becky before she disappeared into China. Now I believed that she was far away and hating me for my boorish lack of generosity. And I dreaded the thought that my doubts might have prodded her to abandon her baby and her home.

Just when Becky was preparing to return to work at Great World after giving birth, the medical complications occurred, and this was no recreational illness; it was quite real. It was determined that Becky's uterus had prolapsed as a result of giving birth to Amanda. Admitted to Queen Elizabeth Hospital, she underwent a hysterectomy and remained confined for ten days. She came home quiet – she declined to see her friends for the first week, until she felt she looked presentable. She seemed to lose interest in Amanda, which shocked the household staff. When I finally saw her, she had accreted enough cheerfulness to be convincing. But Feng had been another problem. He wasn't so mean that he did not worry about his wife and biggest star. But at the same time, he was weighed down heavily by the confirmation that he would never have a male heir. Becky told me that, behind closed doors, he alternately accused her of having failed him and of having conspired to deny him a son. *"There are three ways to be unfilial,"* he had said, evoking the cruel old saying that served self-centred fathers. *"The worst is not to have a son."*

In that foggy-headed week that followed Rudman's acquittal, I wrote the usual slop. I did a rewrite on a wire-service story about the death of poor old Jayne Mansfield in the United States. We carried it because just a couple of months before she had been on what she called a "hit-and-run" trip of the Far East, culminating in one of those profitable gigs in Saigon. In Hong Kong she'd played for two nights at the Kingsland. It was quite sad, her death, because she had been so determined to be a big star despite her slender talents. I had interviewed her. She had worn a tiny miniskirt and a tight sweater and she was one of the most cooperative, enthusiastic subjects I had ever met.

The China Telegraph
June's returning to the UK

June Armstrong-Wright, producer of the popular radio programme "Forces Favourites" is off to Britain on leave. But her many male listeners in the Hong Kong garrison can stand at ease. The programme, broadcast every Sunday at 9:30 a.m. by Radio Hongkong, will be in the able hands of Angela Ernst. Like June, Angela is pleased to receive listeners' letters requesting favourite records.

– PAUL HAUER

There was a small story to do on a study by the Roads Department that small children and teenagers were by far the most likely people to be injured and killed in Hong Kong traffic. I saw such an accident that very week, on Gloucester Road near Fleming. A small boy had been crushed by one of those ubiquitous delivery trucks that ran about Hong Kong with their green wooden flat beds and red cabs. People had gathered round. The parents were nowhere to be seen; probably off at work. Some Chinese children, very young, stood in front of the crowd, silently and gravely considering their dead comrade. Trucks passed on the outer lane of Gloucester Road, each rumbling passage within a few feet of repeating the tragedy on the remaining children.

I covered the Hong Kong government's decision to ban *The Sand Pebbles*. GIS declared that HM Government was concerned the movie would stir up racial and political passions. The ruling disappointed a lot of people, especially in the Hong Kong movie business, because *Sand Pebbles* had been shot largely in the colony using many performers from Shaws, Cathay and Great World.

I heard nothing from Feng. I supposed that he had somehow heard of how I had testified at the trial of a policeman and now considered me irretrievably tainted with scandal. I found out why he was so terrified of scandal from Becky, who had listened to Feng's eldest brother, the failed scholar, when he had drunk too much and was wallowing in another bout of guilt. He revealed why his family had arrived in Hong Kong with so much money after fleeing Shanghai. It was a huge secret in the Feng family. They had been friendly with the Japanese in Shanghai during the Occupation there. They pimped their movie starlets to Japanese officers. The Fengs used Golden Heaven studio sets at night as gambling dens and brothels, rooms decorated in exotic themes. The family would pay the local Japanese authorities handsome complicity dividends, but they took in from Japanese officers much more than they paid out. They bought gold on the sly. Hsiao-foon sent his brothers on journeys across the line from Japanese-occupied territory to Chungking, in Free China, to convert the gold into U.S. dollars. They made a fortune off the Japanese at a time when their countrymen suffered horribly from the occupation. So you can understand that, even twenty-two years later, Feng was not someone who wanted to be around a lot of pointing fingers.

Up at Hong Kong's border with China, freight trains crossing over from China bore inflammatory political posters. Specially detached policemen wore surgical masks against the stink of pigs in the livestock cars. They scraped off broadsheets that read: *"Imperialism and all reactionaries are paper tigers!"* and *"Being patriotic is no crime!"* I went up on the Kowloon-Canton Railway one day to interview Chinese people returning from the Mainland. Travellers from China had to get off at Shum Chun on the Chinese side of the border and then walk across a covered wooden bridge to Hong Kong where they could board trains of the British Section of the Kowloon-Canton Railway.

I boarded the train about a mile down the tracks at Sheung Shui. Sometimes it was a pliers job getting people to talk about what they had seen in China, since they feared reprisals against the family members they had gone to visit there. A couple of men rebuffed me that day. Then I came upon a Mrs. Cheung, who slowly warmed up to telling what she'd seen or heard. She had been in Canton for a month visiting her husband and had a lot to say. She recalled reading a poster on a pillar in the centre of town describing a big punch-up in the market town of Fat Shan, near Canton. Two thousand Red Guards had besieged the office of the Communist Party Committee in Fook Ning Road. The Red Guards, who could barely control themselves, much less a county administration, demanded control of the committee office. They accused Fat Shan's vice-mayor, Tsang Kok, of being an "anti-Party, anti-socialist bourgeois counter-revolutionary." They busted down doors and fought the 700 party workers inside. Another poster, in a filthy food market, alleged that 170 people had been killed or wounded. The poster said that the Red Guards had held a court of their own creation to try party officials they had arrested.

Then Mrs. Cheung suggested that I interview another person,

and she looked behind me, down to the other side of the car. I briefly glanced over my shoulder and saw several people away down the end, so I asked Mrs. Cheung which one she meant. *"That one, over there,"* she said. *"She's just returning from China as well, and I'm sure that she would have something very interesting to say. To Hong Kong people that woman is a famous actress. In the cinema."*

I stood up at once and turned around. There she was, plainly dressed, wearing a head scarf and seated alone at the far end of the car, facing away from me. She was looking out the dusty windows of the KCR train. I went over and stood beside her for some time. Becky failed to notice me because she was intently examining the parched, passing scenery of the New Territories, as if she had never seen it before. We pulled into a local station and she looked up and down the platform, as though searching for someone. I sat down next to her. She turned and looked at me then gave a small start.

EIGHTEEN

Becky didn't want to go to her home, but asked if she could come back to my apartment on Hong Kong Island. She didn't even want to see her baby yet. She had no intention of ever seeing Feng. When we reached Causeway Bay, I took her up the elevator. A housewife wearing a set of day-pyjamas with a brown floral design got on with us and exclaimed when she recognized Becky. She asked Becky, *"So, you're a Communist now?"* matter-of-factly, not as an accusation but more as a fan's comment. Becky said nothing, but looked ahead through the little window in the elevator door, watching the floors drop past as we rose. The car clicked and groaned as we travelled upward. With no responses from Becky, the housewife sighed with boredom, stared indifferently at me and sucked at her teeth over and over. The clicking of the elevator car and the woman sucking her teeth made a tedious rhythm. I couldn't wait to get off.

When we were inside my flat, she was visibly relieved, not just in escaping that woman but also because she said she felt safe with me. I made her a pot of English tea and switched on the reluctant air conditioner. We sat down on the red leatherette sectional.

"Where did you go in China?" I asked her.

"Canton," she said, not really ready to talk. So I told her about the investigations into her disappearance. I told her that Feng knew that she went into China. He had missed a Rotary meeting for the first time because he had lost face. She merely shrugged and played with the teapot lid. She was annoyed that all Feng and everyone else in Hong Kong thought was that she had suddenly discovered politics and the Cultural Revolution.

"Why did you go into China?"

"I'm not a Communist all of a sudden, if that's what everyone thinks," she said crossly. "It had nothing to do with politics, the trip."

"Then why did you go?" I asked.

"I went to see a relative," she said.

"Who?"

"My father."

Becky told me that he had written her a month before. The letters had arrived from Canton; they must have been the ones that Ah-niu had told me about the day I visited her in Becky's kitchen. In them, her father said that he was extremely ill and needed her help.

"Why didn't you tell anyone?" I asked.

Becky did not answer my question in a word or two; the answer was too big.

The last of Hong Kong that Becky saw before entering China was a woman at the side of the train selling Cadbury's chocolate bars from baskets suspended on shoulder yokes. The hawker did a brisk business in last-minute gift-selling to people looking for something to give to relatives in China. Becky was at Sheung Shui station. A few miles down the track was a dour police and customs checkpoint called Lo Wu. There she surrendered her passport to a Hong Kong official in a black uniform who sat at an outdoor steel desk beneath a flagpole flying the Union Jack. He stamped it, recorded her name and gave it back. Beyond that was a railway bridge spanning the Sham Chun River which she had to walk across to connect to the Mainland Chinese train. The bridge was covered with a semi-circular roof of boards. Halfway across there was a slogan on a blood-red linen printed with yellow Chinese characters. It said: *"The liberation of the oppressed peoples of the world is the duty of the Chinese masses!"*

On the other side of the bridge was a cream-coloured building that housed the Communist passport control, a quarantine office and then customs. At the customs room there was a megaphone continuously playing a woman's voice yelling slogans, interspersed with military-like music. The men who worked the customs station were members of the People's Liberation Army and they went about their joyless routines quietly and with dead slowness. Becky glanced out the windows, which were sheathed in slats of frosted glass, like venetian blinds. There were fields of cabbages growing just outside. Apart from the incessant, irritating woman on the public-address speaker, the Chinese side of the border seemed quiet and peaceful.

When she boarded the train for Canton, a brisk young girl in a beret with an arm band identifying her as a Red Guard pushed a yellow pamphlet at her. The paper was cheaply made, fragile and thin, and it almost came apart in her hand. Becky read slowly because the pamphlet was written with simplified Chinese characters, part of a literary efficiency program Mao had ordered. The characters were not used in Hong Kong. The scrap of paper said:

> *Comrades of Hong Kong and Macau, observe the following rules while you are in the Motherland:*
> *Remove foreign clothing and change into those of the 'people's style' in the Motherland. You must shear off hooligan-style and Western-style hairdos. You must not wear shoes with sharp-pointed toes; wear working-class shoes. You must not talk about anything of the capitalist world. If you do not observe these rules, you may find it too late to repent!"*

The huge new railway station in Canton was largely empty. A woman with whom Becky had cautiously chatted on the train up from the Hong Kong frontier had muttered a complaint about how hard it was to get trains beyond Canton and that buses were equally unreliable. Inside the cavernous station was an immense portrait of Mao Tse-tung gazing down on the few arriving passengers. There was another public-address speaker blaring military marches and exhortations to criticize Confucianism, U.S. imperialism and "revisionist roaders." Outside the station there was a big public square festooned with crudely inked linen banners that criticized local officials. There were few people in the square.

Becky was met by a woman named Comrade To. This woman wore an olive-green jacket, blue pants and cloth slippers. Comrade To was from the Southern Film Corporation, a Chinese government-owned studio in Kwangtung province. She took Becky to the Oriental Hotel, just off People's Road. On the way, Becky saw a group of teenagers with red and white arm bands accosting a woman who had come up from Hong Kong on Becky's train. They yelled accusations at her about being dressed in decadent Western clothing. The woman was wearing a pair of tight navy slacks.

The vast Oriental Hotel was a severe-looking building put up by the Soviets when they were still friendly with China. It had a menacing oversized cornice, affected the style of Moscow super-buildings and its harsh air conditioning served up a gelid luxury. Off the echoing stone lobby was a small pool that sprawled through several rooms and was filled with large goldfish that cruised from room to room through gaps at the base of the walls. The public areas smelled of sandalwood soap and must.

After she had settled in to the dour, echoing room, with its furled mosquito net over the bed, tea-bag basket, thermos of hot water and a portrait of Chairman Mao on the desk, Comrade To from the Southern Film Corporation returned. She was correctly distant, distrustful and as chilly as the overly air-conditioned hotel. All she did was take a hand-written letter from a plastic pouch and put it on the small desk. *"You still abide by our agreement?"* she asked. Becky said she did. Comrade To gave her a hand-written letter to sign.

Here is what it said:

> *My flower, my heart's affection!*
> *I must write to tell you how filled with happiness I am whenever I see your picture on my copy of the Quotations! I*

sometimes kiss it when no one is around, for I feel so very alone and want to have you hold me in your arms.

My sweet, dear Chairman, when I hear of the guidance that you give the People in their struggle against revisionist roaders I am so filled with joy and ecstasy I want to weep and laugh at the same time! I have left the evil confines of Hong Kong for the fatherland. I have come to take up class struggle, to stand shoulder to shoulder with the masses. I am loyal only to the masses!

Many people in Canton are conspirators and double-dealers and they are plotting against you. But the management of the Southern Film Corporation, who have convinced me to join the fatherland's class struggle, are loyal to you. They are pledged to expose your enemies to the light of day!

My darling Chairman, I want to come to serve you in your home. I want to cook, clean, wash and help you, provide you with those charms, girlish and womanly, that you are yearning for. The management of the Southern Film Corporation, in solidarity with the masses, will send me to your side at once, there to remain for as long as you want me. The Corporation has enclosed a photograph that shows my dainty charms. Write to me at once, my dear leader!

I remain, your loving Comrade Chan.

Becky finished reading. She wanted to look up at Comrade To and ask why this had to be. But she was too humiliated and just sat quietly for a few moments, fighting back tears. Although Hong Kong movies were banned in China, it was possible for senior Communist Party officials to view them privately and Mao no doubt knew who Becky was. It was so cheap, such a price to pay. Comrade To's affected chilliness became even colder. If she acknowledged that the studio was trying to pimp Becky to Chairman Mao, she didn't show the slightest shame, as if other people were present, listening to what any admission of compassion would say about her politics, and condemn her for it. All she did was snap out a fountain pen that produced an ink the same colour as on the note. *"You had better sign it,"* she said, *"if you want us to tell you where your father is."*

In the darkness of that summer in Canton, Becky had to wait in her hotel room for several days with nothing to do. She was only allowed into the small gardens at the front of the hotel or up to the rooftop dining room for her meals. She sat alone at a big cloth-covered table before the sun came up, eating a bowl of bland congee. The room was almost always empty, except for a small tour group made up of university professors from several Western countries. They sat nearby and excitedly discussed China and its supreme achievement, the Cultural Revolution. "It is a paradise," burbled a bearded man wearing a factory worker's blue hat he'd purchased at the Friendship Store. A day later they had gone, taken a plane to another Chinese city, perhaps, to enthuse about a place they did not have to live in, where they had no idea of the intrigue and revenge that coursed back and forth through every city and every neighbourhood and every alley in the land, a mass poison that terrified millions. Now Becky sat in the dining room completely alone, except for the serving staff, who never spoke with her.

One day the staff ordered one of the hotel taxis around to the front car port and they loaded her in. They gave an address to the driver and let Becky go. No one accompanied her; they didn't have to because there were spies in every neighbourhood, every street, every building. People along the way would report her passing. The radio of the big Russian-built car played songs about sawmill workers expressing their solidarity. *"Save the best beams,"* they crooned, *"for the motherland!"*

The driver let her off in a dank winding street near the Pearl River and told her to walk down the alley to house No. 16. He got back into the car and told her she could get back to the Oriental Hotel via trolley bus No. 3. He was courteous but not warm. Becky watched him drive off, blaring his horn at scores of cyclists cramming the narrow street. She looked around in the street, a little bewildered and very frightened. She did not stand out because Comrade To had given her "people's-style" clothing to wear: a plain white shirt and olive trousers. She hadn't set her hair after washing it, merely pulled it back into a ponytail, and she wore no make-up. She was indistinguishable from any other woman in Canton. And now, dressed like a revolutionary woman, one of Chairman Mao's concubines, she was prepared to meet her father for the first time since she was eight years old.

She stepped through a circular moon gate at the head of the alley. The alley itself was narrow and populated by squalling children who paused to consider her. Women in doorways watched her carefully, either to keep an eye on her for later reports demanded by neighbourhood officials or to see what sort of torment she had brought them. They backed away into the inner shadows of their homes if she looked at them. She passed along to No. 16, a big, decrepit, stucco-covered, four-storey house with a clay tile roof. Its grey façade was mildewed and crumbling. The entrance was very dark and there were bicycles huddled together beneath the stone steps. Toward the back there was a woman, a self-important concierge, seated at a desk with a transistor radio playing revolutionary music. She sensed Becky's unease and preyed on it. *"Wai! What do you want here?"* Becky told her that she had come to visit her father, and showed her the address Southern Film had given her. The woman took her time to read the address and an accompanying letter of permission. *"Bed No. 70!"* she snapped and handed the papers back. She went back to reading a newspaper.

"Where is it?" Becky asked.

"Upstairs!" the woman shouted. *"Do I have to take you by the hand?"*

Becky went up the steps and wandered from room to room, looking in. There were no doors on any of the rooms. Each room had rows of steel beds with small wooden tables beside them. There were cheap pictures of Chinese scenery on the walls or pictures of children dressed as soldiers, or little girls, the Young Pioneers, in bright red neck-scarves presenting bouquets to Chou En-lai on an airport tarmac, a vast Russian-built airliner in the background. The house was a dormitory for single older men. Becky asked a soft-spoken man who was missing two fingers where she could find Bed No. 70. He said: *"The bed numbers rise the higher you go. He must be on the top floor."*

On the fourth storey she looked in and saw him. Even though he looked very old, wrinkled and spotty, she recognized him. He wore a blue cotton jacket, even in the afternoon heat. The shoulders had faded almost to white. He sat up on his steel bed rolling a cigarette. Becky went in and greeted him. He looked at her. It took a moment for him to realize she had come. Then he clutched at his heart with two hands and looked down at his lap.

"They told me you were coming," he said, and tried to get to his feet. He spoke very fast, almost chattering, like a man in a concentrated state of crisis. Becky plumped the dirty, thin pillow behind him. *"I'm very sick. I shouldn't have to work anymore because I'm very sick,"* he said. *"China is a paradise under our great leader. He takes care of the old and sick. But I need special attention, I really, really do. I need help. They make me work."* He went back to his cigarette and asked her to sit down. When he finished he took out a match from a wooden box and lit it. Becky glanced at the match box. *"What did you bring me from Hong Kong?"* he asked.

Becky gave him a few toiletries, a bottle of cognac and American cigarettes, with which he first seemed pleased. But he was trying to play the haughty father expecting homage from his daughter. He enumerated his ailments, paramount of which was his bad heart. Above his head was a cheap fake tapestry printed on rough cloth. It showed the Great Wall sweeping up and down mountain slopes.

His tongue began to loosen even more. *"I'm very sick and they make me work most days, they put me in the back of a truck with a lot of other old, sick men, and take us out to the factory. We make candied ginger root, day after day. I'm in the steam department but I can smell nothing but ginger all the time. After a while you get so sick of it."* He went on and on, as if speaking for the first time in months, cleaning out a built-up inventory of complaints that nobody had wanted to hear. He objected to his co-workers, to the

endless political education classes they had to take in the factory
courtyard before they started work, to the horrific snoring of dormitory mates and to the poor quality of food, to the evil witch
who sat at the desk at the dormitory entrance and even to an incident in which a co-worker lost a finger on a machine that filled
the ginger root jars. They couldn't find the jar with the severed
finger inside so they just shipped it out.

"I've talked to the other men here," he said. *"Maybe you'll have
a word with them, make them see my view."*

Becky asked him what he was talking about.

At that moment, another resident of the dormitory came in
and suddenly Becky's father stopped talking and looked blank. He
turned his head to the other man, who was about fifty years old
and dressed in the same uniform of blue cotton pants, blue jacket and blue cap. The other man went to his little wooden locker
and took out a plastic pouch of cigarettes and removed two. He
considered Becky and her father. Becky's father nodded and
grunted a greeting, offering a cautious, tightly rationed courtesy.
The man returned the same distrustful greeting then went out.

When he was gone and they were alone again, Becky's father
leaned forward to whisper. *"Jeh-jeh,"* he said, using Becky's childhood nickname. It shocked her to hear someone use it after all these
years. *"Jeh-jeh, I have a great secret that I want to share with you."*

"Yes, ba?"

He took out a rolled-up scroll of rice paper that he kept hidden under his bed. *"Tell no one that you saw this,"* he said quietly,
and he peered about, as if there were people spying at them
through cracks in the wall or through the fourth-storey dormitory windows. *"It is very precious and it is forbidden!"*

He unfurled the scroll and held it up. It was half a metre long
and showed a single character:

Becky looked at it without comprehending, then she looked back at her father. *"Well?"* he said, his eyes alive with excitement. *"You can read, I know that you can."*

"It's the number eight," she said.

"Prosperity!" he said. *"It stands for prosperity!"* Becky looked back at the scroll. *"I keep it with me at all times. Sooner or later it's going to come true, if you only do the right things and look out for the correct numbers! I've got to have another bed number. I can't stay in bed No. 70. I simply can't. I've asked to be put downstairs in bed No. 8 but that hag at the front door won't have it. Naturally I told them it was because of my weak heart. And it's true. I can't climb all those stairs. But if only I were down in bed No. 8 everything would be fine."*

After Becky's father abandoned his family, he similarly gave up on Hong Kong. He stood at the high point on the Taipo Road, where the troops of monkeys lived, and looked back down on Kowloon below. He spat mightily in its direction, turned to the monkeys cavorting in the trees and told them that they could have the city as far as he was concerned, and he walked all the way back to China. In Canton, he volunteered as a Nationalist soldier, not because he believed in Chiang Kai-shek's cause and wanted to fight the Communists but because he simply wanted the emoluments that came with steady employment. He was sitting pretty for a while because he worked in the field kitchens, and kitchen workers always made sure that they got fed before the fighting men. Many Nationalist soldiers were barely able to fight at all, so poorly were they fed that their feet swelled from beriberi and their teeth dislodged from scurvy. Becky's father ate better than ever. He told himself that he deserved it, that he had been poor all his life and this war was his great reward. The only time he was truly in peril was when General Lin Piao and his Communist army entered Pinshia on the Canton-Hankow railway and shelled his kitchen. When the civil war ended in 1949 he and millions of other soldiers were discarded. Chiang and his officers fled the Mainland for the island of Taiwan and they had no use for illiterate Cantonese enlisted men such as her father.

When the Communists arrived and rounded up anybody they associated with the defeated Nationalist army, he fled to Hong Kong again. Still wearing his army uniform, he settled with other Nationalist veterans in Rennie's Mill, an isolated settlement outside Kowloon. Rennie's Mill was one of the most squalid, filthy, crime-ridden and destitute refugee encampments anywhere in Hong Kong. It was a place of men in despair, a failed nation's failures. They robbed one another of what little money they had, they killed each other and formed organized-crime gangs for mutual protection and advancement. Occasionally they went into town and, as they did in 1956, stirred up trouble with vicious rioting surpassed in its ferocity only by the events of 1967. Nobody had much use for Becky's father in Rennie's Mill. In a place in which even the despairing worked hard to make a living, he scrounged, begged and gambled. He never changed his clothes because he could not afford to buy any. So for years he wore that faded Nationalist uniform, with its grubby shoulder patch of the Nationalist sun symbol. His one indulgence was to haunt Great World movie theatres and watch Becky. It dawned on him over time that this actress might be his daughter. He went to her premieres for a glimpse of her but he was far too shabby and fearful ever to dare approaching her.

By the early 1960s he had despaired of Hong Kong yet again. He was lured by the Communist propaganda newspapers published in Hong Kong. Someone who could read related that the Red newspapers boasted how every citizen was cared for in the "New China." So he returned, a lost son coming home to the great family. The Communists put him to work, but years of sleeping rough and malnutrition had undermined his health. There was no one except the self-important concierge in his dormitory to take care of him. So he wrote the Po Leung Kuk charity, asking them to trace his daughter. They referred his letter to the Door of Hope Orphanage and, after several years' trying, he became certain that his daughter was the actress Becky Chan. He wrote her at Great World and begged her to come at once.

"People have gone mad here, jeh-jeh," her father said. *"There's a story going around, a terrible story. A man from a dormitory, just like this one, he was walking along Wah Fuk Sai Street, and he was stopped by several Red Guards who complained of his hairstyle. They poured boiling water over his head. Just like that. A bunch of evil adolescents! That's what they did. And they make us go to rallies at the stadium and sit with these children. We had to condemn Tao Chu, the propaganda big boy, who is now evil for some reason. He was in, then he was out. We had to pledge to burn him and make him walk through the streets in a tall hat. And he's a big man in the Communist Party. They say that Teng Hsiao-ping threw himself off a building in Peking and he's dead. If the party couldn't protect Teng Hsiao-ping and Tao Chu how can it protect little men like me?"* Becky's father's voice had risen and she shushed him. Speaking more softly, he started a kind of chant, repeating over and over very quickly: *"What am I going to do, jeh-jeh? What am I going to do?"* He rubbed his hands together and grew red in the face. *"What am I going to do? What am I going to do?*

"I've seen some terrible things, lately, terrible," he continued. *"You don't know what's going on here. You people in Hong Kong live in a dream world with your automobiles and your movies and your chicken meat. We're suffering horribly here."* Canton residents who owned precious family heirlooms acquired before the revolution were hiding them now. Lovely lapis lazuli carvings and black pearl necklaces, paintings on stone tablets had to be kept from the prying eyes of the neighbourhood men and women who spied for the local party authorities. They were all disappearing. There was a man in her father's dormitory who liked to play the saxophone in his factory orchestra. But when Mao's wife took control of the arts, she declared many forms of music and even the instruments themselves were anti-proletarian and decadent. So the saxophonist went out in the middle of the night, sneaked into the public

flower garden near the Oriental Hotel and buried it beneath a mulberry tree. Someone saw him doing it, dug it up and stole it. *"The thief got caught and guess who his accuser was? The man who owned the saxophone! He charged him not with stealing but with owning a decadent musical instrument. The authorities banished the thief to a labour camp in Sei Chong province!"* Becky's father seemed pleased at least with this. *"That saxophonist. We're all watching him carefully. One move against any of us and we'll turn him in smart and quick!"*

The concierge called up the stairs in a brassy voice that it was getting late, that Becky had to leave. Her father looked anguished that she was abandoning him. He apologized over and over for being selfish. She promised to come back the next day.

"Tomorrow, you will tell me about your life in Hong Kong," he said gently. *"Do you have a family?"*

"I'm married —" she began.

"There's a clinic in this neighbourhood and the doctor there said I have a very weak heart. I could go at any minute."

"I'm sorry."

"Any children?"

Becky began again. *"I have a little girl, just two months —"*

"And yet they make me work every day in the ginger root factory. I can't stand on my feet all day!"

Becky asked him if he could get a transfer to another job. Then he blurted it out, what he really needed, why he had written letters to her beseeching her to come to China and see him. He wanted her to take him to Hong Kong.

This took a few moments for Becky to accept but she more or less automatically said, *"Of course."*

Her father started up again, speaking very quickly. *"I'd have to have a separate house, though, to be away from her."*

"Who?"

"Your mother. She's a bad woman, you know: demanding and domineering, always pushing for more." Even though he was feeble he showed an intense hostility, the nurturing of years of grudge-holding. *"Nothing I ever did was good enough. Now she lives with*

you in Hong Kong in splendour, all fat and covered in gems. She probably dyes her hair black to hide the grey. I guess she thinks that's not good enough either. And here I am in Canton, living in squalor, sick and dying all alone —"

"Mamee is dead."

Becky's father showed genuine surprise. Then he drew a mask of indifference over his eyes, looking away distantly, protecting himself from what she had said, resuming the hauteur of the household head.

NINETEEN

When Becky returned to her father's dormitory the next day, he was aloof and distant and he did not want to discuss anything other than the weather. There was no one else in his room so they should have been able to talk freely. She sat down on the edge of his bed and he sat upright, with his back to the wall, occasionally rolling a cigarette from tobacco in his pouch. Behind him was the cheap printed tapestry of the Great Wall, slouching over the mountains of China. They had an awkward start. He refused to hear anything about Becky's mother or the whereabouts of her twin sisters, Man-ling and Cheung-mei, and her brother, Yee. Slowly he began to talk about his ailments, about how badly he wanted her to take him back to Hong Kong and care for him. Then he talked for a long while about the power of special numbers to cure people of sickness, poverty and misery. He even took out his scroll again and he held it like a therapeutic wand. He wandered about in that talk for a while before he fell completely silent.

Becky was furious, and it was in a way that set aside all the formalities of fathers and daughters and those of semi-strangers. She raged at him. *"All mamee wanted was to live,"* she said. *"All she needed was a little money! And after all these years all you can do is sit there with your yellowish outlook and prattle about* your *misfortunes."*

Her father stiffened. *"Who spoiled you so that you talk to your father like that?"* he said. *"Your mother?"*

Becky wanted to hit him, to slap his face and pound his shoulders until he put up a cry of defeat and would then finally listen to her. But she didn't, and he didn't. They only sat there in grim silence, each looking out the window at nothing, both of them isolated and indeterminate in the formality and hostility of the moment.

"*I will tell you how she died —*" Becky said.

"*No! Don't!*" he said. "*She was a grasping, demanding woman! She deserved to die. You know what she did.*" He waved his finger at her uncertainly, with a palsy-like shake. "*She wouldn't give me a moment's peace about money —*"

"*No!*" And at this moment Becky was close to striking the old man, but again she held back. "*She was a good woman. She tried so hard, but it wasn't enough. She was so caring of us after you ran away —*"

"*I didn't 'run away!' I went to seek work —*"

"*And you never came back. You never sent one dollar for our aid and survival.*"

This is what Becky told her father about her mother. She had never spoken to anyone before of this. Her mother was a hard-working coolie. She stayed alive in Hong Kong only by the thinnest of tendons. She lived in an era in which her kind died in the gutter all the time, forgotten amid the great buzzing, swarming tumult of life in the colony. They starved, they grew sick, they gave up. Most made it, but only just. Those who didn't often had no idea why they were fated to fail. Among these was Becky's mother.

Becky told her father that they had remained in the squatter village after he had abandoned them. He objected to the word "abandon" and she told him to be quiet and listen. The village stood in the hills not far from the Wong Tai Sin Temple in Kowloon. Whenever Becky trudged down the stairs of the shanty town she could see the slouching tile roof of the main building below her. Today, you see shanty towns on television news or missionary fund-raising programs: dirty, fly-infested places with foul water passing through the streets, packing-board houses with corrugated iron roofs. You see them all the time so that they seem eternal. But what you don't see is the steep worry, the terrible doubt about simple survival. It is not an eternal place of static disgrace, but a town of many troubles. It is a place of fear. Its smells warn of extinction. When Becky was coming back from helping her mother clean the police station, a vicious dog strayed out of Playing Field Road and so terrified Becky that she refused to walk alone down the street again. So her mother took a stick with her, found the dog and banged it on the head so hard, the dog stumbled and collapsed on the pavement, whimpering. Her mother grabbed at the dog's back, almost lifting it off the ground, and pulled out a swatch of loose hair. She placed the dog's hair over little Becky's heart and rubbed it back and forth. *"There,"* she said in a strong voice that gave confidence and a soft touch that gave comfort. *"Now you have your courage back from the dog that took it away. That dog will never frighten you again."* Becky considered the woozy animal, staggering back to its feet, and yes, she didn't feel afraid any more.

Becky told her father of how her mother spent a few moments with other refugee women in a second-hand goods market, marvelling at sewing machines. Their excitement and sudden optimism cheered Becky and she loved to go with them to look at the machines in a display window, protected from desperate hands by iron bars. It was as if the machines were potent conveyers of good fortune, like the stone statue of Wong Tai Sin in the nearby temple. Pray to the sewing machine and your good fortune could come true.

Even though they stood side by side, the women called to one another in great loud voices, as if they were still talking in the countryside in China, calling out conversations between fields, over great distances.

"They're hiring!"

"The tailor shops!"

"It's piece work but it's good money."

"It's all you need and you can stay home with the kids all day."

"The work flies in the door."

"So does the money."

Becky's mother took up the mood and began saving pennies each week toward the fifteen dollars a used sewing machine cost. It was a goal and it made her happy. Becky even found a little job that brought in five cents a day, filling matchboxes with newly dipped wooden matches in a little cottage factory not far from the village. With little Yee strapped to her back in a cloth baby carrier, she stuffed matches into little wooden cartons. There were Chinese and English words on the boxes but she didn't know what they said. She was only eight years old and she had never been to school. It didn't matter, she would make enough money to help her mother buy that sewing machine. Then everything would be better.

She stood with her mother and the other women evening after evening, discussing intricate details of the sewing machines, comparing makes.

"The Victory brand is best!"

"A woman told me she bought a Singer from overseas and it was far better."

"… the treadle needed to be oiled …"

"… you don't tire your back so much …"

It was almost like a song to Becky, the endless eager discussion, a symptom that things for everyone were going to get better, if only they worked hard.

When Becky's baby brother Yee had his first birthday, the family had a celebration. Her mother had scrounged up a bit of black cotton and she stayed up nights fashioning a marvellous hat. She wouldn't let the other children see it until it was done. On Yee's birthday, she brought it out with a triumphant laugh and placed it on the little boy's head. It was a "dog-head cap." She had folded and sewed the hat so it resembled the head of a dog. Yee was to wear the hat all the time and it would prevent evil spirits who, Becky's mother told her, were not intelligent and would mistake Yee for an animal. They would decide that as such he was not worth harming, and Yee would stay free of trouble. A little jute string went under Yee's throat to hold the cap on and at first he balked at its scratchy roughness. But when he saw the looks of delight on his sister's and mother's face, he realized that he was a pleasing little boy and he started to laugh.

Yee was not the only one to get presents. Becky's mother gave the twin sisters tiny bells that tied to their legs with little iron anklets. The bells tinkled every time the girls toddled about. The iron anklets held the children to Earth, ensuring that they would live, their heaviness would prevent the girls from being taken off to heaven. The happy sound of the little bells were so cheering that the whole family became merry. *"Any day now,"* Becky said, *"we will have that sewing machine!"* And Becky's mother repeated it. They turned it into a kind of song. Inevitably Becky looked around for what little gift she might receive, and she was not disappointed. Rather than receive an ornament, she got a *sam*, a simple but useful blue gown that fastened with a single button on the shoulder. *"It's cool in summer and easy to put on,"* her mother said. But it also had a symbolic value that Becky never forgot. *"Jeh-jeh, no harm will ever come to you when you are dressed like this. Evil spirits and ghosts will see that you are a girl and, like a doggie, you are not worth taking, so you will have a long and capable life."*

Even at eight years old, Becky wasn't sure if she liked that. *"Why am I not worth taking?"* she asked her mother as she paraded about the shack in her new *sam*.

"The spirits and ghosts only want males," her mother said. *"Although with the likes of your father I don't see why."*

Another woman in the squatter camp was caught stealing money from a neighbour's shack. They found her inside clutching an old tin filled with coins. The rightful owners wanted to settle the issue by killing her, but a policeman came up from a station outside the village and took her away.

"My kids!" she cried as she was escorted to criminal court. The wronged family testified against her and she went to prison. Her children were left to starve. A few of the other refugees brought

them food now and then, when they had a little to spare. Once the foreign nuns came up from their mission school and looked in on them. But they did not take them away for care. The children didn't come out for days and no one said anything. Then one morning a vile smell came out of the children's shack.

"*You see?*" Becky's mother told a woman. "*The police are very dangerous. You make one wrong move and your children die!*"

"*It's terrible,*" the other woman said. "*Those foreign nuns are no better.*"

Her mother took very sick with a coughing disease after that. Many refugees suffered from the same thing. The old women of the refugee camp called it a demon at work and they recommended the purgative ritual of buying a rooster to scare away the night demons with its crowing. The nuns called it tuberculosis and they recommended medicine. Becky didn't understand. Her mother was female, so why would a demon make her sick? There was no money to get a rooster or the nuns' medicines. The illness would not go away and it started to claw and scratch away ever greater pieces of Becky's mother's stamina. The disease reached the point where her mother could no longer work.

They prayed as a family to Wong Tai Sin at the nearby temple for help with food, money, work, a return to health. To build their case they all went, the mother, Becky and the little children. Her mother took leftover bits of incense sticks from the sand-filled urn in the main courtyard and rubbed them on her chest, to transfer the healthful ash into her diseased lungs. She took a few more bits to fill a bean pod that she would string into a health-giving necklace.

Her mother yanked Becky's hand as they walked passed the rows of fortune-tellers at tables on the edge of the temple.

"*They have a route to the secrets.*"

"*What secrets?*" Becky asked.

"*The secrets of the way the world works.*"

"*How does the world work?*" Becky asked.

"*Jeh-jeh, how do I know? It just happens. The gods direct it and we pay for it. Demons direct us. They hurt us.*"

"Why do they hurt us?"

"I don't know! Jeh-jeh, I told you I don't. One day you're well, the next day you are sick and the day after you die. You grow rich if you are lucky, you stay poor if you are unlucky. There is no reason why. The gods! If only I could afford to go to a fortune-teller, all would be directed for us."

"Don't die, mamee!"

"I won't, jeh-jeh, not so long as I need to care for you and the babies."

So poor and so lost in a world of harsh fates directed by unknowable gods, Becky's mother lived in a state of dread, a dread that ate her youthful resilience and courage, leaving her a terrified and powerless woman. She had no idea what made it such a vastly cruel world. All she could do was slog through it, and try to accommodate the gods' sadistic direction.

Their little one-room shack was frail and drafty and it rattled ominously during wind storms. During an August typhoon Becky watched as her mother clung mightily to a piece of metal that had come loose from the roof. She pulled down on it to prevent it from ripping right off. Becky forever remembered the sight of her mother trying to keep the tiny house from disintegrating in the storm. She stood in place, drenched from leaks. After the typhoon had passed, Becky went outside with her mother and they saw that the whole shack had distorted in the winds. It was tilted and twisted. She and her mother leaned against a corner and with the help of several men from the squatter camp they managed to shove the corner back and the shack sighed upright again. *"It won't last another storm,"* one of the men told her. *"It will come apart unless you get some work done on it."*

"It will last," her mother said, for she had no means of repairing it.

The man offered to repair the shack. He smirked at her. Becky's mother told him to go away. He came around several nights when the smaller children were asleep and Becky was helping her mother with sewing. He became a pest, offering his services. Becky's mother sent him away. She told Becky that he was a bad man.

Becky woke up one night and found the man in the shack, with her mother. He was lying on her on the platform that served as her bed.

"I hate you," her mother was saying to him.

"Hate me all you want," he said. *"You'll get your house fixed up."*

Her mother only grew more ill until there was nothing left for them to do. She could only sew with a needle and thread and she couldn't make much money with such slow work. Becky kept working in the cottage factory, loading matches into boxes to make five cents a day. It was a shambling building made out of the same packing boards and corrugated iron sheets from which most of the shacks in Becky's refugee town were made. Inside there were rows of home-made tables at which sat little boys and girls with heaps of matchsticks in front of them and little freshly printed cardboard boxes to put them in. Becky's job was to take handfuls of matches and neatly arrange them in the boxes, then put the boxes into larger cartons. The more boxes she filled, the more money she made.

Becky took a place just as a young man came in with a woven basket of matches, which had been dipped in a sulphurous mixture out behind the building. He dumped them on the table and the children went about their work. No one spoke, for they were too busy, too hungry and too tired to talk. They just worked, from seven in the morning until seven in the evening, with twenty minutes off at noon for a bowl of watery soup. Even during the break the little children sat silently, drinking their soup and staring at nothing. Occasionally, one would fall asleep at her work and a brother or sister would nudge her back awake.

Becky came home each day with a five-cent coin in her hand and presented it to her mother. Her mother smiled, took the coin and hugged Becky. *"You are the best little girl any mother has ever had,"* she said. *"One day you will be a wonderful mother."* Becky helped her mother feed Man-ling and Cheung-mei then, exhausted, fell asleep on a pallet on the floor next to her mother.

Every day Becky worked feverishly in the little match factory, as if each filled match box made her mother a little healthier. The box would join others in a carton she was filling, and as she slowly filled up the carton the mother she had in her mind began to smile and sit in front of a new sewing machine. Her mother, in her imaginings, puttered away on piecework for local clothing factories, humming a song and telling Becky how happy she was with the new machine. The money began rolling in and the family moved into a proper flat with a kitchen and a cockloft for sleeping in. And one night, in Becky's thoughts, they had enough money to go out for a meal in a restaurant and they were all very happy.

But these dream-like preoccupations could not last. When Becky came home at the end of the day, having loaded thousands of matches into hundreds of boxes and filling dozens of cartons, she found that her mother was just as sick as ever. Becky's wages for the day, a miserable small five-cent coin, seemed insignificant and she began to despair.

Disaster came when Becky lost her job in the cottage factory. The owner came over to her shortly before noon one day and said to get out. Becky didn't understand – she had stolen nothing, her work was satisfactory. But the owner pointed to another little girl and said: *"She is the daughter of my clansman from China. She's just come."* He paid Becky for a full day even though she had only worked for one morning, but he sent her away.

Then something truly terrible happened to Becky. She had not been paying attention, she must have let her child's mind wander at a tragic, unpropitious moment. Her little brother, Yee, vanished.

Becky wasn't sure if she was supposed to be caring for him. She returned from looking for work and saw that he was missing from his pallet on the floor. His mother was away on an errand and Becky was certain that she had told Becky to look after the boy. She spent an anxious time scouring the neighbourhood. She called his name over and over, crying in frustration and dread. She approached the chilly neighbours, who were too preoccupied with their own desperate needs to do anything to help. No one had seen the little boy in the dog-head cap. The magical hat had failed him! Yee had been taken by evil spirits. He would never come back. She got as far as the nun's mission school but she was too frightened by their European clothes, their demonic blue eyes and bony big noses to speak to them. She came home in terror of what to say to her mother.

Her mother was back when she got home and when Becky saw her, placidly working on a bit of piecework sewing, Becky was convulsed with guilt. Her mother, innocently sitting there, all calm, quiet and steady, unaware of the terrible news that her child had to give her. Becky burst into tears and she fell to her mother's feet. Her mother was annoyed at the noise Becky was making, she had no patience with her at all, and yelled at her to be quiet.

"I lost Yee!" Becky wailed, almost hysterical.

Her mother looked up from her piecework sewing then went back to work in her irritation. *"Yee is not lost. Yee is all right."*

"Where is he?"

Her mother sewed for a while without answering, and it tormented Becky. Where was he then?

Finally, her mother spoke, although she did not stop sewing. *"He's gone to another family,"* she said. *"A new home."*

Becky was confused and astonished, for it had never occurred to her that children would go from one home, one family and into another home, another family. She thought they always remained in one place. How could this be?

"Mameeyah, why is he in another family? Why did he go?"

"Jeh-jeh, don't exhaust me with your questions. I'm tired and sick and I need peace right now," her mother said. But as she spoke there was no more emotion in what she said. She spoke in a flat, steady way that, for Becky, was both calming and alarming at the same time. Becky sat down in a corner and distracted herself with a shoe, pushing it back and forth on the wooden floor, as if it were a truck like the ones she saw down in Kowloon. But the idea that Yee could just go to another family disturbed her. It just wouldn't leave her head. Even worse was the flat unconcern her mother showed. It had to be all right, though, for her mother was not worried about Yee. Everything was fine.

They ate well for months after that – Becky's mother worked very hard to make sure that they all shared one egg several times a week and occasionally even some stewed chicken skin. Becky's little sisters gained weight and began to laugh and cry again, to act like children, rather than the dolorous, unspeaking pair they became when they were hungry.

It didn't last.

There was no food for four days, only water. Becky's mother begged from the mission school and they gave her some rice. She was growing so weak from illness and hunger that soon she could no longer make her way down the steep path to the mission school. Other families in the squatter village contributed what little they could, but it was never enough. There were plenty of other families in the hills overlooking Kowloon who were in similar crises. They rejected her pathetic pleas and told one another she was faking. *"She's just lazy,"* they said. *"Hasn't got a man to do her work."* They wilfully ignored her when she convulsed with coughs and spat foamy blood on the stony ground. *"Just lazy,"* they said. *"We've all got troubles and we still feed our kids."*

Becky's twin sisters stopped talking after a while. They did nothing but lie on their pallet and stare at the walls, blinking occasionally. They stopped having bowel movements and their eyes seemed to grow larger in their faces. From her bed, Becky's mother would look back at them and try to offer a smile. Becky did not know what to do. She did not want to move either, for she was weak from starvation. But she knew that she had to do something or her mother was going to die. They had a brief respite when Becky found a job putting lids on cans of rolled wafers made in a small bakery. All day, she placed tin lids on printed tin containers. At the end the baker gave her three cents and a bag of broken bits of baked wafer, which Becky brought home. Her sisters could barely chew them, so weak were they. But it was like a feast after days of nothing, and again Becky's spirits were boosted. Her mother smiled on her as she ate her bits of wafer. It would be better now, Becky thought. She had solved things. But Becky lost the job after the baker found that she had tucked a couple of good wafers in her pocket to take home. He called her a thief and told her to get out.

When there was nothing left, there was their shack. Becky's mother sold it to another refugee family who wanted to house some relatives who had just arrived from China. They granted Becky's mother a stay of a week. The family ate again, but by now her mother was too weak to do drag herself down the steep shanty-village steps to the food market below, to haggle and argue over the price of the worst carrots, greens and bits of chicken soup bones that were already spoiling. Becky went down, but she did not have the experience or the authority to bargain well, and the money ran out fast.

The night before they were to move out of the shack, Becky woke very late. It was not like her to wake unexpectedly. She was so tired from taking care of the house and her mother that she usually slept through the night. She felt at once that something was very wrong. Then she realized what it was. Her mother was moving about the shack in the darkness. Becky lay there and watched her go back and forth, arranging things neatly. It troubled her and she wanted to tell her mother to get back to bed, but the activity was so strange that it transfixed her. She merely lay on her pallet next to her sisters and watched her mother's shadow move about.

Her mother set all their clothes out on nail hooks on the walls, making sure they were arranged neatly. She set out their rice bowls on the reed mat in the corner where they ate, when they had any food, and put their chopsticks on top of each bowl. She hooked her one cooking pot on a nail in the corner, and it leaned outward, as if to show off the emptiness of its interior. Everything looked so tidy, like her mother was expecting guests to come by and she wanted to present a well-ordered household.

With her arrangements complete, her mother knelt before Becky's twin sisters and looked at them. Becky could quite clearly see her mother's face, even in the dark. It was sunken and wretched. Her farmer's brown face had turned white, the bones of her cheeks stuck out like knobs. The skin was pulled across them in crepe wrinkles, making her look far older than she really was. Becky's young mother had aged into an old woman since they'd moved to Hong Kong from China.

As Becky lay in the dark, she watched her mother take her own shabby, thin grey pillow and creep forward to Man-ling. She kissed the tiny child on the cheek. Man-ling did not stir. Becky's mother softly placed the pillow over Man-ling's head and pressed down on it very hard. She held it there for a long time, Becky didn't know how long, then she lifted it off. She felt Man-ling's neck and put her hand on the girl's chest. She sat and held Man-ling's hand for a moment and considered the tiny child. Finally, she reached down and slipped the iron anklet and tiny bell off her foot. Man-ling would be held to the Earth no more. Then her mother shifted to the left and knelt before Cheung-mei. The second twin woke up and looked at her mother. Becky saw the look on her mother's face. It was distant, removed, dead, the same expression she used to have when she had scrubbed the police station walls. It was as if her mind had left her body. Cheung-mei saw the look too and it frightened her. She began to whimper and kick with her feet, trying to back away from her mother.

Becky's mother made a little sound: *"Sh-sh-sh."* It was that sweeping sound of comfort from a mother that stilled any child's concern. But that night it had lost its power. Becky heard Cheung-mei say in a squealing primitive voice, *"Mamee, no."* Becky's mother held her and pressed the pillow over Cheung-mei's face. Becky saw Cheung-mei's hands go up and down and she kicked her feet weakly. But the little girl had no strength to resist.

Becky's mother removed the little iron anklet and its bell from Cheung-mei's foot then shifted again, to the left, so that now she knelt over Becky.

Becky considered her mother as she knelt there. *"Mamee,"* she said, *"what are you doing?"*

Her mother told her to be very quiet, that she would wake her sisters. But Becky sat up and backed away from her.

"Be a good girl, jeh-jeh," her mother said. *"Don't trouble me. It's late and I'm not feeling well."*

That almost worked on Becky. She instinctively wanted to cooperate, she automatically wanted to help her mother out, to avoid causing trouble and grief. She wanted to be a good, hard-working little girl. But she saw the pillow in her mother's hand. She got to her knees and then to her feet. Her mother struggled to stand and then she reached out. She took Becky by the shoulder of her shirt. They started to fight. Becky cried out and started to slap her mother on the arm. The pillow fell from her mother's hand.

"*Jeh-jeh, don't!*" her mother said.

Becky was so very lost. Why was the shack neat and tidy? Why were the eating things laid out so carefully, as if they were about to sit down for a nice supper? There was even a bowl left out for Yee, who was no longer in their family. Yee was a little boy. Of course, that was why she had given him away. Boys were worth something to families without male children. Perhaps Becky's mother had sold Yee so that they would have food. That was why they had eaten well for a while. But there were no more boys left to sell and it was clear to Becky's mother that her family was now extinct. No one wanted to buy a girl, especially thin, weak and starving creatures like Becky and her sisters.

Her mother came toward Becky again, with her disciplined, blank face. Becky moved into a corner of the shack. "*Jeh-jeh,*" her mother said, "*we can't go on any longer. I'm getting sicker. You'll starve. There will be no one to care for you. I wanted to be a good mother. Now I need you to be a good girl.*"

If she was weak, if she was starving, Becky somehow found the power to slap her mother. And Becky's mother, so broken, so sick and hungry, could not overpower her daughter.

There came a change in Becky's mother's face and she stopped struggling with Becky. She looked at her eldest daughter intently, as if she saw something important and new, something that she had overlooked. She did not speak for a long time, but continued examining Becky's little face as if seeing it for the first time. Finally she spoke sharply, in a loud, dry voice. What she said was: "*Run!*"

Becky stared at her, confused and terrified.

"*Run!*" her mother repeated. "*Run and get help!*"

But Becky remained unmoving, more confused than before.

"*Oh jeh-jeh, do as I say at once! I need you to go get help! Go! Now! Help me!*"

With a task, Becky turned and went to the door. She flung it back and looked at the other shacks in the shanty town. There was no sound outside except a few distant roosters. Starving stray dogs barked in response. Becky didn't know where to go – the missionary school? Bad. The police post down on the main road? Worse. The neighbours? Strangers. To Wong Tai Sin. The god's assistance! She went outside and went down the steep path, hurrying, a little faster now, then faster still, until she began a furious, blind run that ended with a trip on the irregular stones that served as steps. She fell face forward with a cry and cut her hand on some thorns that grew beside the path. The pain burst upon her. She stopped and caught her breath, then stood up.

The fall had cleared her mind, and Becky stood still for a moment. She turned and looked back up the path toward her shack. Despite the darkness she could see quite plainly her mother standing at the door of their flimsy little shack, looking down the foot path at her. Her mother's hand was touching the door jamb. Stooped and haggard, she just looked at Becky. And as Becky saw her mother standing there, she had a terrible clarity. A panic welled up inside of her such that she had never felt before and never would again. It billowed up like an angry cloud of fire.

"*Mameeyah!*"

In the distance, her mother stood there by the door to the shack and she could not help but hear her small child's screeches. But she looked at Becky for a few more seconds with such sadness, such longing and such defeat. She receded into the shadow inside the door and slowly closed it.

Becky screamed again for her mother, "*Mameeyah!*"

Her eyes filled up and she lost sight of things again. She was dizzy and she ran back and forth, up and down the path without purpose or direction, first toward the shack then back down again. She wanted her mother; she had to find help.

She tripped again, regained her feet and started to bang on the door of the first shack she came to. It had a sinister tangle of illegal electrical wires running out of one corner and there was polluted water slushing down a crevice in the hill beneath it. She flung open the door and cried frantically for help. But when the family inside woke up and heard her cry out *"Ta kau meng!"* over and over they had no idea that it was a cry for help because they were newly arrived from Fukien province, where they spoke a different dialect from Cantonese. Becky ran out and farther down the path calling out for help. She stopped at another, but it was a gambling place. Drunken men inside angrily yelled at her to shut up and go away.

She went to the gates of the Wong Tai Sin Temple, but they were locked for the night. Becky stood with her hands on the wrought-iron bars and pulled at them over and over, crying out for the beneficent god to help her in this moment of greatest need. *"Come out and help me!"* she cried to the great stone effigy inside the gates. She couldn't see it from where she stood at the entrance, but she knew his unwavering face, finished and fixed with enamelled stone. Why would he not come down from his podium and help her as he had helped so many others? Where was his goodness, his direction of fates and good fortune? Why had it dried up at this of all moments? *"Come out! Come out! Come out!"* she cried. *"Come out! Come out and help me!"* She placed her head against the cool iron bars and wept for his help for a long time.

Just how long it took for a policeman to find Becky she never knew. The squatters had heard her cries at the temple gates and someone finally brought a police constable up from an outpost in Kowloon. He went into the squatter village with Becky. A nun from the missionary school came along to be with her. The policeman gently asked Becky to show him which was her shack. Men came out of their houses to watch. Women gathered on the path and exchanged speculation about what could have happened. The policeman had the nun hold onto Becky while he went into her shack. He came out after a minute and said to some of the men from other shacks, *"Will you help me cut her down?"*

A moan went through the men and women on the steep path. Two men came forward. Becky stood with the nun silently. She could hear their voices inside, muffled and indistinct. She heard her mother's chair scraped across the floor boards. There was some more discussion inside the shack. Then there were cries and shouts from the men. *"Wai! Watch it, the roof!"* one of them said. As they cut Becky's mother down from the rafter, the whole roof of the shack began to sag. It was such a light structure that the men inside later emerged with only scratches. But as she stood there in the squatter camp overlooking Kowloon, Becky watched her mother's little house collapse in on itself.

After that, the nuns placed Becky in the Door of Hope Orphanage and everything was fine. Probably that was what Becky's mother had hoped would happen after she told her to run away, that the alien nuns would help. And in Becky's new, improved surroundings, she applied herself industriously to the school lessons the nuns provided. She worked very hard in the laundry, she did everything that she was told, and for the rest of her life she would undertake every task. To sweep the dormitories, to wash clothing, to learn how to write Chinese, to take on the English girl's name the nuns gave her, even to speak their language. To learn how to perform opera, to become an actress at Great World, to become Empress of Stars, to marry Feng Hsiao-foon, to become the Goddess of Mercy, ministering to the sufferings of cinema goers so that she might, in the end, find peace for herself.

Her story finished, Becky sat silently on the edge of her father's bed. She had crossed her legs and her elbows were resting on her knees. She couldn't bear to look at her father for fear of his reaction. She looked out the window at the building on the opposite side of the alley. There, a man was in the window of a cramped apartment festooned with laundry, repairing his bicycle. Throughout her story, Becky's father had clung to his scroll like an amulet. Now, he slowly rolled it up and closed his eyes. He sat still for a moment then put the scroll back in its hiding place beneath his bed. *"Ai-ya!"* he groaned *"What kind of a weak and miserable father have I been?"* Becky watched him for a long while as he sat in melancholy silence. Above him, from behind the printed tapestry depicting the Great Wall, a large cockroach had emerged. It waved its antennae about in the air.

TWENTY

Becky told me that her father sat without moving for fifteen minutes following the conclusion of her story. He looked out the window and blinked his eyes occasionally. There were no tears in them, nothing more than a distant, unfocused, unconcluded look. She saw in his dispassionate face the underlying man, the man who had been the father in her early childhood. But his features had changed so: the dark suntan of his farmer's face had yielded to pallor. There were liver spots on his cheeks and forehead and the prominent cheekbones had grown knobby and shiny. His hands were still calloused but the tendons on the backs were prominent, like tightly pulled strings on a *yiwu*. At last, he turned his face back from the window and rummaged around in his pouch for paper and tobacco. He rolled a cigarette, and as he worked he spoke to the air, more as a complaint than an admission. *"What did I ever do to anyone but fail?"* he said. *"Was that such a cruel thing?"*

Becky took his hand and held it. He looked up at her, considered her face, the one he had seen on the motion picture screens of the Great World circuit, looking so very lovely and beautifully groomed. Her hair had been so stylish, her make-up so subtle and beguiling. Now she sat before him unadorned and plain, her hair in a ponytail.

"You must help me," he said. *"You are my only family now."*

"Do you need some money?" she asked.

"I need you to take me back to Hong Kong with you," he said. He said that he was too frail to work the way the ginger root factory wanted him to and that the political turmoil was certain to pause in its national frenzy for a moment to notice him. When it did it would reach down, scoop him up and crush him with its madness. *"I'm going to die if I stay here any longer,"* he said. *"You were the Goddess of Mercy, I saw that film! You took care of the entire world's troubles but you won't take care of your own elderly father. If you really are the Goddess of Mercy then be merciful with me now. Please. I'm going to die if you don't."*

Becky was surprised at how quickly her father had put aside her dreadful revelations to concentrate on his own plight, as if the death of his children and suicide of his wife were minor issues, as if they were dead history of no more relevance. If she had held any rage for her father's disregard for his extinct family, if an entire life of suffering and guilt over her mother's defeat had moved her to hatred for this selfish little man, she swallowed it completely. When he requested – or rather demanded – that she take him back to Hong Kong all she said was, *"I will try my best."* Becky, despite her sophistication and affluence, despite having considered herself an orphan for most of her life, felt the relentless tug of filial piety. It was her duty, no matter what her father had done or not done, to care for him now. And that meant taking him home to Hong Kong.

There was a question of getting him an exit visa. It was far from clear whether Becky herself would be allowed to leave China. Perhaps she would be put on a plane for Peking so she could become one more concubine in Mao Tse-tung's apartments, as the management of the Southern Film Corporation had offered.

Nevertheless, Becky returned to her father the next morning after having made inquiries from Comrade To. The woman had said that the Southern Film Corporation still hadn't decided what to do with her. But she said she could apply on behalf of her father at the city and district government offices. Comrade To warned Becky that she would probably have to stay behind in China and complete her "commitments" to the Southern Film Corporation, even if her father was granted an exit visa.

Overnight, the city's crisis grew much worse.

The taxis at the Oriental Hotel had vanished. Becky waited for a trolley bus to take her down Chong Shan Road to her father's dormitory, but no bus came. The streets were mostly deserted. She was frightened.

She set out on foot shortly after ten in the morning after waiting an hour for a bus. Every small, grimy, mean-looking shop with its shabby bits of merchandise, tea thermoses and wooden tables, had been closed, steel roller doors pulled down over the store fronts. Even the dirty vegetable markets tucked into alleyways were empty. As she walked she could hear tinny and crackling loudspeakers blaring and honking revolutionary music. Becky stopped under an arcade of a long, decrepit grey building constructed forty years before but looking much older. Canton's deserted streets had unnerved her. She saw a poster pasted to one of the pillars of the arcade and she read it. The printing was crude and unclear, owing to a shortage of ink. She understood from it that half a million Red Guards were massing in Canton *"to take control of the situation."* The poster warned that factional fighting between political subgroups of Red Guards would not be tolerated. *"Bloodshed between revolutionaries must stop,"* the poster demanded. Becky knew little and cared less about politics, but she thought the poster's remarks were an extraordinary admission of chaos and infighting among the Communists. The poster warned that people who resisted the call for public order would be punished. The old ones would be "reformed" and the young ones would be shot.

As she walked down the road, she emerged from a long string of arcades beside the People's Cultural Park in the centre of town. She could hear shouts and screams. Occasionally, there was a crashing noise. The park was usually one of the few places in that grimy city where residents could go for fun. They could rent roller skates, listen to music or just visit. When she saw the park, it was a scene from hell.

Young people in shirt-sleeves, teenaged boys and girls, were armed with sticks, knives and bottles and they were all fighting one another inside the park's high steel fence. They were different factions of Red Guards reduced to a vicious hand-to-hand battle. There were hundreds of them. Becky saw two girls smacking each other on the shoulders and face with sticks. There were people on the concrete pavement, lying face down, motionless, with streams of blood running from their heads. Other teenagers were stepping on them and stumbling as they fought one another. A bottle lofted over the crowd and crashed on the concrete. Two boys with knives swiped at each other, both equally matched until someone bumped one of them and the other boy saw his chance and ran his knife into the chest of the other. Becky saw another boy take a girl by the head and run her up against the steel bars of the fence right in front of Becky. The girl gave off a horrendous scream as the sides of her head jammed in between the bars. The boy looked up at Becky, who was only a few feet away. *"Whom do you favour?"* he demanded in Mandarin to Becky. *"Whom do you support, you evil slut?"* He kept holding the girl by the neck even as she screamed, and he tried to wedge her face deeper between the bars. He kept yelling at Becky. *"Whose side are you on? Tell me now or I'll tear your hair out. I'll kill you and your whole family!"*

Becky ran. She ran down to the waterfront and hurried to the left, toward the street that led to the alley that led to the house that led to the dormitory where her father lived, hoping that this madness would not trickle down so deeply as to reach them there. She kept running through the empty streets until she found his alley and hurried down it, tired and out of breath. She stood before the concierge and received a lecture on her foolishness for going out into the streets during a "Party rectification." She asked Becky questions about what she had seen and how she had felt about it, but Becky was wise enough to give vague answers to this wretched back-alley spy. At last the woman allowed Becky to go up to Bed No. 70 and get her father.

"Where have you been? I've waited for so long. I was sure you had gone back to Hong Kong without me," he whimpered. He saw how frightened and tired she was and for once he became sympathetic and tender. He put his arm around her and said comforting things.

They sat quietly in the shared fear and exhaustion. He patted her on the shoulder encouragingly. When she began to recover he asked her if she had secured a visa for him. She said that they had to go across town to a government office and hope that it was open and that they would grant him one. Becky understood that it was unlikely the government office could be open when party members were in the streets bludgeoning one another, yet she relented to his naggings that they should go at once. *"They're working me to death in that factory,"* he said. *"I can't go another day, I simply can't."*

They set out after a small lunch laid on by the concierge and her cook for the men of the dormitory. Becky had to share her father's meal since there was no more food than was barely sufficient for the residents. It was rice, with a few greens and some rehydrated fish meal. Becky could barely stomach it. When they were on the street they moved slowly because of her father's frailty. He complained that they should take the trolley bus but Becky told him they'd all stopped. The screams and noise from the People's Cultural Park had ceased. They walked under the arcade of the Nam Fong Department Store. The red star that surmounted the store's cupola had come loose and hung precariously forward. The windows of the store were smashed, not by looters, for there was never anything in the Nam Fong to loot, but by someone who probably had decided that the department store was on the wrong side of the political struggle.

Father and daughter crept through the streets, north of Sha Min Island, on the Pearl River, and up through the back streets. For the first while, her father talked incessantly. *"What was I to do? You blame me, don't you? I can tell how a woman's mind works and I know that you blame me for what happened to her and the little ones! What was I to do? I was a farmer from Toi Sin. I didn't know anything about the city. All I knew was that it was the only place we could go to. The countryside was a dead place if you had no money. We had to go to the city or perish. When we got there, what do you think I knew how to do? Be a banker or a money lender? I didn't know how to do any of those things. What I knew how to do there were plenty of other men to do it too. There were so many of us we were as worthless as stones. I couldn't do anything.*

And now you blame me. I can tell by your silences. You think it is all ba-ba's fault. But I was just another coolie on the pavement in Hong Kong, a coolie with a coolie family. If we lived, we lived. If we died, we died. You think you're the Goddess of Mercy, well you could starve to death with the rest of us, just remember that. You've no right to blame me for things I couldn't stop. I was a victim of the oppression of the working class! The Communist Party talks all about that, you know. The exploitation of the masses by the landlords! You don't know about any of that! But I was there and my proletarian —"

Her father abruptly stopped his prattle and cried out. They were on the street that ran along the channel separating Sha Min from the mainland. Becky saw a body hanging from a tree over their heads. It was that of a man in his early thirties, and it had been hung by its feet so its arms swayed beneath it. A little farther down was a bicycle, also hanging from a tree. Its wheels had been crushed by a heavy vehicle. Beyond it hung the body of a woman, her face smeared with lipstick. Her bare back carried the character for "decadent" written in lipstick. The dead woman had the broad shoulders of a physical labourer. In the next tree hung a small child by its neck, its noose was a traditional red baby-carrier, embroidered with playful little dogs. From the child's heel hung a paper sign that read: *"Exposed to the brilliant criticism of the masses by his elder sister. Death to traitors!"*

Becky put her hand over her father's eyes and guided him across the street and into a narrow lane. He moaned and cried out as he blundered blindly beside her. Their course took them to the intersection of Tai Hsin and People's roads, where they met a group of angry boys and girls, all of them teenagers. By their arm bands Becky learned that these were members of the "Spring Thunder" faction of the Red Guards, sworn enemies of revisionists, capitalists, exploiters of the working class and their contemporary rivals in the "Red Flag" faction.

"Whom do you support?" a teenaged girl in thick glasses said, jabbing her finger at Becky and her father. *"Tell us now or you will die!"* She seemed almost pleased and self-satisfied with her own ferocity.

"*Tell us the wrong answer and you will die!*" said a boy no more than seventeen. He was holding a picket stick and he swooped it back and forth, cutting the air in the way of a small child with a toy sword.

"*Whom* do you *support?*" Becky asked.

"Never mind!" the teenaged girl said. "*That would enable you to pander to us. We are more sophisticated than that! We understand treachery and we want the truth!*"

The truth was that Becky supported neither Liu Shao-chi nor Mao Tse-tung, the idol-leaders of Spring Thunder and Red Flag. It was not her fight and her father probably had no allegiance either. If they were to answer with the wrong leader's name, they risked being beaten to death right there at the corner of Tai Hsin and People's roads. It had happened to hundreds of people already.

"*Whom do you support?*" a young man with hollow cheeks and a wild look in his eyes screamed. He was almost giddy with the pleasure of controlling life and death, a mastery so denied to ordinary people that its sudden availability seemed to drive him insane. "*If you do not express your true feelings, we will kill you both! Death to traitors!*"

Becky looked to her father for advice. He merely held his hands together in the traditional gesture of kowtowing. That only infuriated the teenagers and one of them stepped forward and slapped his face for making a feudalist gesture. The boy with the picket smacked it on the pavement several times and it made a sharp, cracking noise. He levelled it just above her father's head for a second then raised it to hit him.

"Chairman Mao!" Becky blurted at once. "*We support Chairman Mao!*"

"So!" the girl in glasses yelled in a shrill voice. "*You say that you are Maoists!*" She came over and looked Becky up and down, clearly disapproving of her ponytail.

Becky looked at her father, whose eyes jumped from Becky to the belligerent teenagers.

"*And you, old man?*" the boy with the hollow cheeks said. "*Whom do you support?*"

Becky's father seemed lost, as if the street corner known to every Canton resident had somehow changed beyond all recognition, its dirty, crumbling landmarks vanished and replaced with new ones he did not recognize.

"Whom do you support?"

"He supports Chairman Mao too!" Becky shouted. *"Leave him alone! He's an old man and he's sick."*

"You are Maoists, both of you!" said the girl. *"It so happens that we are supporters of Liu Shao-chi and his colleague, Comrade Teng Hsiao-ping! What do you think of that, Maoist bandits?"*

And suddenly, Becky's weak and doddering father was transformed. His face flushed red and he held both his hands high in the air. *"No!"* he shrieked.

Everyone fell silent and one boy even took a step back.

"I do not support Mao Tse-tung! I am a firm follower of the invincible thought of Comrade Liu! This ... this Hong Kong woman answered for me! And she lied! I understand treachery too! She tried to drag me down with the bandit Mao Tse-tung gang. I condemn her! I am for Liu Shao-chi and Teng Hsiao-ping!"

"Ba-ba, don't!" Becky cried out.

But it was too late to stop him. Perhaps it had been his failing eyes, perhaps it had been his panic, but he had failed to see what Becky had seen on that filthy, deadly street corner. He failed to see the red booklet just peeking out of the trouser pocket of the teenaged girl with the thick glasses. Anyone who saw that would have known instantly who these people really were. Now, the girl slowly drew the book out and held it up for Becky's father to see. In the centre of the red cover was a yellow cameo of Mao Tse-tung.

Suddenly, the group surrounded Becky and her father. The girl who had first challenged them spoke up. *"Death to traitors!"* she shouted. One of the other teenagers took up a chant: *"Death to traitors! Death to traitors! Death to traitors!"* He marched in little circles, a zombie to his own voice. The other young Red Guards struck Becky and her father with their fists and pushed him into the deserted intersection. *"Go, you traitor! We will fix you and all your Liu clique friends!"*

Becky's voice was lost in the chanting. *"Stop!"* she cried. She pleaded with members of the group that her father didn't know what he was saying, that he had been terrified into giving the wrong answer. But no one listened to her. They were too drugged by the frenzied satisfaction of having exposed their very own little traitors to the burning, brilliant light of their loyalty to Chairman Mao. They bound her hands and those of her father and led them through the street. The girl in charge turned to Becky and gave her a look of satisfaction. *"If your father supports the Bandit Liu, then you are as guilty as he is! If the father is guilty, the daughter is guilty. The rot of your whole family must be cut out!"*

Another boy took up a chant, *"The rot of your family! The rot of your family!"* The Red Guards took them to a waiting freight truck on People's Road. They pushed them into it. Inside were other "traitors" who had been rounded up that afternoon. Becky saw her father stumble and roll over in the back of the truck, crying out in pain. His face was very pink and Becky was afraid that he would have a heart attack. The truck lurched into gear and, under the guard of teenaged boys armed with truncheons, the captives were driven off to the north, to an unknown destination. And as they rode in the back of the truck, Becky considered her father, lying there with a red face, howling protests over his sickliness and she had a flicker of betrayal of her own. It was a small flash of satisfaction to know that her father was hurting.

They spent several days in an outdoor compound while their teenaged captors argued over what to do with them. One group wanted to send them to a remote country commune to work in the fields and consider their political mistakes and learn the true revolutionary path as defined by Chairman Mao. But nobody knew exactly how to do that. The other group wanted to execute them to stop the rot of their revisionist ideas from spreading any further. The two groups argued for several days and two boys succumbed to fist-fighting to settle it. Exasperated, the other Red Guards threw the two boys into the compound with Becky, her father and other captives. There the two boys began howling extravagant accusations at each other, slandering each other with allegations of political malfeasance and conspiracy. Then they returned to beating each other and one finally killed the other. No one came to remove the body.

On the third day of their captivity, the teenagers, now led by an older woman, came to the compound and removed many of the prisoners, including Becky's father. They were going to the countryside to be worked to death in farm fields. Becky's father cried and turned red in the face. He pleaded for mercy and kow-towed to everyone idiotically. A teenager kicked him in the leg for this feudal gesture and told him to repent or die. It was a paltry threat, Becky knew, because her father would not last more than a few days at hard labour. He was put in the back of another truck and driven away. Becky never saw him again.

She spent two more days in the outdoor compound, dirty and miserable, hungry, but not frightened any more. There was nothing anybody could do to reduce her any further. The Goddess of Mercy had given everything she could.

Eventually, Comrade To turned up with a stack of papers she pre-sented to the cell's leaders. She lectured them on how they had held prisoner one of Chairman Mao's most favoured allies and that they would soon be planting radishes themselves. She had Becky released at once and removed back to the Oriental Hotel. Comrade To was unsentimental and baldly practical in her expla-nation for securing Becky's release. *"You are valuable to us,"* she said. *"You are our shield from those mad little children."*

While Becky sat in the chilly air-conditioned hotel for anoth-er week, she pleaded with Comrade To to get her father back. Comrade To said that there was nothing that could be done – he had been sent to Anhui province and would not be returning.

A short time later, Comrade To came in and told her that she was being deported to Hong Kong at once. *"Pack your things and go,"* she said. She told Becky that all Chinese cinemas were to remain dark, production would not resume, under the direct orders of Mao's wife, Ch'iang Ching. Motion-picture artists were to spend their time cleansing their thoughts of rightist fantasies and *"black lines."* As a result, the official said, there was no reason for Becky to remain in China. The corporation's leaders were relieved: they were not to be purged but merely unemployed. An order came in from Ch'iang Ching herself that under no circumstances was the Hong Kong actress to come anywhere near her husband, Chairman Mao. Becky was now worthless to the Southern Film Corporation and they wanted her off their hands.

At the frontier, the British immigration and customs officials briefly asked her a few questions but no one could refuse to admit her, since she carried a Hong Kong identity card and had no criminal record requiring banishment. She boarded a British train for Kowloon at Lo Wu and sat on it, staring out the window at things she saw on the platforms at intermediate railway stations trying to piece together an understanding of what had happened to her.

Becky finished her story. I said nothing, for there was nothing to say. After a while I got up for cigarettes, a beer for me and a Coca-Cola for her.

"Do you know where your brother Yee is today?" I asked her.

She said that it was impossible to trace him. She didn't know to which family her mother had given him and there was no way to find what his name had changed to.

After a long silence, she started to yawn, exhausted from her story. She fiddled with the sugar spoon and finally said to it, more than to me, "I've got to get my baby away from him. I have to do that right now."

TWENTY-ONE

Late that afternoon, we went to Becky's home in Kowloon Tong. We buzzed the intercom switch on the black steel gate in front of the house. Ah-niu's voice came on and Becky spoke to her. The electric lock buzzed, I pushed back the shrieking steel gate and we entered the courtyard. Chung Hsiang, the Fengs' little dog, came barking and slobbering toward us until it realized that Becky was there. It turned sweeter. Becky bent down and picked it up and whispered into Chung Hsiang's ear. Several minutes passed before the servant came to the door. She opened it only a little and said that Feng was home and he had instructed that Becky was not to come in. Becky argued with her for several minutes that she had a right to enter her own home. I discreetly stood away from them, pretending not to listen. I happened to glance up and saw Feng standing at an upstairs window, examining me.

Ah-niu went away and after a while she returned and let Becky come in. I was told to stay outside, so I sat on a stone bench next to Chung Hsiang, who panted in the humidity and flopped down in a hairy heap next to me. I glanced at the Chinese characters carved over the doorway of Becky's house: *"Bricks and Mortar of the Nation."*

Eventually Ah-niu came out with a cup of tea and a cookie on a plate and said gravely: *"You are to wait."* I sat on the poet's bench in the little Soochow-style garden then relented to the insistent nudging of Chung Hsiang's wet nose and gave her half the cookie. I took my sports jacket off and leaned forward to look at the koi fish. I tossed the last bits of cookie at them and watched them scramble, their mouths sucking at the surface of the pond with a disgusting sound. I looked at the house. Miss Chin was there. She policed the window, pulling back a lacy curtain, confident that her terrier scowl could prevent me from coming any closer to Feng. It was as if she had been waiting for me to notice her, for once I spied her she dropped the curtain back into place and went away.

Becky never told me what was said in that house on Suffolk Road, Kowloon, in August 1967. But through careful examination of her words for years after, I suspect that she and Feng hammered down a mutual repudiation. I was evidently accused of having drawn Becky into flirtation with the Communists to humiliate Feng and as a cover for my cuckoldry. Becky told Feng that she was leaving him because he was a cruel, venal man too enslaved by his own obsessions to care about hers. She wanted Amanda away from him, she said. The last statements he apparently and variously made were to declare her an outsider, to promise to begin divorce proceedings. He would remove her from the payroll of the Great World Organisation immediately. *"Go work for Phoenix!"* he had said, meaning one of the Communist-controlled movie companies in Hong Kong.

It had to be an hour before the front door finally opened. I stood up as Becky emerged, holding Amanda in her arms. Becky looked astonishingly happy for someone who had gone through such an ordeal. She looked from me to Amanda and back to me again. Ah-niu came out with several suitcases and a sturdy red, blue and white plastic bag full of baby things. Becky brought Amanda over for me to look at. As ever, Amanda considered me gravely. Becky fussed with Amanda's clothing. "I got my baby back," she said.

We turned and looked back at the house. In the window to the right of the front door was Miss Chin, considering us. In the window to the left was Feng, glowering. In the upstairs window was the nursemaid. The whole household was there to drive us out.

Becky turned back to me and said, "Let's go." I held the electric gate open for her and Ah-niu. The servant went to look for a cab on Waterloo Road. While Becky and I waited I said: "Go where?"

"I don't know," she said. "I'll put up in a hotel, I suppose. I guess we need a place to stay for a few days."

I told her that she could come and stay at my flat in Causeway Bay for a while. She, the baby and Ah-niu could take the bedroom and I would sleep in the living room.

TWENTY-TWO

A few days became a few weeks. Ah-niu stayed with us briefly, then returned to Feng's home because we could not afford to pay her. I slept in the front room while Becky and the baby had my bedroom. Every week or so, Becky would laconically suggest moving out and I would tell her to stay, at least until she found a job. She and the baby needed a secure home for a while and I welcomed the company. Becky cared both for Amanda and my long-neglected apartment. Every evening my barren home was newly full with their sound and activity. At first I was unnerved by the change and sometimes irritated by the baby's crying, but I began to look forward to their company at the end of the day. I found it agreeable. Becky needed work because Feng had barred her from Great World Studios in Tsuen Wan and refused to give her any money. The only thing she knew how to do was act.

A few weeks became a few months. When over-the-air television broadcasting began in Hong Kong in late 1967, she picked up work at the TVB studios, acting in dramatic series. To save money she'd take a public bus up to Broadcast Drive to do her shows. But she didn't want to act any more. Bus riders would pester her with questions about her politics and queries about what was going to happen to her TV character. Becky preferred to stay home with the baby. I kept her and Amanda on, despite the constant surveillance from neighbours every time one or all of us came or went. They stared shamelessly at us and sometimes knocked on our door when I was at work, nominally to ask Becky if she needed help with the baby, but really to snoop out what the nature of our relationship was. They thought it was miscegenation, but they had no idea exactly what the combination of our real feelings were. Their prying grew to be too much.

The following spring we moved to Lamma Island, away from the gossip, the noise, and the crowded city on Hong Kong Island. Lamma is a quiet, hilly place several kilometres long, and where all the roads are no more than sidewalks and there are no automobiles. Telephone service had just been installed on Lamma, and Europeans with what later became known as "alternative lifestyles" were moving out to its rural isolation. Especially European men living with Chinese women. The place got a reputation for tolerance and Bohemia. The difference was that Becky and I took a lease on a two-bedroom apartment, one bedroom for her and the baby and one for me.

There, largely separated by water from the urban life of Hong Kong, we could be a kind of family. I took the ferry into Central every morning to the *China Telegraph*. After years of barely making a profit, the *Telegraph* closed in the early 1970s, so I found work at the *South China Morning Post* and added freelance television work to make extra money. Becky and I managed to send Amanda to university in Canada. We have installed two plaques on the door. One is an homage to the patron saint of entertainers, Master Tsang, the other is a domestic slogan in Chinese that was of my choosing: *"A bright pearl in one's hand."* It refers to a man's affection for his wife *"Ai-ya,"* Becky said when I put it up. "You complain I like sugary things."

It has been a quiet life mostly, although we to this day talk about Typhoon Rose of 1971, which ferociously attacked Hong Kong and especially Lamma Island, where we were exposed to the sea winds even more than other places. We spent one night huddled together in a windowless bathroom, for fear that all the apartment windows would blow in and send flying glass everywhere. We set a mat out for Amanda on the bathroom floor for her to sleep on while we kept a vigil in the bathtub. When the electricity failed we read magazines by flashlights, I drank beer and Becky had Cokes. We kept together against a common adversary that we could not fight, only endure. We escaped injury and the damage was light except for flooding that ruined our parquet floors.

Feng Hsiao-foon's fortunes declined after 1967, though not because of Becky's departure. Television devastated the movie theatres in Hong Kong, just as it had in North America. And Feng failed to appreciate the potential of swordsmen pictures which virtually carried his rivals at Shaw Brothers. When kung fu pictures opened new markets in the West after 1970, Feng didn't get it either, he didn't see their opportunity, and the genre passed him by. He died of cancer in 1973. There was a great long funeral procession of hired rickshaws bearing floral tributes, so many that rickshaws had to be brought in from nearby Macau. Some of his Rotary Club pals came, everybody in the movie industry came. A Shaw Brothers executive spoke. But none of the really respectable people came near the funeral. The Chinese bankers, the professionals, the great factory owners, the Europeans, all of them stayed away.

A parade of production executives succeeding Feng couldn't make Great World work. It was a dated business model. By 1976, Great World was out of production and its Tsuen Wan studios sold for redevelopment. Shaw Brothers were left to dominate the local movie industry. On Great World's site now stand high-rise flats. Few of Becky's early pictures survive today. The prints were mostly incinerated to recover their silver. Neither the Hong Kong Film Archive nor the Pacific Film Archive in Berkeley, California, can find a complete set.

Becky gave her last performance in the mid-1970s, on a TVB evening soap opera. It is the curious fate of Hong Kong movie stars to be quickly forgotten by their public. There are no tributes, no charming little encounters with aging fans who run into them at the airport and talk about movies from the past. As little as five years after her retirement, Becky could walk anywhere in Hong Kong in complete anonymity. The most she has done in recent years has been to sit for a videotaped interview by researchers from the new Hong Kong Film Archive. She talked in flat, dispassionate terms about her career, what her work conditions were like and spoke about the roles and stories she appeared in. She didn't say much about what she felt during those years. She rarely did.

I had a succession of occasional close male friends, but I never stuck with them. Like Benoit Ng, to whom I never spoke again, I did not care for these men enough to leave the kind of family I had entered into with Becky and Amanda. I dallied with a Chinese stockbroker who had spent many years in the liberal centres of the United States. He was far more comfortable with, well, what he is than I have ever been. But I backed away after six months. I did not care for him enough even to raise doubts in Becky's mind that I could leave, much less ever commit to doing it. Jack Rudman retired and moved back to Scotland, where he probably continues to fish and read about Wendy Hiller to this day.

Becky was courted by one or two men and I would watch these romances uneasily. As I grew more nervous with their gathering passion and affection, she would step back from them too. Perhaps they weren't the right men for her or perhaps she was not willing to risk the platonic harmony she and I had settled into. She never showed much interest in changing her life from the regular, reliable one she formed with me. We have always maintained separate bedrooms but the household atmosphere was so cordial and friendly that Becky and I are both confident that Amanda grew up in a happy home. It was only in 1984, after the signing of the joint agreement between London and Beijing to return control of Hong Kong to China, that our status changed. To protect my family, Becky and I legally married, extending my Canadian citizenship to both of them. It also helped when Amanda chose to study computing at the University of Western Ontario.

Easily the best day of Becky's life and my own was Amanda's wedding day. After she graduated from Western she returned to Hong Kong and got a job in the information systems department of Jardine Fleming, where she met a young Chinese man, Albert Cheung, who had also studied in Canada. They fell in love and were married in 1991. I wept without shame at the wedding, oblivious to the stares and questions from other guests.

I have always hoped that old age would bring me peace and contentment, especially with the sort of family I belong to. But there are always new anxieties to replace the old ones. I now wonder if I didn't waste my working life, whether I should have been more ambitious. And Becky, to this day, has no release from her torment. On some nights it only grows worse. She has spoken infrequently to me about those moments: "It takes all your energy, all your courage just to push them back far enough so you can go on." But usually she says nothing, only quietly enduring them with as much grace as she can muster.

I can't say that Becky has ever really got better. Her visit with her father resulted in no alleviation of her burdens, no passage through a door. In an irreverent moment she said she had gone through a car wash like those she'd seen in Los Angeles in the early 1960s. There was never any word on her father's fate and the uncertainty choked at her from time to time. She felt guilty that she couldn't bring him out of China. But she felt nothing of the kind of guilt she had for not preventing her mother's destruction. The sadness of her mother's death would come back on certain days, especially during that great annual trauma of unresolved feeling among Chinese everywhere, the lunar new year. Unhappiness still comes over her like an illness and sometimes she takes to her bed for several days.

It is such an easy surrender for her to go into those dark places, those recesses in which she had learned from an early age to inhabit and from which to view the world. It is sometimes everything I can do, that Amanda can do, to bring her back out again. It's always something that's made Amanda worry, even when she was a little girl; and Becky was so afraid that she would repeat the kind of fear in her daughter that she had experienced that she made herself get out of bed and be cheerful. That is enough to correct things for a while. It is easy to go into the shadows, but there is enough goodness in her life to induce her to come back out again. We rejoice when she does. And Becky rejoices too, heartily, happy to be among us. But I can tell, even when she has returned to us, that in small and almost imperceptible ways Becky is holding a spot in those shadows, a place for the person who is never there.

FILMOGRAPHY

Becky Chan's career fell into seven periods: early work, Cantonese starring roles, Mandarin comedies and dramas, two years of big costume epics, a two-year career in Hollywood, subsequent decline following her return to Hong Kong and a single proposed picture in the People's Republic of China, which was never shot. Becky made 190 pictures. The following is only a partial list.

Early bit parts, supporting roles and extra work

Sorrows of the Forbidden City (1948) Mandarin super-production, Yung Hwa Motion Picture Industries

Tales of the Manchu Court (1948) Mandarin super-production, Yung Hwa

Chung Hsiang Upsets the Classroom (1948) Mandarin, Peking opera, Yung Hwa

The Terrible News (1949) Mandarin, United Southern Film Corporation

The Queen of Heaven (1949) Mandarin, United Southern

The Cockatoo (1949) Mandarin, United Southern

Starring roles, Cantonese independents

A Smart Girl (1949) Cantonese, Southern Electric Film Company
    The first in the "Pei-ling" series about a girl who remains
    faithful to a mother accused of murdering her husband.
A Smart Girl Falls in Love (1950) Cantonese, Southern Electric
    Pei-ling meets a brilliant young composer.
A Smart Girl Returns (1950) Cantonese, Southern Electric
    Pei-ling's husband goes blind.

Starring roles, Great World Cantonese unit

The Blue Lake (1950) Cantonese,
Great World Studios
    Great World purchased the
    rights to the Pei-ling series
    from Southern Electric.
Flower Girl (1951) Cantonese,
Great World
    Poor girl becomes a dancer
    before injury halts her career.
Those Kids (1951) Cantonese,
Great World
    Young people foil crooks.

Clap Your Hands (1952) Cantonese, Great World
    Shop girls win the lottery.
The Tram Conductor (1952) Cantonese, Great World
    A working man looks for happiness in the daily grind.
    Award: Empress of Stars at All-Asia Film Week.
Uncle Li (1952) Cantonese, Great World
    A middle-aged widower makes friends with a young woman.
Choose (1953) Cantonese, Great World
    The last Pei-ling picture; about the death of her husband and
    temptation by two rich men, one good, the other bad.

Love Gets in the Way (1953) Cantonese, Great World
> Becky's last Cantonese picture. Their lives in Hong Kong ruined by a misunderstanding, a sailor and a shop girl plot a get-away by sea.

A Mother's Burden (1953) Cantonese, Great World
> A destitute woman sells her daughter, only to be reunited years later when the mother works as a domestic in a rich family's home.

Mandarin dramas and comedies

A Fool in Love (1953) Mandarin, Great World
> An actor falls for a decadent nightclub singer.

Pink and Deadly (1953) Mandarin, Great World
> Becky's first bad-girl role. A rich woman tries to take another's fiancé.

The Rivals (1953) Mandarin, Great World
> Jilted for another woman, a lover goes to work in the other woman's home.

Two Beauties (1953) Mandarin, Great World
> Two young singers vie for success, one in a music academy, the other in nightclubs.

Four Shrieks of a Monkey (1954) Mandarin, Great World
> Quartet of Ming Dynasty stories, including one in which Becky plays a monk reincarnated as a prostitute.

Love on Green Island (1954) Mandarin, Great World, Eastmancolor
> Becky's first colour picture. Period drama about a woman who falls in love with a fugitive swordsman.

The Beautiful Murderess (1955) Mandarin, Great World
  Rich woman is accused of killing her mother.
Police Dossier 408 (1955) Mandarin, Great World
  Adventures of a police vice squad.
The Smile of One Hundred Fascinations (1955) Mandarin, Great
  World
Boastful Women (1956) Mandarin, Great World
Candy Pink (1956) Mandarin, Great World
  Spirit grants a poor woman a magic wish.
Demon Woman (1956) Mandarin, Great World
  A rich woman attempts to make working husbands unfaithful.
The Herdsman and the Weaver (1956) Mandarin, Great World
  Husband and wife are separated by duty.
Temptress (1956) Mandarin, Great World
  Vivacious young woman is wrongly accused of murder.
The Dark Chamber (1957) Mandarin, Great World
  A secretary apparently murders her employer.
Lady Panther Walks Ten Thousand Li (1957) Mandarin, Great
  World
Meteorite of Love (1957) Mandarin, Great World

  Comedy about a hus-
  band-stealing vamp.
Rich But Hungry (1957)
  Mandarin, Great World
The Face of Revenge (1958)
  Mandarin, Great World,
  Eastmancolor
  The legends of Judge Po.
Flames of Love (1958)
  Mandarin, Great World
  A woman's jealous heart
  ruins her family.
Get Out of My Way (1958)
  Cantonese, Great World

Girls Demand Excitement (1958) Mandarin, Great World
The Rivals (1958) Mandarin, Great World
  Two women vie for the heart of an artist.

Mandarin costume epics

Goddess of Mercy (1958) Mandarin, Great World, Eastmancolor
  Expensive recreation of the myth of Koon Yin.
Longing for Worldly Pleasure (1958) Mandarin, Great World,
  Eastmancolor, Award: Empress of Stars at All-Asia Film Week.
  Based on Nineteenth-Century play about a nun who
  searches for love.
White Snake (1958) Mandarin, Great World, Eastmancolor
  Filmed version of the Peking opera.
Behind the Curtains (1959) Mandarin, Great World
  Based on Peking opera *The Butterfly Lovers.*
Memories of a Wasted Life (1959) Mandarin, Great World,
  Eastmancolor
Metropolitan (1960) Mandarin, Great World
Spring in Jade Hall (1960) Mandarin, Great World
  Peking opera.

Hollywood

Almond Eyes (1960) USA-English, Independent, Technicolor
  Feng loaned Becky to American producers for this indepen-
  dent production, which led to offers of representation from
  Hollywood.
Flower Drum Song (1961) USA-English, Universal International,
  Technicolor
  Rodgers and Hammerstein musical comedy about arranged
  marriages among Chinese-Americans in San Francisco.
  Becky was fired for poor attendance at rehearsals before
  shooting began.

Chopsticks (1961) USA-English, Twentieth Century-Fox,
    Technicolour
    The amorous adventures of airline pilots.
Panic on Grant Avenue (1962) USA English, Twentieth Century-Fox
    Drama about Chinese organized crime.
How the West Was Won (1962) USA English, MGM, Cinerama
    Cameo role later cut from U.S. western.

Return to Hong Kong, final years

The Big Doll (1963) Mandarin, Great World
    A Hong Kong department-store mannequin comes to life
    and creates havoc for window dresser.
Don't Bargain with Fate (1963) Mandarin, Great World
    nightclub singer finds love and redemption with a stranger.
The Dark Chamber (1964) Mandarin, Great World
    A secretary apparently murders her boss. Remake of 1957
    version.
The Millionairess (1964) Mandarin, Great World
    Remake of *Rich But Hungry.*
Mangoes and Coconuts (1964) Mandarin, Great World
    Beach hotel owners cope with madcap guests.
That Day at the Airport (1965)
    Mandarin, Great World
Dancing Wives (1965) Mandarin,
    Great World
The Trouble That Money Brings
    (1965) Great World
    Comedy about a couple who
    inherit money and nothing
    but grief.
Love Calms the Goddess (1966)
    Mandarin, Great World
Barren Spirit (1966) Mandarin,
    Great World

The Lady from Swatow (1967) Cantonese, Great World
Long Ago and Far Away (1967) Mandarin, Great World
A woman remembers her unhappy marriage to a rich man and a lost love to an artist

People's Republic of China

Triumph at Li Hsian (1967) China, Mandarin, Southern Film Corporation
Cultural Revolution feature film about putting the masses before personal interests. Never made.

NOTE: Great World switched to Eastmancolor and CinemaScope lenses for all its Mandarin productions in 1960. Cantonese pictures were shot in wide-screen ratio but only occasionally in colour.